Jane had taken off her rain-dappled spectacles, and was gently wiping them with the hem of her dress. She tipped her head back to gaze through the lenses. "They are still spotted. Oh, well, it is of no account. We are so near one another that I can see you quite clearly without them, and there is nothing else in here worth looking at."

George wondered rather distractedly if the ragged pulse he felt raging in his throat was visible to her. "If one thing is certain, it is that *you* are most worthy of being looked at," he said. "You must have the most beguiling eyes, Miss Oxenby." He stopped in horror. Had he really said those things out loud?

"Why, your lordship, the rain has made you most poetical. Thank you for the gallant compliments. You need not have, you know!"

"You must think that fate has contrived to place you here with a madman. I am quite undone by seeing your loveliness so near to me. If only you knew . . . if only I dared tell you . . ."

"If only you dared tell me what?" she said a little breathlessly. Her mouth was a taut bow, and there was a faint spark of something in the back of her eyes. He fancied that if it chanced to meet the spark he carried in his own heart, the two together would kindle a fire which would rage unchecked. He leaned a little nearer her, his mouth leading him forward, closer to the rich, full lips that trembled just a heartbeat away from his. How he wanted to kiss her, and how improper it would be!

"Your lordship!" rang out an agitated male voice. "Your lordship, are you there?"

George realized it must be Fletcher. Whether it was duty or concern which had brought his butler to him at this minute, George did not care. He wanted to wring the man's neck and fling his lifeless carcass down the hill . . .

CAPTURE THE GLOW OF
ZEBRA'S *HEARTFIRES!*

CAPTIVE TO HIS KISS (3788, $4.25/$5.50)
by Paige Brantley
Madeleine de Moncelet was determined to avoid an arranged marriage to the Duke of Burgundy. But the tall, stern-looking knight sent to guard her chamber door may thwart her escape plan!

CHEROKEE BRIDE (3761, $4.25/$5.50)
by Patricia Werner
Kit Newcomb found politics to be a dead bore, until she met the proud Indian delegate Red Hawk. Only a lifetime of loving could soothe her desperate desire!

MOONLIGHT REBEL (3707, $4.25/$5.50)
by Marie Ferrarella
Krystyna fled her native Poland only to live in the midst of a revolution in Virginia. Her host may be a spy, but when she looked into his blue eyes she wanted to share her most intimate treasures with him!

PASSION'S CHASE (3862, $4.25/$5.50)
by Ann Lynn
Rose would never heed her Aunt Stephanie's warning about the unscrupulous Mr. Trent Jordan. She knew what she wanted—a long, lingering kiss bound to arouse the passion of a bold and ardent lover!

RENEGADE'S ANGEL (3760, $4.25/$5.50)
by Phoebe Fitzjames
Jenny Templeton had sworn to bring Ace Denton to justice for her father's death, but she hadn't reckoned on the tempting heat of the outlaw's lean, hard frame or her surrendering wantonly to his fiery loving!

TEMPTATION'S FIRE (3786, $4.25/$5.50)
by Millie Criswell
Margaret Parker saw herself as a twenty-six year old spinster. There wasn't much chance for romance in her sleepy town. Nothing could prepare her for the jolt of desire she felt when the new marshal swept her onto the dance floor!

Available wherever paperbacks are sold, or order direct from the Publisher. Send cover price plus 50¢ per copy for mailing and handling to Zebra Books, Dept. 4107, 475 Park Avenue South, New York, N.Y. 10016. Residents of New York and Tennessee must include sales tax. DO NOT SEND CASH. For a free Zebra/Pinnacle catalog please write to the above address.

PAMELA CALDWELL

SCANDALOUS

ZEBRA BOOKS
KENSINGTON PUBLISHING CORP.

ZEBRA BOOKS

are published by

Kensington Publishing Corp.
475 Park Avenue South
New York, NY 10016

Copyright © 1993 by Pamela Caldwell

All rights reserved. No part of this book may be reproduced in any form or by any means without the prior written consent of the Publisher, excepting brief quotes used in reviews.

Zebra, the Z logo, Heartfire Romance, and the Heartfire Romance logo are trademarks of Kensington Publishing Corp.

If you purchased this book without a cover you should be aware that this book is stolen property. It was reported as "unsold and destroyed" to the Publisher and neither the Author nor the Publisher has received any payment for this "stripped book."

First Printing: March, 1993

Printed in the United States of America

To two great editors,
Ann Lafarge and Debbie Kane:
Who says lightning never strikes the same place twice?

And above all,
to Alexis and Ralph,
who cheer me on, and keep me
steadily supplied with lemonade and love.

Chapter One

"Ooph!"

George Aubrey Tate, Fifth Earl of Sefton, had the breath well and truly driven out of him by a projectile too large to be a dog and too small to be a pony. It came flying out the side door without warning and sent him flying backwards down the three shallow brick steps he had just climbed with some difficulty.

"Beg pardon!" the projectile cried as they tumbled to the ground in a welter of skirts. "Truly sorry . . ."

"Leave off, you silly woman," George said with feeling as his beaver hat slid down over his face. The ankle he had twisted recently was fairly screaming. His attacker scrambled inelegantly to disengage herself from atop him, banging him across the shins with his own walking stick in the process.

"Ouch!"

"Oh! I've hit you with your cane, haven't I?" the anguished female voice cried.

George felt his presence of mind, his *sangfroid*, slipping. "Look here, miss," George said as firmly as he could through tears of pain, "I'm sure your intentions are . . ." George paused, realizing that her intentions could not possibly be construed as other than malicious. "Your intentions need

7

not concern us now," he amended sharply. "Let us simply speak to the moment and . . ."

A pair of hands seized his lapels and his beaver hat slid off the side of his head and into the dust of the Hanover's drive. "Please, you must allow me to assist you," his captor said as she pulled mercilessly at his new jacket.

"No, I needn't!" George said. He made an impatient and ineffectual grab for his hat. "Cease pulling at my clothing, you deranged girl! As long as you are sitting on me, it will avail you nothing to try and raise me from the ground."

The girl went still, though her long brunette curls continued to bob and dance where they had escaped the none-too-clean cap on her head. She stared thoughtfully down at him.

"I'll get off of you then, shall I?"

"Superb!" George snarled. "A veritable jewel of an idea—the ghost of Descartes salutes you!"

The girl squinted at him. "Descartes?" she said uncertainly.

"The ancient Greek philosopher," George snapped. Sprawled ignominiously in his godmother's drive, he found it impossible to be civil.

"My head for the classics was never strong," the girl said, "but do you not mean the *French* philosopher Descartes?"

"Yes, yes," George replied irritably, "only as there is no blood reaching my brain at present, it finds itself unequal to purposeful thought. *Do* get up!"

"Oh! Yes, well, I'm sure I am as sorry as I can be . . ."

"For the love of all that's holy, will you simply arise, you silly female?"

The girl leaped nimbly to her feet, leaving George still spread-eagled on the ground. "I am sure I deserve your censure," she said without the least sign of contrition, "but if you had arrived by carriage or on horseback instead of sneaking in, I would never have passed through the doorway so precipitously, urgent though my mission was."

"I have been rebuked," George said sourly. He got to his

feet by degrees, wincing as his injured ankle took weight on it. "I shall advise my fellow guests to come beating a gong before them, should they be so ill advised—as I was—as to walk through the park from the main road and allow their equipage to arrive separately."

He tapped the ground with his cane and stared hard at the girl. She was of average height and wearing a dress of the poorest poplin, in an awful shade of plum which no female of his acquaintance would wear voluntarily. It was the color of the girl's eyes which struck him forcibly however, for they were the dazzling cool blue of a cloudless winter sky.

"You say you came through the park?" the girl asked, peering around him and squinting into the distance behind him.

George clenched his teeth. The effect of his rebuke, never strong, had vanished altogether. "Yes, I have just said that," he replied peevishly.

"Oh! And did you see some small children along the way—two or perhaps three?"

"If I had, I should certainly have avoided them," George replied, brushing the dust from his sleeves. *"Children* have a nasty habit of oversetting one, and I was endeavoring with my walk to strengthen an ankle injured not long since."

The girl swung round to face him again. "I suppose you mean for me to be much lowered by that remark," she said, "and I promise that I shall be, only it must be later, for I must find the children just now. Please excuse me."

She ducked around him and set off again, only to stumble over the beaver hat still lying in the drive. Incapable of ignoring his instincts, George reached out to catch her hand and keep her from falling.

"Oh! Thank you," she said breathlessly. She turned and the wide blue eyes stared guilelessly up at him. "I'm sorry— was that your hat I stepped on?"

"Only my newest and best," George said drily, surveying the wreckage of the expertly turned crown, "but what are twenty-five guineas after all?"

At last he appeared to have made an impression on her. Her eyes widened.

"Twenty-five guineas?" she exclaimed. "But that's unconscionable! Who would have the effrontery to charge twenty-five guineas for a hat?"

George released her hand and said frostily, "You have left aside an equally important consideration, which is to say, what fool would *pay* twenty-five guineas for a hat? No, no," he said, holding up his hand to silence her as two patches of color appeared on her flawless cheeks. "For the purpose of hastening to a conclusion this less than flattering exchange, I will answer that question. *Myself. I* paid twenty-five guineas for it. I will thank you to hand it to me before you can do it more harm."

The girl turned and peered about uncertainly. "Yes, if you will just point it out to me."

George stared hard at the hat, which, had it been a snake, would have bitten her, and waited. She glanced at him with a puzzled frown when no reply was forthcoming. At least she resorted to feeling about with one foot.

George reached down and snatched the hat before she could graze it with her foot and do it more harm. Really! It was most unlike his godmother to retain the services of inept persons. She might be parsimonious and therefore perennially understaffed, but those servants she *did* employ were generally more able than this one.

"What on earth is your name, young woman, and if you need spectacles, why do you not wear them?" George demanded.

"Jane," the girl replied without blinking, "and I *do* wear them, only not when I am here at Canfield, for my Aunt Eugenia has particularly desired me not to. She says that they are far too unfashionable."

"Your aunt?" George asked in some confusion. "Then you are a Hanover relation?"

"Not in actual fact," Jane replied, ducking her head. "My calling her 'aunt' is by way of convenience." She glanced

10

around worriedly. "Please, I really must excuse myself and go in search of my charges. If they are not outside then they are surely playing with their bandalores somewhere inside and something will end up broken."

George tapped his cane imperiously. "Please explain yourself."

"Well," Jane said, casting her gaze around uneasily. "I have played at battledore and shuttlecocks with them, and spillikins, but when those pastimes failed to divert, I turned them to making paper ships. It did not entertain them above half, only they said it might be jolly to see if they would actually float and when they disappeared, I began to think they might have gone off to the ornamental fountain, only if you did not see them, then they cannot have, and are probably engaged in playing with the one object they were strictly enjoined from . . ."

George clenched his teeth together through most of this speech. When he could not forbear it another instant, he stopped her by clearing his throat loudly. The girl paused and looked up at him.

"I meant, young woman, what is the precise nature of your relationship to Lady Eugenia?"

"Oh! Well, a little plain spokenness would have served your purpose better," Jane said with surprise. "It is only that we are near neighbors, and when she asks for my assistance, I am only too happy to come to her aid."

George detected a false note in her answer and lifted one brow in his most quelling manner. The girl whom it was intended to quell, however, had begun sidling toward the door. George realized with an unpleasant start that the girl desired most earnestly to be quit of his company. It was so unusual an event in his life that for an instant he could not entirely bring himself to believe it.

"Young woman . . ." he began.

A crash emanated from the house, followed by a roar not unlike that which might come from a large bear being baited mercilessly. The girl turned and her mouth went round with

11

surprise. Her lips were the soft pink of oxalis in bloom but her cheeks had suddenly lost any hint of blood.

She made a strangled sound and flew through the open door and down the corridor within. Her cap flew off and bounteous dark brown curls went streaming down her back, throwing off sparks of red and gold in the sunlight from each bay window she passed. The black and white marble squares of the floor put George in mind of a chessboard as he took a hasty step inside and landed on one. A footman or two leaped nimbly out of the girl's way as she neared the junction with the main hall. Mere pawns, George decided, and then the queen herself came sailing around the corner under full canvas.

"Jane," said Lady Eugenia. Her tone was sepulchral, her face suffused with displeasure. The girl in the lackluster plum-colored dress skidded to a halt some steps short of the mistress of Canfield as the roar of indignant youth being unfairly dealt with echoed down the stairs.

"I was just searching for the boys, Aunt Eugenia," Jane said. The riot of hair framing her flushed face made her look more like a mistress lately tumbled than a nanny or a governess.

"They have broken my Sèvres cache pot, the one I most particularly favor," Lady Eugenia said severely, "and they have been abominably cheeky in explaining how it came to happen. It does not seem to have made the least bit of difference that I charged you with only one task the whole of this day, Jane. I make allowance for your inexperience but I simply cannot conceive of how even *you* can have let them run riot in the upper gallery."

George shook off a fleeting terror, an echo of the fear that same voice had induced in him in his salad days.

"Godmama," he said nonchalantly. "I perceive I am come at a bad time for you."

That august lady pivoted with such grace that George could only admire her lightness of bearing. "George!" she exclaimed, her expression transformed from aggravation to welcome. "How delightful it is to see you! Indeed, how could you imagine that your arrival could ever be inconvenient?" With hardly a pause for breath, his godmother descended on him. "I am, of course, enchanted to see you, but how is it that you arrive at our side door?"

"I sent my coachman on without me and walked in by the home farm road. I took a fall on the hunting field some weeks past and require light exercise for rehabilitation."

George tucked his cane under his arm and began to remove his gloves without haste. His hostess made a sharp gesture with one elbow and a footman approached George. George pretended not to notice the signal, only thanking his lucky stars again for his own major domo. Neither Timothy nor any of the numerous footmen who served under him would have required so much as a blink from the earl to prompt them to so obvious a duty, no matter how unconventional or unexpected the guest's arrival.

George bestowed a scant smile on his godmother as he handed his bits and pieces to the dilatory footman. "I trust my arriving late has not caused you any inconvenience? My ankle, you know," he added politely, all the while thinking how much more delightful an extra night in Clarisse's arms had been than an evening of listening to girls barely out of the schoolroom play abominable set pieces on the piano in his godmother's salon.

Lady Eugenia beamed at her godson. "We—*I*—am so pleased to have you as a member of the party that anything you do must suit us extremely. You have missed only one day, and though I believe the entertainments and diversions I concocted were excessively well received, I flatter myself that they were the merest prelude to the delights we shall have for the remainder of the week."

Pure ennui swept through George as he contemplated the prospect. If there was even one person there whose conversation interested him for longer than the time it took to butter a slice of bread, he would be astonished. He kept a firm grip on his cane when the footman would have taken it.

So nonplussed was the young man that George felt in imminent danger of having to wrestle the liveried servant for the right to retain his own possession. At last the footman backed away with only the earl's hat, gloves and buff driving coat. Using his cane with more than ceremonial purpose, George started the long walk down the gallery, his already ill humor further strained by the contest.

Lady Eugenia fell into step beside him. "I regret to say that there is no precise entertainment or plan for this afternoon. We are to have our little country dance tonight and I thought it best to allow everyone to rest." A worrisome thought appeared to strike her. "I do hope your injury won't prevent you from standing up with at least a few of the young ladies. They are most of them, of course, beneath your notice, but I believe there are a few you will find quite up to the mark."

George forced a civil smile onto his face. Compared to the incomparable Clarisse, they would be the merest drabs. "Naturally I will endeavor to partner at least a few," he murmured.

Behind his godmother, the girl in the abominable plum-colored dress made good her escape. She was a fetching thing, George decided, or would be if she paid any attention to her turn out. Her slippered feet disappeared up the stairs and he had the feeling that he had just had the most interesting experience he would have all day, albeit an exasperating one.

". . . and then there are the Percival girls, Julia and Judith. I believe you may have met them in London during the last season. Neither of them took, but I cannot imagine another season will pass without some announcements being made. They are of the Hampshire Percivals, you know, and worth quite ten thousand pounds per year. But of course," Lady Eugenia added merrily, "that cannot signify to one of your consequence."

George managed a tight-lipped smile. "Whether it is a question of too little or too much, it must always be a consideration."

Not for the first time, George wondered what on earth had possessed his otherwise rational Mama to choose Lady Eugenia Hanover as her only son's godmother. He conveniently forgot that he had perpetuated the connection by agreeing to allow Lady Eugenia to bring out his sister Portia with her own girls, but his widowed mother would never have cast off that duty and gone to Italy unless George had accepted the arrangement as head of the family. They reached the main reception area and George judged it time to touch on that arrangement, and the main reason for his visit.

"And my sister Portia, she fares well?" he asked.

"Oh, more than well," Lady Eugenia assured him, tapping him on the arm with her fan. "Depend upon it, she will be happily spoken for before this season ends. I would not—*could* not—fail in my duty to dear Fanny. Her daughter is as dear to me as my own girls, as you must know."

"And so I do," George said, knowing full well that Lady Eugenia had done her daughters no disservice by welcoming Portia into their midst. Who knew better than she that the presence of an heiress would bring more suitors within proposing distance of her own two girls? "And is Portia about?"

Lady Eugenia shied like a horse encountering a water jump. "Indeed not!" she exclaimed. "I have given all the girls strictest orders to spend the afternoon resting quietly, so that they will all be in looks for tonight. I sent up lavender water compresses for them to put on their eyes, too, to take away any hint of puffiness."

George tried to think what dissolute activity might have produced puffy eyes in strictly chaperoned young girls, but failed. He, on the other hand, had had a very tiring night.

"If you will permit, my dear godmother, I will follow their example and retire to my room until this evening."

"Dear George, of course." Lady Eugenia said, her face wreathed in smiles. "I am quite sure your man will have made everything ready for you. It is one of the comforts one can be sure of in London—finding adequate servants, I

15

mean. Here in the country it is lamentably different. Either they consider themselves to good for service or they are too simple-minded to be adequately trained."

"I must take your word for it," George said drily. He thought again of the girl with the piercing blue eyes. The truth was that she was quite the most distracting thing he had seen since he'd first laid eyes on Clarisse, though Clarisse was more in the traditional style of what passed for beautiful.

"That girl," he said, impelled by curiosity, "Jane. Does she come to you often?"

"Jane Oxenby? Oh, as often as need be," his godmother said airily, "but as you can see, she's not much better than nothing, only one cannot seem to *hint* to the Sherwoods how much one would appreciate it if they were not quite so devoted to their children as to bring them *everywhere* they go." Her brow wrinkled and then cleared as she recalled the subject at hand. "Of course, Jane was not raised to service, not at all. Her father married a *most* unsuitable woman while on the Grand Tour and the family refused to acknowledge the union. I'm afraid Jane has led rather an odd life. She is sadly unable to keep her opinions to herself. And she *will* laugh right out loud in the most vulgar fashion! I only offer her the chance to come to Canfield because I feel sorry for her."

George kept his reaction to that piece of information to himself as he took leave of his aunt outside the chamber reserved for him. If he was thinking of the right Sherwoods, their children were bound to be execrable brats, and the blue-eyed girl were better to take refuge in a cave than accept the job of caring for them. He allowed Henry to strip away his neck cloth and pull off his boots. Settling down by the window with a glass of good wine and a novel, George congratulated himself on having avoided the rest of his godmother's guests for one more afternoon. Soon enough he would have to face them, and ascertain whether there was any truth to the disturbing rumor that had reached him in London that Portia was on the verge of attaching herself to a cash-poor country squire.

A dark look settled over his lordship's face as he contemplated the thought of a fortune hunter marrying his sister. It was an irksome duty, being obliged to see to the welfare of his sister, but one he meant to discharge as well as he knew how. It had been a near thing with his other sister, Horatia, now happily married and living in America, but she had fallen prey to the blandishments of an awful rogue out to get his hands on her money. If George had exercised more attention, it would not have reached the pass it had. It was an error he did not intend to duplicate.

George crossed his stockinged feet and gazed out over Canfield Park. Approving a husband for Portia would take special care, for she had neither looks nor conversation to recommend her. Portia was the sum of all her parents' more unfortunate traits, but George knew his mother had done her best with her third child, her ugly duckling. It was just that her best had not been enough.

The effects of the wine coupled with his long walk put George into a doze. He fell asleep wondering what the result might have been if the effort put into Portia had been expended on that girl Jane instead. . . .

"They say he's an awful rake," Imogene Hanover whispered.

Her twin nodded vigorously. "And that he makes love to all of the married ladies but none of the unmarried ones," Emmaline added.

Imogene giggled and colored up prettily. "But how shocking it would be if he *did,*" she exclaimed. "And how divine . . ."

Julia and Judith Percival looked at one another and smiled knowingly. *They* had been out for a whole season and could set these poor country mice straight. Keeping their voices low so as not to give their hostess reason to look in on them, they imparted their superior knowledge.

"It is not the current earl but his father of whom you speak," Julia said archly. "All of London knows what a roué *he* was. They say that wagers were made at White's on the number of married women he would seduce before a husband finally caught up with him."

"But none did!" Imogene protested. "Mama has told us he died while racing his curricle on a moonless night."

Julia resisted the titter that rose to her lips, not wanting to offend poor, naive Imogene. "Yes, but racing to get away from a husband," she said, "*and* his pack of hounds. It was the *on dit* of the season when it happened."

"Indeed, I have heard it said that he was such a prodigious philanderer that we shall never see his equal again," Judith said loftily. She did not add that it was her own mother who had made the remark, and that Judith had heard it while eavesdropping at her mother's salon door.

All four girls had craned in a most unseemly manner for the best view of the earl as he had come striding down the avenue leading from the home farm. Jammed shoulder to shoulder in the box window, they had sighed over his proud bearing, his fine profile, his broad shoulders, each privately wishing that he would make love to *her*. What a coup it would be! The excessively handsome, terribly wealthy Earl of Sefton dangling after one's self!

"Perhaps his father's reputation makes him unsuitable for any girl with a very strict notion of what is proper," Emmaline ventured timidly.

"I think it reflects well on him that he does not pursue the married ladies or the unmarried ones," Judith said. "It will puff up the consequence of whoever does marry him by that much more—and he *must* marry eventually. I declare, *I* would have him."

"Tish tosh!" Julia put in. "As if he would even look at you." She was the elder by a year and felt entitled to squelch her younger sister's pretensions. She cast a conspiratorial look at her circle of listeners that caused them to lean in closer. "My brother has told me that his lordship keeps the most divine mistress, and that *that* is why he has no interest in marrying."

Imogene and Emmaline gasped in unison. "No!"

Julia angled her head in what she knew to be a becoming way and looked at them from beneath her lashes. "Egan has seen her on the street and declares that she is so beautiful he quite forgot to breathe while she was in sight."

Judith forgot to be annoyed that their brother had not shared this marvelous piece of intelligence with *her*. "Who can she be?" she squealed. "What is her name?"

All three girls waited breathlessly for Julia's description but it never came. Instead, their conversation was cut short by the arrival of the sister of the very man they were discussing. Julia kept her composure the best of them all but even she jumped noticeably. Portia always moved so quietly that she barely stirred the air as she passed.

"Lady Eugenia," she said in a whisper, "is coming."

All five girls were prostrate and breathing deeply when Lady Eugenia paused to look in on them, but in four virginal breasts lurked the hope that the dangerously handsome, dangerously masculine Earl of Sefton would show her some special attention that night—not enough to put her friends in a pet but enough to make the evening an unqualified success.

Only Portia did not share their aspirations, quite natural since it was her brother the others sought to attach. Portia lay bathed in gloom. She too had caught a glimpse of George approaching, but from a bay window in the gallery where she had been waiting in hopes of talking to the overworked Jane Oxenby. Not to anyone—not even her only friend, Jane—could Portia confide the terror she had felt when she learned that her brother would shortly be joining the party at Canfield.

In every endeavor, George excelled to the exact degree that Portia failed, which was to say, utterly. She did not mind comparisons—those she had long ago learned to live with. With a beautiful sister, a charming mama, and a brother who was considered to be on a par with royal dukes as husband material, Portia had even become accustomed to a fair amount of veiled pity.

No, George's arrival did not inspire terror because she was the ugly Tate, the banal Tate, the Tate who would never amount to much, but because George loved her, and wanted only the best for her. Like everything else in her miserable existence, it was all upside down. Any other girl would have been glad to have George as a brother. Among his friends were all the brightest beaux, including the royal dukes whom he so outshone.

But Portia would have preferred it if George had not bent so much of his attention on her, throwing her back into the pond, as it were. She did not wish to be shown off, though she knew George was only prompted by the best of intentions. No, it was less that Portia wished for, not more. Only to Jane had Portia managed to convey how she longed for a quiet life where her deficiencies and shortcomings could pass unremarked. Portia was quite sure she could never screw up the courage to explain it to George, and even more sure that he would not approve of the one man who thought she was fine just as she was. Jonas was, in his way, as imperfect as Portia was in hers; even Jane, who was his cousin, did not quite like him.

Portia had prayed earnestly that some dreadful affliction would seize her, or that some contagion would carry her off before she was obliged to face George again. Even as she repeated that forlorn prayer, she heard the rustle of skirts and knew that the maids were carrying in the warm washing-up water. It was time to begin getting ready for dinner and Portia realized with a sinking feeling that she had not managed to contract so much as a chill.

Chapter Two

"Is there no way to make that popinjay understand that his attentions are not welcome?" George said, smiling pleasantly around clenched teeth. He nodded to an acquaintance passing by. His sister quivered like a sapling in a strong wind and drew her shawl tighter around her but said nothing.

Across the room, Sir Jonas Biddle had tapped his finger to his nose, winked, bobbed, and otherwise signaled his interest in having Portia join him so blatantly that an onlooker might have thought them already married. Apart from a few dances at the beginning of the evening, George had kept Portia securely lashed to his side all night, but Biddle persisted in making a spectacle of himself. His loud voice carried across the open floor when the musicians paused.

"And anyone who pays his grooms more than that deserves to be horsewhipped," he was saying to a young dandy with shirt points so high that he had to turn his entire body to see anything to his right or left. "And as for maids, I cannot see why one should pay them at all! Why, they sleep in until all hours and then act as if it were *our* job to serve *them*."

George began to think that the *best* that might be said about Biddle was that he was a fortune hunter. In fact, George would have welcomed an unvarnished fortune hunter at that moment, provided that his lack of money was his sole blemish. What he got, however, was Lady Eugenia sailing toward him with a young female in tow.

"George, may I present Lady Judith Percival? She is quite sure you will not recall her from your ball at Sefton House. Such a crush—but everything, *everything,* that one could desire!"

"But of course I remember you," George said smoothly to the dark-haired girl. He couldn't remember ever having seen her before in his life. He took her hand and bestowed a light kiss on the back of it. Out of the corner of his eye, he saw Jonas Biddle hot-footing it across the dance floor toward them. There was nothing he could do to forestall the inevitable so he accepted it with the closest thing to grace he could manage. "Lady Judith, would you honor me with this dance?"

"Oh, your lordship," she said breathlessly, "with pleasure."

Try as he might, George could not sustain a conversation with the girl. He was too distracted by watching Jonas Biddle pounce on Portia and sweep her off onto the dance floor. Dancing was only one of many things Portia did not do well, but under Jonas Biddle's domineering guidance she looked even clumsier than usual.

"I see that you are interested in your sister's partner," Judith said, peering up at the Earl of Sefton in a way she hoped was flirtatious without being pert.

"What? Oh, forgive me," George said, annoyed to be caught out. It was one thing for Jonas Biddle to be mannerless, but quite another for himself to forget what was proper.

"We have all noticed that she is . . . comfortable in Sir Jonas's company," Judith said.

George gritted his teeth. "Yes, quite," he said. "I feel that way about my favorite hunter, too, but I would not marry him."

"Oh, indeed, you are too droll!" Judith exclaimed with a trill of laughter that set George's nerves on edge. "Of course we are all hoping you will do no such thing. What a hardship it would be to us unmarried females to lose such a bachelor as yourself, and to a horse!"

This one wasted no time in coming to the point, thought George. He forced himself to smile. "I am sure you exaggerate my worth, Lady Judith. One so lovely as yourself must have so many offers that you are quite dizzy with them. Surely mine will not be missed."

Judith preened discernibly. "La! I think you put me to the blush, my lord. I did not mean to suggest for an instant that I expected any such attention from you—not that it would not be most welcome," she added with a lighthearted smile.

"But you are being most unfair, Lady Judith," George demurred. "Am I not showing you my regard at this very moment?" George executed a turn and had a clear view of Jonas. His round cheeks were the color of overripe tomatoes, and a sheen of perspiration covered his upper lip as he manipulated a pale Portia around the floor. *Pompous, pushing popinjay!*

"Indeed! And I am sure the other young ladies are gone quite the greenest shade one can imagine—envy, you know," Judith said with a titter.

George smiled at her with just the degree of pleasantness to indicate acquaintance but not attachment. Lord, but these conversations ever took only one turning! It had been fully ten months since he had last been obliged to stand up with an unmarried girl. Ten months was a pitifully short span of time—either that or his memory was lacking. He could have sworn he had had more or less this same conversation at *that* affair, and with at least four different young females.

He managed to keep enough of his wits in the foreground to finish the dance and still uphold his end of the conversation, but he was quite sure he hadn't said anything scintillating. Of course, it would have been wasted on Lady

Judith Percival if he had. He restored her to his godmother and bowed before making a surreptitious exit. He needed at least a few moments to himself away from the presence of the matrimonially minded.

It was a good deal cooler in the rotunda at the top of the staircase. Galleries led off east and west, and George made a rapid surveillance, trying to decide which corridor was less likely to have attracted those looking for an improper moment or two alone in one another's company. His eye fell on a figure in a chair just inside the east corridor.

It was the girl who had run him down that afternoon. Her head was slumped to one side in a most peculiar manner and one arm hung limp at her side. George hastened to her and knelt down. He pulled off his white evening gloves so that he could touch her wrist with bare fingers. She did not stir but the strong pulse there relieved him on at least one score.

"Miss Oxenby," he whispered, not wishing to draw the attention of a footman who was passing by.

Her eyelids flickered but she took a deep breath and drooped deeper into the embrace of the chair. Quite seriously alarmed now, George gently took hold of her shoulder. The flesh there was warm and marvelously soft beneath his palm.

"Miss Oxenby! I say, are you all right?" he hissed. He gave her a little shake that made her head wobble.

"Hmm?" She smiled ever so slightly and adjusted her head so that it was supported more fully by the back of the chair. "Go 'way, nanny. Not time yet . . ."

"I say, Miss Oxenby," George said a little more forcefully.

A little frown creased the smooth skin between her eyebrows. They were very pretty eyebrows, he noted, with just the right amount of arch to them, and lustrous, like the hair curled and piled carelessly on top of her head. She sighed and nestled into the chair. George began to suspect that he was dealing not with the vapors but with exhaustion.

"Miss Oxenby, please, you must wake up," George said,

growing desperate. He put a fingertip under her chin and lifted her head, but it obeyed gravity and he was forced to use his whole hand to support the weight of it.

Jane came awake to the feel of masculine fingers under her chin. "Oh!" she said, staring into heavy-lidded, deep blue eyes. Her own eyes were not fully open but she felt quite sure it was the same man she had collided with that day. The high forehead and proud, almost hawkish nose fit her impression of him perfectly.

"So you are with us after all," he said. "I began to be quite worried." George's relief betrayed itself in a smile.

Jane couldn't help smiling back. "I'm sorry. Did I give you a fright?" she asked.

George cleared his throat. "Not precisely," he said. He found he was a little embarrassed, now that she was awake, to be kneeling at her feet like a suitor.

"I didn't *mean* to fall asleep," Jane said. "It's just that, well . . ."

"You were tired," George said absently. Her eyes were absolutely mesmerizing, drawing him into their clear depths.

"Well, as a matter of fact, I . . ." Jane searched for the right words but couldn't find them. He was looking at her so *oddly,* his face so close that she could see every line and angle easily. He had a stern sort of male beauty that could not fail to inspire admiration.

"As a matter of fact, you arose very early this morning, worked hard all day and are now at the end of your strength," he supplied in an even tone, his eyes never leaving hers.

Jane disengaged her hand from his. She found the steadiness of his gaze unsettling. "If you will just step aside, I'll walk around a bit to revive myself," she said nervously.

George felt the strain in her voice. "Of course, Miss Oxenby." He rose to his feet. An emotion he only vaguely recognized as mortification coursed through him. "I did not mean to detain you."

Feeling considerably more at ease now that he had moved away, Jane laughed. "That would be quite impossible to do," she said. "The sum of my evening is to sit here so that I can do any service any of the ladies might require of me."

George gazed down at her and thought of what it might be like to be at the beck and call of his godmother, or of someone like Lady Judith Percival. He shuddered inwardly. Though unfailingly polite to his own servants, he had never until that moment considered what it might be like to *be* one.

"And what of the gentlemen?" he said, thinking he might engage her and spare her the necessity of waiting on anyone. "Are they to fend for themselves? May they not speak for your services?"

As soon as he said it, he realized she might place the wrong construction on his words, but she was either too innocent or too forgiving to do so. Instead, she laughed. It sent a warmth through him.

"I believe any number of footmen are within easy call," she said, "so if you will excuse me . . ."

"Why is it that you desire so earnestly to be rid of me?" George said somewhat plaintively. "We have encountered one another only twice and yet each time you no sooner see me than you do your best to be away from me."

"Well, you are an invited guest and I am a . . . a *factotum,*" Jane said. "My Aunt Eugenia would not thank me for diverting your attention."

"And if *I* decide that—as her guest—I *wish* to have you divert me? Say, perhaps, to walk the gallery with me and amuse me with some inconsequential conversation?"

Jane moistened her lips thoughtfully. "Then it might be all right, I suppose."

"Good!" George declared. He offered her his arm imperiously. "Now we shall stroll and you shall be, for the moment, Miss Oxenby, *not* a factotum."

Jane hid her giggle behind a small cough as she slipped her hand over his forearm. Lady Eugenia was forever reminding her that men did not at all care for females who laughed at them.

"Does the music and dancing please you?" she asked. He would be bound by politeness to say yes, and that would keep their conversation on safe ground.

"I suppose they are tolerable," he said, "but I found it necessary to absent myself for a while. The aroma of fortune hunters abounds."

Jane thought of her cousin Jonas and chuckled. "I suppose it is a necessary evil. Are you not also hanging out for a rich wife?"

"Isn't everyone?" he asked lightly.

"Since you have rescued me from being a factotum, at least for a little while, perhaps I could help you," Jane volunteered.

"In what way?" George asked, highly entertained.

"Well," Jane said, "I spend a considerable amount of time among the young ladies. I could perhaps—without violating any confidences, you understand—convey the ladies' feelings towards you—who might favor your suit, who prefers another. I feel sure you must already know well enough who has a fortune and who has a mere competence, so that I would *not* endeavor to tell you."

George fought to hide his smile. What a refreshing creature she was—so matter of fact about fortunes and competencies! He felt sure that Lady Judith Percival knew within a percent what his income was per year, and yet she would undoubtedly turn handsprings rather than admit it.

"It is a generous offer," he said. "Let me consider whether I should accept, thereby placing myself in your debt."

"Oh, pooh!" Jane declared. "I should be doing the others a service. You are not ill-favored, and I daresay there is an heiress or two who would think you worth her fortune."

"Ah, you flatter me," George said with a twinkle in his eye.

"Indeed, I do not," Jane said promptly. "I am sadly lacking in that art. Well, the truth is, I don't have the stomach for it. I am all in favor of simple courtesy, but as for humbug and fiddle faddle . . ."

"You find yourself sadly lacking?" George suggested.

"Quite," Jane agreed. A vision in puce appeared at the head of the corridor. "Oh, dear, it is Aunt Eugenia!"

"You had better go then," George said. "My godmother is a formidable woman but you may safely leave her to me. I have a topic to discuss with her which will undoubtedly distract her thoughts."

Jane walked away quickly, back to her lonely chair next to an overgrown aspidistra. George watched her go. She was clothed in a high-waisted evening dress in an orangish-red shade horribly at odds with her coloring. George, who had a well-developed sense of style, decided that Miss Jane Oxenby was truly a victim of poor fashion judgment. What she *did* possess, however, no dressmaker could supply. The Earl of Sefton found himself much restored by his encounter with Miss Jane Oxenby, and went forward to meet his godmother with renewed good humor.

George placed a few light pencil strokes into the picture of lillies he was drawing. He worked quietly but not with any degree of concentration. Too much else competed for his attention.

After parting company with the charming *factotum* the night before, he had forced himself to spend half an hour in Sir Jonas Biddle's company, to see if he could discover any redeeming quality in the man which would make it possible to consider him a candidate for Portia's hand. Not a single attribute had been evident. To the contrary, Jonas had become even more fulsome and annoying, which George would have previously laid money was impossible. Even worse, Portia had cleaved to Jonas as if espaliered to him.

Unless George acted, and acted quickly, he feared he would soon be saddled with a brother-in-law he would as soon consign to the Outer Hebrides as have to Sefton House for Christmas dinner. The thought of being forced to raise glasses in a toast with a country squire who smelled faintly of bad boot black made George feel quite nauseous. He knew without fear of contradiction that if Jonas came to the capital, he would be dubbed with some awful sobriquet by the pundits. Just as George himself was known as Selfless Sefton over a less than flattering and best forgotten incident, Jonas would be labeled within a week of his arrival. In fact, the more George thought about it, the more likely he thought it that Jonas would be known as Bad Boot Black Biddle. It had the alliterative flair the wits favored.

No one had dared refer to George as Selfless Sefton in many years, at least not within his hearing, but his own memories of the incident which had engendered the name still covered him with shame. It was fortunate that he had not yet reached his maturity when the episode had occurred. His youth had blunted society's censure and the passage of time had blunted society's memory. Only in George's mind did the incident still burn bright.

He eased his stiff ankle by flexing his leg, knocking over the leather portfolio leaning up against his shooting stick. He did not care for the turn his thoughts were taking and was just wondering whether he might not as effectively escape the other house guests by simply strolling Canfield's park when he saw a flash of movement beyond a hedge.

He stayed carefully still, suspecting he might be drawn into a walking party if he made his presence known. He heard no chatter, no whistling, no clues of any kind as to who might be approaching. Soon enough, though, he had his answer, as Miss Jane Oxenby hove into view. Suddenly he found he wished his peace to be disturbed after all.

"Why, Miss Oxenby, do you mean to run me over again?"

Jane slowed and glanced about before squinting in his direction. "Of course not," she said. "Actually, I had not even noticed you there."

"I rather thought you had not," he answered, standing up, "but then that is precisely the circumstance that led to your oversetting me yesterday."

She did not appear to think that required an answer. "You are quite some distance from the house," she said. "Are you lost?"

"Indeed I am not, Miss Oxenby. I have come out here for the purpose of sketching. I had to walk some distance, though, before I found a subject that interested me," he said with somewhat less than complete truthfulness.

The girl began to move toward him. "And what did you find?"

"Those lilies over there," he said. She glanced around nearsightedly and George realized that her best chance of seeing the lilies was in his sketch. "Would you care to see the result of my efforts?" he asked, holding out the paper.

Jane took it and held it up to her face. George watched her, reflecting that with each additional meeting, he found her more and more handsome. She had a long, almost Grecian neck, and an aggressively straight nose that joined the forehead at the bridge with such a no-nonsense finality that it must make anyone cautious, for though the overall impression she created was one of femininity and youth, the bridge of the nose warned of far sterner stuff within.

The prominent cheekbones would be bound to disqualify her from being thought a classic English beauty—they hinted at Mediterranean antecedents—but the exquisite line of her finely formed mouth made the artist in him long to discard the top sheet of his sketching book and begin to draw her. Alas, he knew that his only skill lay in botanical subjects.

He was so absorbed in observing her that he was startled when she declared, "It is quite good. Your grasp of detail is commendable."

George smiled. "Why do you not wear your spectacles when you are at your leisure?" She handed the sketch back and walked several paces away. *There! She was distancing herself again!*

"The truth is, I find it convenient not to while I am still on the grounds of Canfield. I am neither a servant nor a guest, and without my spectacles I find I can quite easily detach myself from situations that would not otherwise be completely comfortable."

George admired her good sense and candor at the same time he was drawn back to scrutinizing her face. The irises of her large blue eyes were encircled by a darker corona, lending a piercing quality to her gaze. It quite transfixed his feet to the ground, even though he knew she could not see him at all clearly. That much he knew because her earnest gaze was focused slightly to the left of his nose.

"It occurs to me, Miss Oxenby, that you and I have not the benefit of a formal introduction. I have the advantage, in that I have already inquired as to your name from my godmother. Do you not find yourself curious as to *my* identity, or have you likewise taken steps to find out who I am?"

"No, I took no such steps," she admitted. She dropped her gaze and stared at George's neckcloth. "There was no point. As I have already informed you, I am not here at Canfield to socialize."

"Did it not occur to you to wonder about my character when you proposed to help me find a rich wife—whether you might be aiding some dastardly villain?"

Jane laughed. "I perceived in your voice and manner that you were a gentleman and so did not scruple to offer what little help I could. Besides, my aunt is a woman of the strictest niceness. You would not be here if there was any whiff of scandal attached to you."

George could not fault her reasoning but an imp drove him on. "Do you not find yourself at least a little curious about my apperance?"

Jane cocked her head to one side while she considered it,

no more self-conscious than a dog which swivels its head about, wondering if it has heard or only imagined the cry of a woodcock nearby. To see a refined young woman behave in so natural a manner rocked George.

"Well, perhaps a little curious," she finally said. "I already know that you are above average height by some two or three inches—no bad thing in a man—and from your outline, I perceive that you are well-made. Your coloring is dark, and your hair is inordinately shiny."

George repressed a laugh. "Are there standards for such things, Miss Oxenby, that I should be judged and found excessive in that quality?"

"Oh, I did not mean to say so," Jane demurred mildly. "In fact, your valet seems to feel that you are precisely what is to be hoped for in every category by which a gentleman may be judged."

George reflected on that for a moment. "You have heard my valet speak of me?"

"This morning, yes, when I went belowstairs to read the newspapers, as I like to, with the housekeeper. She is my old nurse's sister."

George puzzled on that for a minute. "Then how, since you did not know my identity, did you know that Henry was *my* valet?"

"Oh, quite simply because he spoke of the ruination of your lordship's clothing, and in particular, the beaver hat of which you are—*were*—so fond. In despairing of it altogether, I collect you have made your valet a very happy man. He proposes to have it repaired and means to wear it himself."

"So you are in possession of all the facts regarding my identity?"

Jane nodded slowly, struck by the deepness of his voice. He had moved several steps closer, within an arm's length. His face was little more than a blur to her, though, since he was standing with his back to a very bright spring sun. For a man of his rank to freely admit that he required a wealthy bride had been no more than a snippet of truth admitted to a nobody. It was not unusual at all, of course, for a nobleman to require new wealth to restore encumbered or crumbling estates.

Yes, she thought, I know who you are, but not why you are showing such interest in me, who has neither rank nor fortune. Instead she said, "I believe I had better be going. Since you know your way back to the house . . ."

He stepped closer. "And if I did not?"

Jane pulled her cloak tighter. "Why, then I would have been glad to show you the way," she said. "As it is, I am expected elsewhere."

"And what if I requested your presence here, much in the same spirit as last night, to while away some empty moments?"

Oh, dear, Jane thought, *now I am afraid I understand all too well why you are taking an interest in me.* "Then I should say to you that I am not at liberty to entertain you," she said. "In point of fact, I am on an errand."

George quirked an eyebrow. "Then perhaps you would not mind if I strolled along."

Jane cleared her throat. "As it happens, I am on my own time," she said uneasily.

"And you would prefer not to spend time in my company unless obliged to?"

A faint flush appeared on her cheeks. "It is not that, precisely."

"I assure you, Miss Oxenby, you are quite safe in my company. Your assessment of me was correct. No hint of scandal attaches to me because I have never given anyone the least cause for complaint—at least where well-bred young ladies are concerned."

She lifted her head and studied him with interest. "I suppose there can be no objection then," she said at length.

"You mean you can think of no other reason to turn me

down," George said.

"No, I meant what I said. You may walk with me if you care to, but we must part company at the edge of Canfield."

"Ah! An air of mystery! I like it, Miss Oxenby. It suits you. You are the lady of gentle birth fallen on hard times, after all, are you not?"

Jane started walking. She did not even wait to see if he joined her. "My father always said that concocting fanciful stories to explain perfectly ordinary facts—a thing I did rather a lot of at a certain age—showed a want of intelligence," Jane said.

"Your point is well taken, Miss Oxenby. I perceive that I have offended you."

"Not at all," Jane replied. "It is only that your characterization misses the mark."

"And you do not intend to enlighten me."

"I see no point."

George drew a deep breath. She was not being elusive for the sake of creating mystery. Of that he felt sure. He had been trying to elicit more facts to support his supposition, but she was not playing the game as she ought. If he had so baldly attempted to draw out another young woman on the subject of herself, he would have been obliged to listen to a history that commenced with her birth and ended only with yesterday's dinner menu. They walked on in silence.

"This is the boundary of your godmother's property," Jane said at last, stopping at a stile. She turned and offered him her hand.

George realized he had not begun to breach her reserve. What a maddening creature she was! And yet so beguiling, with her forthright manner and incomparable face. "Miss Oxenby, I would be a very poor sort of man if I let you go on alone." He gestured around. "We are in the middle of nowhere. Wild animals might come and drag you off."

Jane laughed. "I hardly think so. You have been listening to Uncle Harry's hunting stories, have you not?"

George took her hand and bent over it. He looked up, his eyes brimming with mischief. Now she could *not* pull away. "Indeed I have not. No, I am only pointing out what any sensible man would—that you will not be entirely safe without me."

She smiled and withdrew her hand from his grasp. "I begin to believe—your disclaimer to the contrary—that I am not safe so long as you are near."

George edged a step closer. With the stile behind her, the girl had no choice but to stand her ground. Her eyes widened.

"And now, Miss Oxenby, I will emancipate you only if you explain why it is that I must go no further with you. Does the neighboring landowner not look kindly on the Hanovers? Would one of their guests not be welcome on his property?"

"I do not believe that to be the case," Jane said reluctantly. "They deal tolerably well with one another."

"Well, then, what is it?"

Jane sighed. "This property belongs to someone for whom *you* do not care," she admitted. "You may encounter him and then you would not thank me for not having warned you, for it would provide him with an opportunity to further the acquaintance."

The Earl of Sefton raised one eyebrow. Truly, Jane thought, he was devastatingly handsome. She ignored the uncomfortably heavy beating of her heart. With his title and his looks, he could lay claim to any feminine heart in the isle. She determined that it would not be hers, for nothing could come of it. When he *did* set up his nursery, it must be with someone whose rank more closely parallelled his own—and whose fortune made up for his own lack of one.

"Well?" he asked. "You have my complete attention. Are we to talk in riddles and conundrums or will you name this person?"

Jane licked her lips. "It is Jonas Biddle, your lordship."

George did not move, but behind his eyes, had he but known it, was the look of a man who has been dashed in the face with cold water. Jane perceived it immediately but the earl prevented her from saying anything palliative by speaking first.

"Am I so transparent then?" George asked icily. He straightened abruptly and clenched his hands together behind his back.

Oh, dear, Jane thought. She did not at all care for the Earl of Sefton in his haughty, high-handed guise. He was charming when there was a glint of humor in his eye, but this autocratic, hard-edged man sent a chill through her. It was ten times worse than the quivery feeling Aunt Eugenia's scolds produced, and that was quite bad enough. She stepped onto the first rung of the stile and turned only when she had taken a calming breath.

"I know that you dislike Jonas because of what your sister has told me," Jane said carefully. He raised his eyebrows in inquiry and she went on. "Portia reported to me the substance of your conversation with her after the ball last night."

"Did she?" he asked coolly. "Did she indeed? I perceive that you enjoy a rare friendship with my sister."

"If by that you mean that she talks to me, then yes, I suppose it may be true," Jane admitted.

"Come, come, Miss Oxenby. To be disingenuous does not suit you. I am persuaded that behind that wide open countenance resides a penetrating mind. Of course you are aware that Portia does not talk readily with others. Why, I could not elicit above half a dozen words from her last night."

"Perhaps she felt your mind was already made up on the subject," Jane suggested.

"And perhaps she never says more than a half-dozen words to anyone on any subject," he countered sharply. They were the words of a man hurt to discover that the sister he loved could more easily confide in a stranger than himself.

Jane clasped her mittened hands together. "I feel I must defend her," she said. The earl's lids dropped over the deep blue eyes. It made his expression all that much more forbidding but Jane persevered. "Just because Portia does not communicate so volubly as other girls her age does not mean she does not have a host of thoughts and feelings. She knows her own mind and I find her quite sensible. And," she added, "she is quite sensible of what your position must be, too. She simply disagrees with it."

"I see," George said drily. "So, on the strength of her half-dozen words, I am to intuit that she is sensible, that she appreciates my position, and that she nonetheless prefers Jonas Biddle above all others." He paused, surveying her. "What I am unable to determine on the strength of this very slim evidence, however, is what she sees in him that would serve to amend my own impression of him as greedy, grasping, ill-bred, loud and domineering. The man has not the least shred of erudition, manner or conversation. She cannot even have fallen in love with a pretty face, for Sir Jonas resembles nothing so much as a stump which has yet to be pulled from the ground!"

Jane's spine stiffened as his lordship's words gathered momentum and anger. She did not care for her cousin, but to have a stranger denigrate him made her want to point out any virtues in him that she could. Since none sprang to mind, she was reduced to an angry retort. "I see! And all this you have determined in one short evening!" The earl opened his mouth to respond but Jane rushed on. "Yours must be a dizzying intellect that you can so easily penetrate the mysteries of a human soul upon such short acquaintance!"

"Miss Oxenby, you are quite the most shining example of feminine sense it has been my fortune to meet—leaving my mother aside. Kindly use that prodigious brain of yours to delineate the fine traits in Sir Jonas that make you champion him so warmly. I swear, I am longing to be persuaded to take another view of him."

Jane was struck dumb.

"Miss Oxenby?" the earl inquired when a long silence had passed.

Jane took a gulp of air. "What virtues my cousin may possess in my eyes or in yours must count for nothing when compared to Portia's opinion," Jane declared with spirit. "I suggest you ask *her*, only you will have to do it in a considerably milder manner than you are currently using with me, since bullying her will not serve."

Out of all this intelligence, George heard only one thing. "Your cousin!"

Jane regarded him as steadily as she could, sick that in the heat of the moment she had revealed a connection she abhorred. "Yes, he is my relation," she said unwillingly.

The earl's face hardened. "Why, then, Miss Oxenby, I believe this very edifying exchange is at an end. I could not collect how an otherwise sensible female could see value where none existed, but now I perceive the way of it. I beg you will forget the bruising things I have said about your cousin. I would not have said them had I known who you were."

"I will not be able to forgive them," Jane said, tipping her chin up.

"I did not ask for your forgiveness," the earl pointed out, "as I feel there is nothing unfair in the assessment I have made. I merely ask that you forget them, and only consider the offense you might have been spared if you had but advised me of the connection before this."

"Must your acquaintances provide you with a list of family and friends prior to conversing with you then, so as to avoid hearing them slandered?" Jane asked hotly.

The earl's face went a degree colder. "That, I think, deserves no answer." He lifted his hat and made a slight, stiff bow. "I will not detain you further."

Chapter Three

Jane returned from her errand to the Dower House in a considerably worse frame of mind than when she had left. In fact, she had been in an agreeable mood all day, right up to the point when she had encountered the Earl of Sefton, and even—if she were to be honest—some minutes into their interview. But when the conversation had turned to Jonas, she had been put completely out of countenance and stayed so for the rest of the day.

Nanny had not been deceived by her attempt to dissemble either. Not for anything would Jane have had Nanny guess what was amiss. Fortunately for Jane's peace of mind, Nanny was not so omniscient as Jane had always imagined. Instead, that formidable but good-hearted woman had leapt to the conclusion that Jane was being run into the ground by That Woman. For as long as Jane could remember, Lady Eugenia Hanover had been "That Woman" to Nanny, for failing to have championed Jane's mother in society, with the result that any chance she might have had of being accepted was lost.

Even the brisk walk back through the sparkling spring day failed to dislodge Jane's uncharacteristic gloom. When she arrived at Canfield, Jane paused outside the garden door to dispossess her boots of the mud they had acquired when she had cut through the fields rather than risk another encounter with the Earl of Sefton. Jonas loomed out of the doorway and Jane jumped in the act of taking off her mittens.

"Jonas!" she said on a gasp.

Jonas smiled at her unctuously. "I have been awaiting your return, cousin. I wish to speak with you most urgently."

"You must make it brief," she said irritably, her nerves still ajangle. "I am sure I am wanted upstairs."

"Jane, Jane," her cousin said with ill-disguised reproof, "would you not rather be your own mistress than be ruled by Lady Eugenia? Reconsider my offer!"

"You mean to be the paid housekeeper of my childhood home?" Jane said tartly. "That does not at all suit my notion of being my own mistress."

"But Jane, you were born to the management of such a residence. You must be all that I could desire in a housekeeper for Longchamp."

"But you are far from being all *I* could desire in an employer!"

"You cannot seriously mean to go on as you are! Trimming hats and doing fancy stitchery for pay when you are not hanging about here accepting charity! I declare, it shames me when I think of it, and I shudder when I think of its coming to anyone else's attention. Only think—at least as my housekeeper you would have security!"

"Would I?" Jane asked cryptically.

"Of course! And I am convinced that my need for a housekeeper will soon become urgent. I am sure—quite sure!—that I made the best of good impressions on my prospective brother-in-law last night. Why, he spent nearly an hour—a half hour at the very least!—at my side. Everyone remarked it! It was tantamount to his giving his blessing to my suit. There can be no reason for coyness between us, Jane. You know full well it is Portia I seek to attach, and she has a great fondness for you. I am persuaded you would be happy with us. And with the, um, improvement in style one anticipates upon marriage, it is doubly important that I have a housekeeper born to the manor. Not only that, I fancy his lordship would not turn down an invitation to spend some time at Longchamp, prenuptially, as it were, and I must have a housekeeper of exceptional talents to please one of his extreme refinement."

Jane clenched her jaw through this little speech with its self-congratulatory air. She could not abide the thought of being under Jonas's dominion. And if Jonas thought he had the Earl of Sefton in his hip pocket, he was sadly mistaken, but then that was more or less a condition of life for Jonas Biddle. Jane did not regard it as her job to put him in the right of it.

"You will have to please the Earl of Sefton without help from me," she said tersely. She turned and went into the house.

Jonas struggled to keep pace with her down the hall. "Only consider! As my housekeeper, not only would you be assured of security, but respectability, too!"

Jane rounded on him in a temper that now found a better target than her own self. "I am sure I do not worry for my reputation!" she snapped. "And it is extremely bourgeois of you to suggest that I should! I was *born* the daughter of a baronet, while you have only inherited your title, so perhaps you are to be excused, but pray do not vex me further on the subject. I grant that my father took no trouble to teach you what anyone must have known you would need to know, but just because he did not is no excuse for you to act like a lout. *You* knew any time these past ten years that there would be no male heir to Longchamp, and to the title! You should have taken it on yourself to learn what it means to possess an estate and a title! You may start by repairing the roof of the Dower House. You say you live in fear of being shamed by us. Pray think how you will be regarded if anyone should learn that Nanny and I are forced to sit under an umbrella inside our own house whenever it rains!"

Jonas seemed to wilt under this withering fusillade but he was not completely undone by it. Having received my lord Sefton's favor the night before had boosted his own sense of self-worth. "I say, Jane, that's coming it a bit too thick!"

But he was speaking to thin air.

George wished, not for the first time, that his godmother had not chosen to wear vertical stripes of ruby red and apple green. The high-waisted, slim-skirted style that suited young figures so well did not at all lend itself to one which was thickening alarmingly in the middle. As Lady Eugenia stalked the morning room, the colors of her dress made him bilious and the shape suggested small puppies wrestling inside a rolled-up carpet.

"But Jane could not possibly be spared!" her ladyship was exclaiming, her unnaturally black ringlets dancing indignantly.

George sighed and shifted in his chair. He did not mean to be brooked and was politely allowing his godmother's wrath to run its course. "As she would be accompanying Portia, there would be correspondingly less work here. And of course I do not intend setting out before your house party shall have ended," he added generously, "so you will not be without her while your need is greatest."

"Oh, George, it is too bad of you!" Lady Eugenia protested as if he hadn't spoken. "I vow, I have all my own plans in train. Portia will meet eligible men of the first stare in London, depend upon it!"

"But that is precisely what will *not* answer," George said. His manner was all patience but his left foot twitched. "I see now that she is too easily outcountenanced. I wish to start her out slowly. By taking her to Bath, and so early in the season, I assure that she will not meet with any Pinks or Blades or Dandies, or any other overweening types. She will be introduced to quiet, sensible men who do not see London

42

as the pinnacle of all that is great."

"But George, it is so unnecessary," her ladyship said pleadingly. "You know that all the girls have quite set their hearts on a London season!"

"I do not stand in the way of any but my sister," George said implacably.

Lady Eugenia's eyes puddled up most unbecomingly. "I declare, I have had the keeping of Portia for less than three months and already I have failed dear Fanny."

George suppressed a shudder. "Nothing of the sort!" he said bracingly. "Portia is a difficult case. It would not reflect well on either of us if she goes off with the first man she meets out of the schoolroom. My mother would say so, too, if she were here."

Eugenia sniffed. "Perhaps we ought to recall her from Italy."

"Indeed we shall not," George said firmly. "The climate and the scenery are having exactly the effect one hoped for. You must have had your own letters from her indicating how much improved she is. She wore her weeds with grace and bravery, and I will not see her deprived of this well-deserved holiday."

"Of course not," Lady Eugenia echoed faintly. George's tone was that of a despot. If Fanny had kicked over the traces, perhaps she had done so to escape her tyrannical son. Lady Eugenia cleared her throat. "You must do as you see fit, George, but I had so hoped to fulfill your expectations . . ."

"I did not say that you had not," George said quite reasonably. "I have every hope that Portia will join you in London later, but she must be put at lower fences first. It is by far too tame in Bath for even Portia to take fright."

"I am sure I hope you may be right," her ladyship said with no great conviction, "only perhaps it has not occurred to you that you place your whole reliance on Jane accompanying you, which is by no means a sure thing. She has no clothing

43

suitable for going into society, or rather not enough, for I fancy we have fitted her out well enough for a country party!"

To George, who had fully intended doing something about Jane's wardrobe anyway, that could not be a serious obstacle. "I rather think she will want to go," George said, "especially once she is persuaded that under no circumstances will I allow Portia to become engaged to her cousin until she had made the acquaintance of other eligible men!"

Lady Eugenia looked at him in some confusion. "What can that have to say to the issue?" she asked. "Surely whether Sir Jonas marries Portia or another can be of no significance to Jane."

"*No* significance?" George asked, raising one eyebrow cynically.

"Well, none that *I* can see, at any rate," Lady Eugenia responded uncertainly.

"We shall see," George said. "All that must count is that she is my conduit to Portia's thoughts. I can only hope that she will recall Diogenes to mind in performing that office and be scrupulously honest."

Lady Eugenia was a good deal more forthright with Jane than she had been with her godson. "You cannot and you must not! Why, he is bound to pull my budget and your Uncle Harry will never consent to make up the difference!"

"But if it is only for a month or two, as you say he intends, then they will be back in London by the beginning of June at the latest," Jane suggested hopefully. "That will not be too late for a presentation ball."

Her aunt whirled. "And if it is?" she demanded. "I place no reliance whatever on Hanover putting on such a lavish display as George would be bound to. Why, even without George's hand in it, the staff of Sefton House would know what was owed to appearance. The staircase! Only consider the staircase, and what a setting it would be for Imogene and Emmaline!"

Jane squinted as she tried to imagine what two identical blushing schoolgirls might look like trussed up like turkeys in court gowns and receiving the *ton* at the top of the mythological staircase.

"Really, Jane, what a most unbecoming expression," Lady Eugenia snapped. "Do try not to screw your face up so!" She pulled a day-old flower out of an arrangement and began pushing the remainder around the vase irritably. "I would never have consented to bring Portia out with my own two had I known what a sad pass it would come to! Of course it was understood that George would stand the expense for all three, for Harry and I could not hope to match the style expected for Portia! And now—no!—it is not at all what Fanny would expect of me. What is the world come to when a bachelor contemplates bringing out his sister? A shabby business!" She yanked another daisy out of the obsidian vase and dropped it carelessly to the floor. "Why, you are not to be thought a suitable substitute for someone like myself. Depend upon it—the boy has temporarily lost his mind! To take his sister to Bath without the guiding hand of an experienced woman! On no account must you do it, Jane!"

Jane's head ached horribly. She could not follow her aunt's arguments. Did she mean that Portia ought not to go to Bath at all, or that if she went, it should only be with Lady Eugenia and her daughters as companions?

She hastily excused herself and hurried off without making any answer. Feeling sick to her stomach, Jane went down the staircase, passing several footmen and a maid working to sweep the carpet and buff the banisters back to a high gloss. By ten, all the servants would have vanished into the nether regions of the house, so as not to spoil the illusion that the great house renewed itself each night by magic. Jane felt sure she was the only one up and about besides Lady Eugenia and the servants.

45

Lady Eugenia's words still raced through Jane's mind like bees escaping from an overturned hive. The prospect of going to Bath as Portia's companion had seemed like a marvelous dream when Portia had first whispered of it last night. Jane had lain awake in the small room assigned to her and tried to imagine the splendors of Bath. Of course, Cheltenham and Brighton were far more fashionable now, but for a genteelly-raised girl who had had no coming out and no presentation—and never would—Bath during the season loomed very like Nirvana.

But then, even before Lady Eugenia had expressed herself so passionately on the reasons why Jane must not go, Jane herself had already begun to perceive obstacles. Nanny relied on her to make the trips to and from Coddington for the handwork which both did, and they could not afford the loss of income if Jane were to go away for any length of time. And of course, there was the question of clothes.

Oh, if only it hadn't been for the war with France and the dreadful inflation which followed! Jane's small trust from her grandmother would not have sunk so low in value, her father would have had more cash to leave her at his death—all, all! would have been so much more bearable. Of course, Canfield would still have been entailed away to Jonas. There was no escaping that unpleasant fact, though her father had succeeded very well in avoiding any discussion of it while he lived.

Jane felt so low in spirits by the time she reached the conservatory that she threw herself into a small settle and shriveled into the cushions. Only a scold like the one Lady Eugenia had ladled out could rob Jane of the pleasure of sitting by the glass and absorbing the rays of the April sun.

Jane hated the side of herself that quaked and quailed when she was scolded, but she had never yet managed to eradicate it. Her sweet, gentle mother and quiet, fond papa had not prepared her for the vicissitudes of standing up to characters who unleashed their passions so violently. Even at the Abbey School in Reading where she had received her schooling, even there Jane had been made to feel that gentle words and soft tempers were valued. She had never had to endure so much as one rebuke from dear Miss Marlowe.

Jane could only marvel when she recalled her conversation with the Earl of Sefton. Somehow she had found the courage to stand up to him, albeit over a small thing, and only for a minute. She suspected it was because he conducted himself with such civility, though even *his* extreme courtesy had only been strained by Jonas. Jane sighed. Who would not be put out of all patience by Jonas? She nestled deeper into the cushions and let the sun warm fingers made unnaturally stiff and sore by the incessant needlework she did with Nanny.

Abovestairs, the Earl of Sefton yawned and examined the cream-colored cuff of his top boots. "They do not strike you as being just the tiniest bit *yellow,* do they, Henry? I swear, either this country light works a deception on my eyes or I shall be forced to change bootmakers."

Henry stood up stoutly to the issue. "It may be, your lordship, that I added a bit too much champagne to the mix."

George raised his eyebrows in languid doubt. "Or it may be that our hosts have stocked the cellars with an indifferent champagne."

Henry stifled an apologetic cough. "Begging your lordship's pardon, but that is always possible." The small valet, hardly less dapper than his master, judged it best to say no more.

"I shall be needing Wofford presently," the earl said, still examining his booted legs in a desultory fashion.

"Very good, your lordship. Shall I send for him?" Henry asked with perfect aplomb, as if the earl's secretary was merely in the next room and not in London.

"Rather see to it that my writing things are laid out. I will give you the dressing of me, Henry, for precisely fifteen minutes more, and then I simply must hare off to see what joyous occupations present themselves today." The earl adjusted his neckcloth with a sardonic twitch, observing Henry's pained reflection in the glass. "It is of no use whatever to make that face, Henry. What, I ask you, *what*, are we to gain from spending the customary two hours on the process?" The valet maintained a stoic silence and the earl spoke for him. "'Standards, my lord. We uphold standards, no matter where we may be.' Well, that bird won't fly here, Henry. We go to Bath soon, and then you may rig me out just as you see fit."

Henry's brow wrinkled. "Bath, my lord?" It was clear from his expression that Bath ran a poor second to returning to London. "I'm sure it is my pleasure to go where your lordship chooses to go."

"Don't gammon *me*, Henry," scoffed his lordship good-naturedly. "Take solace, however, in the fact that our mission in Bath will almost certainly require me to don knee breeches at some point." Henry drew in a sharp breath and gazed hopefully at his employer. "It's no good turning those puppy dog eyes on me, Henry. I stop short of *that*."

Henry's face fell but George managed to quell his mirth until he had exited the chamber. A valet brought along in the years when powdered hair was *de rigueur* would forever yearn for its return. George thought highly of Henry and would oblige him in all respects save that one. George ambled down the staircase, up a hall, and into the breakfast room, nearly tripping over a tin of fender polish left near the grate.

"Beg pardon, your grace!" a small housemaid cried, darting out of sight before he could thank her for the added ennoblement.

Perceiving that he was far too early for breakfast, George cast a regretful look at the sideboard and saw there was not so much as a bowl of fruit to select from. He sighed heavily. Trusting that the chocolate a footman had delivered earlier would sustain him for at least another hour, George set off in search of the library. Seeing the well-dusted books cheek by jowl in Harry Hanover's library put George in mind of his secretary.

Wofford had been with George some five years, an academic unable to flourish in academia after some sharpish questioning over the true authorship of a treatise on the use of fish imagery by Shakespeare. If Wofford said he had written it, George was not the man to question him, for Wofford had shown himself to be scrupulously truthful in the conduct of his employer's business. It was only owing to Wofford's extreme attention to detail that George had been made aware that his new hat cost twenty-five guineas, Wofford having insisted on going over what appeared to be a large bill—even for the earl—item by item.

Cambridge's loss had been George's gain. It was with utter confidence that George sat down and scrawled off a brief note directing Wofford to inquire into the availability of suitable accommodations in Bath, and the whole raft of other requirements needful for a successful sojourn in that town. He replaced the pen in the standish and sanded the paper. Henry would be piqued that the earl had not waited and used his own paper upstairs, but that was a trifle.

Enormously cheered that he had at least done one useful thing with his day, George wandered off to peruse the conservatory. The gardens outdoors, he had already discovered, were a dead loss at this time of year, the Hanovers seeing no purpose in cultivating flora which bloomed at any time of year when one might reasonably still be lighting a fire at night. Who, after all, would see and appreciate the blooms?

A blob of plum caught his eye in the conservatory, a curled-up, sleeping blob as it happened. George felt a twinge of tenderness for the blob, its sweet, straight nose so determined even in sleep. The cheeks looked a tiny bit chalky in the sun and George frowned. It would be as well for Miss

Jane Oxenby to spend a month or two in Bath as his guest. He settled into a chair opposite her and began to study her coloration with an eye to the clothes he would order made for her. He had decided that Portia would appear almost exclusively in white, but Jane was a different matter. She was young, but not *very* young, and he could enjoy more liberty with color. Ever a man of fashion, George began to think he might actually enjoy this venture.

Jane awoke slowly and felt the heat of the sun on her left cheek. She smiled, her earlier bad humor quite vanquished by the short doze. What a pagan pleasure it was to be so warmed by the sun when outside, nature was still clothed in only the merest hint of green! She pulled in a long deep breath of warm air and turned her face so that the sun could caress both cheeks. She made a contented murmur in her throat, not even trying to open her eyes just yet.

George smiled. What a natural she was! He steepled his fingers and swung one booted foot ever so slightly, a signal to any of his contemporaries that he was engaged in hatching a plan for some amusement. The word would go round the room like fire when he was in this contemplative state, that no one was to disturb Sefton on any account. Among his greatest larks had been the notion to hire Astley's Amphitheatre for an evening, substituting himself and his friends for the usual performers.

My Lady Grey had made a most charming and extraordinary bareback rider, a fact which, had it become known to her elderly husband, would surely have brought on a fatal attack of nerves. It was the earl himself who shone brightest, however, his athletic physique the envy of all the other gentlemen endeavoring to keep up with him in performing the acrobatic mounts and dismounts. Some more than others were made to feel that they had essayed too much, and were known to have nursed broken or bruised limbs for some weeks afterward, but none denied that it had been a splendid notion and a capital success.

In that same fertile mind, there was now forming a plan to make Miss Jane Oxenby the toast of Bath. It was conceivable. It could be done. And it would suit his own purposes to a turn, for how much easier it would be for Portia if she were not the object of all eyes. As the friend and constant companion of Miss Jane Oxenby, though, she would do admirably. There was no question of Jane being thought a beauty; the earl rather thought he was the only one who might be brought to that conclusion. But to have her pronounced an Original was within reach. He must apply himself and think of some ingenious scheme. The first one which occurred to him brought a smile to his lips. He decided it would do very well and bethought himself no further.

Jane came slowly awake with the conviction that she was not alone. Her wandering gaze discerned a figure seated across from her.

"Your lordship!" she exclaimed, and hastily sat up.

"Ah!" he said with gentle humor. "You see how we progress, Miss Oxenby. You not only perceive my presence but you are in no danger of running me down."

Jane repositioned her lace tucker with a smile. "The worst danger you face is missing breakfast, I should imagine."

"You have breakfasted already, Miss Oxenby?" he inquired politely.

"Some time ago," Jane said, combing her fingers through the heavy mass of curls surrounding her face.

"Enchanting," the earl murmured.

Jane glanced up. "I beg your pardon?"

"Nothing," the earl demurred. "A thought which found my tongue. Tell me, Miss Oxenby, have you any obligations—other than to my aunt—which would preclude you from accompanying my sister and me when we remove from here to Bath? That is to say, I wish you would do us the honor of coming with us as our guest."

Her fingers stopped working through the brunette tangles, all glittery with the reds and golds of the sun in them. "I am afraid I cannot," she said with a trace of wistfulness. "There are so many obstacles that I would bore you with the telling of them."

"Perhaps you think me easily bored," the earl suggested. He leaned back. "That is not the case, at least where you are concerned."

Jane smiled. "You seek to flatter. It was prettily done, your lordship, but to no purpose."

"My purpose is too important to allow me to accept your first answer. I wish you will permit me to keep the subject alive," George said. "Please excuse me if I offend by persisting when you have quite clearly said no."

"Oh! I am a rough and tumble sort where such matters are concerned. You could not offend me if you tried—you are far too refined. Everyone says so." George's shoulders shook. "I have said something to amuse you?" Jane asked.

"No, nothing," George said with a gentle cough. "I wonder if you were being quite truthful when you told me you had no gift for dissembling. Am I laboring under a delusion or did I not offend you over the matter of your cousin?"

"Well, no, not offend precisely. I am obliged to admit that he does not always make the best of impressions."

"Then why defend him?" the earl asked, lifting one eyebrow.

"Because you mentioned him as a suitor for Portia. In that context, I believe it is fair to say he has a number of assets."

"You begin to sound like my banker," George murmured.

"Well, marriage is a matter of assets and liabilities, is it not?" Jane said with feeling. "Where Portia is . . . lacking, Jonas makes up."

"Ah! I collect you do not refer to money. Please continue, Miss Oxenby."

Jane straightened her shoulders and went on bravely under the earl's polite scrutiny. "Well . . . Portia does not at all like to be the center of attention whereas Jonas thrives on it. Portia is content to listen while Jonas feels the need to speak at length on every topic. I perceive that she is comfortable in his shadow. It may not be what one likes, but it is the truth."

George sat up and eyed Jane with interest. "You are indeed an astute observer, Miss Oxenby. Tell me though— just because the hen is shy, must she be joined to a rooster that crows all day long?"

Jane chuckled. "Assets and liabilities, your lordship."

George rose and strolled toward a potted stephanotis just beginning to bud up. Keeping his back to Jane, he gently fingered its leaves and said, "To be quite candid, Miss Oxenby, I would pay a great deal of money to protect Portia, and assure her happiness. Some might say it was wise to spend a small sum to protect a larger sum, by which I am convinced you must realize that I mean Portia's fortune."

"I'm sure no one would fault you for that," Jane said reasonably.

George shrugged his broad shoulders and spoke without turning back to face her. "I have another sister, Horatia. She nearly made a disastrous liaison through my inattention. I knew very well that the man who pursued her was a destroyer. He would have plundered her innocence and then her fortune, but I thought she would see through him as easily as I did."

He turned to face Jane again. Though he was too far away for her to see his face clearly, Jane perceived from the set of his jaw that he was frowning.

"And so you averted it?" she asked.

"Narrowly," he said quietly. "Very narrowly. He had persuaded her to run away with him. I caught up with them within the day and used all the currency accrued to me by virtue of friendship and position to cause the matter to be overlooked by anyone who knew of it." He gave a small, dry laugh. "Ah, and so we are back to banking. Note, I used my currency."

Jane smiled uncertainly. His voice was solemn and yet she

perceived that he meant to make a joke. "I am sure you were grateful to have it to use."

He moved back toward her. "Though there is no obligation on your part to remain silent, I hope that I have some small currency with *you*, Miss Oxenby, and that you will forget that I disclosed these facts to you. Even my godmother has no inkling of the incident. Horatia is now married to a man of merit, and living happily in America."

"I am honored to have been taken into your confidence. Of course you may rely on my discretion."

"Thank you—I felt sure I could. And of course, you may easily guess *why* I shared the story."

"Yes," Jane said regretfully. "To make it nearly impossible for me to say no yet again to accompanying you to Bath."

George laughed, a rich, full sound that echoed in the conservatory. "Oh, Miss Oxenby, you need not look so rueful! Indeed, I would not place you under an obligation to me by so underhanded a trick. You deserve better than that."

"Perhaps," Jane said dubiously, "but I apprehend that the trick has been played nonetheless." She looked up, naked appeal in the clear azure eyes. "But it will not do, your lordship. I feel your position most keenly, but you must relent and acknowledge mine, too. I cannot go, I *must* not go!" She arose and began to pace distractedly. "It would be wonderful to go to Bath, but . . ." But once she returned, Lady Eugenia would make her regret it for years to come. No—she could not say that. *How to put him off?* "Spring is so very rainy and I simply cannot go off and leave . . ." *No!—it would not do to tell him that she was the one who hung buckets and mopped and carefully kept Nanny from getting wet and chilled when the roof leaked.* "I know I cannot be the only one to whom Portia will talk of her inmost feelings and—"

"'Ware!"

Jane pulled up abruptly, within an arm's length of having collided with his lordship. "Beg pardon!" she stammered, staring up into the heavy-lidded eyes.

"No harm done, Miss Oxenby," George said. "Indeed, I would have caught you gladly."

Jane felt warmth rising to her cheeks. "Sorry," she said unsteadily.

"It is nothing. Now, you said something about the season being rainy. Is it your health that concerns you?"

Jane shook her head, unable to break free of the spell of his nearness.

"Then we go on to the second item, namely whether Portia can be induced to place her confidence in another. Will you accept my word as one who has known her for eighteen years that she will not do so? You are a first, Miss Oxenby. If I may address a delicate subject, I would ask if money—or the lack of it—enters into your deliberation?"

Jane nodded again, this time in the affirmative. Such a finely wrought nose, such majestic brows! The careless sweep of dark brown locks across the noble forehead! The jaw carved out of the stuff of Mount Olympus! Jane began to feel quite giddy.

". . . whatever you require, including clothing. I told you I am prepared to pay any amount of money to assure Portia's happiness. I would not feel I had done my best for Portia if I did not enlist your aid. Say you will do it, Miss Oxenby, not least because I will never countenance your cousin's suit until I have satisfied myself that Portia is making an informed choice."

Jane heard only one word in three with any comprehension but she knew well enough what he was asking. She felt so peculiar that she could hardly credit it. What *was* the matter with her? She had been fine only a moment ago!

The lips sculpted by the gods themselves parted. "Miss Oxenby? Are you quite all right?" He put his hands on her shoulders, concern etched in every magnificent feature.

It was thus that Lady Eugenia found them.

Chapter Four

In the end, she said "yes," simply to be assured of escaping Lady Eugenia's vicinity for a protracted length of time. Finding her hugely eligible godson in the act of making love to hopelessly ineligible Jane Oxenby had so enraged Lady Eugenia that she was not likely ever to forgive Jane, on whom she placed the entire blame for the incident. Was George not notorious for confining his amorous attentions to Cyprians? If there was dalliance afoot, it was because Jane had given his lordship to understand that she was willing.

Jane shuddered as she recalled that and a thousand other horrid things that Lady Eugenia had said to her after recommending that George go and partake of breakfast. George had looked to Jane for an answer, which had come out as a whispered "yes," and then he had taken himself off, drawing Lady Eugenia along with him, with some affable remark about the fine collection in the conservatory. He cast a speaking look over his shoulder as he went, indicating he would seek Jane out for further conversation later, but it was Lady Eugenia who found Jane first, up in her tiny bed chamber under the rafters.

She waxed long and eloquent on all Jane's deficiencies, swelling with rage like one suffering the effects of a venomous snake bite. Only Portia's arrival had cut the tirade short. As soon as Lady Eugenia departed, Jane dissolved into a flood of tears, which Portia dried away. She patted Jane's hair and stroked her shoulder as if she were the senior of the two, and not the junior by seven years.

Portia had heard enough of what Lady Eugenia had to say to Jane to know that George had been caught nearly *in flagrante delicto*. It buoyed Portia up no end to imagine George committing such folly as to fall in love with someone so wholly ineligible as Lady Eugenia seemed to think Jane was. It gave Portia reason to hope that George could be brought to understand how *she* could desire to wed someone wholly ineligible in *his* view.

Not until the chaise and four with the earl's crest arrived to take them away did Jane draw a free breath. It was a long wait, ten days during which George took himself off to choose from among the accommodations his secretary deemed acceptable in Bath, and to tend to myriad other matters. Despite the imminent separation from Jonas, Portia passed the time with an air of suppressed excitement about her which Jane could not help but wonder at.

Nanny professed herself skeptical of his lordship's -intentions and asserted that no good could come of allowing That Woman's godson to carry Jane off. She hinted strongly that she should come along, but Jane gently commended her to remember her gout and stay where she was, and then proceeded to set that lady's heart to palpitating by pressing money into her hand.

"And what the source of *this* is I can imagine," Nanny said indignantly.

"It is only what his lordship thought fitting for me to have as pin money in Bath," Jane replied. "He has guessed something of my circumstances."

"Pin money, eh?" Nanny said with a frown. "I hope that's the truth of it, for you are far too pretty to accept money from him unless it is all clearly understood what the money buys."

"Oh, Nanny! You are so funny!" Jane laughed. "As if anyone but you could think me pretty!"

Nanny clucked at her. "Do not underrate yourself, my girl," she said severely. "You will soon enough discover that you are fair game in a town like Bath!"

Jane rose and gave Nanny a fond peck on the cheek. "I only hope that you may be right," she said, her eyes twinkling behind the gold-rimmed spectacles that suited her so well. "I do not like the apothecary in Coddington, our clergyman is already married, and none of the eligible gentlemen farmers in the shire can afford to take a wife so impecunious as I."

"I'll not like it!" Nanny declared. "Not a bit of it, and I shall not rest easy until you come back to me safe and sound!"

Jane thought again of Nanny's words as the earl's chaise rolled down the tree-lined avenue of Canfield, and out onto the main road. She had seldom felt safer. Her host had infuriated Lady Eugenia by bending over Jane's hand and inquiring with a sparkle in his eye whether the wait had been unbearable. Now Lady Eugenia and her wrath lay behind, and a lovely adventure lay ahead.

The earl had chosen to ride and was mounted on a blood bay, a sight that Jane very much wished she could see better. She patted the reticule that contained her spectacles. Perhaps she would have a chance to see the earl from a window sometime, when she could wear them unobserved, but in the meantime, she kept them tucked away. If Lady Eugenia considered them too unfashionable for a party at Canfield, how much more unfashionable they would be in Bath!

Portia said little, beyond mentioning that it was a fine day. Her footman, Manning, and abigail, Stoke, came behind in a large coach with all their baggage and, of course, George's valet. Jane thought she might explode from the sheer pleasure of it all as they passed Barnby-in-the-Willows, the world a bright splash of budding greens and yellows beyond the chaise windows.

Jane gave some thought along the way as to what might be done with Portia's hair. She was as fair as her brother was dark, and it lent her a certain insipidity. It would be well to add bold-colored ribbons to her hair, and Jane decided she would ask Stoke to experiment with more elaborate coifs, too, to add some presence to the slight, pale girl.

The only wonder was that Portia did not appear paler, having been forced to wave good-bye to Jonas as he stood on Canfield's stair. *He* had been a study in ill-disguised dismay when Portia had informed him of George's plan, but Jane had contrived to give the pair some moments alone—at great cost to her peace of mind, lest Lady Eugenia discover it—and the two had somehow resigned themselves to what must be.

The chaise turned west at Balderton to join the main road, and then the coachman pointed the horses south. They passed Farndon and Hawton, Thorpe and Syerston. It was all familiar to Jane, who had traveled this same route to school. Once past Coventry, though, where the earl had announced they would break their journey for the night, it would be new to her. Jane reached over and squeezed Portia's hand for sheer happiness. Portia smiled shyly and returned the pressure.

"I hope this will not be very disagreeable for you," she ventured timidly.

Jane laughed. "As many times as you have said that, I have assured you it will be my pleasure. What must I do to convince you once and for all?"

"I am near to believing you," Portia admitted, "especially when I see that you are in such looks today. Your eyes are positively sparkling."

"There! Then you have your answer, for I am not the least bit feverish. If my eyes are sparkling, it is because I am happy."

"I only wish I could be as happy," Portia said softly, casting her gaze down.

"You shall be," Jane said firmly. "You will like to see the sights in Bath, and you will find there is nothing but pleasure to be had from the concerts and dances and such."

"I shall do my best to be good company for you," Portia said faintly. "If only Jonas will join us in Bath . . ."

Jane saw nothing to be gained from encouraging Portia in that line of thought, and succeeded in distracting her with a discussion of new hair styles.

They stopped just short of Leicester for lunch, at the Boar and Hound. Despite the fact that the earl's chaise was excellently sprung, and the coachman instructed not to push the pace, Jane was very happy to be handed down by an effusive landlord. The ladies were shown to a private chamber where they could relieve themselves and freshen up. Portia expressed a desire to lie down for a bit, for, as she declared, even the smoothest of rides made her head ache. Jane left her to the ministrations of Stoke and went downstairs again, being exceedingly hungry.

When she walked into the parlor reserved for their meal, the earl was seated by the window, perusing a newspaper. He immediately arose.

"I trust you are comfortable so far?" he inquired politely.

"Most comfortable," she assured him, "though Portia is somewhat done in. I fear she is not as reconciled to this separation from Sir Jonas as she would have you believe."

The earl's mouth tightened. "She would do well to save any vapors and airs on that score for a more sympathetic audience than myself."

Jane shrank from his tone. "I do not think she means her infirmity to be perceived as a performance," she said, keeping her chin up with an effort. "She means to make the best she can of circumstances, only she is insufficiently fledged in concealing her true feelings to present a completely unaffected face to the world."

An unconvincing smile crossed the earl's countenance. "I hope that Portia *does* mean to make the best of things, for I will not tolerate any failure to put her best foot forward."

"She will, you know," Jane declared, nettled. "Just because you do not feel that she has bestowed her affections wisely does not mean she is not a good-hearted girl. She is sensitive, she is kind, she is—"

George held up his hand. "I am quite sure I take your meaning, Miss Oxenby. I do not need to be lectured on my sister's good points, I assure you."

"I think perhaps you do," Jane said passionately. She was thoroughly riled by the suggestion of laughter in the earl's voice.

"I assure you, I appreciate my sister's finer points at the same time that I am unwilling to minimize her failings. To that end, I have concocted a plan for our stay in Bath," George said. He gestured toward a table set with a drinks tray. "Will you have some ratafia while I describe my scheme?"

Jane felt her indignation deflating in the face of the earl's courtesy. "Very well," she said reluctantly.

The earl uncorked a decanter of straw-colored liquid and poured as he spoke. "We are agreed that Portia prefers not to be center stage, as those in the theatrical profession might say. Keeping in mind Portia's extreme shyness, I have a plan that will put the focus on you instead."

"Me?" Jane echoed in surprise.

"Yes. I hope you will not mind it too much." He smiled winningly and handed her the glass of ratafia. "But then, I am persuaded that you are made of far sturdier stuff than Portia, and can easily rise to the occasion."

Jane smiled uncertainly. The merriment in his lordship's face and the intimacy of his address gave rise to an odd flutter in her chest. "I pray you will tell me what you envision."

"Come sit with me," the earl said, leading the way to a

61

window seat. "I undertook this sojourn in Bath as a regrettable necessity, Miss Oxenby, but I begin to think it may prove very enjoyable. This ratafia is quite passable, is it not?"

Jane, who had been about to take a sip from her glass, burst into giggles. The earl inclined his handsome head toward her, his heavy-lidded eyes alight. "You find the ratafia amusing?" he asked.

Jane controlled herself with an effort. "Oh, not at all," she declared. "It is just seeing you make such a game pretense at drinking it—as if you drank it every day! In truth, I do not like it myself, though it is considered a ladies' drink. My father taught me to prefer port."

The earl smiled, revealing smooth, evenly aligned teeth. "It is my belief he did you a great favor."

"Oh! I don't believe he set out to do so," Jane replied matter-of-factly. "It was only that after my mother's death, he found it difficult to recall that there was still a female residing in the house—I came home from school when we learned my mother had died while on a trip to Italy—and he always ordered just what it pleased *him* to drink, and nothing else. I grew quite used to it though, I assure you, but I have not been used to drink it of late."

"He has been dead some years?" the earl inquired gently.

"Four."

"And his passing left you in somewhat . . . straitened circumstances."

"More than somewhat," Jane admitted. "Quite shockingly close to the edge, in point of fact."

"Just so," George murmured. He deemed it best to leave the indelicate subject behind. It occurred to him that if his plan succeeded, Jane might well emerge from this stay in Bath with a wealthy husband in tow. She was fresh and witty and very striking. To the discerning, such traits in a wife would outweigh any lack of mere money. He cleared his throat.

"Since you have informed me of your preference for port, I shall see that it is served this evening. Now, allow me to tell you the idea I have had for making you the center of attention." The earl crossed one long, elegant leg over the other. "I believe I may safely characterize myself as a confirmed bachelor. That is society's conclusion, too, and one which it is quite well justified in drawing, as I do not ever intend to marry."

"But I thought you had the intention of seeking a bride who could bring you a fortune! That you were in need of money!"

The earl's mouth twitched. "Have you discovered any deficiency in my style of dress or travel that would support that conclusion? If you have, I beg you will point it out, for I would like to redress it at the earliest opportunity."

"No, but . . . but you said it to me!" Jane stopped to search her thoughts. "Or at least you did not correct me when I suggested . . ."

George watched her trying to recall exactly what had been said. How delightful she was, so ingenuous at times and yet so sharp of mind overall! "I take full responsibility for misleading you," he said. "It was such a marvelously unexpected role to have thrust upon me that I could not resist playing the pauper, if only for an evening. No, Miss Oxenby, I am quite wealthy, very eligible, and exceedingly determined never to marry."

"But that is nonsensical!" Jane said. "You must want to have children, a son to whom you can pass on the title, at least."

George's nonchalance fell away and his expression was a shade more guarded. "I have my reasons and my mind is quite made up. I beg you will let me take you into my confidence this far and no further. It bears on my plan or I should never have brought it up."

Jane felt heat rise to her cheeks. "Of course! I did not mean to pry or offer any impertinence."

"You did not." George idly twisted the black grosgrain ribbon which held the quizzing glass he so rarely used. "I beg your pardon if I have caused you any embarrassment."

Jane nodded, her azure eyes so large in her face that they made her look almost elfin. "I am sure you have said nothing that needs to be forgiven. Please go on."

"I propose that when we arrive in Bath, I escort my sister and her good friend, Miss Jane Oxenby, everywhere, and I will make it plain that I find you devastatingly attractive. I plan to fall in love with you, you see—very publicly and quite hopelessly. It will deflect attention from Portia, for I am known to be a man who will throw his heart over a fence but never over a female."

He paused and Jane gazed at him, her thoughts racing as she considered the ramifications of the plan. Portia was known to have a fortune so suitors would still seek her out, perhaps all the more easily if such a grand romance was being conducted at her elbow. "Of course," Jane said in admiration. "It is a splendid idea."

"Then you have no objection?" he asked, a little surprised that she had acquiesced so easily.

"None at all," she declared. "It is, after all, in the service of a higher good, is it not?"

George bit back the first of several retorts that sprang to mind. She made it seem as if it would be something of a penance to have him make love to her! "I suppose you could interpret it that way," he said mildly.

"What is not exactly clear to me," Jane continued, "is what response I ought to have to this . . . this attention. Am I to be flattered? Shall I pretend to return your feelings or not?"

"It will be more interesting if you are cool to me," he said. "All of Bath will be watching and expecting complete capitulation on your part. How much more delicious for them if you keep me waiting outside the draper's, and seem indifferent to the fact that I dance with no one but you.

Besides, it might create a scandal if you reciprocated my regard while we shared the same roof."

"Oh! How very right you are," Jane declared. "It's clever of you to have foreseen that."

"However, you need not fear *true* scandal will be occasioned by our living under the same roof, for I have desired my Great Aunt Serena to join us in Bath."

"Oh! Then you do not truly need me!" Jane said.

"On the contrary, I need you very much," he said with a smile, "for all the reasons I have outlined. Great Aunt Serena is in no way capable of providing companionship to Portia, nor can she bear her company. The truth is that Serena is deaf as a post and suffers from the most regrettable case of lumbago. One could conduct orgies of Caligula-like proportions in a house where she was the nominal chaperon—which, of course, we will *not* do!—without her any the wiser. Nevertheless her presence will signal to the world that we are not dead to appearances, nor will she vex you or Portia with questions, or require you to spend time in attending her. Great Aunt Serena is a remarkable soul who will be delighted to exchange the view from her window in London for a view of Bath, provided we do not actually require her to leave her room."

"I see," Jane said, much struck by the picture he had drawn of his eccentric relative.

Portia joined them shortly after, followed by the landlord, who served them himself, solicitous to the point of tedium. It was a harbinger of the reception they received when they pulled into the White Stag that night. A light rain had begun falling in midafternoon and the damp crept into the carriage despite a sheepskin on the floor and lap robes. Portia declared herself thoroughly chilled when they alit, and the entire hostelry was thrown into a flurry of activity. Wilcox, the proprietor, was a short, cadaverous man who nevertheless fairly carried Portia in to stand by the fire in the best parlor.

"I assure your lordship that the ladies will be most comfortable," their host said. "Fires are lit in their chambers already, the sheets are as dry as can be, and my missus will see that hot bricks go up when the ladies retire."

"I am sure you will see to it all," George replied politely. "And my servants—please see that they are well looked after, too."

And that was the true Quality for you, as Wilcox later told his wife. They thought of those that served them in the next breath after themselves. Nothing was too good for the earl in Wilcox's view, which was why he took the trouble to tell him that he had turned away several sporting gentlemen earlier that day.

"I told them your lordship had spoken for all my best rooms for tonight and recommended they try the Sterling instead," Wilcox informed George.

"And did they?" George asked politely.

"Not before they'd claimed they knew your lordship. One gent said I was to tell you that he would call on you here, a Mr. Creighton, he said his name was."

A sudden smile lit the earl's face and Wilcox knew he'd been right not to put a flea in the gentleman's ear.

"The devil you say! And what is Roger doing in Coventry?—that's what I'd like to know!"

"He says to me, tell Mr. Tate—for that's what he *would* call your lordship," the landlord said apologetically, "tell Mr. Tate I'll call round later this evening."

George gave a bark of laughter. "He would, the impudent scamp! Call me Mr. Tate that is, but he was not incorrect, Wilcox, so you need not worry that I will take offense. Mr. Tate! That is Roger all over. Why, if he had dared that while we here in the Guards, I'd have had him cashiered!"

"A Guard were you, sir?" said Wilcox admiringly. "I might have known, sir, what with your bearing and height."

"And were Mr. Creighton's companions similarly impressive?" George inquired. "Tall, broad-shouldered, keen of sight? One with sandy hair that would not behave if it were dressed with lard, and another with curly brown locks that would be any woman's envy?"

Wilcox beamed. "The same, your lordship! I perceive your lordship knows them all."

"Oh, yes, I know them all," George said, chuckling, "I know them all for the blackguards they are. Take care, Wilcox, lest they tear your establishment apart. Never let rooms to them, as you value your property. But all shall be well tonight. As their former senior officer, I shall keep them well in check. When the ladies retire, I shall require you to keep us well-supplied with spirits. If they are smuggled, so much the better, for these are palates which will appreciate the finest."

Wilcox looked momentarily scandalized. "Why, I never would! Begging your lordship's pardon, but such things have never crossed the threshold of the White Stag! However, Mr. Creighton did drop a word in my ear about perhaps playing cards here tonight with your lordship and I fancy I have laid my hands on a cask or two which will not displease."

"Stout fellow!" George declared.

He rubbed his hands in anticipation of an evening spent with old friends and went upstairs to allow Henry to repair the ravages of the road. His valet replaced breeches with pantaloons, top boots with elegant evening shoes, and gently assisted his noble employer into a splendidly tailored coat of blue superfine. With a clean neck cloth freshly tied by his lordship, the effect was all any gentleman's gentleman could have hoped for. Henry watched with barely concealed awe as the earl carelessly brushed his gleaming dark brown hair into a style many a lesser man would have wept to achieve in twice the time.

"Marshall, Willoughby and—dare I say it?—that dog, Creighton, appear to be in Coventry on what will un-doubtedly prove to be some havey-cavey errand," George announced as he set the brush down on the dressing table.

He gave his neckcloth one last twitch and turned to face his valet. "No one will appreciate better than you, Henry, that there is little use in your waiting up for me."

Henry repressed a smile. "No, of course not, your lordship."

George forbore to remonstrate with his valet for the smirk and went downstairs. Jane and Portia were already settled by the fire, having decided not to change for dinner.

"Poor Stoke is all in," Portia said by way of explanation. "We have sent her off to eat and retire early."

"That is what comes of allowing our mother to foist Grandmama's abigail on you," George said, turning his back to the fire.

Portia looked faintly shocked. "But how could I not?" she protested. "Stoke has been with the family for ever so long! She would have been heartbroken had I not wanted her services after Grandmama died."

"What a lamb you are, Portia! Stoke would have been pensioned off, and would be living happy as a grig at Sefton Hall," George said.

Portia looked quite thunderstruck at the notion that she need not have accepted the services of an abigail so elderly that it was Portia who waited on her as often as she waited on Portia. "Oh!"

Wilcox scurried in after a polite knock, bearing a large roast of lamb, and two boys followed him with side dishes. The travelers sat down to eat *en famille*, with George carving. Jane thoroughly enjoyed the meal and the company. George gently twitted Portia on a number of scores, which Jane soon saw was his way of making his young sister talk. The table had only just been cleared when there was a great noise and halloo-ing from the front of the inn.

George threw his napkin aside and said mildly, "I perceive that Roger, John and Hugh have arrived. You remember Roger Creighton, do you not, Portia?"

Portia fluttered her hands unhappily. "Oh, yes! But I beg you will excuse me. I feel suddenly fatigued."

"Nonsense!" George declared. "Stay and become re-acquainted, and help me introduce them all to Miss Oxenby."

The room was soon filled with three strapping men, whose presence, added to the earl's own, fairly overwhelmed Jane. Portia blanched as first one and then another of her brother's friends bent over her hand. They paid their addresses to her handsomely but Portia could scarcely make any intelligible reply, flushing and stuttering with self-consciousness.

John Marshall was the quietest of the three, but could not be trusted for an instant not to do mischief, or so said George when he made the introduction, "He once caused my duty horse to be dyed black and then convinced my batman that the real animal had been stolen as a prank. Poor Bates rousted half the regiment and accused them of theft before someone thought to wake me." He eyed the sandy-haired John sternly.

John Marshall had the goodness to look shame-faced for just an instant before saying, "But you must allow, Sefton, that it was well worth it. Do you remember? Bates gibbering like a madman and you still in your night clothes, trying to keep your fellow officers from stringing him up for bringing false charges?"

"And you, sly dog, calm as you please, drawing a bucket of water and washing the animal in front of us all. I always meant to thank you for that, you know, because nothing else had the power to rattle Bates after that. He felt he had seen the worst and that mere warfare was anticlimactical by comparison."

John Marshall grinned and leaned his rangy frame against the mantlepiece. "I made a pony on that, too. Roger said Bates could never be fooled into thinking a horse of a different color was a different horse altogether. Don't know as I would have gone to all the trouble if not for him."

Roger Creighton accepted the tribute with a nod, his Adonis-like face grave. "True, true. I think—no, I'm sure—that's how it went. Mustn't blame John."

Hugh Willoughby slapped Roger on the back. "I am persuaded you planned it all from the beginning."

A lazy grin split Roger Creighton's face. Even without her spectacles, Jane could tell that he was by far the handsomest man she had ever seen. The earl possessed a craggy, rugged sort of masculine beauty, but Roger Creighton's was the sort of face one expected to see carved in marble by the masters.

"And what ill-conceived notion brings you to this part of the world?" George asked.

"Tish tosh—as if I was ever up to no good," Roger said without any apparent offense. "We repair to Charlcombe, old friend, where we will endeavor to keep Hugh from further dissipating his fortune with unwise wagers, at least until there is a new moon and one can reasonably hope that his luck has turned."

"This is a new remedy for an old problem," George remarked, "unless a new moon also brings a new quarter, in which case I quite see the sense in your plan."

"Exactly!" said John Marshall with enthusiasm. "I knew you would see the way of it. Splendid fellow, George," he declared to no one in particular. His unruly blond hair flew every which way, glinting in the fire's light and framing a plain but appealing face.

George unbent himself from the chair he was sitting in and stared with obvious interest at the lime green waistcoat being worn by Hugh Willoughby. "You know, dear boy, if you wished to pare expenses, you might have spared us all that . . . that garment."

Hugh looked down in surprise. "Don't like it, do you? Well, I daresay it will do for a stay in the country." His face brightened. "I say! Won't you come with us? More than enough room!"

George smiled. "I am obliged to take the ladies on to Bath, gentlemen. May we hope to see you there instead?"

"But what splendid luck!" Hugh exclaimed. "Charlcombe lies no more than a fifteen-minute ride from Bath. Oh, the dreary prospect of rustication takes on a new cast! And Father will be pleased if I do my duty in the town." His fresh young face glowed with happiness at the thought, his auburn locks, styled à la Grecque, lending even more grace to what was already a pleasing countenance.

"Do you stay high or low, George?" inquired Roger.

"High," the earl replied. "I confess, I wanted my stable conveniently close so that I could escape the confinement of town at will, and no such arrangements were to be had lower down."

"Capital, simply capital!" Roger said. "Would do the same myself. Makes it a dashed sight easier for one to call, too. May I hope for the pleasure of a dance or two at the assemblies, Lady Portia?"

Portia colored up and whispered some reply, all of which was lost in the sound of a log collapsing between the andirons in the fire.

"Should like to claim a dance myself," John Marshall added, his hair bouncing vigorously as he made a bow in Portia's direction.

"Likewise," Hugh Willoughby added, his hazel eyes crinkled up in a charming smile. "After all, George's sister!"

Portia was, by this point, quite scarlet and quite bereft of speech. The earl smoothly interposed himself. "My sister is overcome by your kindness but she will naturally stand up with you all. Gentlemen, allow me to present my sister's very good friend, Miss Jane Oxenby."

"Your servant," Roger declared, a speculative look on his handsome face.

Hugh bent over her hand. "My pleasure," he said warmly, peering up from beneath long, dark lashes.

John Marshall fairly galloped to Jane's side. "En-

71

chanted," he declared merrily. "Won't we be the happiest of parties in Bath?"

Jane was gratified but in no way mistook their attentions for more than mere politeness, since George's friends soon turned back to his sister. Portia made gargling sounds in her throat in response to their renewed attempts to converse with her and Jane soon contrived to exit, bearing Portia away with her. Upstairs, the younger girl gave way to nerves which had been strained to the breaking point in the parlor.

"I cannot!" she cried in anguish. "You see how it will be! All of George's friends and all the persons who would *like* to be George's friends will flock around us in Bath. I will be introduced to countless people—men!—who will be forever paying me compliments and attempting to conduct light, amusing conversations. I cannot endure it! It is too dreadful!"

Jane began to undo Portia's dress. "But how nice for you," she said soothingly. "You need only smile and nod. They will do the rest."

Portia peered over her shoulder, her eyes brimming with unshed tears. B—but don't you see? I—I will *still* have to think of *some* things to say! And it will be truly h—horrible being made to dance in p—public!"

Jane helped Portia into a night rail while wondering whether to tell her of the earl's scheme. For a girl of Portia's nervous disposition, it might be worse knowing that a deception was being carried out, especially as it was for her benefit, and Jane decided not to say anything to her unless the earl suggested it first.

"You are seeing spooks and goblins where none exist," Jane said kindly. "If you will only take things one step at a time and not anticipate disaster before the fact, I am persuaded it will not be so awful as you think."

"But these three! They are just the first of many, and though I know perfectly well that they are all kindness, I could not even *speak* to them! You saw how it was! How am

72

I to go on in Bath?"

Jane shushed her and soothed her and promised she would never leave her side in Bath, until at last Portia allowed herself to be tucked into bed. The landlord's wife had wrapped a hot brick in flannel and put it between the sheets where it would warm Portia's feet. Jane arranged the plump covers over Portia and sat back against the pillows.

"Oh, what am I to do?" Portia whimpered. She insinuated herself into the curve of Jane's arm like a small child.

"You will do very well," Jane assured her. "Your brother has not undertaken this stay in Bath as a punishment for you," she pointed out. "He expects you to do your best, but he will not persist if he sees that you have tried and are miserable."

"You do not know George as I do," Portia said darkly. "He has no idea what it is to be less than perfect, and so he has no pity for those of us who cannot possibly live up to his high standards. Our mother has even said he can be arrogant at times. Of course, she would not dream of saying that to his face! She adores him, and of course, I do, too, but he is not an easy man to live with."

Jane let Portia ramble on and made encouraging noises whenever she could, until at last Portia had spent her anxiety in words and dropped off to sleep. The fire had warmed the room nicely and Jane nodded off, to. She awoke sometime later when the fire was burning low. Chilled and achy from sitting in an awkward position for so long, she disengaged herself from Portia, anxious to seek out her own bedchamber. She was grateful that the earl had engaged a private room for her, since Portia gave every evidence of being a restless sleeper.

In the hallway, candles which had been lit earlier were guttering low, and Jane realized it was very late. She shivered and hurried along the corridor, only to hear herself hailed by Stoke from further along. The elderly abigail apologized for asking, but would Jane mind fetching another hot brick for her? She swore she would be too stiff to arise in the morning if she continued the night without one.

Jane did her best to accede pleasantly, reminding herself that it was better to be able to help one who suffered from aches and pains than to have them oneself. She took Stoke's brick and felt her way back along the corridor to her own room. The fire was low but she got it going again with wood left on the hearth, and laid both her own by-now cold brick and Stoke's on the andirons. Changing into a night rail, she huddled by the fire and waited, knowing that the more fully warmed the bricks were, the longer they would throw off heat. The warmth of the fire made her sleepy again, and when she felt her eyelids drooping for the third time, she withdrew the bricks with a tong and swiftly wrapped them in the flannels.

Carrying both bricks for extra warmth, Jane felt her way back to the abigail's room, counting doors as she went. The corridor was barely lit by the one remaining candle, and Jane particularly disliked darkness when not wearing her spectacles, it being doubly hard to distinguish anything in shadows without them. She accepted Stoke's thanks and started to feel her way back along the corridor. At the sixth door, she stopped and pushed inward. The fire was burning exactly as she had left it, bright and high, and Jane gratefully closed the door behind her.

Kicking off her slippers, she pushed the brick down beneath the covers and crept under them, surprised to find the bed already quite warm. She maneuvered the brick lower with her feet and felt a sudden shock as her foot came into contact with a leg not her own, and a hairy leg at that. Jane recoiled in alarm. She was undoubtedly in the wrong room, and furthermore, the bed was already occupied by someone of the opposite gender!

"Ho!" said a masculine voice. "Who's come to warm me then?"

The words were slurred but the voice was unmistakably

the earl's! Jane scrambled frantically to reverse directions but a hand snaked out beneath the covers to encircle her waist. The earl kept a firm grip on her as he raised himself on one elbow and inspected her with bleary eyes.

Jane felt a furious blush rise in her cheeks, for the earl wore no night shirt, no night cap—nothing! His broad chest was bare except for a liberal covering of dark hair, the shoulders sleekly muscled and formidable. Jane tried to stammer out some explanation, squirming all the while to escape his grasp, but the earl merely grinned down at her.

"What a nice surprise," he murmured.

"Sir! Your lordship!" Jane babbled. "You mistake me—I am in the wrong room. I apologize, I—"

"Not at all," he said. "I won't hear it. So pretty! Where else should you be? What better place than here?"

Jane began to feel quite panicked. There was a strong suggestion of liquor on the earl's breath. How did one reason with a man in his cups? "I mistook your door for mine—it's quite dark in the hall, you know!" she said swiftly. She edged toward the side of the bed but made no progress against the confinement of his hand. "I should be in my own room."

The earl's grin softened to a seductive smile, his naturally heavy-lidded eyes dropping to further shutter his gaze. "No, don't say so. I like you here." He took in the high, lace-trimmed collar of her night rail. "Do you know, that is the first thing you have worn that suits you? And yet I am bound to say, I wish you did not have it on."

Jane stared at him, aghast. He was clearly inebriated. "Please, your lordship, release me," she said pleadingly. "This is most improper. You are not yourself."

"No, not at all, and thank God for it," he agreed lazily. "Old Wilcox said no smuggled liquor under his roof, but—devil take him!—it was. Nantes brandy, best I've ever had . . . but why are we talking about Wilcox?" His smile deepened as he studied her. "Those eyes! Those lips! Nothing for it but to kiss you," he said thickly, and before Jane could take evasive action, his mouth came down on hers.

Jane received the touch of his lips with the profoundest shock. Warm and dry, they pressed into hers, and a lightly stubbled cheek rubbed her cheek. It was not at all unpleasant.

"Mmmmm, Jane—you are heaven," he murmured, pulling back. "You are Jane, aren't you? 'Course you are. Why else would I be kissing you? That's the plan."

Jane could only stare up at him, telling herself that she should be mortified. Except that she wasn't.

"Your lordship . . ." she whispered faintly, "you mustn't."

"George," he said firmly. "You must call me George, and I'll tell you why," he said confidentially. "Because I'm going to kiss you again."

Jane felt pinned to the spot by disbelief, the pace of her breathing increasing as she watched his face descend again. Every single detail of it was plain to her. Her lips pursed up to form the word "George," and then it was too late. She let her eyes close and melted into his kiss.

His hand caressed her waist and he moved over her, his body blocking out the fire's light. Jane felt warm and dizzy and limp all at once as the earl pulled her up against him. She put up a hand in halfhearted protest but it met with the hard, furry wall of his chest, which only served to further confound her senses. Blood thrummed in her ears as his lips caressed her mouth insistently. At some point she realized she wasn't breathing and took air in through her nose. At last he pulled away.

"Oh, my!" she exclaimed breathlessly.

"So delightful," the earl whispered. He traced along her cheek with his lips. His breath ruffled the hair at her temple and tickled her ear. "So soft . . ." He reached her ear and began to roll her earlobe between his lips. "Mmmmm."

Jane closed her eyes in a dim haze of pleasure. The sheer bulk and weight of him surprised her, and made her think—in a vague sort of way—how futile it would be to resist him.

76

He made another deep sound in his chest and she felt his hot, humid breath on her neck, and then what must be his teeth nipping at her earlobe.

She knew she must make some move toward going. "Please, your . . . George," she managed to say, "you must leave off what you are doing."

"Leave off?" He sounded puzzled. "Why? Do you dislike it?"

"Not precisely," she whispered as he kissed her neck and brought his hand up to cup her shoulder. She groped in her mind for a way to explain why something which struck her as so pleasurable must end. The best she could manage was, "Were I a man, I should be obliged to call you out for taking such liberties."

He chuckled, a rich, full-bodied sound that rumbled through her. "Ah, but if you were a man, I would not be doing this." He slid down to pay further attention to the base of her throat, using his hand to open the top of her night dress. Jane felt a flutter of dismay and reached up with some nebulous idea of pushing his head away, but her hands betrayed her, stroking his hair in what could only be considered an encouraging way.

"Oh, much better," the earl muttered against her neck. "You smell like . . . like . . . spring. How can a *person* smell like spring?" He nuzzled her collarbone, his lips pursuing the line of it as he pushed aside her gown.

Jane was now entirely consumed by the war within— what she wanted versus what must be. What she wanted was running so far ahead of what must be that it was not going to finish even a distant second unless she acted soon.

"Your lordship . . . George," she said desperately, addressing the top of his head. Firelight gleamed on the waving, sleek, dark brown hair, and she tried to push him away, but her wrists had gone all soggy. Instead she found herself twining her fingers through the richness of his hair. She was rewarded by another deep sound of satisfaction from him.

"No, this is not right . . . please, I beg of you, stop . . ." Even to her own ears, the words sounded spurious.

The earl shifted his weight so that both his hands were at her shoulders and she saw with a shock that her night rail was undone nearly to her breasts. "S'very right," he muttered, working the cloth with his thumbs so that her throat and chest were exposed. "Want you."

"No!" Jane cried. The heat of his lips and the rasping of his beard sucked the wind out of her and the protest lost whatever pale conviction it might have had. He angled across her and trailed a steady stream of moist kisses up her throat, ending at the opposite ear, which was treated to a gentle nipping. "Oh, that is—"

He paused long enough to interrupt her. "S'nice, that's what it is."

The feel of his chest with its dense mat of hair brushing against her own bare skin was so extraordinary that she was left speechless for a full minute, during which time the earl was engaged in nibbling at her eyebrows. Jane sensed that she was losing ground without moving an inch. *What was one to do!* He was three parts drunk and she knew it was up to her to put an end to this highly improper interlude.

The earl moved slowly and with great deliberation to kiss her again. Jane felt the heat of his lips melting her will to resist. He might be drunk as a tinker but she was not, and yet she felt as if she might be. A spinning head, a dry mouth, a trembly, hot feeling in all her limbs—but she had not drunk a drop of any spirit all night. How was one to account for it? The one truth which stood out clearly in her otherwise foggy brain was that she very much wanted to be kissed by George Tate, Earl of Sefton, and *had* wanted to be kissed by him for some time now. He obligingly gathered her in his arms as this simple fact lodged itself dead center in her consciousness.

"Jane, Jane," he murmured, "you are intoxicating." She shivered in reaction to this impassioned declaration. He pulled away and peered down at her uncertainly, his breathing uneven. "You are so quiet! Have I frightened you, little one?" he asked. He drew one finger along the curve of her breast where it swelled out from her night rail, provoking another shiver. "You are cold? But the remedy is at hand—you must have some of Wilcox's very excellent brandy!" The earl turned his head and called out loudly, "Henry!"

Alarm bells began to ring in Jane's torporous brain. "Do hush!" she begged in a loud whisper. "You'll wake the whole house! And on no account must Henry find me here!"

"Nonsense," the earl said, his handsome head wobbling for a moment as he slowly focused on her again. "I want you here. Henry has no say in the matter."

"Oh!" Exasperation cleared Jane's head and gave wings to her wit. "Let me go and I shall get the brandy myself," she insisted.

"Wha' for?" the earl said unsteadily. "Henry lives to please me—he'll tell you so himself. Would be vastly displeased *not* to be called."

"It's late, I tell you," Jane said firmly. "He is fast asleep in his bed. *I* will get the brandy." She pushed away from George's side just as she heard the urgent tread of footsteps coming down the hallway. With a quickness born of desperation, she arrived at an alternative plan of escape. She leaped from under the covers and slipped beneath the bed before the earl could stop her.

There was a discreet rapping at the door. "Your lordship called?" came the muffled inquiry.

"I want some brandy, Henry."

The valet gently pushed the door open and peered around it. "Immediately, your lordship. Any certain type?"

"The Nantes." There was a long pause. "Henry?"

"Yes, your lordship?"

"Where is Miss Oxenby?"

The valet responded as courteously as if he were accustomed to being awakened every night to answer simple-minded questions. "I cannot say for certain, your lordship, but I would hazard a guess that she is asleep in her bedchamber."

"But she was just here," the earl said somewhat forlornly. "The brandy was for her."

"Does your lordship not then require the brandy?" Henry asked, disdaining to enter further into the subject of Jane's whereabouts.

"But she was here just a minute ago," George persisted.

"Just as you say," Henry agreed. "Will that be all?"

"Well, she was," George said petulantly.

The earl was known for having a deadly temper when he drank too much, which was seldom, but none who had witnessed it ever forgot it. Henry softly closed the door and mused on what an odd—and yet welcome!—departure it was for his master to hallucinate after imbibing heavily. As the valet settled back into his own bed, he hit upon the only logical explanation: the brandy the earl had been drinking was French. The French were an odd lot, as everyone knew, and Henry supposed it was not to be wondered at if their brandy induced imaginary perceptions in a man.

Unlike his valet, George did not have any such weighty intellectual dialogue with himself. He fell back against the pillows when Henry left the room and whiffed the air. There! It was inescapable—Jane's scent was still around and about him. His body still quivered with the feel of her body up against his. Where the devil she had got to was a question that would have vexed him a great deal longer had it not been for the advanced hour and the huge quantity of brandy he had drunk. His eyes drifted closed irresistibly, and he was quite incapable of hearing anything by the time the latch was lifted and a shadowy figure departed the room.

Chapter Five

When he awoke the next morning, George did not hold it against the brandy that he had been so overcome by it as to molest a refined young woman under his protection. Indeed, upon learning that he and his friends had not—amazingly enough!—breached the second cask their host had procured for them, George asked Wilcox his price and had the cask added to the rest of his chattels in the luggage coach. As he sat nursing his aching head in the coffee room, however, the more important issue of what to do about what had happened tried him sorely.

His first question of Wilcox that morning—looming much larger than the acquisition of the Nantes brandy—had been to ask if the ladies were still abed. Upon being assured that they were, he set about rehearsing a speech which he hoped would mollify Jane, if anything could. He relied heavily on his assessment of her as good-natured, intelligent, and not in the least missish. He was prepared to grovel on his knees until they were bloody, if need be, to procure Jane's forgiveness. What he had done was unthinkable, inexcusable! He could only hope that his memory served him right and that he had done no worse than he remembered, which was bad enough.

He, who was never at a loss for words, struggled mightily

to think of a suitable apology. He forced another cup of coffee into his unwilling mouth and stared dismally at his top boots. They were too bright by half—he would have to speak to Henry. Such a sheen could only hurt one's eyes. He passed fully an hour in wretched contemplation of the debacle to come, reflecting that if it had been anyone other than Jane, he would not have cared nearly so much. But Jane! That he held her in such high regard on such short acquaintance was itself ominous, and the realization tied his tongue in knots when at last she made her appearance.

"Good morning, my lord!" she said brightly.

George goggled at her like a stupid stripling. She wore one of Portia's dresses, a pale blue that did nothing for his sister but suited Jane to perfection. No hint of censure or reproof could he read in her expression.

"Portia charged me with telling you that she would not be more than another fifteen minutes in coming down," she said cheerily. She paused and looked him over. "Are you quite well, your lordship?" she asked sympathetically. "Your color is less than . . . wholesome."

George opened his mouth and tried to launch into the speech, the opening of which he knew well enough, having repeated it in his mind at least forty-five times in the last hour, but nothing came out.

Jane helped herself to some eggs from the sideboard. "Oh, well! Perhaps it is just the light in here. You know that I do not see at all well without my spectacles, and most especially not in dim light. La! What a time I had finding my bedchamber last night!"

George drew himself up. He was twenty-eight: not eight, not eighteen, but twenty-eight, and honor demanded that he own his misdeeds. "Miss Oxenby," he began stiffly, "I believe there is something which occurred last night for which an apology of the most comprehensive nature is owed."

Jane paused in the act of conveying a forkful of eggs to her mouth and regarded him with mild curiosity. "My, but how serious you sound! Is it that you played cards with your friends? I am sure you are perfectly entitled to your own entertainments. After all, you have engaged to devote yourself entirely to Portia and me while we are in Bath. I am sure that the prospect is not wonderful to you, being a bachelor accustomed to pleasing himself at all times. Your magnanimity in this venture must excite approbation in everyone who learns of it."

George labored with difficulty to keep his mouth from dropping open. Was it possible that what he *thought* had happened *hadn't* happened? But no! There was a . . . a look in her eyes. Was she tacitly conveying her willingness to overlook the affair? And if she was, could he accept it? He wrestled with his lesser impulses for a moment and then he bethought himself of a noble reason to follow her lead.

"You are all delicacy," he said, bowing low. "I would not cause you further . . . embarrassment by dwelling on the events of last night."

"Oh, I was ever one for looking to the future," she said blithely. "I see nothing to be gained in taking offense where none is calculated."

"Indeed, none was," he said with feeling. He turned his back to the fire and reflected that the day was going rather better than he had had any right to hope. Still, there was one matter left unresolved. "As to something you said earlier, about your spectacles—I wish you to know that there is no bar, in my view, to your wearing them. In fact, I think it nonsensical not to."

Jane's eyes sparkled as she spooned some marmalade onto toast. "Truly, I believe it would be wiser, since we are now departed from places where familiarity alone will guide my steps."

George laid his elbow on the mantlepiece and felt a grateful peace settle over him, a welcome antidote to the tension of the past hour. What a splendid girl she was!

Excellent white teeth nibbled at the toast and George was reminded of what he had been endeavoring so hard to forget, which was the taste and the feel of those lovely lips beneath his. He shook himself.

"Please, wear your spectacles at all times," he said fervently. "I will not hear of it being otherwise."

Wofford made the ladies a handsome bow as he ushered them into the front drawing room of the accommodations the earl had selected. "And the ladies' bedrooms are located on the second floor of the house," he was saying, "though they are by no means as small and ill lit as is customary in these houses. For the most part, houses in Bath seem to reflect the vainglory of mankind—all for show and little eye toward practicality."

Jane nodded and walked past him. What an earnest man he was!—and much higher in the instep than even the earl, if one were making comparisons.

"This room is lovely," Portia managed to say in response to Wofford's obvious lingering.

Jane cast her eye about. Cerulean blue drapes hung at the four windows which fronted the street, windows which stretched from nearly floor to ceiling, and let in a vast amount of sunlight. The two end windows were draped with plain cream silk, and the theme was repeated in the settees and various upholstered chairs. There was even a pianoforte in one corner of the huge room. It was difficult to see why three persons required such a large house, but Jane felt a touch of excitement over the grand scale on which the earl apparently intended them to live.

"It is marvelous!" Jane declared. "Truly beautiful!"

The secretary drew himself up. "So kind," he said in pleased accents. "I trust it is everything you hoped for."

"Oh, I hoped for nothing at all," Jane said. "I had not the least idea what to expect. I assure you, I would have been content in much less splendor than this!"

"Then I must be thankful that you have allowed *me* to order affairs," came the earl's voice from the doorway.

Jane spun around, her slippered feet carrying her forward over a Turkey carpet of blues and creams and magentas. "I believe I have found a little piece of heaven in this room," she said gaily.

"Surely not as wonderful as all that," the earl declared, smiling.

Jane laughed out loud, unable to subdue her happiness as her Aunt Eugenia would have said she ought. "More wonderful!" she said. She slipped her arm through Portia's. "Shall we not be the happiest two females in Bath?" she asked. "Three—no, four!—handsome gentlemen already engaged to stand up with us at the assemblies, subscription libraries on every hand, concerts, lectures, exhibitions, theatre, shops, Sydney Gardens . . . why, any more entertainments and we should be exhausted from pleasing ourselves!"

Portia dimpled up, her face almost lively. "Why, Jane, we need not *do* all of those things! It was only that Mr. Wofford thought we might like to *know* of all the activities open to us."

Jane jiggled Portia's arm. "But of course we must do all that is open to us! Must we not, your lordship?"

George strolled into the room, a faintly amused look on his face. "If I had know you would be so overcome by the positively bucolic pastimes in Bath, I would have endeavored to find an even more quiet resort for our stay."

"No, I will not allow you to have it that Bath is bucolic," Jane averred. "When we crested the rise, the design and proportion of the town below fairly took my breath away! It is quite the most gracious, sophisticated place one can imagine."

"Only if one has not seen London or Brighton or—"

"I refuse to listen," Jane said stoutly. "Come, Portia, your brother is being provoking. I vow, we must retire to our rooms or he will coax me out of my good humor."

"Oh, you misapprehend," Portia giggled. "George is just . . . George. He is forever talking to me in this manner."

"Quite right, Portia," the earl murmured. "Now, if you will allow, Miss Oxenby, I have a program to propose for today which I hope will meet with your approval."

"Very well," Jane said with mock severity, "I suppose we shall hear you out."

"So obliging." He turned to the secretary. "Wofford, please tell Fletcher that we require a cold lunch within the hour. You will dine with us?"

"Most kind," Wofford said, bowing stiffly and exiting the room.

"Now," the earl said, languidly withdrawing a snuffbox, from which, to Jane's knowledge, he had never withdrawn even one pinch of snuff, "we must draw up an order of march. Since we have traveled by such easy stages, I trust you two will not be too fatigued to accompany me into the heart of the town, to Milsom Street."

"What are we to do there?" Portia inquired a little fearfully.

"Set your mind at ease," George said. He flipped open the enamelled snuffbox with one, long elegant finger and gently pushed the snuff around, releasing a faintly spicy odor into the air. "It is nothing you will dislike. In fact, I believe you may even enjoy it, for we are going to visit a mantua-maker or two. You, Portia, may have whatever strikes your fancy, but we are going primarily to decide on frocks for Jane."

Portia raised her eyebrows and looked hopefully at Jane. "That would not be altogether unpleasant."

"Good! Then it is settled. If you ladies will excuse me, I believe I will look further into the matter of the stabling of my horses while we await luncheon."

"If you please," Jane said hastily, "I do not need any dresses. Or rather, if you wish me to have one or two additional so as not to shame you with my appearance, could not Portia and I simply attend to it by ourselves?"

George closed the snuffbox with a tiny snap and looked at Jane with interest. "Why, may I ask, do you wish to go alone?"

Jane felt the color coming into her cheeks. "I think it would perhaps make the wrong impression if . . . if . . ."

"Ah!" the earl said with a look of dawning comprehension. "If an unmarried man should be seen to be purchasing articles of clothing for an unmarried lady? Has someone perhaps planted that suggestion in your mind, Miss Oxenby? Someone with a rather overheated imagination?"

Jane pushed her spectacles further up her nose, a gesture calculated to buy her a minute in which to compose herself. "Well, not precisely, no," she replied with less than complete candor.

"Oh, but I think someone has," George said in an infinitely bored voice that suggested that such notions were beneath his regard. "Allow me to assure you that no impropriety can attach to the circumstance of me accompanying my sister and her very good friend on a shopping expedition, and only the mantua-makers need know to whom the bill is sent."

"No," Jane said meekly, "I can quite see that." Her gaze flew up to meet his. "And no one would dare to ask—would they?"

His rather hard face softened. "They would have me to reckon with if they did," he said, as though that were a complete answer. He excused himself and strolled out through the double doors which let onto the marble vestibule.

"No one would," Portia volunteered when he was gone, "I mean, question him on such a score. He is considered one of the finest amateur boxers in all England," she added with a touch of pride.

Jane laughed. "Does that keep all animosity at bay? Or do not his foes consider using weapons with which he is not so skilled as with his fists? Pistols perhaps, or swords?"

Portia looked shocked. "R—really, Jane," she gasped, sitting down abruptly on a satin sofa, "you must not say such things!"

The laughter died on Jane's lips. "Why, Portia, dear, I have greatly offended you somehow. Please! Forgive me!" Jane sat down beside her and clasped her hand.

Portia's fingers were limp and cold, and she stared at Jane in disbelief. "Can you really not know?" she whispered.

"Not know what, dear one?" Jane said, vigorously chafing Portia's hands between her own.

"About George, about . . . about how he came to be called Selfless Sefton?"

"No, I am quite sure I have never heard him called that," Jane said. "Recollect that we have not known one another long, nor do we move in the same circles."

"Of course," Portia said on a long exhalation, "but you must on no account ever say anything of the kind to George—regarding pistols or swords or . . . or dueling!"

"Why, then I shall not," Jane assured her.

"Oh, it would be the most awful thing imaginable if you should! It has all quite died down now but it might so easily be resurrected by the maliciously minded!"

"What on earth can you mean?" Jane asked, much mystified.

Portia frowned. "I am not sure it is quite right that I should tell you," she said worriedly.

"Then you must not," Jane said with perfect equanimity.

"No, I shall," Portia said with sudden decisiveness. "It is too important for you *not* to know. It happened many years ago and I know of it only from what I have overheard, since no one would speak of it openly." She paused and nibbled on her lip. "I believe our father had some sort of an argument with another man over an affair of honor. My father refused to give the man satisfaction and this man continued to blacken my father's name until it came to my brother's ears.

He was young at the time, younger than I am now, but he called the man out."

"But that is heroic, surely," Jane said.

Portia's warm brown eyes met Jane's and in them was a look of deepest sorrow. "I believe—that is, I do not know precisely—that the misdeed of which our father was accused was one he had, in fact, committed. The accuser was content, though, merely to wing George, after which my brother was sent abroad for a time. In his absence, he was labeled Selfless Sefton for having put himself forward in our father's stead. It was an epithet of greatest derision, for everyone seemed to have known of our father's . . . guilt, except for his own son."

Jane sat motionless, considering it. "Well, I do not hold with that," she said at last. "It was most unkind in anyone to blame George at all. *He* did not commit the misdeed. He only defended the family's honor!"

"Only," said Portia sadly, "there was no honor in this particular case."

Jane patted Portia's hand consolingly. "It is in the distant past now. Let us not dwell on it. I am sure George does not."

Indeed, Jane reflected when they walked out later, it was greatly to be wondered at that there had ever been a blemish on the life of George Aubrey Tate, Earl of Sefton. His rugged handsomeness took her breath away—the proud, firm jaw and the high forehead, the bold, dark brows, and most of all, the deep blue eyes, hooded over as often as not by the lids, concealing his private amusement or cynicism. His tallness was somewhat intimidating, his broadness through the shoulders definitely so, and the fineness of his bearing and dress could only lead one to conclude that nothing at all untoward could ever have touched him—if one did not know better.

Ahead of them, Portia walked beside Mr. Wofford, listening as the secretary delivered a commentary on the architectural history of the town. ". . . and also built the

Royal Crescent in 1775, but Bath quickly became so fashionable that many other architects were drawn to it. John Jelley designed Campden Crescent in 1788, and Lansdowne Crescent—where you are residing—was designed by John Palmer the following year. Ah! Here we have an aspect which will allow you to appreciate fully the work of . . ."

His voice faded as they proceeded around a corner. "Poor Portia!" Jane exclaimed when she was sure they were out of earshot. "Mr. Wofford is the most serious-minded individual it has ever been my privilege to meet!"

George gave a dry laugh. "If my sister will not speak up, she must resign herself to listening to whatever her companion chooses to discuss."

"Still," Jane sighed, "I think that sort of lecture a steep comeback for having made one small remark regarding the Grecian portico surmounting our door."

The earl did not reply, merely smiling, and turned the conversation to more convivial subjects as they wended their way down the long hill into the center of the town. Jane expected him to be bored by their visits to the shops in Milsom Street, but she was greatly surprised. He reclined in the chair offered to him by the mantua-maker and began to discuss the latest issue of *Le Beau Monde*, and the merits of various costumes illustrated in it. The modiste eagerly entered into a detailed discussion with the earl, perceiving that here was a man of great sensibility. It seemed that nothing but white muslin would do for Portia, but that his lordship would be pleased to consider pastels for Jane, and before she could easily comprehend it, Jane found herself being measured and turned this way and that for the earl's eye.

"Lavender sarsenet for that one, I think, and let us have a pelisse for it, too, with a facing of deepest yellow. And we shall require a black gauze cloak. Shawls to blend with all the rest will have to be looked for at the draper." Jane began to grow quite bewildered by the profusion of detail—trims and laces, beaded jet and plaited ribbons, satin roses—but the earl went on in his smooth, authoritative way until he professed himself satisfied that nothing had been over-looked.

They left the mantua-maker, escorted to the door by an extremely pleased owner, and despite the throngs of shoppers in Milsom Street, the rest of their purchases were made in short order. At each stop, the earl's air of quality inspired the chiefest of the clerks to come forward and attend them himself. They purchased in two hours what must have taken two days for anyone less imposing and decisive than the earl. Bonnets, parasols, fans, gloves, stockings—silk, at a guinea a pair!—all followed, as well as reticules, ribbons and, lastly, slippers. Jane submitted to have her feet measured at the shoemaker's, where her very best nankeen half-boots were deftly unlaced and the earl decreed that she should have one pair of every variety of slipper and shoe to be had ready-made, owing to the press of time.

"As to handkerchiefs, scents, combs, hair ornaments and the like, I trust you and Portia may have the pleasure of lingering over such selections tomorrow perhaps, or the day after," the earl said as he escorted them once more into the light of day.

"I hardly know how to thank you," Jane said. "I only hope I may remember what goes with what so that I do not embarrass you, or spoil the nice effect of the ensembles you have chosen."

The earl gestured in his imperious way for Wofford to lead off with Portia down the crowded thoroughfare. "I have no doubt that you will look most charming in any combination of pieces," he said diplomatically, "but I have been wondering if I should not engage another abigail to assist you. I brought staff up from my country residence, leaving my London residence fully staffed, since I anticipate making some short journeys to my town address while we are here.

However, among my staff at Sefton Park, there were no additional abigails. I have told Wofford to engage a hairdresser to call on you and Portia as often as you require one, but would it not be best to engage another abigail to assist Stoke?"

"Oh, no!" Jane exclaimed. "I am quite horrified by the expense you have already been to today, to fit me out. You must not add to my indebtedness by increasing staff on my account."

"My dear Miss Oxenby, I assure you that the addition of one more abigail to my household will not be the ruination of me."

Jane saw the gleam of humor in his eye. "Well, perhaps it wouldn't," she answered, smiling up from under her lashes, "but I think it might upset a comfortable balance that exists in our boudoir. Portia, Stoke and I manage quite well, and the addition of another abigail might overset our happy arrangement."

They rounded a corner and came onto Bond Street. "I defer to you in this, as in all things," the earl said mildly.

"You do no such thing!" Jane countered.

The earl laughed then. "How very kind in you to point out the falsehood," he said. "I trust you will always keep me honest, though in becoming so, I fear I may concurrently become unsuited to move in polite society."

"Oh, you mean you dare not be honest? I suppose that if you have a great many wicked and unsuitable thoughts, that may be so," Jane agreed.

The earl stopped and smiled down at her in a way that made Jane's heart twist just a bit. "The salary of another abigail would not ruin me, Jane, but your candor may!"

"I believe you are well embarked on your course of drawing attention to us," Jane replied with a mischievous smile, "for there is not a soul within fifty paces who does not long to know the source of our mutual laughter, and to hear every word of our conversation!"

The earl did not blink but she saw a change come over him, a subtle shifting into a more public persona. "Just as you say," he said softly, "but I did not mean for that to begin today. For any compliments or pretty attention I have paid you this afternoon, you have only yourself to blame."

Jane had to still the flutter his words sent through her, maintaining her lighthearted countenance. "I will reconsider this conversation at my leisure," she said, "and try to discover if there was anything of a complimentary nature in what you have said."

The earl let loose a chuckle and resumed walking toward Portia and Wofford, who were waiting at the curb for them. "I suspect you might like to rest now," he said, "and if you would not, I know my sister will."

"I perceive that you are presenting me with no alternative," Jane said with a smile. "I will rest."

The earl summoned two sedan chairs. "These stout lads will take you back up the hill in comfort," he said. He gave the address to the bearers and watched Portia and Jane take their seats. "Ah! One last detail," he said to Jane. "If I might have your spectacles for a short while. I promise they will be restored to you by dinner time tonight." Jane reluctantly handed him the gold-rimmed spectacles and then the bearer whisked the chairs away before she could ask why he wanted them.

Jane discovered when they arrived back in Lansdowne Crescent that she *was* tired, and reflected that the lack of her spectacles took some of the pleasure out of inspecting the house anyway. She and Portia mounted the stairs to the second story and discovered their separate bedchambers at the front of that floor. The earl, Manning informed her, had his own suite of rooms on the third floor. Stoke and the footman had contrived to unpack and arrange their belongings so that there was nothing left to be done. Jane fingered the elaborate embroidered counterpane on her bed and chose to recline instead on an elegant Grecian couch by the window.

Portia took herself off to pen a letter to Jonas, telling him of their journey and giving him their direction in Bath. Jane had some misgiving regarding the latter, but she knew that the earl had already given orders to Wofford to enter their names and direction in the books at both the New and Lower Rooms. It would serve as a notice to others that they were open to receiving callers, and also allow the masters of the two assemblies to pay them a welcoming visit. If Jonas should come to Bath, he could easily discover their direction by examining the registers. Jane sighed and reflected that she was in Bath in the role of confidante, not jailer, and waved Portia off. Jane meant to write to Nanny, too, but at very limited intervals, owing to the cost of the postage which Nanny would be obliged to pay at the receiving end, at least six pence. Though Jane had given fully three-quarters of her pin money to Nanny, it would not do for that excitable lady to squander it in receiving news that was as likely to alarm her as to entertain her. When they assembled for dinner, George announced that they would go and pay their respects to Great Aunt Serena, who had been firmly established in a bedroom at the rear of the second floor just prior to their own arrival. Jane was quite astonished when she caught her first glimpse of their chaperon. Great Aunt Serena was, quite simply, the *roundest* woman Jane had ever seen. She was tiny, well under five feet, and dressed all in pink—pink slippers, pink handkerchief, pink cap, pink tucker, pink fan.

A huge tin of sweets graced the table next to the invalid's chair she occupied, and a pile of novels occupied a stand on the other side. She giggled when George made the introductions in a near shout, and she held out a plump, white hand for Jane to clasp.

Great Aunt Serena added to the difficulty of conversing with her by whispering her replies, while one was forced to shout at her to be heard. They did manage to make some conversation, centering chiefly around a book Serena had read recently called *The Female Quixote, or the Adventures of Isabella.* Jane was forced to admit she had not read it, which turned out to be a blessing in disguise, for Serena happily regaled them all with a detailed description of its plot.

Every so often, Great Aunt Serena's hand edged toward a box of bonbons but then she would withdraw it with a swift, regretful glance at her visitors, as if she did not wish to share the bonbons and could not bring herself to be so rude as to eat them without offering them around. Jane had to clamp down on a fold of her inner cheek to keep from laughing, especially when she caught George's eye and saw that he too had noticed the reaching and withdrawing motions, and was hard pressed not to laugh. When they rose to take their leave, Serena's relief was evident. Though she invited them to visit her anytime, it was apparent that she was quite content with just the company of a large raw-boned woman who was her companion, and who said not two words to any of them. Jane never did discover the companion's name, and rather thought she had not been meant to.

Dinner proved to be a good deal more awe-inspiring an affair than luncheon had been. The earl restored Jane's spectacles to her with a word of thanks, and led the way into the dining room at the rear of the first floor. The large mahogany table which had earlier been split into smaller tables was reformed into one large one, and china and silver sparkled in the light of numerous tapers. Wofford did not join them at this more exalted meal, a subtle reminder of his lesser station.

"Oh, dear!" Jane exclaimed as she took in the Wedgewood dinner service and saw that there was to be a footman in attendance at each place. Little could be spoken of in front of the servants, other than the most innocuous topics. In the end, she drew the earl out on the subject of the linen, silver and dishes which had, of necessity, been brought from Sefton park. The repast was quite bewildering in its scope, from salmon with shrimp sauce to sweetbreads and chicken fricassee, all beautifully presented, to Maids of Honor pastries and a syllabub decorated with spring violets for dessert.

"If we are going to dine like this every evening, we shall have to order the mantua-maker to let out every dress which was ordered today," Jane declared as she set aside her napkin at last.

"Oh, we shall be taking any number of bracing walks, and making energetic forays into the surrounding countryside," the earl said with a gleam of humor in his eyes. As the solitary male, he did not linger over a decanter in the dining room but went directly to the drawing room with Portia and Jane when the last cover had been removed.

"I quite like this informality," he said, settling into an armchair.

"Before you imagine that you enjoy informality, I think perhaps you should make an effort to experience it," Jane said wryly as a footman lit the last of the fifty or so beeswax candles in the room.

"I apprehend you mean that I should go off with the gypsies, or some such romantic thing," George remarked mildly. "It wouldn't do, you know, having peers of the realm off living in painted carts and roaming the land. Portia, ring the bell for Fletcher to bring the tea, and when you have done that, you had better sit down and discover if that pianoforte is in tune. I think our guest needs the charms of music to soothe her."

Portia sat down at the instrument and said apologetically, "As I do not have my folio, I will have to play from memory."

Jane leaned forward and said with enthusiasm, "Then may we hear one of the sonatas by Dr. Haydn? I know you have practiced them to perfection." Portia ducked her head in modest disclaimer but Jane would not allow her to escape praise. She turned to George and said, "Portia copied out in the fairest hand you can imagine all of Dr. Haydn's piano sonatas while she was at Canfield, to say nothing of spending hours playing them."

The earl raised his eyebrows. "Can this indeed be so, Portia? Our mother will be very pleased."

Portia did not answer but played very prettily for nearly half an hour, and then excused herself on the ground that she was fatigued. Jane watched her receive a lighted candle from Manning at the foot of the stairs and ascend before turning to the earl. "Playing the pianoforte is one of the few things Portia is naturally gifted at, and yet, I own it is wonderful to me how she works so diligently to play even better."

The earl regarded her for a moment, his expression reflective. "I think I am fast learning the secret of your appeal for Portia, and it is quickly becoming your appeal for me, too. Yours is a happy, conciliating spirit that nevertheless speaks its mind. That is a rare quality, Miss Oxenby. I wonder if the world is quite ready for you."

"What wondrous nonsense you spout!" Jane declared. "I do not doubt that the world can well cope with my poor self."

"Oh, Jane, what a dance we will lead them," he said with a thoughtful smile. It was the second time that day that he had made use of her given name without benefit of any honorific, but he seemed not to notice. "Your clothes—as well as a little surprise of my own devising—will be delivered two days hence, and then we will see if the lesser universe of Bath is prepared for Miss Jane Oxenby. I propose we waste no time in beginning our deception then."

Jane went to bed that night with a troubled heart, for in the pleasurable afterglow of the earl's remarks had come the realization that she had already begun to be a bit in love with him. Trying to pretend that she did not return his regard when he paid her public court was, she feared, going to require more theatrical skill than she possessed.

Chapter Six

George eyed Jane at the center of a cluster of young bucks. She lifted an exquisite, long-handled cloisonné quizzing glass, one of five he had had made for her, and responded to something that had been said. Her remark produced a round of laughter. John Marshall was among the besotted, George noted, as was Hugh Willoughby. Several other Corinthians lounged about on the fringes of the group, like the fragments in a comet's tail. Across the room, Mr. Le Bas, Master of Ceremonies of the Lower Rooms, regarded the scene with a satisfied air.

The earl judged it time to cease his skulking about the perimeter. It had started as a calculated, dog-in-the-manger act, but over the past few weeks, he had grown into the role. As Jane's potential suitors grew in number, George felt his temper grow more precarious. He had been too clever by half, he now realized, in concocting a scheme whereby he publicly adored Jane Oxenby while his sense of honor constrained him to hold back any private expressions of regard until she was no longer living under his roof.

On the whole, though, the plan had started out well enough, with the resurrection of his ankle injury. "Naturally," he had explained to Jane as he partnered her at their first assembly, "if I am able to stand up only a few times, I must, perforce, dance with the ladies in my own party first."

"Why, you gammon them all," she had protested. "Your ankle is long since mended!"

"But only you know that," he said, his eyes merry. "Will you unmask me? Make a liar of me in the eyes of the world?"

"I cannot make you a liar," she replied. "That you have done yourself!"

"Then it is put to rest," he said. "We can enjoy one another's company and conversation without ruining your reputation."

"Ruining my reputation?" Jane exclaimed, nearly fumbling the steps of the quadrille. "And how were we going to do that, pray tell?"

"Very simply. If I did not have a disabling injury, my failure to dance with anyone else would mark you as a shameless flirt. No one could doubt that someone so obviously enamored of you—as I will shortly be seen to be—could have failed to ask for your hand in marriage. When we do not announce our forthcoming marriage, you will be thought heartless and beneath contempt!"

Jane laughed heartily at that, drawing more than a few shocked gazes. George schooled his face into a bland smile, secretly delighted to have amused her so. And now, after numerous promenades on the Crescent, picnic expeditions to Monkton Combe, fancy balls, dress balls and concerts, Jane was a success. Anyone who had not thought her wonderful at the outset had revised his opinion after watching the way the Earl of Sefton danced attendance on her. She was generally considered to be, upon closer inspection, tolerably handsome, clever in conversation, easy and unaffected but never overly familiar, and uniquely stylish in her choice of clothing and accessories, especially the enameled lorgnettes. Everyone strove to duplicate the latter, but never managed to use them with the consistency and manner that made them so pleasing in her hand.

It was accounted a great shame that she had been abroad

for some years, and so had not come into society earlier. Murky tales circulated about her ancestry, which people hastened to confirm based on very confidential knowledge from so-and-so, who had it on good authority from another, who had heard that . . . until it all had the power of certain truth. She was thought to be quite well off, her mother an Italian countess and her father a brilliant but retiring horticulturist. What details were not forthcoming in the usual way, the avidly curious felt free to manufacture. The foremost fact in society's eyes, however, was that the heretofore unattachable Earl of Sefton was smitten, and his regard was not—so far as anyone could tell—being returned in kind. So vastly entertaining was it that no one could pass a day without acquiring some fresh information on the subject.

Yes, Jane was an unqualified success and George was tasting victory, but it was bitter fruit. The trap he had unthinkingly created was squeezing him tighter and tighter, forcing him to stand passively by as Jane was swept away on a tide of popularity, and further and further from *his* reach. George inhaled deeply in an attempt to settle himself and made his way to Jane's side.

"Miss Oxenby?"

Jane glanced around. "My lord! I did not see you there!"

"That is because I have only just come to be here," George said evenly. "I have been out to stroll in the night. It is singularly beautiful. I thought I would come and offer to share it with you."

"Now, George," Hugh Willoughby protested, "Miss Oxenby was just going to tell us what a Bullet Pudding is. Don't say you're going to take her away!"

Jane stood up and touched Hugh's arm lightly. "It's a very silly sort of entertainment," she said teasingly. "I vow, I am surprised you have not already encountered one! I promise I will tell you all about it before you are very much older."

"You must," Hugh said enthusiastically. "I could have my

cook make one up, build a jolly little party at Charlcombe 'round the thing. You did say it was a bit of a game, didn't you?"

Jane laughed. "Indeed, though with Boney riding high just across the Channel, I believe seeing a former Guardsman playing a game that entails nosing about in a dish full of flour must create a crisis of confidence in our national defense!" Jane turned to George. "There! Now I am ready. Where is Portia? I am sure she would like to join us."

George glanced across the room. "She is with Roger, and that harmless little puppy—what's his name, Digby? I daresay she is perfectly content as she is."

"Oh, but so was I," Jane pointed out. Her gallants traded glances over the subtle affront.

George knew that a week ago he would have regarded it as masterful, calculated to convince their audience that she did not return the earl's regard. Now he found it maddening. "The slight headache you complained of when we left this evening," he said with a trace of annoyance, "I worry that it will return unless you have some time away from this crush."

Jane looked up at him with a dazzling smile. "Why, if you had not mentioned it, I believe I would not have remembered it at all. How kind!"

He took her arm in a somewhat firmer grasp than he had intended. "But that is my main occupation, you see, to keep watch over you and see to your health and well-being . . . and to that of my sister."

"I cannot recall," Jane said innocently, her blue eyes brilliant as jewels by the light of the assembly's chandeliers, "did Portia have the headache before we left, too, or was it only me?"

George felt a muscle jump in his cheek. "No, it was only you. Now, will you take my arm?"

She let herself be led away docilely enough, but cast a wistful smile back at her admirers. George took a route through the anteroom, where card tables occupied all the outer walls, and some very deep loo was being played, judging by the piles of money at the corner of each table. The earl threaded his way past numerous persons who would have detained them but for the very clipped "Good evening" his lordship offered.

"Oh, my," Jane whispered impishly, "you are at your most quelling tonight!"

"They are all sycophants," George retorted as they reached the double doors leading onto a colonnaded walkway. "It would be well if *The Bath Journal* listed them: 'so-and-so just arrived from London, a raving sycophant, and also the so-and-so's of Small Littleton, horrendous toadeaters.' Besides," he added mendaciously, "I have a toothache."

Jane recalled how Nanny's temper changed for the worse when her gout flared up, and was instantly solicitous. "I'm sorry!" she said. "I had no idea. You said nothing, and gave no sign of it."

George felt his heart soften, not because of her apology—which he did not deserve for a toothache which was as fictitious as her headache—but because her focus was entirely upon him for the first time that evening. "No, not to worry," he said, patting her hand where it lay across his forearm. "I think I may go to London, however, and have it seen to on Monday."

"Oh! Well, I suppose Portia and I may find something entertaining to do at Lansdowne Crescent," Jane said, a little dismayed but endeavoring not to show it.

George laughed, his mood improving. "You needn't act as if you must withdraw into purdah just because I leave town! You are quite well launched here, and you may stroll the Crescent and meet acquaintances without accusations of impropriety. For that matter, you may certainly attend the public breakfast at Sydney Gardens on Monday. Portia will enjoy the music, as always, and you will like to walk the pathways rather than sitting while I sketch."

"True," Jane said.

"And of course, I believe there are still some shops in Bond Street and perhaps also in Bath Street where you and Portia have not managed to buy the last of their merchandise. Milsom Street, naturally, you will not trouble to visit, for they cannot have recovered yet from your last visit."

"*You,* I believe, had better take the brunt of *that* criticism," Jane said airily.

They reached the end of the walkway, where the torchieres created as many shadows as circles of illumination. "I think I must be seen to be taking your hand," George said lightly. "Play along with me, do you, for I think those odious Musgroves are watching from afar. We can rely on them to embroider the tale of our tête-à-tête, and at the same time, we are quite safe, since no one will know precisely how much of their tale to believe."

Jane smiled up at him, putting her hand into his large one trustingly. "I will feel quite fitted out for a career on the stage when we have done with all of this," she said under her breath. "I think Mrs. Siddons can have nothing on me now. Famous though she may be, she cannot have the advantage of performing under such *realistic* circumstances as I do."

George smiled down at Jane, quite melted by her fetching little chin, the alabaster skin that glowed from within, and the long-lashed eyes that met his with such probity. "Indeed, you put me in mind of her when we were inside just now. You had me so convinced that you did not want to come out with me that I wanted to wring your neck!"

"Did you?" she asked. "*That* would have drawn everyone's notice. I wish you had!"

"Oh, Jane, Jane—what am I to do with you?" he sighed. He leaned forward and softly kissed her on the forehead.

Jane gave a little hiccup of surprise. "Well," she said a bit unsteadily, "if the Musgroves are still anywhere within the shire, I suppose that will be reported to one and all. The effect should be at least as good as if you had wrung my neck publicly." He didn't answer, merely looking down at her with an enigmatic expression, and she went on. "Will you be in London long?"

"No, just one night, but I'll leave Wofford for you, in case you have any misgivings about being alone. He would certainly be an unexceptionable escort should you decide to sally forth, except of course, if you go shopping, in which case Manning would be the one to take. As Portia's footman, he is not used to quite so much activity as she has embarked on recently, but he will manage. I actually believe she has almost acquired the knack of being mildly flirtatious. You have made it seem so easy to attract admirers that she has garnered her courage and attempted to do likewise." His voice sounded a trifle strained.

"Is your tooth bothering you dreadfully?" Jane asked tenderly. "You needn't wait until Monday, you know. If you went up tomorrow, I daresay the surgeon would wait on you."

"I daresay he would," George replied absently, "but, no, it's not as bad as all that. I will not trouble him on a Saturday."

"Hugh and Roger and John can look after Portia and me quite capably while you are away. I am sure they would sleep across our doorway if we asked them to."

"Jane," the earl began in quite a different tone, "I don't mean to dictate to you, but will you try not to be swept off your feet by Hugh?" He didn't wait for an answer but went on. "He's a good man, don't mistake me. I should be happy to see Portia joined to him, but not you."

Jane felt an unpleasant jolt. "If he is good enough for Portia then I fail to see why . . ." she began stiffly.

He squeezed her hands in his own, effectively stopping her. "It's that he's not good *enough* for you," George said quickly. "You deserve someone who can match wits with you. Hugh would bore you silly within a year."

"Oh."

"Look here, the matrons will have us married and the parents of fourteen children if we don't go back inside soon," George said with a quick look over his shoulder.

"Yes, all right."

They walked along the paving stones in silence but the earl stopped her just before they reached the anteroom. "I forgot one of my reasons for bringing you out here," he said. "I wanted to thank you—in private—for all that you've done for Portia. She is a tolerable success, you must own."

"I will not dispute that," Jane said, "but she still means to marry Jonas. She is doing her very best to please you but it has not affected her feelings toward him."

"Time will tell," George replied, his expression hardening, "but she has discovered that she can make conversation, accept compliments, and dance without tripping over her partner's feet. Along with a fortune and a naturally sweet disposition, it may encourage another, better, man to offer for her, and then, who knows?"

Jane fiddled with the fringe on her shawl and said softly, "Portia believes that a true attachment is forming between us, and *that* is why she is putting forth the effort to mingle. She thinks that if she is more independent, it will free us to spend more time together."

"Ah," George said. He was quite unable to think how to respond. He could not say that *he,* at least, truly *was* forming an attachment—not now, not under the circumstances.

Jane hesitated and then went on. "I did not like to tell Portia the truth since she is of a somewhat nervous disposition. I thought it could only make her more nervous to know we were enacting a charade, and it has worked as you thought it would—only not quite the *way* you thought it would—and you must allow it would not work at all if Portia knew, for she would not have made the effort she has in order to support a charade, and then we would have to think of some other way to . . ."

Jane trailed off, looking up at the earl uncertainly. He was regarding her with a bemused smile, but there was a hint of tenderness in his expression, too. It had become more difficult with each passing day for her to pretend that she didn't welcome his touch, his smile, his every look. She knew the hopelessness of Portia's ambition though, of the earl's implacable opposition to marrying, saw how he deftly turned aside all the matchmaking mamas. It could avail nothing to admit, not even to herself, that she had fallen in love with him. She looked down at his long, patrician fingers as he took her hand again.

He too kept his gaze fixed on their joined hands and said, "I suppose that my sister is young and romantic. I was foolish not to anticipate that she might think it a true attraction, even though," he added slowly, "she has seen us in private and must know that . . ."

Jane looked up and their eyes met. ". . . must know?"

". . . must know that we are only good friends," the earl said emotionlessly, his heavy-lidded eyes further shadowed by the uneven light from the torchieres.

"Of course," Jane said softly.

A quick breeze sent a corner of her shawl flying and she snatched at it. The earl's hands followed hers, as if reluctant to lose the contact. He helped her to resettle it around her shoulders, lightly grazing her neck with his fingers and sending a flush of heat through her. Striving hard to conceal her reaction to his touch, she said, "You must nevertheless hold to your end of the bargain with Portia. She has done everything you asked of her, and more. If at the end of it all, she still wants Jonas, you are honor-bound to accept her wishes."

A second too late she saw the fire in his eyes, the proud flaring of his nostrils. He dropped her hands as if they had burned him.

"I do not require a lecture on the nature of honor," he said icily.

The depth of his fury left her breathless with shock. He

turned abruptly and went in through the doors without another word. Jane felt her face go crimson with mortification. Now she must somehow find the courage to walk back in alone. It was some minutes later when Roger Creighton appeared, nonchalantly blotting a suspiciously dry brow.

"Ah! Miss Oxenby! I perceive that you also found it insufferably hot inside."

Jane managed a tepid smile but knew that with the way her hands were shaking, she would not be able to so much as open her fan, never mind wield it to any good purpose. It was up to Roger Creighton to perpetuate the pretense, a task he fulfilled adeptly.

"You must allow me," he said, holding out his hand. She managed to disengage the satin cord of the fan from her wrist. He snapped the fan open and wafted some air in her direction. "Much better, I'm sure you are agreed," he said in an even tone. "Shall we go in again?"

He offered his elbow and Jane slipped her arm through it. "Thank you. You are too kind."

"Hate to disillusion you," he drawled as they walked back through the card room, "but I am not kind at all. It ain't in my line. A good joke, a saucy bit of gossip, an excellent claret—that's the sort of thing that speaks to my heart."

"No, of course," she said. "I can quite see that being called kind must make you seem stodgy and ruin your dashing image. I apologize."

"Thank you, Miss Oxenby," Roger said solemnly, the corner of his mouth twitching ever so slightly. "Knew I could trust you to understand!"

"You are bored, *chéri*, so bored. I see that you are," Clarisse said, pouring another cup of tea.

The earl smiled absently over the top of the paper he was

not really reading. "Perhaps."

Clarisse was not a stupid woman. She knew perfectly well that her *bel ami* did not wish to talk, but she had no intention of letting him go before she plumbed a certain topic.

"It must be the company of all those so boring persons in Bath, no? Is it very dreadful for you there?"

"Hm? Oh, not so bad."

Clarisse looked at the cinnamon pastries she had ordered the cook to make because George had once said he liked them, and carefully considered whether she should allow herself one more. But no—she must be sure that her waistline gave no cause for complaint.

"I saw Roger Creighton last week," she said lightly. "He took me up in his curricle. Was that not nice of him?"

"Very," George murmured. He held out his cup and Clarisse refilled it with the special blend of coffee she ordered for him from Twinings.

She leaned forward on her elbows and smiled her most enchanting smile. "He said he saw you in Coventry and that you had a very jolly evening, but that Bath was going to be not jolly at all."

"Well, it's not as bad as all that," George said. "When it comes to diversions and amusements, Roger has rather high expectations. It is not a trait which stands him in good stead most of the time, and most certainly not in Bath."

"Oh, my! How very stern you sound!" Clarisse laughed. "Roger said he rather feared you were becoming . . . domesticated. I think I perhaps see now what he meant."

The earl frowned but immediately lightened it into a smile. Clarisse reached out for his hand across the small, chintz-covered breakfast table. Here in her morning parlor, decorated with yards of exquisitely printed cottons and papered in a rosebud pattern above the bleached wainscoting, the earl looked almost fearsome. Dressed in a coat of rifle green that stretched to perfection across his wide shoulders, he had an air of masculinity completely at odds with the decor.

George glanced about. "I would understand that remark if Roger had ever seen me *here.*"

"Oh, *chéri*—do you dislike it excessively? I vow, I will have it changed immediately."

It seemed as if she had finally succeeded in gaining his undivided attention.

"Good God, no! Not if it means we must see any more of that wretched little man," the earl said.

"Oh, the vicomte?" Clarisse asked, batting her eyes in mock innocence.

"Vicomte!" the earl snorted. "If he's a vicomte, then I'm the brewer's apprentice!"

"Just as you say, darling," Clarisse replied demurely. A man in a temper was preferable to a man indifferent. "If there is to be any redecorating, I will engage to find someone else to advise me." Clarisse was still secretly grateful to Trevor for undercharging on the decoration of the house, coming as it had early in her relationship with the earl. Trevor had been wise enough to know that one job done at cost could easily lead to many more commissions at substantial profit.

George rose from the table. "I believe the fog will be sufficiently lifted now for me to start for Bath."

Clarisse rose, too. "Shall I have the porter run on ahead and tell your coachman to put the horses to?" She slipped her arm through the earl's. "He could even drive back here and pick you up. Think of the time you would save. We might even be able to . . ." She raised herself to the tips of her toes and whispered in the earl's ear. ". . . and then you might have to stay yet another night, for I think one cannot be too careful with toothaches."

The earl smiled in a distracted way that made Clarisse's heart sink. He had not responded to her salacious hint, and added to the uncharacteristically cool response he'd shown in bed the night before, it sent a chill of misgiving through her.

He accepted his hat from her butler. "I assured my sister I would not be gone more than one night," he said, congratulating himself on remembering not to name Jane as the person to whom he had actually made the promise.

"How lucky she is to have such a devoted brother!" Clarisse sighed. "But her gain will be my loss. I will be so lonely for you, George!" It was a trifle melodramatic but it drew no offer from George to change his plans. Clarisse decided to throw caution to the wind. "Did I not hear Roger mention that your sister has a companion? Could she not keep her company, this Jane Oxenby?"

George withdrew his arm from Clarisse's. "She is a friend, not a companion," he said stiffly, "and she is *Miss* Jane Oxenby."

Clarisse smiled brightly. "Yes, of course. She is something of a new friend?"

"My friends away from this house are my affair," he said, drawing on his gloves.

Clarisse began to feel that she could do no right. "Of course," she said, laying a conciliatory hand on his arm. "I am sorry, George. I did not wish to suggest that you need answer to me for anything."

"No," he said, looking down at her, "I don't suppose you did. I rather think you know the rules of the game too well for that." He gave her a perfunctory kiss on the cheek and signaled the porter to open the door.

As her benefactor strode off, Clarisse was left wondering at the change in him. She swiped aside a tear that sprang from true feeling, for she loved George Tate, Earl of Sefton. It was not politic to do so in her position, but she did. She had cherished a hope that, in time, he would come to feel the same for her, but something had changed. Clarisse put out a hand to support herself in the doorway as a tight ball of fear grew inside her.

She had thought it amusing when Roger described the badly-dressed country nobody who was traveling with the earl and his sister, and pitied George for having to put up with his tongue-tied sister and her unsophisticated companion. Not until Roger Creighton had set her down at Lackington's book shop in Finsbury Square did he mention that he rather thought—not positive, mind you, but he rather thought!—that he had seen the "nobody" slipping into George's bedchamber shortly after George went up to bed and a little before Roger's groom had come in search of his master.

As the earl disappeared from view, Clarisse's fear expanded. She was appalled at the realization that she had just acted very much like a wife questioning her husband about the existence of a mistress—and she had been soundly rebuffed.

Jane strolled along the paths of Sydney Gardens, surprised and yet pleased to find herself all alone. The turnout for the public breakfast was substantial this Monday morning, as was usual during the season. She had left Portia sitting with James Digby and his sister, Lavinia, and Wofford, all of them happily drinking tea and eating cakes and rolls to the accompaniment of French horns and clarinets. Jane repressed a shudder. As much as she enjoyed Portia playing the pianoforte, she did not enjoy music in all its forms. French horns positively made her teeth ache, but since saying so would be neither complimentary nor constructive, Jane had not expressed herself on the subject. The further she walked from the exquisite gazebo that housed the musicians however, the happier she was.

Happy, that was, within the limits of her ability to feel that emotion after the events of Friday night. The earl had ignored her return to the ballroom and requested introductions to several unmarried females, all of whom he had taken onto the dance floor, to Mr. Le Bas's extreme gratification. That Jane had come back in on Roger

Creighton's arm had escaped no one's notice, and more than a few had been overheard to say that Miss Jane Oxenby looked a trifle less vivacious than usual.

Unfortunately for Jane's peace of mind, the evening had not been far advanced when the earl had taken her outside, so she was forced to endure another two hours of surreptitious surveillance. The earl, on the other hand, finished a set of country dances and announced his intention of going off to a private gaming club for the balance of the evening. His marked attentions to other females followed by his early departure made the situation more remarked than it had already been, for it suggested a lover's tiff. Jane had put on her bravest face and jested and laughed with Hugh Willoughby, who, she thought rebelliously, was excessively nice, and would not bore her at all if they married.

Jane gently shook herself free of her recollections. Sydney Gardens was lovely, the jonquils and forsythia at their peak, and away from prying eyes of over a thousand guests at the dress ball, she was able to acknowledge to herself that Hugh Willoughby would no more suit her as a husband than Father Christmas. No, before she had fallen in love with George, she had merely been unmarried. Now she was unmarriageable, for no one could suit her but him.

Jane was pierced with sadness. She tried to convince herself that it was better to know the happiness of cherishing someone so utterly as she cherished George Tate than never to have loved. Not knowing his reason for not wanting to marry did not keep alive a faint hope—as it might have in one with less common sense—that the earl could be brought around. Even if he *did* change his mind and marry, she lacked the background, the polish, the refinement, and the strict sense of propriety that he would require in a wife. Neither was she a beauty, not by anyone's reckoning. It would be, quite simply, a mesalliance, not perhaps a *shocking* mesalliance, but a mesalliance nonetheless.

A few tears moistened her eyes and she walked on

determinedly, hoping that her pace would generate enough breeze to dry them. One never knew when one might be observed, and she did not wish to dab at her eyes in so public a venue as Sydney Gardens and have it reported later that she had been seen crying near the labyrinth, or wherever it was that her steps had carried her. She passed an artfully formed grotto and tried to orient herself. The outer perimeter of the gardens had been made into a bridle path to accommodate those who preferred promenading on horseback, and Jane saw that she was nearly atop it. It made her think of Roger and John, who had announced their intention of riding over from Charlcombe that morning. She had no sooner begun to wonder what had become of them than she heard their voices, faint at first and then growing stronger as their horses ambled along the path.

"I saw her just last week," she heard Roger say. "She's more beautiful than ever."

"I liked it a sight better when one could see her anytime one liked for the price of an opera ticket," came John Marshall's reply. " 'Course, she'd never look twice at a cove like me—'twas the only way for me to fasten my eyes on her. What a voice—an angel! And that hair, like the sun shining on clouds. What I wouldn't give for an evening with her!"

"Worse luck," Roger said casually. "She's as devoted to George as ever. Damme if she don't love 'im! For her part, I think she means to marry him."

"Only she *couldn't!*" John protested in shocked accents. "He wouldn't! Not by God that she's not everything a man could want, but . . ."

"Quite," Roger said drily.

The horses were nearly abreast of the grotto now and Jane hoped the two men would pass by without glancing over the hedge. Her head ached as if a band of metal had been drawn progressively tighter around her temples.

"But if George don't mean to marry her—and we both know he can't!—then he must marry *someone*. Sefton Hall,

113

Sefton Park, Sefton House—it's a damned lot of property, you know, Roger, a damned lot. He must, despite all that fal-de-ral about never marrying, find a good little breeder to get himself a few heirs on—maybe Jane!"

Jane felt her cheeks flame and wished that they would move on, out of her hearing.

"Not Jane, I think. She ain't taken with him in any case— only female I ever saw who resisted his charms. As for the rest, do you really think it's fal-de-ral?" Roger asked. "I'm not so sure. There's no need for him to leg-shackle himself if he don't want to. Horatia or Portia could easily provide an heir to the title."

"Hadn't thought of that!" John exclaimed. "'Course they could—no reason in the world why they shouldn't. But, I say!—George is such a stickler for doing the proper. Could he be satisfied to see one of his sisters' brats carry on the line?"

"Can't think why not," Roger replied. "It would be a sweet situation, with the incomparable Clarisse to keep him entertained while his sisters produce some candidates. Right time comes, George looks over the crop, picks out a likely one, pays his school fees, hires him a bear leader for the Grand Tour and then introduces his heir to the *ton*. No inconvenient wife, no blubbering infants in the nursery, no jelly-encrusted hands mucking up his precious staircase. Gad! The more I think on it, John, the more I wish I had sisters to take the burden off *me!*"

"Well, of course it would be all right for *you*," John remarked, "but I can't imagine George doing anything less than his rightful. Why, don't you remember the time he insisted that *we* take a turn at early guard duty?"

Roger laughed. "Well, we *were* Guardsmen. It only disagreed with you because you'd shot the cat the night before. Dare say if you'd stayed sober you wouldn't have minded."

"Not the point, dear boy, not the point!" John said in

aggrieved tones. "Point is, George is a man who always takes the moral high ground. Well, take his club! Who else do you know who'd refuse to join White's just because they'd carried a bet he didn't approve of on their books?"

Jane heard Roger Creighton's dry laugh. "Not just any bet, old man—that you must allow. No, a wager that was carried forward several years running, one that made sport of his father's . . . *sport,* shall we say? It was a grand bet, legendary really, but even *I* can see how George would be bound to take umbrage. He is a principled sort, no getting around that—principled enough for both of us, I sometimes think. Whenever I find myself mired in immorality—not infrequently, you understand—I always pause and reflect that it can be laid at George's door. He got too much conscience and it left none over for me. Happy enough state for me, though, mind you."

"As you say," John agreed. "Poor George—how he suffered over that whole Selfless Sefton business!" Then on a more practical note, he added, "He's had the luck of the devil ever since, though, you must admit! He won the fair Clarisse, his horses never lose, and he has only to pick up a pair of dice and they roll to please him. And look at Wattier's—it was nothing before he gave it his patronage, or nearly nothing, and now it's the greatest gaming club in London! You have to say that it's a stroke of the greatest good fortune that he was willing to sponsor us, Roger. We should never have seen the inside of number eighty-one Picadilly without he vouchsafed us."

"It's the inside of thirty-two Half Moon Street I'd like to see," Roger sighed. "You know, it would suit me admirably if George ever gives up the songbird. I'd give her my *carte blanche* in a minute—just take over the nest, as it were."

"Well, for someone in his shoes, he's been damned grouchy lately," John grumbled.

"Clarisse," Roger said succinctly. "If she waited day and night for you in London, wouldn't it put *you* out of sorts to be hanging about here, rigged out in knee breeches and drinking tea until eleven half the nights of the week?"

"Ah!" John said, sounding a good deal startled. "I see your point, old man!"

Their voices began to grow fainter but Jane didn't relax. She remembered to keep breathing, but just barely, inhaling and exhaling mechanically as she absorbed what she had overheard. When she could no longer hear even a hint of their deep, male voices, she walked to the nearest garden bench and settled herself on it carefully.

George had a mistress, a beautiful mistress who loved him. And presumably, he loved *her*. Why else would he object to marrying and producing heirs in the usual way? He had said he had his reasons for not wanting to marry, that he was a man known for throwing his heart over a fence but never over a female.

Jane remembered how he had phrased it in the coffee room in Leicester as clearly as if it had happened yesterday, mainly because—she now realized—she had already been more than halfway in love with him then. She now understood that he *could* throw his heart over a female, *had* thrown his heart over a female—just not one he could marry without a scandal. And the Earl of Sefton was not a man to create scandal.

As Jane walked slowly back toward the entrance of Sydney Gardens, she perceived that conceit made a very good tutor. She had told herself that she had no designs on George Tate, that he was beyond her in every way, but she now felt with every painful beat of her heart the patent falseness of her self-directed lies. If she had truly accepted that the Earl of Sefton would not fall in love with her, she would not now be suffering so horribly over the news that his heart was already committed to another.

Chapter Seven

"He is coming here! He is coming here!" Portia cried. Stoke endeavored to follow her young mistress's head, arranging her hair into a style which would suit the elaborate hat she meant to wear out walking. The smell of singed hair rose from the heated curling tong in her hand.

"Oh, your ladyship," the abigail said resignedly, "I simply cannot do this, not if you flop about like a mouse that the cat's got hold of."

"Portia, sit still—do," Jane admonished with a half-hearted attempt at sternness. "That bonnet will not look at all well if your hair isn't styled properly."

Portia disregarded both admonitions, reading on from the sheets in her hand, and Jane noted wryly that Jonas had not troubled to write over the first lines at right angles, as most people would, to save the receiver the expense of paying for more than one sheet to be delivered. "Oh, he says that he is sure he will not like Bath—just as I was sure *I* would not!—but that he will make the effort for my sake." She raised sparkling brown eyes and gazed at Jane. "For *my* sake! Is that not the most romantic declaration?"

"Very," Jane declared dryly. "Does he say whether he has arranged for lodgings yet?" She half feared her cousin would expect an invitation to stay with his "future brother-in-law."

Portia studied the letter, her face quite as animated as Jane had ever seen it. "Yes! It is all fixed—he is to have a set of rooms in the Axford." She looked momentarily crestfallen. "But that is so far from us!"

"I'm sure he knows what is best for him," Jane said, hoping that white lies were not counted against one on Judgment Day. She rose and took the comb and last remaining pins from a frustrated Stoke. "Now stay still and we will finish your hair in a trice."

The abigail stood by with a long-suffering expression, prepared to settle the hat on Portia's head. It was far too fancy for Jane's taste, with strawberries, cherries, brightly colored lace, a bit of grape vine and some ruching, but Portia had trimmed it herself in what she was sure was the very latest style. It made Jane faintly dizzy even to look at it.

"Are you quite sure, dearest?" she asked dubiously when the creation was seated on Portia's head.

"Oh, who cares about a silly old hat when Jonas is coming?" Portia said worshipfully.

"Fine talk from the one who sat up until all hours this week working on it and then declined to stroll the Crescent yesterday in order to finish it!" Jane declared, feeling suddenly old. Portia's youthful passion only served to point up her own lackluster state.

"Pho! Let us just go down and see if George does not approve," Portia said. "And if he does not, then I shall turn to Roger Creighton for an opinion. You shall see—they will all admire it excessively! And Lavinia Digby will beg me to make one just like it for her!" And so saying, she tripped gaily out of the room, leaving Jane to follow.

Jane descended the stairs with a great deal more reserve than Portia. It was wonderful to see the improvement the news of Jonas's impending arrival made in Portia, but it did nothing to blot out the misgivings which assailed Jane when she thought of what George's reaction might be to the news. Jane pondered with great diligence how she might excuse herself from the day's walking expedition altogether.

George had returned from London just as taciturn as when he had left, and had closeted himself with Wofford for long hours ever since—tending to estate matters, he explained. Jane had done her best to act as if nothing had changed between them, but she found it difficult. It had become the earl's habit to escort them to the various routs and balls and drums, stand up for a few dances and then excuse himself to spend the rest of the evening at a private gaming club. He always returned for Portia and Jane at the close of the evening, however, and continued to play the role of hopeful—but noticeably more subdued—lover in public. In private, though, they had not resumed the easy informality she had so enjoyed before. She longed for that quite as much as she longed to tell him that she loved him, and to hear him say he loved her in return. The stern and formal stranger who shared the house with them was not the George Tate she had fallen in love with.

Even now he waited for her at the bottom of the staircase, looking bored and restless, and tapping his walking stick on the marble floor.

"Your lordship has not been waiting long, I hope?" she asked. The earl turned and she imagined, just for an instant, that he was glad to see her, but the illusion was fleeting.

"Not above a quarter of an hour," he replied politely.

"Then you must be quite out of patience with us," Jane said. Determined to chip away at some of the frost surrounding their relations, she added, "Only conceive how much longer you might have waited if Portia had made *me* a new hat. It must have been quite five of the clock before I could have made myself appear outside the boudoir in it."

"Indeed?" George murmured, his mouth twitching. "Then surely we would have had recourse to using the word *boudoir* in its true and original sense—'to sulk.'"

"Thrust and parried!" Jane declared, and then asked in a conspiratorial whisper, "Truly, is the hat not atrocious?"

The earl smiled at last. "Truly, it is."

Jane let Fletcher bow her out the door and fairly danced down the front steps to where Portia waited with the Digbys and the trio from Charlcombe. George followed more slowly but she rejoiced when he took up the position on her left elbow and they led the party off to stroll in the Crescent fields, the fashionable green slopes in front of the Royal Crescent. They greeted others out to take air, and talked of inconsequential things. Jane took great delight in the occasional trenchant remark the earl made in so low a voice that she knew it was meant only for her ears. His sense of humor and powers of observation being keen, he seldom failed to make her laugh.

Jane began to feel quite restored to good spirits, except that each time she remembered that Jonas was coming, she started like a badly trained gun dog when its master fires overhead. She squelched the thought but it kept returning, leaving her nerves in a sadly tattered state.

Another several days went by, during which time George escorted them to the subscription library, attended a lecture with them at the Lower Rooms, and took them to the Theatre Royal. Still, remembering their quarrel at the ball, Jane could not bring herself to tell the earl about Jonas's imminent visit. When Portia herself said nothing further about it, Jane convinced herself that it had merely been another of Jonas's many grandiose schemes—all bluster and no action. It was the only conclusion which gave her any comfort, for it was no good hoping—as she had for a space— that he would be turned away by the masters of ceremonies if he came to Bath. No, he would be welcomed at either assembly, for they were not at all like Almack's, where, as Aunt Eugenia had often said, three-quarters of the aristocracy went begging for an invitation. That truly was open only to the cream of society.

But Jane had reason to regret her reticence, a monumental reason, on the occasion of the regular Fancy Ball at the New

Rooms on the following Thursday. A kind of ease had crept back into her dealings with George, leavened by the humor which both shared. They had just managed to separate themselves from James Digby and his sister Lavinia when Jane looked up and saw Jonas entering the room.

"Oh, no!" she whispered, lowering her lorgnette.

"What is it?" George asked with a quick look of concern.

Jane whirled to face him, her face pale with strain. "There is something I have neglected to tell you which can wait no longer," she said tremulously.

"Surely it is not that you secretly admire Lavinia Digby?" the earl exclaimed with an attempt at lightheartedness. "Did we not just decide that her simpering is exceeded only by her tittering?"

Jane tried to respond with a similar breeziness, but failed. "Oh, no, n—nothing of the kind," she stuttered. "It is only that, well . . . there is someone here whom you will not be pleased to see."

The earl raised the dark, sleek eyebrows that he used to such good effect on persons who sought to extract from him that which he did not wish to give. "Really? That can hardly be your fault, surely—or has the master solicited your advice in deciding whom to admit?"

"Oh, please," Jane said, digging her fingernails into her palms, "do be serious for a moment!" She was afraid he was going to spy Jonas before she could break the news.

"Oh, Jane, I thought we were agreed that the only way to enjoy oneself at these affairs was to find the humor wherever possible! Have you been gammoning me all this time?"

Suddenly his eyes narrowed as he gazed at something past her shoulder. A look of deep displeasure formed on his face and Jane felt a sick sensation in her stomach. She turned just in time to see Portia hurry across the open floor in a *most* unseemly fashion and arrive at Jonas's side with an ecstatic expression. Jonas clasped her hands in his and smiled down at her possessively. It was a spectacle no one could have missed, and very few even pretended that they weren't watching raptly as the Earl of Sefton's rich sister acknowledged someone who looked very like an *arriviste*.

"Did you know of this?" the earl asked without looking at Jane. His voice barely concealed his anger.

"I did," Jane said, finding courage from some unknown source. "I tried to find the right moment to tell you, and then I began to hope it was only more of Jonas's hot air and that he would not actually—"

"I say, do you know that fellow?" Hugh Willoughby asked, coming up behind them. "Dashed lot of nerve taking your sister's hand like that if you don't."

George turned and said with deadly calm, "He is Jane's cousin."

Hugh glanced at Jane through his quizzing glass. "You don't say!"

Jane managed a sickly smile. "Yes, it's true."

Hugh looked across the ballroom and frowned. "Why does the fellow wear his clothes too small? Is it some new fashion in the country?"

Jane wanted to reach out and take George's arm, steady herself on him, but she did not dare. "I believe he may have simply made use of my father's wardrobe," she whispered. Her voice began to crack on the last words and she felt her eyes tearing. Jonas was undoubtedly wearing her father's evening clothes. Perhaps he had worn them at Lady Eugenia's ball, too, only she had not been able to see that without her spectacles. It was bad enough that her father was dead—to see Jonas in his clothes was desecration.

"Steady on," George said in quite a different tone of voice than the one he had just been using. He held out his arm and Jane thankfully slipped her hand through it. "We will get through this in the best style we can manage and talk about it later," he said softly. To Hugh he explained, "Jonas inherited the family estate."

"Pity!" Hugh remarked.

"Dearest Jane!"

Jane's spine stiffened and indignation overcame grief. "Jonas," she said, nodding. His face was suffused with color, though the ballroom was not excessively hot, and he was panting like a man who had just run a race.

"I am so very glad to see you," Jonas puffed. "And your lordship!" he said to George, "How extremely happy I am to have a chance to renew our friendship, and how pleased I am to see your lordship's sister again." Since Jonas was at that moment clutching his lordship's sister as if she were a piece of luggage and not a freestanding human being, it was hardly to be wondered at if his lordship did not respond to this greeting with enthusiasm.

"Sir Jonas," was all he said by way of acknowledgment.

The master of ceremonies, who had followed Portia and Jonas, bowed to George. "My lord, this gentleman claims your acquaintance."

"It is true that we have been introduced," the earl said smoothly.

"An acquaintance of yours must always be a welcome addition to the company," the master said. He bowed again. "I will leave you to enjoy one another's company."

Only Jonas and Portia seemed likely to fulfill that ambition.

"Oh, George, is it not wonderful?" Portia breathed. "Jonas has come all this way only to see me!"

"Extraordinary," George murmured. "Quite remarkable." Except for the rigidity of the arm on which her hand rested, Jane might have believed the earl was quite unperturbed to find Jonas in their midst.

"I expect we shall be seeing a great deal of one another, my lord," Jonas said with an ingratiating smile.

"But damme!—who *is* the fellow?" John Marshall's voice carried clearly to them as he and Roger Creighton came through the packed room toward the party. "I'll swear, George's man dresses better than that fellow."

123

Jane felt ready to die of shame but the earl was impassive, not betraying by even a quiver that he had heard the remark. Roger attempted to shush John Marshall without success. "Damned public dances!" John was saying. "Why should a man be obliged to socialize with someone who don't even dress as well as his own valet?"

The earl greeted them politely when they came within range. "Roger! And, of course, John. Allow me to introduce an acquaintance of ours—and Jane's cousin—Sir Jonas Biddle. Sir Jonas, Mr. John Marshall and Mr. Roger Creighton, late of Her Majesty's Guards, and swiftly bound for perdition."

Jane suppressed a watery smile, knowing that in his way, George had just rebuked them both for approaching and obliging him to make the introduction. Roger immediately perceived the earl's displeasure and adopted an attitude of cool civility that conveyed his understanding of the situation. Jonas, hearing that both men were plain "misters," proceeded to condescend to them in a way that must have riled even the meekest-spirited man. John appeared too much the worse for drink to comprehend the slight, but Roger Creighton's handsome features became a rigid mask. Hugh Willoughby did not miss it.

"I say, George, don't you intend introducing *me* to your friend?" he said stiffly.

"Naturally," George said. "Sir Jonas, allow me to present Lord Hugh Willoughby. It is at his estate—or rather his father's—that Mr. Creighton and Mr. Marshall make their stay."

"Ah!" Jonas said, looking quite pumped up by the information that Hugh was also a member of the nobility. "Your father—who is he? Perhaps I know him!" he declared, for all the world as if he knew and was known by everyone of any account.

"And then again, perhaps not," Hugh said coolly. "The Duke of Darby?"

Jonas's mouth dropped open and then snapped closed again.

"No," Hugh drawled in a most quelling manner, "I rather thought not."

Jonas was not long in recovering. "The Duke of Darby!" he exclaimed. "Well, I am certainly glad to make your acquaintance, Lord Hugh! Very glad indeed!"

Hugh smiled, a tolerant, faintly amused smile. "I don't doubt it, Sir Jonas. Your sincerity does you credit. I am, by the way, the eldest son."

Jane wanted to drop right through the floor with embarrassment. She was not used to flying in high circles—indeed, she had not even been aware that Hugh was destined to be a duke one day—but she knew that *anyone,* even easygoing Hugh, must dislike to be so patently toadeaten. Why, oh why, could Jonas not see that?

The musicians began to play and Jonas begged Portia to accompany him out to the floor. Neither of them thought to glance over to see if they had the earl's approval, for if they had glanced neither would have moved from the spot. As it was, George watched his sister be dragged off and drawn around the floor in Jonas's ham-fisted embrace without any outward sign of the rage that had his arm trembling.

"Really, George," Hugh remarked, "what an odious man! I do believe I shall have to claim the next dance with Portia."

"And I think I must be next," Roger Creighton added.

John Marshall felt himself being stared down. "Why are you all looking at me like that? It's because I'm a trifle bosky, isn't it? Well, a man shouldn't be made to drink tea half the night. 'Tain't right and I won't do it!"

Roger drew him aside and quietly explained to him why he was going to ask Portia to dance, while Hugh went off to stand nearer the dance floor.

"I'm sorry I didn't tell you earlier that Jonas was coming to Bath," Jane said quietly.

"That is past mending now," George replied, never taking

his eyes off his sister, "though I would appreciate knowing your cousin's movements in future at least as soon as *you* know of them."

"Yes, of course," Jane murmured, thinking it a well-deserved reprimand.

"He is contemptible, utterly contemptible," George said coldly. "What an abomination it is to see my sister dance with him!"

"Oh, please do not say so," Jane begged. "Your hatred of him is irrational, and is bound to drive Portia into his arms."

The earl looked down at her, his eyes dangerous with reined-in feeling. "How can you have just witnessed your cousin's boorish performance and still maintain that my dislike is irrational?"

"It is not that! I quite agree with you that he is boorish, but if you disapprove of him too strongly and too publicly, it may make him a figure of sympathy in Portia's eyes."

"Do you know," he said calmly, "I believe you had better allow me to keep my own counsel regarding this matter."

And Jane watched, sick at heart, as he spent the next hour doing exactly what she had hoped he would not. When Portia returned after her first dance with Jonas, the earl reminded her firmly but pleasantly that she had promised the next dance to Hugh. Puzzled but unresisting, Portia kept the engagement she hadn't known she had. She had no sooner finished *that* dance than Roger Creighton took her arm and whisked her away. Jonas attempted to cover his dismay when he was denied access to Portia time after time.

Jane was not surprised to see Portia grow increasingly agitated. Jonas ventured to ask the earl if Portia were free any time that evening and George responded by flagging down the passing James Digby, whose name he could scarcely call to mind in his anger, just so he could thrust his sister into his arms—anyone's arms, in short, other than Jonas's. Undaunted and uncomprehending, Jonas struck up a conversation on horseflesh with the earl, who was a noted judge of all things equine. Even to Jane, who knew little of horses, Jonas sounded sadly misinformed, and the earl made only terse replies, and only to unavoidable questions.

Much to Jane's relief, the earl declared the evening at an end early. Portia looked to be on the verge of tears and Jane hurried her through the throng to the ladies' tiring room, where they retrieved their cloaks and slipped their pattens over their dancing shoes.

"George is being perfectly horrid," Portia said, her eyes brimming as Jane knelt at her feet. "He's not even giving Jonas a chance!"

"Yes, I know, darling," Jane said soothingly. She laid a hand on Portia's knee. "I will talk to him later and see if he cannot be brought to see your point of view."

"I hate him!" Portia cried. "He's being beastly and I hate him!"

"Oh, dear," Jane said. It was quite as animated as she had ever seen Portia. "I quite agree that he's being unreasonable, but please—you mustn't fly into a passion or it will only set his back up more."

"*His* back! Much I care for *his* feelings! What about *my* feelings? And all this when Jonas has extended himself for my sake! He says that the rooms he took on Lady Eugenia's advice are not at all the thing. They are small and cramped, and he is excessively uncomfortable there, all on account of me, and oh!—I wish I were dead!"

Jane wished George could see his sister at that moment, for then he would surely have realized the depth of her unhappiness. Jane gathered the younger girl in her arms and felt as if her own heart would break.

"Oh, Portia, dear, I am so very sorry! Depend upon it, we shall find some way to resolve this. Come, dry your eyes and we will go out with our heads held high. You must take your leave of Jonas calmly." She dabbed at Portia's red-rimmed eyes with a scrap of lace as the girl regarded her miserably.

"It will not make Jonas's lot any easier if he sees you are unhappy."

"I suppose you are right," Portia said. "Still," she added defiantly, "I will not pretend that I am in charity with George!"

"No," Jane agreed, her heart sinking, "I am sure that would be too much to ask."

They rejoined the earl and Jonas pressed an invitation on Portia to go walking the following day. "And you, too, Jane—you must come with us," he added magnanimously.

Portia was just opening her mouth to say "yes" when George said, "I think my sister will not join you." He looked down at Jonas as if he were little better than an insect. "She is engaged tomorrow."

"Then perhaps I may call the day after?" Jonas suggested hopefully.

"That will not suit either," George said without even looking at him. They had reached the carriageway and Bates, the coachman, was holding the earl's matched grays in hand with some difficulty. "I think you will find that your sojourn in Bath must go forward without our company, as we have made plans which it will not be possible to break for all the time between now and when we are due to leave."

He took Portia's hand and fairly boosted her into the elegant landau with his armorial bearing on the door. Portia could see that even in the extreme of the moment, Jonas was unable to contain his admiration for the fine vehicle, avariciously scanning the mahogany shutters, the morocco cushions, and the silk spring curtains inside. The earl handed Jane in and followed, drawing the curtains as he tapped on the ceiling with his cane.

They were not more than ten feet from the curb when Portia burst into tears. "How could you!" she sobbed. "To say that we cannot . . . that he cannot even call on us . . . oh!" She buried her face in Jane's shoulder.

Jane was angry, but one look at the earl's face served to

128

convince her that the earl was even angrier. His jaw was set in grim lines, his eyes like obsidian by the light of the japanned lamp.

"You will obey me in this, Portia," he said coldly, "else we shall remove to London and you will finish out this season by attending no balls except at Almack's, where you can rest assured Jonas Biddle will not be admitted." He pulled the curtain back again and stared out into the night. "When one sees the effect of the easy access to be had to the assemblies in Bath, one appreciates Almack's as one never did before."

This only served to amplify Portia's sobs and Jane glared at George, but to no effect, for he continued to stare out the window. The trip back to Lansdowne Crescent was accomplished in silence unbroken by any sound except Portia's sniffling. Stoke, whose upper limit of wakefulness was eleven-thirty, received them in some surprise but also gratitude, for they were fully an hour and a half earlier than she had anticipated. Jane slipped off her cloak and hurried back downstairs. She saw Fletcher going into the drawing room with a tray and paused to consider what she would say. Then, before her resolve was tempered by too much thought, she went through the doors. The earl was just filling a pouch with gold guineas from the tray held by the butler.

She paused inside the doors and glared at the earl. "You were shockingly rude tonight," she declared without preamble.

The earl looked up and met her gaze, his face expressionless. "That will be all, Fletcher. Tell Bates to walk the horses."

"Immediately, my lord." Fletcher sketched a bow and backed out of the room, reluctantly pulling the doors closed behind him.

The earl bestowed a distinctly glacial look on Jane as he tucked the kidskin pouch into the inner pocket of his jacket. "If you wish to have some conversation with me, I will arrange to wait on you after breakfast in the morning," he said.

"After breakfast!" Jane snorted. "It is plain to see that you think it no small thing to be lodged next to a tigress. You have so infuriated your sister that even now she is flinging breakables around upstairs! You have turned the mildest, the gentlest of girls into a . . . a . . . *hellion!* Really, your lordship, how could you have been so insensitive, so dictatorial, so . . . so . . ." Jane choked on her indignation and had to draw a full breath before she could go on. "Portia is young. All one has to do is say 'no' to something and she is bound to rise up against the injunction. You were insufferably high-handed tonight!"

"Was I?" George asked calmly. "Then I suppose it must have been necessary. It is not my custom to be so."

"Of course it is! You are the most high-handed person I have ever known. You have the knack of getting whatever you want with a word or a look. Everyone around you jumps to do your bidding. Ordinarily you use that talent just as you ought, but tonight was a different case!"

"Is there a point to all of this?" George inquired coldly. "Beyond an indictment of my character?"

"I am trying to tell you that if you had deliberately set out to promote a match between Portia and Jonas tonight, you could not have succeeded better. Could you not simply have let matters take their course?"

"I did not care to see where the course might lead."

"But your opposition has merely fanned the flames!" Jane insisted.

George stared at her, considering. "What effect do you suppose it might have on this romance if Portia's money was to be kept in a trust administered by me even after she was married?"

Jane's mouth opened and then she seemed to stop and think about what he had said. "I'm not sure," she replied, looking perplexed. "If you wish to know, then I suppose you

130

should simply announce that you have arranged matters in that fashion and await their reaction."

George rolled a loose guinea in his hand. Four years of Jonas's ineptitude had not improved an already modest estate. Longchamp needed maintenance and improvements to become truly profitable—he had had Wofford make discreet inquiries. He knew from what Wofford had discovered that Jane lived in virtual penury, in a dower house that had seen much better days, but did Jane stand to gain if Jonas prospered? It was the unanswerable—and unaskable—question. He hefted the guinea in his palm. "I do not have that luxury," he finally said. "The disposition of her money is governed by my father's will, which decrees that it comes to her in its entirety upon marriage."

"To Jonas, is what you're thinking," Jane said.

George nearly smiled despite his anger. Her bluntness always diverted him. "Yes," he admitted, "but I have always been prepared for the fact that Portia's husband would take control of her money."

"Then what is the problem?"

"I had hoped that the man whom she chose would be someone whom I could like, someone who did not manifestly pursue her only for financial gain, and above all, someone who would make her happy."

"*That* is why I have been urging you to moderation!" Jane exclaimed. "You cannot possibly know the answer to that last in the current climate. If you will allow them to spend more time in one another's company, without breathing fire and brimstone each time they so much as look at one another, you may discover—and *they* will certainly discover—whether they suit or not."

"And as for my other objections?"

Jane shrugged. "What would you have me do? Transform Jonas into someone he is not? If you cannot like him, you cannot like him. He certainly aspires to better himself through marriage—that I won't deny. But perhaps for all

131

that, he might make a very good husband for Portia."

George regarded her for a long minute. She still stood braced where she had stopped upon entering the room, her jaw thrust forward dangerously and her feet planted solidly. It would have been unattractively mannish in any other woman, though in her it was not, but then very little about her struck him as wrong. Was she right? *Was* he being irrational?

At last he said, "I watched my mother endure a marriage which became increasingly less happy for her, a marriage which was made for every reason but love. I swore that I would do all I could to see that my sisters did not suffer likewise. Then, in giving Horatia free rein to seek out a man whom she could love, I let her fall into the arms of a man who would have taken her money and made her miserable."

Jane softened noticeably in response to his words. "Perhaps you have reason to be cautious," she said, "only don't, I beg you, create new problems in attempting to redress old ones." Her hair, which was not cut short to conform to fashion, had begun to cascade down from the formal arrangement the hairdresser had contrived, and her cheeks were stained pink with emotion.

George found himself drawn into her guileless blue eyes. The wide openness of them invited him to believe her, to accept her advice as sound. "You accused me of breathing fire and brimstone tonight," he said in a lighter voice. "You were breathing more than a little fire yourself just now, you know."

Jane smiled uncertainly. "I may have been," she admitted, "but then, you asked me to accompany you to Bath so that I could represent Portia's views to you. I could not have done that faithfully tonight without some fire. She was quite transformed!"

George let out a short laugh. "I had occasion to witness some of it myself, you will recall." He so wanted to be on good terms with Jane that it was easy to let his anger slide

132

away. "Will you have some port?" he asked, moving to a tray which held a decanter and glasses.

The anger appeared to go out of Jane. "Yes, please, I will have one glass, but then I must go see that Portia has settled."

It was a truce they both desired. Later, when Jane had gone upstairs, George sat alone in the drawing room, forgetting that he had been on the verge of going out again. Not until Fletcher cleared his throat and asked if his lordship still required the carriage did George remember he had issued orders for Bates to keep the horses moving. It was so unlike him to forget the welfare of his horseflesh that it took him aback.

The explanation was obvious enough. He had been remembering the way Jane had looked that night, the way her hair had caught the candle's flames and made the fire live again in its strands, the way her face had glowed in the golden light while they drank their port. He had had to resist the urge to reach out and touch her cheek, or take her chin in his fingers and kiss the sweetly shaped lips.

It was an urge he had not felt for a woman of his own class in many years. Knowing that everyone lived in expectation of his following in his father's footsteps, he had become almost inhumanly circumspect in dealings with women of his own rank. He had kept aloof, permitting himself to form relationships only with women of the *demimonde*. His very aloofness had inspired women to more and more flagrant attempts to attract his interest. The result was that they all bored him, and in time his aloofness became genuine.

Jane had slipped in through a crack in his defenses, taken root, and begun to grow in his heart almost before he had realized what was happening. She had intrigued him, always drawing away, running to be somewhere else, to *do* something else, *with* someone else. He let out a muffled crack of laughter. It had been an illusion. Jane was no more aloof than a spring rain, and just as direct and uncomplicated and refreshing. Coupled with her good sense and compassion, her outspokenness and her humor, she enchanted him.

He pinched out the flame of a candle, methodically rubbing the still-hot wick between his thumb and forefinger. It burned his flesh, reminding him that he could still feel pain as keenly as anyone. The romantic adolescent he had been had been devastated by the discovery of his father's dishonorable conduct, but his own romantic ideals had merely been buried, not destroyed. That rather shattering realization had come to him within the past few days, but the issue of trust could never be forgotten—everything turned on that frail pivot. What he felt for Jane must be kept below the surface for the time being. But even submerged, it had the power to hurt.

Chapter Eight

Portia began the next day in a considerably less wrathful mood than she had ended the night before. Several days passed during which she did nothing to arouse alarm in anyone's mind, merely acceding to whatever plan George or Jane put forward. Within a week, though, Jane examined her heart and found that it was troubled, for although Portia was behaving in a perfectly characteristic fashion, there were one or two inexplicable happenings that did not inspire confidence.

Manning, Portia's footman, went out, ostensibly to collect post, at least twice daily, but a casual question put to Wofford over breakfast one morning netted Jane the information that the mail was delivered only once a day at the post office in Bath. That inconsistency troubled Jane, especially when coupled with the fact that Portia had gone out shopping several times by herself, always waiting until Jane was busily engaged in some activity that could not easily be broken off. It was always for some trifle, and she always took Manning with her, but after she went off to purchase her third bottle of Steele's Lavender Water in as many days, Jane's uneasiness hardened into definite misgiving, not least because she herself could not imagine using even one bottle of that particular scent in a year.

The next few days found Jane completely at liberty to accompany Portia anywhere she might decide to go, at any time of the day, though she took care to seem engrossed in a novel by Mrs. Radcliffe. Thus, when Portia announced her intention of going off to acquire some buns at Sally Lunn's famous pastrycook shop, Jane set aside her book and announced that it would please her to accompany Portia for the sake of the exercise. Portia made a number of crafty attempts to deflect Jane from her intention, but could not be rid of her. Jane felt very much like a burr under the saddle of love by the time they departed from Lansdowne Crescent, and not at all anxious to learn what sort of wrongdoing could inspire Portia to such contortions.

Vague suspicion was one thing but proof positive was another. Portia bought the buns without any great show of enthusiasm and then grew increasingly agitated as they strolled in the direction of the Pulteney Bridge. Finally, she confided that she had just recalled something else she required, and would Jane be patient and wait just there for one moment? She flew off before Jane could even inquire as to her destination and Jane, after a moment's hesitation, hurried after her.

She just managed to catch a glimpse of Portia's fair head as it disappeared into a draper's shop not normally patronized by the *ton*. Jane ordered Manning to wait outside and detected an uneasy look in his eye. It occurred to her that he was quite young, young enough to be sympathetic to Thwarted Love. It took some minutes of browsing through the drapers in an offhand way before Jane discovered what she had ardently hoped she would not.

Portia was nervously ordering various ribbons and trims at the backmost counter, scarcely bothering to look at them as the clerk presented the items for approval, while Jonas hovered at her side. They spoke in earnest undertones, and Portia, for one, wore her heart on her sleeve.

Jane took a gulp of air and strode forward, saying breezily, "Oh, Portia! You've found those trims for the hat you promised me! How kind!" Portia whirled and gasped, but Jane—though she had previously conducted deceptions for public consumption only with a master—did not let Portia's amateurishness throw her. "And Jonas! Only fancy meeting you here! I dare say my Aunt Eugenia has charged you with making some purchases on her behalf while you are in Bath. Has Portia been giving you some advice? She is the cleverest hand imaginable at trimming hats! You would not credit the stunning bonnet she finished only last week! Will you walk with us as far as Meyler's? Portia has desired them to hold a book for her."

And still chatting on in that manner, Jane maneuvered them both out of the shop by an elbow apiece, with an airy instruction to Manning as they passed him to go in and collect her ladyship's purchases.

"How dare you!" Jane hissed when they were out of earshot of other pedestrians. She nodded to a passing acquaintance and pinched Portia to make her do the same. "Your behavior surpasses all understanding!" she went on in an undertone. "As an unmarried female, you skirted the boundaries of what is proper by even corresponding with Jonas—which I forbore to point out at the time—and now I find you having assignations contrary to your brother's express wish! It is unacceptable in the extreme! And Lady Montfort is a notorious gossip! I daresay your brother will have heard that we were together with Jonas in the town before we even set foot back in Lansdowne Crescent."

"You are making far too much of this," Jonas protested. "What possible harm can there be in . . . ow!" He broke off abruptly as Jane delivered a savage pinch to his arm.

"I only wish I dared do more," she exclaimed in a low, furious voice. "If I could do so without being observed, I would box your ears for you! You and your sanctimonious lectures on *my* respectability! Owing to your sad lack of judgment, it is very likely that Portia will be pronounced a hoyden before the day is over. If she is not, it will only be because there are no particular events at either of the assemblies today. We can only pray that by the time the majority of Bath's fashionable residents *do* come together again, something even more shocking will have happened to eclipse this!"

Jonas took one look at Jane's expression and seemed to think better of protesting further. She detached him from their company outside the subscription library and made a brief show of going inside, lest anyone had overheard their announced intention in the drapers, and then started home. Jane set a bruising pace up the hill which left Portia and Manning winded. She climbed the staircase to the second floor and pointed Portia toward her chamber without another word.

Manning she dealt with summarily also. "In future, you will collect the post once a day only, and if her ladyship asks you to deliver, or collect, any additional messages, I expect you to come to me and ask whether I, too, have any messages." She stared hard at the anxious footman. "Have I made myself abundantly clear?"

"But . . . but I am supposed to take my orders from Lady Portia," he stammered, in a game attempt to defend custom.

Jane discovered an unaccustomed fierceness in herself. "You may accept that order from me or I can arrange for you to hear it from his lordship's own lips," she said, trying to emulate George's bland but crushing style.

Manning went the color of a blanc mange. "Oh, no, your ladyship," he said hastily. "There is no need for—"

"Good," Jane said firmly.

She turned and went up the staircase to the third floor. Wofford had a bedchamber on the top floor, but he discharged his duties to the earl in a room set aside for that purpose at the front of the third floor. The earl's bedchamber and sitting room occupied the remainder of the floor. Wofford rose from his desk at the sight of her.

"Good day, your ladyship," he said, looking a good deal startled to see her in the earl's private domain.

"Will you kindly inform the earl that I must speak with him at his earliest convenience?" she said.

"Wofford, will you excuse us please?"

Jane jumped as the earl's cool, commanding and seemingly disembodied voice emanated from a shadowy corner of the room. Then she saw that he was seated there in a high-back chair of dark red leather. He arose and nonchalantly gestured toward a settee by the window.

Jane ignored the invitation. "I have come to speak with you about Portia," she said. "Something must be done."

"Must it?"

She took in his apparel in one sweeping glance. He was impeccably attired in riding clothes, by which she deduced that he had plans to visit the party at Charlcombe. "It is all well and good for you to amuse yourself and go where you like, when you like, but the whole purpose of our being in Bath is threatened, and the outcome hangs in the balance," she declared darkly.

"Really? I did not know that a simple round of shopping could give rise to such drastic and far-reaching results. But no—I see that you are distressed enough and do not need to be teased. Tell me what troubles you, and I shall do what I can to remedy it."

Jane, who had been about to wipe the languid look off his face by telling him precisely what had taken place, found that his sympathy unhorsed her. "You must compromise on the issue of Portia's seeing my cousin," she managed to say, "or disaster may befall."

George barely heard her, thinking how remarkably handsome she looked in the soft light issuing through the windows. He thought of the Italian masters who swore by the merits of northern light for its constancy, and the way it revealed detail. Here was an exquisite piece of work indeed, but who now living could do her justice? He found himself hoping it was a question that would have to be answered in the very near future.

He collected himself with an effort. "Disaster, did you say?

Then we must avert it at all costs. What do you propose?"

"Could you not allow them to further their acquaintance without precisely giving it your blessing? Perhaps Jonas could join us for some informal outing, and you could see how he conducts himself away from more formal events. I own, it is not a great deal more pleasing than his conduct in society, but it may serve to soften your attitude toward him some small amount—*or* Portia may discover that he is not at all what will suit her. Please, your lordship, or you risk creating a rift between you and your sister that no amount of wishing to the contrary will bridge."

He clasped his hands behind him. "Very well."

"Very well?" Jane echoed in surprise. "I did not expect . . . that is, I thought you would . . ."

"Say no?" He smiled. "There is merit in what you say. I have decided to place my trust in your judgment. For as long as I can bear to spend time within hailing distance of your cousin, that is how long I will allow Portia to rid herself of this infatuation."

Jane felt faint with relief. She thanked George profusely and hurried downstairs to prepare Portia. "I have just spoken to your brother," she began. "I did not tell him about the events of this afternoon." She held up both hands to stop Portia from flinging herself around her neck. "Do not thank me! I did it as much for *my* peace as for yours, but I insist that you go talk with your brother. If you approach him in the right spirit, I think he may allow Jonas to spend some time in your company."

Portia's face was luminous with happiness. "Oh, you are surely the best friend in the world! Only what am I to say to my brother?"

"It will help if you say quite clearly that you know he does not care for Jonas. Ask only that he keep an open mind. Oh! You know the sort of things he will want to hear. I am sure he is ready to listen to you, if only you will talk to him in a reasonable way. He does not wish to hurt you, you know. He simply thinks Jonas is not worthy of you."

Portia sighed. "But that is exactly what is wrong! He has an inflated notion of my worth."

"I am sure you are quite as worthy as he thinks you," Jane said gently. "He is not a fool. He knows very well what your worth is."

On that bracing note, Portia went off to request an interview with her brother. She returned fifteen minutes later wreathed in smiles. "It is agreed that Wofford will write to Jonas and ask him to accompany us to Monkton Combe for a picnic, only we are to invite James and Lavinia Digby also, so that we are not conspicuous."

The day was so lovely and warm that it made Jane quite dreamy. She set her spectacles aside and reclined on the picnic blanket which had been spread by one of the three footmen who were on hand to serve.

"Oh, I feel so wonderfully idle," she sighed. "No needlework to do, no duties beckoning me to the still-room, no herbal tonics to be concocted, no cordials to be distilled."

George smiled. "Is there, in fact, a still-room belowstairs at Lansdowne Crescent? I admit, if there is one, I have yet to discover it."

Jane rolled over, playfully crossing her ankles in midair, forgetting for the moment that Lady Montfort was looking on from not far away. "I have yet to discover it, too," she said with a mischievous look. "It is altogether charming to live in an establishment and not be obliged to have a hand in its running. All seems to run just as it should in your household. I am agog with admiration, but tell me, who orders the meals and consults with the housekeeper each day?"

"I do. It is an abbreviated form of the ritual my mother was used to conduct, but it serves well enough. I rely a great deal on Fletcher when I am at my country seat, and in London, my major domo is extremely competent, and of course, Wofford sees to the accounts. I'm sure there are some who would say my establishments suffer for the lack of a feminine hand, but if there is some deficiency, society has been too polite to draw my notice to it."

"How on earth did you learn to do it?" Jane marveled. "Did your mother teach you the way of it?"

"Oh, Lord, no," George laughed, leaning back against a tree. "I was just turned twenty-one and I determined to do it all on my own. I thought it would be very shabby indeed to attain one's majority and establish a bachelor's residence with one's mother as aide-de-camp! Besides, my mother finds the running of a household a distasteful necessity. She is more inclined to want to see to the gardens, or sketch or paint. She runs a house with great energy and style, as she does everything to which she sets her hand, but it is not a source of joy to her."

"Then she is a woman after my own heart," Jane declared.

"Yes," George said thoughtfully, "I rather think she is." Then in a lighter tone, he added, "She is in Italy at present. She adores all things Italian—the painting, the music, the countryside—but until now she has not been at liberty to make an extended stay there. She has become quite adept at speaking Italian, too."

"Oh! There is Lady Montfort glancing in our direction," Jane said in an undertone. "I believe there is a hint in her expression that we ought to be leading the younger members of the party off on some improving expedition."

"If you detect such a look on her face, it is only because she is too indolent to lead them on such a tour herself," George said under his breath. "Depend on it, she would run us as thoroughly as I was used to order men in my regiment about, if only we would allow it. Still . . ."

"We must?" Jane said regretfully.

"Not if you don't wish it," George said with a twinkle in his eye. "I'll outflank her." He returned a moment later, saying, "The younger set is breaking off its game of Oranges and Limes and *we* are going to attend from the top of that hill over there while they descend into the valley under our watchful eye. My bad ankle, you know," he added with the

142

same kind of rueful charm that had undoubtedly done in Lady Montfort.

"What a perfect scoundrel you are!" Jane exclaimed. "I only hope that you can still recall which ankle was injured so that you can do some judicious limping without being caught out!"

When they were seated on the knoll of a steep slope which led down to a stream some way below, Jane said reflectively, "I do not believe that either of us is a great deal older than the rest of this group. Why do we *feel* so much older, do you suppose?"

The earl did not reply at once, engrossed in comparing the outlines of the sketch on his easel with the vista below. He added another touch before replying, "In my case, I suppose it is having gone to war. A man cannot, of necessity, return from such an experience as young as when he went out."

After a short, considering silence, Jane said, "Yes, I can quite see that. I still remember vividly the accounts in *The Times* by that man, Robinson. One felt almost as if one were there." The earl's mouth compressed a little but whatever thought he had he kept to himself. "You were not hurt in the action?" she asked.

"Nothing of consequence," he said, "but war leaves marks on one's soul if not one's body. The hell of it is that the Iron Duke has not yet done with Boney, and so many more are bound to discover how inglorious a pursuit war may be." Then in a lighter tone, he said, "And what is the explanation for the old head on *your* shoulders?"

"Nothing so epic, I am afraid," Jane said. "Oh, look! There they are, just past that copse."

"They will have to expend no small amount of effort coming back up that hill," George remarked. "They shall be glad to have their suppers and be tucked into bed early tonight."

"Oh, no!" Jane protested with a gurgle of laughter. "That's coming it entirely too thick! I can't allow you to sound so elderly as that."

"Elderly, is it, my girl?" the earl said with a devilish smile. "I've a good mind to join them after all."

"What! And put up with Lavinia Digby's laugh?—which I believe you dislike intensely though you are by far too good-mannered to say so. And then there are the Montfort twins—Lady Montfort must have the servants feed them raw meat! I have never seen such enormous, hulking boys in my life! I own I did not quite like to let them kiss my hand for fear they would relieve me of it with one bite."

"I shall be sure and inform Lady Montfort of what a splendid opinion you have formed of her sons," George said drily.

"You'll do no such thing," Jane said. "Imagine! Not one but two of them to feed! How Montfort's purse can have stood the strain all these years, I do not know. I suppose it is for the chance of having someone else feed them that Lady Montfort accepted your invitation today."

"It was extended under duress, I assure you," George said with the flicker of a smile. "I am sure she employed some of Torquemada's techniques on the Digby parent to prevail upon her to ask if the twins might also join our party."

"I did not think it was because you wished the twins to pay court to Portia," Jane said with feeling. "Torquemada himself could not have wished *that* fate on her!"

George erupted in laughter. "And now that you have cleverly managed to point out that there are even less-acceptable suitors for Portia's hand than Jonas, you will address the first issue we took up. Come now, and make a clean breast of it. How have you come to be such an old soul?"

Jane sat thinking how to answer him for several minutes, during which he pencilled in additions to his sketch.

"I don't *feel* like an old soul," she said at last, "only I suppose that not going to parties and doing all the frivolous things these other girls have had the chance to do has made me more serious."

"Did you not go to any of my godmother's entertainments?"

"Lady Eugenia's? I suppose I might have done, only she would not acknowledge my mother, so I did not wish to go to Canfield while my mother still lived." George raised an eyebrow in inquiry and Jane drew a deep breath. "My mother was Italian—very beautiful, very full of life—and she was already married, with two young children, when she met my father."

George's hand stilled. Here was fodder for scandal indeed. Jane met his eyes, seeking censure or acceptance, but he schooled his expression to simple interest. It seemed to satisfy her, for she went on.

"She was married young, against her will, to an elderly duke, and quickly provided the heirs he sought. She was not yet twenty when she met my father. He was on the Grand Tour, and when they met at a ball, they fell in love instantly—or so my mother always said." Jane smiled as she gazed out over the valley and George relaxed, not knowing how tense he had been for her sake. "The duke agreed to grant her a divorce provided she laid no claim to the children. She never spoke of them, but I think she must have been sure that their father would give them a good and happy upbringing. She was such a loving parent. I don't believe she would have left them, not even for my father, otherwise." She paused.

George waited for her to continue but she seemed lost in thought. He added shading to his sketch while he considered what he ought to say. He could not pretend that the story did not shock him. It did. And yet, Jane was merely an innocent aftermath.

"Did you . . . *dislike* your parents for bringing you into the midst of such a . . . a situation?"

Jane looked at him in surprise. "No. How could I? I could only have been born to them out of their love. If they had not loved, then I should not be here to judge."

George inclined his head toward her gravely. "You are

145

right, of course. Forgive me—the question was one that should not have been asked."

"Well, it *was* an interesting question," Jane said.

"So your mother was not received by your father's friends?" he said in a gentle attempt to get her to continue her narrative.

"Quite true. My mother grew a little lonely as time passed, and she began to spend some part of each year in Italy, with my father's blessing. He went with her a few times, and I have a vague recollection of being bundled along with them one time, when I was quite small. Very little stays in my mind except that Nanny Kent went with us, and she dressed me so warmly that I thought I should melt before we ever left England. And then!—we arrived in Italy and my mother insisted that I be allowed to run about in little except a shift. It was quite the most wonderful sensation, running free in the sunlight and the warmth. But it was ultimately a sad trip for my parents, for my mother's parents refused to receive her, and that had been her object—to present her new husband and daughter to them, and to be forgiven. My father never went again. He could not bear to see my mother's pain, I think, and besides, he was a devoted agriculturalist, and did not like to leave Longchamp for protracted periods of time." She was still for a moment and then she sat up a little straighter. "Is that our little group at the stream now?"

George, who had not taken his eyes off Jane's face while she spoke, had to force himself to look away. "Yes, I believe so. They seem to have encountered another party, too—yes, I am sure their ranks have swelled."

"Good," Jane said. "It will keep them out of mischief, having to display to advantage for others." She lay back, quite unable to summon the energy to keep upright. The prospect of this day had induced no small amount of apprehension in her, largely owing to anxiety over how Jonas would behave, but he had not been too doltish or mannerless, and Jane was able to relax. She had achieved one of her chief ambitions early in the day, taking Jonas aside on the pretext of strolling to an outlook some ways from where the picnic was being laid by the earl's servants. She had given him a quieter, more well-reasoned set-down regarding his conduct in encouraging a young female of quality to meet him in the town unchaperoned. If he had not perfectly understood the depth and the breadth of that trespass beforehand, he went away with a firm understanding of it. She had likewise made it clear that through her good offices, his reputation with the earl had not suffered for it, and that it was also at her insistence that Jonas was being allowed further acquaintance with Portia.

"But, I say, Jane," Jonas protested, "why should one of my degree, with a title and an estate, be made to come cap in hand just to pay my address to Portia—or require *your* intercession to do so? Not," he added hastily, "that I don't appreciate it."

"Because you ninnyhammer, the fact of your being a baronet does not give you entrée to court where you like. The earl is a society leader, and his sister an heiress, their family prominent for more generations than one can count, and one simply may not walk up and say, 'How'd'ye'do? May I be a member of your circle?' Your ascension to a title in no way guarantees admittance to the *ton*. Oh, Jonas, how can you not know any more of these matters! *I* did not go into society but I could not help know *something* of how people go on, if only from reading the newspapers."

"Oh, them!" Jonas said scornfully. "Don't hold with them—what's not blather is all useless facts one's never likely to need."

Jane covered her exasperation with an effort. "That's as may be, Jonas, but on one point, we must be understood! I have intervened with the earl to earn you an opportunity to see Portia, and to make a better impression on him than you have heretofore. I will not have my trust abused, nor his. Am I making myself quite plain? There are to be no more secret meetings—and if Portia is such a gudgeon as to have agreed to them, then you are all the more to blame for not having quashed the idea. You must promise me that your dealings will all be aboveboard hence forward."

Jonas looked a little petulant but acceded, and even summoned from somewhere the grace to thank Jane for her efforts on his behalf before they came in view of the others. George, during that same time, had been the recipient of a similarly well-intentioned lecture. Lady Montfort had seized on the opportunity of his being unengaged for two whole minutes together, to buttonhole him.

"I dislike above all things to be a tale bearer," she began, her bosom swelling with righteousness, "but since your mother is a particular friend of mine, I could not fail to acquaint your lordship with some few items of information."

"I am all ears, your ladyship," George said politely. It was a wonder to him how many women had styled themselves "particular friends" of his mother the instant she had left England's shores.

"Your sister has but recently left the schoolroom so it may be that she did not appreciate the gross impropriety of meeting Sir Jonas alone in the town—though I can quite see that he has your lordship's permission to pay his addresses to her! It gave me cause for alarm, for I am aware of it having happened several times, and with not even the footman along. Jane Oxenby is a lovely girl—one can hardly credit how she has taken!—but she can not be quite as well up to snuff as one would like if she thinks Portia may meet with Jonas under those circumstances. I am so glad to have a chance of conveying this to your lordship directly, for I know your mother would tell you the same if she were here."

George was carefully formulating a reply which did not involve telling Lady Montfort to take her interfering ways and go to the devil, but that lady was not nearly quit of all her shot. "But of course, your mother is *not* here, and that is part of the reason for the . . . shall we say *dilemma?* Jane is only lately released into society herself, I apprehend, and the circumstance of her sharing a roof with you and your sister is another thing one does not quite like to see, begging your lordship's pardon. And this cohabitation is most particularly liable to be taken amiss—by those with an unkind bent of mind!—in light of your apparent tendre for Miss Oxenby."

George drew breath to speak but Lady Montfort was unstoppable. "You must—simply must!—find it in your heart to forgive me for being so very forward in speaking to you in such a personal vein, your lordship, especially as it is your mother with whom I enjoy a close relationship, and not your lordship, but I am persuaded it was entirely needful that you hear what I have had to say."

George had heard as much as he was prepared to hear. "Naturally I recognize that your motives are of the finest," he said with chill civility, "and I will think what is to be done regarding my sister. As for the propinquity of Miss Oxenby to myself, I think one need only point out to those with—how did you so eloquently convey it?—those with an *unkind* bent of mind, that whilst I certainly admire Miss Oxenby, Miss Oxenby in no wise returns that sentiment in equal measure. *And,*" he added severely, "I would trust that both Miss Oxenby's unblemished reputation and my own would preserve us from any criticism on such a head."

Lady Montfort fanned herself vigorously, finding it curious that one could feel so overheated when being addressed so coolly. "Of course! It is just as you say. You are a person of such refinement and sensibility that one felt sure one need not say anything, but how could one fail in one's duty, to at least . . . !"

"Indeed, ma'am," George said, with a smile intended to disarm, "only I am sure you have also overlooked the presence of my Great Aunt Serena who is staying with us but never sets foot from the house owing to her lumbago."

"Oh! I had not realized . . . that is, I am sure I was never aware that she . . ."

"No, of course not," the earl said civilly, "and yet within our four walls, we never cease to be aware of her."

George redeposited a very flushed Lady Montfort with Mrs. Digby with every appearance of just having had the most enjoyable chat one could imagine.

Lady Montfort later said of the earl to Mrs. Digby, "He is in every particular as nice as one would hope from his manner and appearance." Mrs. Digby had not for a moment supposed othewise. The chaperonage of two lively, fatherless children had begun to wear on her, and she was forever singing the praises of the earl to any who would listen. James had taken to emulating the earl—who would have been any mother's first choice for such an office—and Lavinia had come along beautifully as a result of just a little of his lordship's kind attention. Both things taken together, the earl had, albeit unknowingly, taken a good deal of worry off Mrs. Digby's thin shoulders, and *that,* she said comfortably to Lady Montfort, had been even before his lordship had been so kind as to invite them along on special trips. And as for today!—why, anyone knew he need not have invited herself, for only a trip undertaken in closed carriages would have occasioned comment, whereas his lordship had seen to it that all the ladies were most comfortably situated in open conveyances while the men rode alongside. No, she did not feel in need of a lecture on the earl's virtues, and those who questioned his lordship's living arrangements were, to her mind, those who were the recipients merely of his civility and not—to their extreme vexation—his particular friendship. For her part, she would believe no ill of him, nor ever would.

The earl, meantime, sat blissfully unaware that the two ladies at his back were so deeply involved in assessing his face, his conduct, his manners, and—in the case of Lady Montfort—his fortune. Jane had fallen asleep and the earl had ceased to make even an attempt to sketch, merely watching her face as she smiled sweetly at whatever dreams consumed her. He longed to possess himself of her hand, and drop an occasional kiss on her brow, but those privileges belonged only to a husband. He aspired to that position with a longing that almost overcame good sense.

Engrossed by such thoughts, George failed to notice the first few drops of rain that fell. By the time he became aware that a deluge threatened, his servants had already assisted Mrs. Digby and Lady Montfort to the shelter of a tree, and were covering the carriages with lightly waxed cloths packed in trunks against just such a contingency. Below he could see the last of the younger group disappearing into an ornamental folly that had been their declared goal. With no one's welfare to see to except his own and Jane's, George eyed an outcropping of rock beneath the brow of the hill. Tall grasses shielded the interior from view but he felt sure there was sufficient room within to keep them both dry.

He roused her gently and grappled with his own emotions as he steadied her down the slope into the unexpectedly spacious bower. Seizing some of the grasses and twisting them, he provided a clean, dry mat for Jane to sit on. Still bemused with sleep, she sat down and smiled at him in the languid way of one only half-awake. George instantly regretted that he had thought it the best course to seclude himself with her. Lady Montfort's warning had made it clear that nasty, prying minds were ready to place the worst possible construction on any time they spent together away from public scrutiny.

Never had George felt more in need of the inhibiting influence of public scrutiny. His stomach was doing a peculiarly unsettling dance. It was not the result of tainted food, as one might have hoped, but was entirely due to Jane Oxenby. He delivered a stern admonition to himself, composed of about two parts sermon and one part threat, all aimed at subduing the burst of libidinous thoughts which were running riot in his mind, and making highly improper suggestions to his body. He had never experienced anything quite like it.

"That came on quite suddenly, didn't it?" Jane remarked.

"Eh?" George wrenched his attention away from her ankles, for she had taken off her spectacles, which were dappled with rain, and was gently wiping them with the hem of her dress, revealing slender ankles with delicately curved bones. "Sudden, you say. Why, yes—I suppose it was," he managed to say.

She tipped her head back to gaze through the lenses. "They are still spotted. Oh, well, it is of no account. We are so near one another that I can see you quite clearly without them, and there is nothing else in here worth looking at so I need not wear them for the moment."

George wondered rather distractedly if the ragged pulse he felt raging in his throat was visible to her. "If one thing is certain, it is that *you* are most worthy of being looked at," he said. "You have the most beguiling eyes, Miss Oxenby." He stopped in horror. Had he really said those things out loud? She was gazing at him with a soft smile on her lips and a quizzical look in her eyes.

"Why, your lordship, the rain has made you most poetical," she said. "Thank you for gallant compliments made when no one is about to overhear them. You need not have, you know!"

George stared at her blankly. "Need not have? I have never had a lady tell me I need not have complimented her."

"It is undoubtedly force of habit on your part which causes you to compliment me. I daresay you have never before so sincerely complimented a lady who did not deserve it."

He could make no sense at all of her words. Why would he not compliment her? She was the object of all his dreams, waking and sleeping. He reached out and touched the hair which had come loose from her pins and was cascading down her neck. She shivered and her eyes dilated, but she said nothing, merely staring at him uncomprehendingly.

"You must think that fate has contrived to place you here with a madman," he said. "I am quite undone by seeing your loveliness so near to me. If only you knew . . . if only I dared tell you . . ."

"If only you dared tell me what?" she said a little breathlessly. Her mouth was a taut bow, and there was a faint spark of something in the back of her eyes. He fancied that if it chanced to meet the spark he carried in his own heart, the two together would kindle a fire which would rage unchecked.

"Oh, words!—what words I would use," he said a trifle dazedly, "but they would not begin to convey that which I wish to say to you." He leaned a little nearer her, his mouth leading him forward, closer to the rich, full lips that trembled just a heartbeat away from his. How he wanted to kiss her, and how improper it would be!

"Your lordship!" rang out an agitated male voice from above. "Your lordship, are you there?"

George had to think where they were for a minute and then he realized it must be Fletcher. Whether it was duty or concern which had brought his butler to him at this minute, George did not care. He wanted to wring the man's neck and fling his lifeless carcass down the hill. Barring the satisfaction of turning his otherwise much appreciated butler into carrion, the earl decided that he would be satisfied if Fletcher simply went away, so he kept silent.

"Your lordship!" Fletcher cried again, sounding a good deal more alarmed than before.

George felt the inevitability of the summons even as Jane regarded him with an oddly arrested look on her face. He drew breath to respond and then decided it would answer better if he made an appearance outside.

"Ah, your lordship," Fletcher said. "How very glad I am to have found you." He straightened his back and announced, "One of the young people has desired me to find you and say that the Lady Portia cannot be found."

Chapter Nine

The earl took a last, fleeting look at Miss Jane Oxenby, sitting so charmingly in their bower, robed in a demure yellow which had made it seem as if the sun were shining in the grotto where he had been on the brink of declaring his love for her. She gazed at him in inquiry, waiting to know the reason for the interruption and smiling sweetly in that vague, detached way she had when she was not wearing her spectacles. It wrenched at him that whatever trouble awaited could undoubtedly be laid at her cousin's door. Not wishing to unleash his anticipatory anger on her, he turned away.

"Fletcher, convey Miss Oxenby to where the others are sitting and see that she is kept warm and dry."

Disdaining the umbrella the butler held out, the earl strode off toward where the grooms had tethered the horses. As he mounted, he became aware that one of the Montfort twins had lumbered after him. Which Montfort it was George could not have said, for there was not a groat's worth of difference between them. The one behind him, however, was bursting with some information which he proceeded to disgorge in a torrent.

"I'm sorry we didn't stay with them, your lordship," he blurted out, "but they kept straying further and further behind, and I own that none of us could endure Sir Jonas's prosing on about bottomland and pasturage and enclosure and . . . and what-not. He was attempting to educate us all about a plan he had in mind for the improvement of his own acres, and, well . . . sir!" The burly youth looked up at George with a plea for understanding.

"I apprehend that you found it a great relief to be rid of them, what with having to keep a civil look on your face and thinking of polite things to say when you were bored senseless?"

A flood of relief washed over the Montfort boy's face. "Just so, sir!"

"Recall that to mind if ever you are tempted to go on at dinner about your day in the hunting field," George said drily. "Now tell me what, if any, attempt was made to find my sister."

The Montfort boy brightened, glad to be able to report that they had had the presence of mind to form a plan. "My brother retraced our steps and Digby stayed in the folly with his sister. I came to inform your lordship of what had taken place."

The rain was slackening somewhat and as the Montfort boy heaved himself onto his cover hack, which, of necessity, resembled the chargers of old which could carry knights in full plate armor, George took stock of the terrain below. It was a skill he had sharpened to a high degree in the Peninsula, and he quickly ascertained that there were only one or two spots where his sister might be out of sight of where he stood. He put his horse to and rode the downhill course in such bruising style—as young Montfort later recounted to his admiring and envious friends—that even such a noted horseman as the Earl of Sefton must have been thought to come to grief.

And yet somehow he did not. Young Montfort, press his horse as he might, could not keep up, and so he was not privileged to see the circumstances in which Lady Portia was discovered, and no details were forthcoming from either the earl's grimly set mouth or from her ladyship's own lips, blue with cold, when at last they rejoined the party. The dainty muslin dress in which her ladyship had begun the day was entirely soaked, and quite half of it was liberally covered in mud. What shoes she might have worn were now gone, and the earl unburdened himself of his sister in what Monty Two—as the younger twin was known to his chums—later told Monty One was a very brusque manner indeed. Since Monty Two had no very high opinion of girls anyway, Monty One took that to mean that the earl had probably pitched her ladyship into the carriage head first. Sir Jonas Biddle, when he arrived, looked only a little better than Lady Portia, but like the earl and his sister, seemed disinclined to say much about what had transpired.

Miss Oxenby took charge of the sopping heiress, who was adding her tears to the rainwater already cascading down her face. The combination of being chilled and crying did no very great justice to a naturally pallid complexion, and Portia's face was soon mottled in shades of red and white. Coupled with hair flattened to her head and red-rimmed eyes, her ladyship presented such an altogether unappealing picture that Monty Two wondered how even such a cod's head as Jonas Biddle could wish to attach her, fortune or no.

It did not materially change the outcome of the day that neither Montfort boy's opinion of the match was solicited, for the earl was in such a cold fury by the time he had sent his coachman off toward Bath with his sister and Miss Oxenby in one conveyance and Lady Montfort, Mrs. Digby and Lavinia in the other, that his implacable opposition to Sir Jonas could not have been made one degree stronger by corroboration from a third party, even if the third party had been the Almighty.

Lady Montfort had little to say on their return journey, a reticence which the earl had no doubt would be redressed by an excess of volubility in the days to come. He was everything that was civil, seeing that the ladies were provided with protection from the rain, which had lessened to almost nothing and showed signs of being soon over. It would, in fact, have suited most of the party better to have lingered where they were until the storm abated, but the earl's countenance did not encourage discussion of any alternate plan to immediate departure.

Jane apologized to the undergrooms for the deplorable condition of the carriage's interior when they debarked in Lansdowne Crescent. Accustomed to waiting on Lady Eugenia, Jane could not help but see the matter from the perspective of the servants. She knew that in all likelihood they would remain awake most of the night attempting to restore the carriage to pristine condition by morning. As she led Portia inside, she thought she detected a flash of gratitude from one of the postilions. Somehow, the orders had already been given for a warm bath to be drawn, and Stoke was waiting for them, wringing her hands in despair. But it was in the drawing room that the real drama was played out some hours later, when Jane descended for dinner and found herself alone with the earl.

"Portia is quite snug and comfortable," Jane said, "but I am sure she will be the better for having her dinner upstairs and going to sleep immediately. She and Jonas will no doubt share a laugh over the whole matter tomorrow."

Her attempt to make the incident into a mere peccadillo brought a dangerous glint to the earl's eyes.

"He couldn't even manage to accompany my sister on a simple stroll in the countryside without leading her into danger!" The earl's wrath lent a measure of volume and intensity to his words that had Jane cringing.

"Well, no great harm has been done to her, you must admit," she ventured. "And it was not Jonas's idea for her to walk along the bank of the stream, after all . . ."

"Do not defend him to me, if you please, Miss Oxenby," the earl said in a quieter but equally dangerous voice. His deep blue eye were shuttered by lids dropped halfway over them, and his lips were thinned out in a grimace that marred the perfection of his stern male beauty. "Your cousin told me he had been endeavoring to explain to my sister how moisture content alters the character of soil, and he took advantage of the rainfall and its effect on the riverbank to drive the lesson home. What use Sir Jonas imagines my sister will make of a knowledge of soil dynamics is quite beyond my ability to grasp, nor do I care to speculate. The fact is that I found my sister mired in mud nearly to her knees, and in imminent danger of being swept away into the stream." He paused and flicked away a speck of dust on his sleeve, drawing a calming breath as he did so. "I think you will own that I did all that I could to make a success of this day. I extended every possible courtesy to Sir Jonas, and planned an outing in a milieu which I anticipated would suit him. And what was the outcome? Your cousin made a complete disaster of it, exposing my sister to both danger and ridicule in the process. I trust you will not cavil when you learn that I sent him away with the clear understanding that he is not to set foot within my house again, and that he may not address my sister, nor even approach her in public. A walk! Dear God in Heaven, the man is hopeless!"

Jane had been anxiously biting her lip throughout this speech. "I did not mean to defend him precisely," she managed to say, "and I did not realize until just now that Jonas encouraged Portia to tread on the softer soil. Portia told me a rather different story, one in which Jonas figured as a hero for having saved her from her own clumsiness. And she was quite enchanted to be taken into his confidence regarding the science of soils."

The earl snorted in a derisive and wholly unconvinced way. "I suppose it may be true that love is blind, but I had not, until now, thought it could descend into the moronic, too."

Jane flew past the most obvious interpretation of his words and exclaimed, "So then you admit that your sister could sincerely be in love with Jonas? That it is an attachment with more substance than mere infatuation?"

The earl regarded her steadily for a moment. At last he said, "Miss Oxenby, I find myself averse to displeasing you in any particular. However, I collect that you wish to preserve the hope of yet another day dawning on this *affaire du coeur*. I beg you will not. There is not the slightest chance of that happening. It is over, Miss Oxenby, irretrievably over. I urge you to reconcile yourself to that fact, and to whatever effect it may have on the future of Longchamp, your cousin, and yourself."

"Myself?" Jane asked. "How do you imagine that my fate is in any way bound up with Jonas's?"

His expression took on a gravity she had never seen there. "Just as Portia is my sister and her future is therefore of concern to me, so must one suppose that Sir Jonas's future concerns *you*, as he is your closest living family member."

Jane gazed at him blankly. It was too ludicrous to think that the earl seriously supposed her connection to Jonas in any way approximated his relationship with his sister. It seemed a good moment to say the obvious, however. "I do not deny the tie, but I am not advancing Jonas's cause out of familial feelings. I merely represent his cause to you as I would do any other suitor under like circumstances," she said. "I have made every attempt to be impartial."

"That, of course, is what I had hoped for," he replied, his eyes appraising. "Nevertheless, I find myself at a standstill. I cannot permit Portia to continue to see Sir Jonas, and I place no great reliance on her forming any other attachment while she imagines herself to be the centerpiece of a Cheltenham tragedy with him as its protagonist. I had thought earlier of returning to London and introducing Portia there, but I now find myself inclining toward the idea of returning her to the schoolroom until my mother's return."

"Oh, you could not!" Jane exclaimed. "It would be, of all

things, the most lowering! That is, I perfectly understand that Portia is not precisely out yet in society's eyes, not having made her curtsy at the Queen's Drawing Room, but—"

"Then there can be no harm done if she quietly retreats from society for another year," the earl interposed smoothly.

"No harm?" Jane was beside herself. "How can you imagine for an instant that Portia will not react against what you propose? Naturally she must oppose it, for it is a step backward. Any girl's self-respect must suffer when she is told one minute that she is fit to move in adult society and then the next it is announced that she is being returned to the care of a governess! How she must shrink with humiliation if you pursue such a course!"

"I should vastly prefer her to shrink with humiliation in private, and for a short duration, than to see her obliged to endure the humiliation of being Lady Biddle for the rest of her life. Portia's natural refinement would assert itself within six months of their marriage, and she would discover that she held Jonas in the liveliest contempt. She would, quite properly, charge me then with failure to protect her from her own youthful folly." There was annoyance in the commanding voice, and around the eyes.

Jane sighed. "I am afraid I have failed miserably in my capacity as confidante to Portia and advisor to you." She looked up and met his gaze unflinchingly. "I regret that I have put you to a great deal of expense and trouble to no good purpose. I was not at all altruistic when I agreed to your proposal that I accompany you and Portia to Bath, and now my own selfishness comes back to haunt me." The earl opened his mouth to respond but Jane shook her head ever so slightly. "Please let me finish. I wished to see a bit of society, and indulge in the happy pretense that I could take my place in it, despite the unhappy circumstances of my birth. I feel like the worst sort of fraud at this moment, your lordship. My first responsibility was to you and your sister, and I have not reconciled either of you to the other's position, and I have therefore failed you utterly."

"You did not—could not!—fail us," the earl said, his tone now gentler. "I hold you in the highest regard, just as I know Portia does, and I assure you that the circumstances of your birth do not weigh with me! If you have failed to mediate between my sister and me on this issue, it is because it is a task which would have taxed Solomon, or perhaps Job is the man I mean, for patience is the quality most called for at this juncture. You are by far too sensible to seriously believe you are in any way to blame, and I will not see our friendship come to any harm over so unworthy an issue."

George infused his words with a warmth which his earlier remarks had lacked. Jane looked up at him hopefully. "I will accept that what you say may be true. May I ask what your immediate plans are?"

George twirled his quizzing glass at the end of its ribbon. "I thought I would give the household orders to commence packing at the end of the week, with an eye to a Friday departure by ourselves, with the servants to follow."

"Friday," Jane repeated a little breathlessly. A painful tightening in her chest robbed her of further speech for a moment. The earl and Portia would go on to London, and the Lady Serena, of course, and she would return to Longchamp, or more precisely, to the old and leaky dower house she shared with Nanny.

"Does it not suit you to depart on Friday?" the earl asked with a touch of concern. "I have no particular plans. I could as easily move the departure forward or back."

"Oh, back, if you please," Jane said on a rush of air. "I . . . I should not like for anyone to think that the events of today have driven us away within the week. That is, I think Portia would feel keenly that she was being rushed from the scene of the debacle and be all the more humiliated for it."

The earl nodded. "If you think that an unfavorable interpretation will be placed on an earlier departure, then by all means, let us delay until, say, Monday."

"Thank you," Jane said gratefully. As they went into dinner, she prayed that she had not revealed herself in voice or face. It was not to spare Portia a precipitous retreat from the scene of disaster that Jane had requested the later departure, but to allow herself to spend a few more precious days with George Aubrey Tate before their paths diverged forever.

"Oh, and Fletcher, tell the cook that the sauce on the partridges was curiously bitter last night."

"Very good, your lordship." Fletcher perceived by his master's abstracted air that he was now immersed in other thoughts. After waiting in silence for a moment for a formal dismissal, the butler judged that his lordship had forgotten his presence. He departed and made his way as rapidly downstairs as decorum allowed, so that he could make a written list of all the things his lordship had desired him to do. It would be a not inconsiderable list, concerned as it was with the closure of the house on Lansdowne Crescent and, a few months hence, the arrival of a house party at Sefton Hall.

Fletcher would not have dreamed of discussing his lordship's business with chef—who was French, in any case!—or any of the numerous footmen and maids, but he did manage to hint to the housekeeper, without being vulgar, that he rather thought his lordship might be of a mind to marry soon. "And like as not, you know who it may be."

Mrs. Briggs nodded sagely. Like any housekeeper, she was addressed by the honorific "Mrs.", and she had come to believe over the years that she actually knew about the wedded state simply from having enjoyed the title. "I daresay she'll do well enough for him. He's bit, sure enough, and nobility these days thinks a match made for love will suit 'em best. I hope they may be right, for I don't hold with it!"

Fletcher waited until an approaching footman had passed by before replying. "I've watched him man and boy and I'm that glad he's found someone so pleasant and cheery—and not a bit top-lofty either, for all she's Quality. Reminds me of her ladyship, she does."

"It'll make life easy for us if she is," Mrs. Briggs said with feeling. "Do you reckon he'll wait until herself is back from Abroad?"

"Not for the askin'. You know well enough her ladyship ain't expected back until year's end, and when I sees that faraway look in his eye this morning as he's orderin' up this house party, I thinks to myself, now here's a man in love, and gettin' fit to pop the question. No, it's my belief that if his lady love says yes, there'll be a weddin' before the cat can lick her ear."

George was thinking very much the same thing at that moment, though in distinctly different terms. Wofford awaited with estate matters but George was inclined to let him wait awhile yet, as he pondered the plan he had conceived for bringing Miss Jane Oxenby back within his bailiwick after their departure from Bath. He rubbed a finger thoughtfully across his cheek, encountering a slightly rough spot where Henry had equivocated with the razor that morning.

George had devoted much thought the night before to the circumstances upon which he might build on the solid foundation of friendship between Jane and himself. He had gone on foot to the gaming club which he had found most convivial in Bath, and had taken advantage of the mental calm which always claimed him when he was engaged in rolling the dice, to think further upon the matter. He had earned a reputation as a "regular cool one" wherever he gambled, since he never seemed to care whether he won or lost. In fact, he did *not* care, which, perversely enough, produced more winning rolls for him than all the connip-tions, spells and imprecations employed by others.

Several hours spent at the tables gave George ample time to savor the precise moment when Jane had betrayed her attachment to him. Most women who desired a closer acquaintance with him badly overplayed their hands, but Jane had never exhibited anything more than friendliness, and so he had been left wondering if he had any hope of ever being more to her, at least until last night. And then . . . and then!—she had, with one heart-stopping word, revealed herself.

Friday. In those two syllables, and in her eyes, had been the emotion which he had been hoping to see. No one who had been there could have mistaken it. She was loath to leave him. And so he had gladly extended the time of their departure. The memory of the look on her face inspired a happy heat in his chest, a schoolboyish giddiness that would have astonished those who had watched him at the tables last night, coolly rolling for anything up to a thousand guineas a time. If he had been more sure that her heart belonged to him, he would have told her that all she need do was say the word and they could stay in Bath forever, that he would *buy* Lansdowne Crescent if she wished it, but it seemed to be risking too much to declare himself so fervently on such slim evidence.

The plan to assemble the most convivial of his friends at Sefton Park had come to him later, on the walk home. Once the season ended, they would be happy enough to fill the numerous bedrooms of Sefton Hall, for to be seen in London in August was a horrific fate. He would ask some terribly respectable married woman to act as his hostess—a sop to the likes of Lady Montfort and her references to impropriety. Then he would prevail on Jane to join them, and within the safety of numbers and amidst the flirtations that permeated any country-house party, he would declare his love and attempt to extract a like confession from her. From there it was but a short step to an acceptance of a marriage proposal.

"If your lordship does not wish to attend to this business, I shall withdraw," Wofford said.

George turned away from the window in some surprise. "Ah! I collect from your pained expression that I have kept you waiting for far too long. Come, let us go to with a will then, and we may yet finish in time to see it all in today's post."

"That would be impossible, I regret to say. It has already gone."

"Has it? Is the hour so far advanced then? Well, then it shall go tomorrow, for I will not waste another day over it."

"It is hardly waste, your lordship," Wofford pointed out with a trace of reproach. "I have succeeded in cross-checking and verifying the land agent's report for the first quarter and I expect you will want to see it yourself, and authorize payment of the two hundred and fifty pounds now due the agent. In addition, there are the pensions to be paid, to the ex-gamekeeper as well as Nurse Ralston, the allowance for your Uncle Augustus which should be transferred to his bank in Marrakech—"

"In the earnest hope that he will stay there," the earl remarked dryly. "Yes, yes, I know these are necessary and important items, Wofford. Spare me your disapprobation."

In a voice from which nearly all censure was stripped, the secretary went on. "There is also a complete accounting from the village schoolmaster of this term's expenses for books and coal, as well as a letter asking what he is to do about the children who wish to further their education at the . . ."

George settled back in a chair and listened with half an ear. The problems and the pensions varied hardly at all from one year to the next, and unless something unusual were added, such as the six hundred pounds it cost to repair the church steeple the previous year, it would all pass through his brain with scarcely any need for thought.

One thing did rouse his interest, but it was on the street. Manning appeared on the pavement below in the earl's distinctive blue and yellow livery, and George leaned forward in the hope that he was preceding Portia and Jane out of the house on some errand. He had not seen Jane at breakfast, having arisen late himself, and that omission had left him with the sense that he was tending to everything but that which was most important.

He found himself fantasizing as he waited, picturing himself in a dressing gown paying a morning call on Jane in her boudoir at Sefton House—which he would have redecorated expressly for her when they were married. He pictured her against a backdrop of cobalt blue silk, festooned to frame her headboard. She would be sitting up in bed, drinking chocolate and sorting through the various invitations and letters on her tray. And her hair would be loose, full and glorious, with perhaps just a bit caught up in a ribbon.

He would send her maid away and sit on the edge of the bed. Her eyes would still be heavy-lidded with sleep, softening the startling effect of the dark corona that surrounded the cool, clear blue of her irises. The thick eyelashes would sweep the lenses of her spectacles as she smiled at him, and he would reach out and remove them. Her eyes would widen and soft laughter would form in their depths when she realized that he meant to make love to his own wife in the bright light of day.

George felt a tremor pass through him, the vision in his head as real to him as the room in which he was sitting. How perfect it would all be if he could but persuade Miss Jane Oxenby to become Lady Sefton!

It was with no small amount of disappointment that George saw Manning move off down the street alone. The footman carried what looked like a letter, nothing unusual in itself, but when Manning returned with another letter a half hour later, George supposed that for once Wofford had erred, and that the day's post had only just been delivered.

Chapter Ten

George looked up and repressed his irritation at being disturbed. Bates, his coachman of many years standing and his batman before that, hovered on the threshold of his study. George motioned for him to come. If Bates had business with him which could not wait, he would as lief hear it here in his study as in the stable yard. Wofford looked a question at the earl, which George answered in the negative.

"You may as well stay, Wofford. I perceive that Bates is here on an errand of some importance, and I may very well have need of you if that is the case. Well, Bates?"

Bates looked gravely at his employer, for whom he had the highest degree of liking, as well as regard. "I hope it may be nothing, your lordship, but one of the undergrooms, a reliable lad, reported a conversation to me which I believe it's needful for your lordship to judge for yourself."

George slowly laid aside the pen with which he had been signing the bank drafts for pension disbursements. "Did he? Well, then I suppose I had better hear it."

"If your lordship pleases, it was with that gentleman as come out to Monkton Combe with us, stoutish fellow who couldn't sit his horse very well, begging your lordship's pardon."

"No need to beg my pardon," George said coolly, perceiving that Bates could only be referring to one person. "The fellow is ham-fisted. What of him?"

Both Wofford and Bates had observed the earl's brilliant, heavy-lidded eyes narrowing, and Bates drew a short breath before continuing with some trepidation. "He passed by on the street back by the stables today, sort of casual-like, and said something to Freddy—that's the boy I was meaning when I said an undergroom—about them high-steppers you have ordered up for tomorrow. He said he reckoned he'd be setting a stiff pace for somewheres soon and was desirous of knowing where he could hire animals that would match them for speed." Bates snorted. "Of course there are none such, and so Freddy told him. No one but a jolly head would think that such cattle could be had for hire, and werry few for sale, too, as your lordship well knows!"

"Quite right," the earl said, his lips thin. He rose and strolled to the windows overlooking the crescent. Presently he turned. "Bates, I want you to send to London for that new post chaise I ordered. I fancy I recall you saying it was all done and just sitting in the mews awaiting my approval before the crest is added to the door."

"Yes, my lord," Bates said, "that is exactly the way of it."

"Good. I will expect it here, still *sans* crest, you apprehend, at the earliest possible moment." The earl fixed a piercing look on his head coachman that added anxiety to trepidation, for his tone of voice had already conveyed that the matter at hand had deeply angered him.

Bates rapidly calculated the time necessary for a fast horse to reach Sefton House, horses to be put to, and the chaise to accomplish the return journey. His lordship interrupted this line of thought with an abrupt question.

"The chestnuts I bought at Tattersall's last month—can my sister have any knowledge of them?"

Bates concealed his surprise at this odd question. "I think not, my lord, as they have been kept in London since you purchased them, and her ladyship has been away since then."

"Very good," the earl said brusquely. "Use the chestnuts

then. I expect complete discretion. Put the boys in plain livery—I'm sure we have some about—and arrange for the horses to be stabled at the Swan, and the chaise kept there also."

"But my lord, the chestnuts?" Bates protested. "At a public house when we have ample room here in your lordship's own—"

The earl stopped him with a crackling look. "See to it, Bates. You are a good man. I need not worry that my horses will suffer for being stabled at a public house while you are in charge. In any case," he said, softening his expression a little, "I do not anticipate keeping them there for very long. And keep my second best team on the post road to London. Do not bring them on when Thursday's drive is done." He turned his head and stared out the window. "They will make their move quite soon, I feel sure."

"Their move, your lordship?" asked the coachman in confusion. "Then you *do* mean to bring the chestnuts on here?"

But the earl was no longer attending. He grasped his hands behind his back, emphasizing a musculature across the back and through the shoulder that patrons of amateur boxing matches would have recognized as the source of power behind his lordship's punishing right. Bates exchanged looks with Wofford. After a long period during which the earl said nothing, Bates soundlessly let himself out. It was, he would later tell his wife, as if the earl had left the room and been replaced by a demon, so fiery and fierce had been the look on his face.

When at last the earl spoke again, it startled his secretary.

"Wofford, I believe you are about to go away and take care of some business for me in London."

"Indeed, your lordship, I would be glad to, though I know of no—"

George turned suddenly. "Where has Bates gone?" he demanded.

"He thought your lordship had done with him," Wofford

said. The earl's manner was most unsettling and the secretary endeavored to keep a composed mien. There was every suggestion that the earl, who in general was pleasant and reasonable, even gay at times, was well into a temper the like of which had not been seen since the abortive elopement of Lady Horatia. In general, the earl's temper manifested itself as an implacable determination to have his will obeyed, coupled with a dangerous degree of politeness. His brilliant, heavy-lidded eyes naturally made him look somewhat contemptuous, but now they glittered with something much worse.

"Wofford, Mr. Creighton has a valet with pugilistic talent. I have even sparred with him on occasion as a means of keeping fit. He also has a knowledge and an aptitude for the low life which will serve us very well in the circumstances. I wish you will take yourself off to Charlcombe and ally yourself with this individual. Tell Bates that he is to take you there first thing in the morning, but that the manner of your departure should be consistent with a journey to the capital. That is the story you will give out, incidentally, that you are embarked for London. Inform Bates that he is to stop one night at a posting house on the London road before returning here, to strengthen the impression that he has been to London and back. I myself will come to Charlcombe tomorrow evening and explain to Lord Hugh why you must stay there for the time being, and to Roger why it is that he must lend us his valet. I want that individual to follow Sir Jonas Biddle, and to alert you the instant it appears he means to leave Bath." He turned and looked at his secretary. "If my preparations seem somewhat labyrinthine, I assure you, they are not."

Startled, Wofford replied, "Indeed, my lord, I have never known any of your schemes to go awry, nor have I ever known you to be wrong. I would not dream of contradicting or criticizing you."

The earl looked at him, his expression of grim determination giving way to a kind of bleak unhappiness such as

Wofford had never before seen on his employer's face. After what seemed an interminable time to Wofford, staring—as he felt—into the face of another man's torment, the earl said, "I wish that you were right, Wofford. It is unfortunate that in this case, I am obliged to tell you that you are quite wrong, and that I made a grave error. I allowed something to progress which should have died aborning."

"Well, I have no taste for it, but if you wish to hear Mr. Burdett's lecture, I am happy enough to go with you," Portia said. "Oh! This entire section is quite hopeless!"

Jane reached out and took the cutwork from Portia's hands. "It is not so bad as all that. Let me just go over a few stitches here and there and I fancy no one will think it less than perfect. What did Horatia say in her letter?" Jane asked by way of diversion.

"Oh, I have given it to George to read," Portia said.

"Well, I did not mean for you to read it aloud to me," Jane said with a teasing note. "I only wondered if she was well."

"Oh, you mean the baby, no doubt," Portia said in an offhand way. "From what I can tell, all is just as it should be. And I *would* read you the letter if I still had it."

"Nothing is more natural than that you should have given it to your brother. I only thought that since you replied so quickly there might be some exciting new development," Jane said, concentrating on her stitches.

A letter had arrived some weeks before from Horatia in America, announcing that she and her husband were expecting a child. It had cut up Jane's peace, reminding her of Roger Creighton's remark that the earl need not beget a son of his own but could choose a nephew as his heir. George had proposed a toast to the forthcoming baby at dinner, highlighting his pleasure at the news and presumably, the uninterrupted liaison with his mistress which it presaged. Jane did not very much want to talk about Horatia and the baby anyway, so she let the subject of this latest letter from

171

America drop. Instead she asked, "Have you given any thought as to whether you would like to attend the dress ball at the Lower Rooms on Friday?"

"Only if I had something new to wear," Portia said, "and besides, Lavinia Digby had thought of having a small informal entertainment at their accommodations on Friday."

"Who does Lavinia intend to invite?"

"Oh, she has not given it much thought, I am sure. You know what Lavinia is like! But the Montfort boys will surely want to come, and James would be there," Portia said airily. "I quite like James. He is very agreeable, even when one is out of sorts, or not feeling quite up to making pleasant conversation."

"I have always thought so. There! What slight irregularity there is to the stitches will be unnoticeable after the first washing and blocking. Now, whether or not Friday is devoted to a home entertainment or a dress ball, I think we must see what is to be done to refurbish your dresses. Stoke mentioned that a new silver tissue underskirt might improve that deep lavender dress that becomes you so."

"You mean the one that does not make me look as hideous as some of the others," Portia sighed.

"Oh, what a shocking thing to say," Jane said. "You could not possibly be hideous no matter what you wore!"

Jane set to work to jolly Portia out of what seemed like a fit of the sullens, finally prevailing on her to go down into the town to look over what materials might be used to bring new life to gowns grown stale to the eye. Portia asked if Manning might be spared to take a note to Lavinia's asking her to meet them if she could, to which Jane readily assented. Her mind was quite elsewhere. Whether Lavinia joined them, whether they went to the ball or to the Digbys on Friday, was all a matter of indifference to Jane. Today was Wednesday and Wofford had already been despatched to London that morning, and the servants had begun making discreet preparations for leaving. While Portia was easily distracted by some bright yellow kid gloves and a Dunstable straw bonnet trimmed with satin rosebuds, all Jane could think of was how soon they would be leaving.

The fact that Lavinia never joined them in no way seemed to diminish Portia's pleasure in the shopping expedition. It was likewise quite remarkable to Jane how easily Portia had accepted Jonas's banishment. Given her own distress at being parted from George soon, Jane concluded that Portia's feelings for Jonas could not have run so very deep after all. She hoped that Portia would never know the anguish of facing separation from one she truly loved, and ardently wished that *she* had been more on her guard against falling in love. Such reflections did little good, however, and Jane resolved to keep herself too busy to think about it until their departure. George dined with them and then went off for an evening of cards with the party at Charlcombe, leaving the undercoachman to drive the ladies to the Theatre Royal, where Mr. Burdett was to speak on the miracle of modern inventions.

The effort required to conceal the stormy emotions within her breast left Jane quite enervated at evening's end. When they arrived back at Lansdowne Crescent, Portia retired immediately, leaving a grateful Jane to her own thoughts.

Portia was up early, in time to report to Jane that her brother had appeared in the breakfast room dressed in the prescribed garb of the Four Horse Club and prepared for a fast bowl into the coaching station at Salt Hill for the club's monthly luncheon there. Jane had never even heard of such a club and Portia, though bored by it through long acquaintance, informed Jane that its members comprised all the most notable whips, and that they wore outlandish driving costumes, of which blue and yellow striped waistcoats and spotted neckcloths were only the most objectionable features. It was Portia's opinion that the club's members had assembled it from among clothes judged too vulgar to be worn to a cockfight.

"Though I will say that George looks a little less ridiculous than most of his friends in that rig out," Portia confessed, "but only because the Sefton livery is blue and yellow, and so his tiger seems to be dressed to accommodate his master, which gives the whole affair some small measure of at least appearing to have been planned."

"Very small indeed, I collect," Jane laughed, observing Portia's disapproving grimace. "You are quite as high a stickler as your brother for appearances, you know."

Portia looked at Jane, her eyes wide. "Do you think so? I own, I have always tried to be so but when one is faced with the example of a beautiful mama who dresses so exquisitely that everyone quite faints away at the sight of her, it almost seems as if one were better off not to make the effort."

Jane laughed. "How awful for you! My mama was beautiful, too, so I know exactly what you mean."

"Except that you are quite lovely yourself. You can cut a dash if you choose."

"If I had the means and the position to do so, you mean," Jane reminded her gently.

"Oh, as for that, you need only marry the right man, which would be no great trick for you," Portia declared blithely.

"You are a shameless flatterer! I thank you for the vote of confidence but it could not happen the way you suppose."

"Whyever not?" Portia replied, looking surprised. "I had thought at one point to have you as my sister-in-law but I have since seen that you cannot care for George as much as he may admire you. That still leaves any number of men who would attach you if they could. Hugh quite likes you, you know, and everyone can see that Roger is an admirer, which although Hugh will one day be a duke, carries more weight than Hugh's admiration since Roger is such an out and outer."

"What an awful expression to hear from a young girl's lips!" Jane said, laughing. "Wherever did you learn it? No! Do not tell me—I am sure I do not wish to know. As for Hugh and Roger, I am very grateful for the kindness they have shown me, especially at the public balls, but what you cannot be expected to know is that the circumstances of my birth and my parentage are such as most disqualify me from aspiring to any higher rung in society."

"Oh, stuff!" Portia responded. "Why, some of the most shocking things have happened in our own family—indeed, I told you one of them—and no one has ostracized us. As long as one is amusing or clever, one need not worry about such things."

Jane smiled tolerantly. "My own experience suggests quite otherwise. Some people, most people, I think, care very much about one's background. But there!—let us not talk of unpleasant things that need not concern you." She poured another cup of tea and took it up, saying, "Your brother will be driving quite a distance away. Is Salt Hill not north of London?"

"He says it is a hundred miles from here, but by good roads, so he considers it a mere nothing. He posts his own horses along the way so there will be no reason he cannot arrive in time for lunch and then be back in Bath in time to change for dinner. He took me up once when he was planning on setting a spanking pace. I own, it was the most exciting thing I ever felt! The wind fairly rips at one when George springs his grays. Of course, he favors gray, and so all his driving horses are gray."

"Well, I sincerely hope he *and* his grays will not end up in a ditch today!"

"You need not fear that any harm will come to him," Portia said with sisterly pride.

It pleased Jane to hear it, for she had feared Portia might harbor some residue of resentment toward George over Jonas's banishment. "Have you heard anything further regarding Lavinia Digby's plans for tomorrow night?"

Portia glanced at her blankly and then recognition lit her face. "Oh! Well, I have not, but it is of no consequence, for George asked me to tell you this morning that he particularly wishes us to attend the dress ball tomorrow night. It will be the last assembly of any note before our departure and he wishes us to say our farewells."

In the event, Portia felt unwell on Friday afternoon. She complained of a vague achiness and took to her bed. When it was time to dress for dinner, she declared that she could not possibly contemplate arising, but begged Jane to go to the dress ball, particularly as George had been so insistent.

"I shall lay here quietly, and Stoke can sit with me. No harm shall come to me, and I do so wish you to have one last nice evening," Portia said. "I shall send Manning with a note to the Digbys, telling them that if I feel better later, I will endeavor to join them in Beaufort Square. You must know that I would not entertain any idea of coming to the ball late—Mr. Le Bas would be bound to react very badly if I arrived untimely—so if you come home and I am not here, you will know that I am feeling better and having a lovely time with the Digbys. I am sure James will see me safely home, so you need not wait up."

Jane smiled, rather sure that Portia was not at all unwell but had merely contrived a way to attend Lavinia's small party as she preferred, rather than the dress ball, as her brother had desired her to. Jane was quick to tell George at least part of the truth, which was that Portia was not seriously unwell and that they need not scruple to stay home on her account. The earl accepted her explanation without comment and offered her his arm for the stroll into dinner.

George sat across from Jane at the table and entertained her with a highly amusing account of his mad dash to Salt Hill and back. Jane smiled and nodded, feasting her eyes on his face all the while. She concentrated on memorizing small details, like the minuscule cleft in his chin that was only noticeable in the right light, and the way his rich, deep brown hair waved back from his high forehead. How she loved him!—and never more than when he talked as he did now, in a self-deprecating and clever way, making his accomplishments seem amusing when other men would have been unable to resist boasting of them, or at least describing them in such a way that one was left in no doubt as to the storyteller's prowess with a phaeton and four.

She went upstairs briefly before they left, to fetch her fan and cloak, and to say goodbye to Portia. The earl's sister had eaten some soup and bread from a tray brought up by Manning, and given the footman a letter to carry to the Digbys. Jane paused on the threshold, thinking that Portia looked almost pretty tonight, with a becoming color to her cheeks, and bright, shining eyes. It was on the tip of Jane's tongue to wish her a happy evening at the Digbys, but she kept the thought to herself, knowing that Portia would not then have the satisfaction of thinking herself quite so clever. It was a small deception, and Jane thought no worse of Portia for it. Indeed, it seemed refreshingly high-spirited in one who had, until recently, been so very timorous.

When Jane descended again, she was surprised that the earl was not waiting for her. The front door was just closing and she supposed it was only Manning leaving with the note for the Digbys. It was fully five minutes before George emerged from the back of the house, coming, rather curiously, through the green baize doors that were the demarcation between the servants' territory and the master's portion of the house. He apologized tersely for the delay and accepted his cloak, hat and gloves from Fletcher.

The earl was singularly silent in the carriage, his jaw set as he gazed out the window, and Jane was reminded of another evening, when he had been at the limits of his patience over Jonas Biddle's conduct at the assembly. He had been absorbed with the view outside the carriage *that* night, too. She castigated herself for drawing such a silly parallel, and reminded herself that George was under no obligation to be charming and witty on her account, especially after he had exerted himself to entertain her at dinner.

It was clear from the opening dance that he had little interest in the ball, and Jane wondered why he had told Portia he particularly wished them to attend. He was as engaging as always in his address, but to Jane—who fancied she knew him better—he seemed abstracted. Hugh, John and Roger were there, but they did not require leave taking, as they would undoubtedly be reunited with George in London quite soon, and Mrs. Digby was absent, as Jane had supposed she would be. The evening seemed quite pointless to her after tea had been served and individual parties were encouraged to break up. The earl handed Jane over to Hugh with a light remark about saying farewell to Mr. Le Bas and disappeared.

Hugh partnered Jane through a quadrille in excellent style but she found it nearly impossible to concentrate on his conversation for seeking out a glimpse of the earl. It was all a bright, multicolored blur without her spectacles, however, and she had to wait until she was seated again to bring her lorgnette into play. It availed nothing, though, for the earl was nowhere to be seen. Roger and a few other gallants formed a court around her as they had done on numerous other occasions, but all Jane could think was that she had been living in a fairy tale which was soon coming to an end.

When George had not returned at the end of an hour, Jane supposed he had gone off to try his luck at cards or dice. He was completely within his rights to do so, of course, but Jane felt let down. She had foreseen a magical evening, something to cap the months just past, with memories to be savored in years to come, of dancing with the Earl of Sefton, and being courted by him, even if it was only a charade. Now it was too clear that the enchantment had been an illusion, and that the earl did not intend to perpetuate the illusion of a courtship now that there was nothing to be gained by it.

Once Jane could no longer evade that realization, she wanted nothing more than to leave, but Hugh, John and Roger all insisted on one last dance apiece. Hugh went in search of George for her afterward, returning with the intelligence that the earl was enjoying an extraordinary run of luck at the tables—even for him!—and would she consent to being driven home by himself instead?

That George would not even break away from his gaming

to escort her back to Lansdowne Crescent as he had always done was the final blow. All of Jane's misery focused on that proof that he did not care for her at all. Tonight, when the ruse was at an end, he had made that manifest by a lack of even common courtesy. Jane could not bear to be pitied, and she turned Hugh's offer aside with thanks. Bates could drive her home in complete safety, and that way Hugh need not leave the ball. Blinking back tears too ready to be spilled, Jane let Hugh walk her to the carriageway and hand her into the earl's equipage. She squeezed Hugh's hand in farewell and assured him that she would be all right, for it was clear from his worried expression that she had not succeeded entirely in keeping her unhappiness a secret.

What she found when she arrived at Lansdowne Crescent chased away all thoughts of her own unhappiness in the blink of an eye. She had expected either to find Portia in bed still, or a note saying that she had—wonder of wonders!—recovered sufficiently to go around to the Digbys' humble little soiree.

Instead, Jane discovered an empty bed in Portia's room. Portia herself was still very much within the precincts of the house, however. That Portia had not expected to see Jane was evident by the way she started and turned pale when Jane walked through the door of her sitting room. She was dressed in traveling clothes, though somewhat clumsily, by which fact Jane knew that she had not entrusted Stoke with her plans, and she was attempting to clutch a letter behind her back.

"You are going out?" Jane inquired coolly.

"N—not as yet," Portia stammered. "I . . . I . . . what are you doing back so early? I mean, I trust that the ball was not ended early?"

"Oh, no, it will go on until eleven of the clock as usual, which I am sure you counted on," Jane said, briskly stripping off her elbow-length gloves. "Do you think that pelisse quite the thing for Mrs. Digby's salon?" Without waiting for an answer, she went on. "I expect that letter will explain the mystery of why you are dressed for a journey. It was for me, wasn't it? Or was it for your brother?"

"Letter?" Portia echoed, her voice cracking. "Oh! You mean this!" She slowly brought the letter into view from behind her back. "It is just the one from Horatia. I was reading it again."

Jane held out her hand. "Then you won't mind if I read it for myself. I recollect that your only objection to my reading it was that you had already given it to George."

"And so I had," Portia said nervously, "only I asked for it back and—"

"The letter," Jane said. She reached out and took it from Portia's trembling fingers.

She scanned it briefly. Portia had obviously labored long over it, for it included some elegantly turned phrases meant to tear at the reader's heart. It failed in that regard, for Jane's heart had turned to stone the instant she had seen what was afoot.

"I had better see the other letter then, hadn't I?" Jane said. "The one in which Jonas has spelled out the particulars of your elopement?"

"There . . . there is no such letter," Portia said, her chin stuck out in childish defiance. "I cannot con—conceive of what you mean."

Jane unfastened her cloak and flung it across a chair. "Very well, I will search for it." She found it almost immediately, rather pathetically obvious among the other papers on Portia's writing table. It appeared to be devoid of writing but its surface was oddly wrinkled. Jane held it in front of a candle, ignoring Portia's gasp.

"How did you . . . how could you know?" Portia exclaimed.

If she had not been so angry, Jane would have laughed. "Did you and Jonas imagine you were the only ones who knew about secret messages? I learned quite a number of useful things at school, including how to write secret messages in onion or lemon juice, though I learned *that* from

180

the other girls, not the masters. Did you seriously imagine you could fool anyone over the age of twelve with this silly trick? Have you written all your letters to him in this mode? I swear, I shall positively *flay* Manning for continuing to deliver them for you! He has not been to the post office or the Digbys once this week, has he?—merely back and forth to Jonas's lodgings!"

The tears which had been gathering in Portia's eyes suddenly broke loose, accompanied by a heartrending sob. Jane turned her back on the weeping girl and read the message from Jonas. It described the rendezvous point in great detail—by the three Lombardy poplars in the garden of the last house in Queen's Parade—and urged Portia to arrive no later than half past nine *"for we will need a fair start if we are to reach GG before Those Who Will Likely Pursue You."*

Jane crumpled the note in her hand. She had never been so furious in her life. That Jonas should betray her trust! No, she vowed, he would be taught a lesson! When Portia so ardently wished to marry him, and none of their friends stood in their way, it ill-behooved him to resort to such a distasteful and clandestine scheme. It was only George who barred their way, and Jane knew he could be brought around sooner or later. Why, his lordship, the Earl of Sefton, cared more for his fast horses and even faster women to long endure the overseeing of his sister's life!

Having found herself equally and inexplicably as angry with George as with Jonas, Jane flung the note to the floor with shaking hands and went in search of Fletcher. She asked the butler to bring the housekeeper to her, and Manning, but in the event, only Mrs. Briggs could be found. Jane was not surprised, and rather thought that if Manning was as intelligent as he seemed to be, he would already have taken himself off the instant he realized the scheme must have been discovered. She desired Mrs. Briggs to lend her the household keys for a short while, saying airily that she had somehow locked her bedroom door. That lady complied readily enough, though much astonished by such an unusual request.

Jane quickly climbed the stairs and locked the two doors leading to Portia's chambers. The younger girl was still sobbing and did not even notice, but all Jane cared about was that Portia could not now leave Lansdowne Crescent. Returning the keys to Mrs. Briggs, Jane thanked her civilly and wished both the senior servants a good night. They stared after her, open-mouthed, but she scrupulously kept an expression of unconcern on her face as she mounted the stairs again. It was vitally important that none of the servants suspect that anything was amiss, and most especially not *what* was amiss, or the story would be bound to get out and make the rounds, destroying Portia's reputation as surely as if she had actually run away with Jonas.

It lacked only forty-five minutes to the agreed-upon hour of meeting in Queen's Parade and Jane sat down in her small sitting room to consider what to do next. From down the hall she could hear Portia's distraught sobs. Just for a moment, Jane let herself think what a welcome relief it would be to burst into tears herself, and then she sternly pushed aside the impulse in favor of deciding how best to frighten the life out of Jonas.

He must be roundly scared off from ever contemplating so harebrained a scheme again, not least because she had championed his cause. She decided she would meet him herself, and give him such a set-down as would make him wish he had braved his lordship's temper and done his proposing in the right quarter in the first place. Jane picked up her fan and snapped it open, waving it angrily to cool herself.

She could not be ruined by an assignation with Jonas, she who was his close relation, and she could effectively deliver the needed reprimand without completely undoing the graceless buffoon's chances of ever marrying Portia by revealing his stupidity to his intended's brother. Jane

182

thought he had already succeeded too well in that regard without any help from her, but it would not do, for Portia's sake, to poison the well for all time by adding to the damage.

Portia was safely out of the way, which left Jane only Jonas to deal with. It occurred to her that she would be best off to pose as Portia and let Jonas take them as far as the first posting house before she revealed her identity. Otherwise the noddy head would undoubtedly return and attempt to finish the job. Besides, if they only went as far as the first posting house, she and Jonas would be back in Bath before dawn, and no one the wiser, particularly if she put on a morning dress beneath her cloak, and desired Jonas to set her down within walking distance of the house. Then she could walk in, pretending that she had let herself out and was merely returning from an early morning stroll.

She thought briefly of simply letting George handle the whole matter, but she decided that that course was too fraught with danger. Sending a footman to desire the earl to return home early would give rise to comment, and if she left a note of explanation, he might pursue Jonas and do something in the heat of anger that he would not do after a day's sober reflection. That she was afraid of the earl's temper was undeniable. She was put quite out of countenance by *anyone's* temper. She tried for a moment to think honestly whether what she proposed to do was really done out of concern for Jonas and Portia's prospects, or because she sorely wanted to avoid a confrontation with the earl. She was compelled to admit that the latter weighed more heavily with her at this moment. Besides, the same course of action answered both needs.

She heard the large clock in the front salon downstairs chiming the hour. She had effectively removed Portia from events. If she were to similarly remove Jonas, she would have to act now. Terror of the earl's finding out what the viper—whom she had encouraged him to encourage—had been about to do propelled Jane to her feet. Terror, mixed with a liberal dose of her own righteous anger at Jonas, caused her to shake all over. Disregarding the unpleasant symptom, Jane changed swiftly into a morning dress and threw her black gauze cloak over it. With a dark shawl made into a mantle, she would be indistinguishable from Portia, providing she was not called on to speak.

The clock chimed the quarter hour and Jane began to be concerned that George would return and discover the plot—not unfolding as planned, but not quite at an end yet either—and she went quickly to Portia's door. Rapping on it softly, she whispered, "Portia, it is Jane. Can you hear me?" There was an anguished choking sound which she took as a disgruntled acknowledgement. "I am going to go and tell Jonas that the elopement is off. I have locked your door and I hope you will have the good sense to simply wait until I return and let you out in the morning. If you ring for Stoke, you will have to rouse the whole household before she awakes and hears you, which would ensure that everyone would know of your misadventure. Do you understand? Your brother is still out and need know nothing of all this. I assure you, this is for the best, truly. Nothing good would come from such a shameful beginning."

This last was met by a renewed burst of weeping and Jane looked at the door with a touch of exasperation. She could only hope Portia would eventually see the sense in what she said. Jane turned and made her way down the staircase like a phantom. Fletcher had posted an underfootman by the front door to come and alert him when the master returned, but the young man had nodded off, either by accident or because he was confident his keen ears would hear the earl's carriage through his dreams. Jane passed through the front door like a puff of smoke and was gone.

Chapter Eleven

The Earl of Sefton was not normally a patient man but he allowed himself to be guided by experience, which suggested that anything which could be done during the light of day was rendered ten times more difficult by darkness. Unless she had changed her mind, Portia would be here very soon, but the darkness of the night was undoubtedly slowing her steps. He pushed his hat well down and resisted the urge to pace the distance to the corner of Brock Street, for it was from that direction that Portia would have to come. The chestnuts were growing restive but Freddy had them in hand for the time being.

George gnashed his teeth in silent seething. The very word "elopement" had the power to make him feel violent. Jonas Biddle had been dealt with accordingly. That stout young bumpkin would awake in the morning in an innkeeper's basement with a head very much the worse for Blue Ruin. It might then finally occur to him that the friendly ostler who'd offered him a glass or two of gin hadn't been so wonderful a fellow after all, and that the horses he'd sworn were being harnessed had never existed.

Devil take him! George didn't give a damn what Jonas Biddle thought or felt the morrow. By the time the odious country squire awoke and let out his first moan, George meant to have his sister safely in London. Roger would have his valet *cum* ostler back, and after two consecutive days of full-out activity, his horses would have the day to rest up for a return trip to Bath on Sunday.

The only regret in all this, George thought, was that he had been obliged to abandon Jane at the ball. When Portia had begged to be allowed to attend the dress ball, George had known the game was in motion, for never had there been a girl likely to want to attend a fancy ball at the height of the season. He had intercepted Manning carrying Portia's missive to Jonas. It had only confirmed that they planned to be away this very night. Manning he had dismissed without a character; he wondered if the footman knew how lucky he had been to be turned away without a horsewhipping, too.

Roger, John and Hugh had covered her ably for him at the ball, he was sure, but George still regretted the necessity of leaving Jane so uncivilly. In his initial surge of anger, he had been inclined to hold Jane to blame for allowing the two love birds to reach a state where they could think that elopement was a good solution. Then reason had asserted itself. Jane had openly urged moderation on him all along—she would be the first to deplore underhanded tactics. He had taken comfort from that thought and absolved Jane of any complicity, making it possible for him to greet her with an easy mind at dinner, even when she had delivered the expected news that Portia was too unwell to join them. It seemed like eons ago now, but he had loved making Jane laugh, and seeing her lively and lovely face across the table. He wished that instead of participating in a damnable hoax these last months, he could have been courting her in earnest.

But that must be postponed for yet a while longer.

Now he must deal uncompromisingly with Portia. He would not have scandal cloaking their house again. His father's conduct had been infamous, and George's naive response had served to bring even more ridicule on the name of Sefton. Nothing else could be allowed to mar it, and it was his duty as the head of the family to see that nothing did. If, when Portia came of age, she still wished to marry Jonas Biddle, George knew he would have to swallow his pride and see his sister wedded to a fortune hunter, but for now, he did not have to countenance it, and he would *not* countenance it.

On another head, George felt a great deal more optimistic. He loved Jane Oxenby with almost painful intensity. If he could make her his countess, he felt it would go a long way toward redeeming the family name, for he loved her so utterly that no one would suppose for a minute that *this* Earl of Sefton would look outside of his marriage for female companionship.

George had just come around to this happier thought when he saw a dark figure hurrying down Brock Street. He snapped his fingers to attract the attention of the groom. Freddy nodded and stepped to one side in anticipation of a quick start, as his lordship had said was needful.

Just seeing Portia's furtive manner, the way she kept her head down and clutched at the cloak to keep her face hidden proved to George that she knew what shame attached to elopement. It was as well for his cause, because she evidently did not have any romantic notions of being swept up in her beloved's arms and kissed under the circumstances. Instead she paused nervously some feet from the carriage. This was the sticking point if there was one. He gestured toward the stairs and held out his gloved hand to assist her.

Portia glanced around one last time and fairly leapt into the chaise. George quickly put up the stairs and mounted the driver's box, all without a word being exchanged. The chestnuts jibed momentarily as Freddy let go of their heads, but then they felt the steadying touch of George's hands on the reins. Just as quickly as the earl felt sure he had established a proper contact with their mouths, he gave the horses the office to start. Freddy jumped onto the box behind, and they were leaving Queen's Parade behind.

George felt a grim satisfaction. Portia was being taken from the scene without so much as a whimper of protest. This second trip to London in as many days would tax not only his horses but himself, which was to the good since it might serve to blunt the fury he was feeling toward his sister at this moment. Little fool! For all she knew, she might have just taken flight with the devil himself! George had thrown a heavy cloak over his multicaped driving coat to make his outline more like Jonas's, but with his hat pulled down low on his forehead and not a word spoken, he could have been anyone. It reinforced George's conviction that Portia was too ingenuous to be allowed to decide whom she would marry.

Inside the chaise, Jane chased away white spots of dizziness. Tension had nearly undone her. At the top of Brock Street she had remembered her spectacles and snatched them from her face lest the lenses catch the light of a street lantern and betray her identity to Jonas. Still quite breathless with apprehension, she lay back against the cushions. No lantern had been lit within the post chaise, a wise precaution against anyone's recognizing its occupant, and her breathing slowly returned to normal.

Bath to Gretna Green was over three hundred miles as nearly as Jane could figure, but she had no intention of riding above a tenth of those miles. No, she calculated that at the first change of horses, they would have covered a sufficient distance to reliably deflate the scheme. She would make herself known to Jonas, deliver the scold she was *boiling* to throw in his face, and force him to return her to Bath. Or perhaps, fearing the earl's wrath, Jonas would hire some other conveyance to take him on to Longchamp without delay, while allowing Jane to return to Bath in this one.

Jane detected that they were leaving town already, and making good speed on the more open road. She was a little surprised, for she would have guessed that her cousin was an indifferent whip—but perhaps he was only sitting next to a hired coachman. She considered herself lucky that Jonas had not spoken, nor desired to sit inside with her. The post chaise swayed only slightly from side to side, and the forward and back motion was not uncomfortable either. Plainly Jonas meant to make good time without making his bride-to-be ill. Beneath her fingers she detected the softness of Moroccan leather seats and cushions, and she could smell the rich fragrance of wood polish. Such quality and comfort were unusual in a hired conveyance. Along with the lap robe and a hot brick at her feet against the chill of a spring night, it all made Jane think a good deal higher of Jonas than she desired to at that moment, for he had contrived to carry his beloved off in greater style than Jane would have credited.

Still, he was sadly lacking in his brain box if he thought he was going to succeed. Even if Jonas had the temerity to come about and return for Portia, George would certainly have arrived in Lansdowne Crescent by the time Jonas back-tracked, and meeting one's love in Queen's Parade was far different than spiriting her out of a locked room in her brother's house, and from under her brother's nose! Jane did not think even Jonas so lacking in intelligence that he would undertake such an endeavor.

No, nothing of moment could go wrong from this point forward. The worst that could happen was that Jonas, in a pet over being thwarted, would leave her stranded, but Jane was prepared even for that eventuality. She patted her reticule again and heard the reassuring clink of coins. It was the last of the expense money George had given her, and it would be adequate to pay her return fare to Bath via stage coach if need be.

Jane took a deep breath and allowed herself to believe that all was truly going to turn out for the best. Her terror of George's finding out subsided, her anger at Jonas was momentarily set aside until it could be unleashed, and deprived of the two strong emotions, Jane was left feeling limp. Putting on her spectacles, she adjusted the shutter at the window so that she could watch the fields and hills beyond, bathed in light from the wan half moon. One hour passed, and then two, but despite blowing up the toll gate keeper and passing onto a post road, they hardly slacked speed at all as they passed first one and then a second posting house.

Certain that by now they had gone well beyond the point where she need worry about Jonas returning to Bath to retrieve Portia, Jane began to grow fretful. She knotted and unknotted the fringe of her silk shawl, and wondered whether Jonas meant to drive the hired horses into the ground. Another hour passed and she knew that even the best-bred horses in the world must soon reach the limits of their endurance. She finally heard the groom up behind blow on the yard of tin again. Leaning forward, she saw a posting inn ahead on the left. The post chaise began to slow, and by the time they entered the yard, a fresh team of gray horses was already being led out. Jane was relieved that they were stopping, but still felt troubled for some indefinable reason.

The carriage drew to a halt and tilted as someone jumped down from the forward perch. Not knowing whether it was Jonas or merely a coachman, Jane waited, listening to the voices outside. Considering that it was well after midnight, the response to their arrival was nothing short of astonishing. Jane concluded that Jonas must have greased a great many palms to inspire this level of service. When no one else descended from the driver's box, Jane reached for the door handle, prepared to alight.

"Oh, yes, m'lud, it's a great pleasure to have the keeping of your lordship's horses," she heard a man saying. "Such blood as this ain't often easy to handle, what with their owners treatin'em like pets, but these!—why, they've been brought along proper, that's certain."

Jane's hand froze at the sound of *m'lud*. Then, just as she realized he had also said "your lordship," she heard the deep and unmistakable voice of the earl.

"I am sure my head coachman will like to hear it. He saw many a life lost in the Peninsula due to a horse improperly trained to duty under fire. It gave him a particular dislike of bad actors."

Jane could scarcely breath. George! What in God's name was she to do?

"The Peninsula, eh?" said the landlord. "I daresay you was in the Hussars, a horseman like yourself! It's a rare treat to watch our lordship handle the ribbons, as I said to my wife yesterday when you was a-pullin' in for the change."

Jane's heart was racing so fast it threatened to burst, but George sounded as relaxed as if he were out for a Sunday drive. She could just picture the languid air with which he was conducting the conversation, his finely carved lips in a polite half-smile.

"No, the Guards," he replied, "but only owing to a wager which I lost—some friends of mine having proposed it while I was less than fit. Ah! I see that the change is complete. I regret making such a request at this time of night, but I must ask that the chestnuts be hot-walked for not less than a half hour."

"Yes! Certainly, m'lud!" the landlord cried. "A half an hour at the very least! May I interest your lordship in some food and drink? My wife took the liberty of preparin' a tray . . ."

"No, I thank you," the earl replied smoothly. "My business in London is pressing. I must be there before first light."

"Them grays is prime goers," the landlord said enthusiastically. "You'll have no trouble doin' it, which ain't a thing I could say about many!"

Jane heard the earl's booted feet crunching on the fine chips of stone which covered the yard. She quickly roused herself from paralysis to reach out and snap the shutter closed. Shrinking back against the seat, she prayed with all her might that the earl would not open the door.

The carriage tipped and then centered over the axles again. Jane released a pent-up breath and sagged against the seat as the post chaise pulled out onto the roadway. Tears sprang into her eyes and she cursed herself for a coward. Once or twice she had withstood the earl's temper, and even made quite a good show of defending her position, but *this* was altogether different. George would be furious—of that there could be no doubt. She could only suppose that he had gotten wind of the elopement and decided to take preemptive action himself. Mile after mile passed beneath the post chaise as Jane thought all around the problem of what to do. She found herself crying from sheer nerves, and dabbed at her cheeks until they were raw. George would be incredibly angry to find that she had known of the plot. Would he even give her a chance to explain what she had done, and why? Lacking certainty that he would, Jane swiftly decided on a course of action which would obviate the need for a face-to-face discussion: she would simply wait until they stopped to change horses again and slip away unseen, out the door opposite where the earl stood.

But she had reckoned without George's prime horseflesh. It seemed their powers were limitless, and the carriage raced on through the night without stopping. A few times she heard the horn sound as they approached a toll gate, and Jane crouched against the door, hoping for a chance to leap from the post chaise when they slowed to pay the toll. But a brief survey of each toll gate revealed that the cover to be had around or even near it was scanty at best. If she left the post chaise, she would immediately be conspicuous, and the toll collector would certainly raise a hue and cry that would reach the earl's ears.

In a lather of fear and increasing tension, Jane waited helplessly. The best she could hope for—and hope was thin on the ground at this point—was to slip away unseen when they arrived in London. In the capital, she knew, buildings

192

Now you can get Heartfire Romances right at home and save

Heartfire Romance

Get 4 Free Heartfire Novels: A $7.80 Value!

Home Subscription Members can enjoy Heartfire Romances and Save $$$$$ each month.

ENJOY ALL THE PASSION AND ROMANCE OF...

Heartfire

ROMANCES from ZEBRA

After you have read HEART-FIRE ROMANCES, we're sure you'll agree that HEARTFIRE sets new standards of excellence for historical romantic fiction. Each Zebra HEARTFIRE novel is the ultimate blend of intimate romance and grand adventure and each takes place in the kinds of historical settings you want most...the American Revolution, the Old West, Civil War and more.

SUBSCRIBERS $AVE, $AVE, $AVE!!!

As a HEARTFIRE Home Sub scriber, you'll save with you HEARTFIRE Subscription You'll receive 4 brand new Heart fire Romances to preview Free fo 10 days each month. If yo decide to keep them you'll pa only $3.50 each; a total of $14.0 and you'll save $3.00 each mont off the cover price.

Plus, we'll send you these novel as soon as they are publishe each month. There is never an shipping, handling or other hid den charges; home delivery i always FREE! And there is n obligation to buy even a singl book. You may return any of th books within 10 days for ful credit and you can cancel you subscription at any time. N questions asked.

Zebra's HEARTFIRE ROMANCES Are The Ultimate
In Historical Romantic Fiction.
Start Enjoying Romance As You Have Never Enjoyed It Before...
With 4 FREE Books From HEARTFIRE

TO GET YOUR
4 FREE BOOKS

MAIL THE COUPON BELOW.

Heartfire Romance

FREE BOOK CERTIFICATE

GET 4 FREE BOOKS

Yes! I want to subscribe to Zebra's HEARTFIRE HOME SUBSCRIPTION SERVICE. Please send me my 4 FREE books. Then each month I'll receive the four newest Heartfire Romances as soon as they are published to preview Free for ten days. If I decide to keep them I'll pay the special discounted price of just $3.50 each; a total of $14.00. This is a savings of $3.00 off the regular publishers price. There are no shipping, handling or other hidden charges. There is no minimum number of books to buy and I may cancel this subscription at any time. In any case the 4 FREE Books are mine to keep regardless.

NAME _____

ADDRESS _____

CITY _____ STATE _____ ZIP _____

TELEPHONE _____

SIGNATURE _____

(If under 18 parent or guardian must sign)
Terms and prices subject to change.
Orders subject to acceptance.

HF 111

GET 4 FREE BOOKS

HEARTFIRE HOME SUBSCRIPTION
SERVICE
P.O. BOX 5214
120 BRIGHTON ROAD
CLIFTON, NEW JERSEY 07015

AFFIX
STAMP
HERE

sat hard upon one another, so she might have a chance to be away from the chaise and blend in with other early occupants of the street before the earl or his servants even noticed her. With care and a great deal of luck, Jane felt she might contrive to escape undetected.

As dawn neared and the sky lightened, Jane perceived a new threat. If they *did* stop and the earl alit, he would see at a glance that his passenger was not Portia. Jane burrowed down with her head on the Morocco cushions and pulled the shawl over her head, feigning sleep. It had been a long and wearying night, however, and when at last the post chaise drew to a halt in front of Sefton House, her sleep was no longer feigned.

George unbent his long legs and leaped to the pavement, wincing in pain. In the gray, predawn light, Belgrave Square looked quietly elegant, a bastion of peace and privacy, but it was entirely illusory. Footmen and parlor maids were already at work in each huge domicile, and any of them might glance out one of the numerous windows and spy a struggle as the Earl of Sefton forcibly escorted his sister into the house. Several of his noble neighbors took their places in Parliament, but the news of a forcible repatriation in Belgravia would far outstrip any other news so paltry as, say, confiscation by the French of more British goods.

Thus, George was glad to see his major domo already awaiting his arrival. His message had said to be ready at any hour of the day or night, and Timothy had not conveniently assumed it meant anything but exactly what it said. His major domo greeted him and opened the door of the post chaise, letting down the stairs as George stripped off his driving gloves and felt the uncomfortable return of circulation to fingers which hours of gripping the reins had reduced to numbness.

George's arms ached and his feet hurt like the devil from

193

hitting the pavement after hours of sitting. He glanced inside the post chaise and saw a motionless figure entangled in a cloak and shawl. Seeing Portia slumped over and sleeping like a baby when he himself was exhausted did not improve his temper. "Take my sister inside, please, Timothy. On no account is she to leave Sefton House without my express permission, even if you are forced to lock her in. Is that clear?"

"Perfectly, my lord," Timothy replied, his face expressionless.

"Oh, and Timothy, all your best discretion, if you please."

"Naturally, my lord," his major domo said with a bow. "And would your lordship care for some breakfast?"

That almost made George smile. "And wake the wizard belowstairs before dawn? I think not, Timothy." He shrugged off his driving cape and retrieved his evening cloak from the driver's box. Timothy helped the earl to settle it around his shoulders with so much aplomb that one might have thought he routinely robed his master on the sidewalk in front of his house. "Thank you, Timothy. I believe I shall walk around to my club. There may yet be some interesting play going on, and there will certainly be some excellent drink. I do not know when I will find it convenient to return. I will send a note round if I want dinner."

"Very well, my lord."

And with that, George strode off toward Grosvenor Crescent, which let onto Picadilly. He tested the edge of his control and found it sorely wanting. He knew it would be profoundly counterproductive to talk to his sister while the events of the night were still fresh in his memory, and the fatigue engendered by a sleepless night would cloud his reason. He knew he must be rested and calm when he spoke to Portia.

Picadilly was all but empty, and Green Park on his right still somnolent. A certain heaviness in the air suggested that rain might be on the way, but that did not suit his plans for returning to Bath, so he thought instead of the journey just completed. First the chestnuts and then the grays had made a splendid run of it. George breathed in deeply, savoring that fact, and the fact that he had managed to subvert Jonas Biddle's plans. When he arrived at Wattier's, there were a few of his particular friends still at the tables but the smell of freshly made coffee lured him to the lounge. There was some desultory talk of countermeasures to be used against the French, but George followed it only until the steward delivered a letter to him.

It was almost certainly from Clarisse, as all ticklish correspondence, including that from one's mistress, was best directed to one's club, and away from the prying eyes of secretaries, butlers, and wives. It was on a tray, facedown, a precaution against another man recognizing a familiar handwriting, but for George, who had never and would never carry on an affair with another's man wife, the safeguard was unnecessary. He turned the envelope over idly, realizing he had no interest in its contents. He had not even given a thought to driving around to Half Moon Street, though a warm bed and an obliging lover waited there.

He had barely thought of Clarisse in the past two months, and even the one brief visit he had made to her had been more out of habit than desire. Strange, he thought, when she had previously been such a fixture in his life. But it was Jane who came to mind now when he wished to share a thought or ask an opinion, Jane he could not wait to see again when he was away from her. Jane, with her proud, straight nose, and the crystalline blue eyes that glowed with humor whenever they shared an unspoken joke, the ivory brow which creased in agitation when she was telling him something she thought he would not like to hear, and the sweet mouth that trembled when he looked at her the way a man should look at the woman he loved.

George allowed himself to be drawn into a game of cards, and later, into a breakfast the likes of which could have been had in no other club in London. Sleep became imperative following the substantial meal, and George stretched out in a corner chair.

He awoke considerably refreshed sometime around dusk, and the staff discreetly offered him a change of linen and a razor. Dinner and some deep play occupied him for several hours, but at last he knew he was only putting off the inevitable. He declined the porter's offer to whistle up a hackney and set out for Belgrave Square on foot, welcoming the light rain that helped to clear his mind.

He entered his own house convinced that he was calm, but as he looked at the staircase and thought of going up it to confront his sister, he knew he was not. He let a liveried footman take his cloak and went into the library, where Timothy had had the foresight to order all the candles lit against his master's return. George's hand and eyes were steady as he broached his third bottle of brandy that evening. The first two had not kept him from winning three thousand pounds from a Johnny Raw at the gaming table, and this third would in no way impair him from doing the duty that awaited him. Portia would be an easy mark in any case.

She had had many hours in which to rue her mistake in daring to run away with Jonas Biddle. Her fear would, he hoped, make her more than willing to do as she was bid now. But what was best to do? He could return her to the care of her recently discharged governess, send her to finishing school in France, or perhaps Switzerland, or ask his godmother to arrange for her presentation along with her own daughters as originally envisioned, and launch her into London society, or—most convenient of all—hire a companion and a courier and ship her off to join their mother in Italy.

The last thought, though not something he would do, put George in a vile temper. His mother deserved better than to have her maternal obligations thrust upon her via international courier, and he was damned if he would play jailer to a girl who had no more sense than to run off in the night with Jonas Biddle, who in all likelihood would have ruined her and negotiated a settlement with him afterward. George set his glass down and climbed the stairs with no charity in his heart.

There was no light showing beneath the door of the room that had been prepared for Portia's use when their mother had closed up her own home and gone abroad. George wondered if Portia could already have retired. He knocked and received no answer. He knocked again.

"Portia?"

Still there was no answer. He turned the knob and the door gave way. Setting foot inside, he immediately perceived that the holland covers had not been removed, nor the fire lit. Baffled, he turned.

His major domo watched apprehensively from the second-floor landing. He saw that things were not as his lordship expected them to be. It was a circumstance Timothy daily lived in dread of—"let everything be to his lordship's satisfaction" were the exact words that formed a part of his nightly prayer. It looked as if the Almighty had failed to intercede on behalf of a lowly major domo this time. Timothy drew himself up and moved to the foot of the stairs. If there was one thing that would worsen the situation, it would be to be behindhand about it. His lordship appreciated a goer.

"If your lordship is looking for the female . . ."

George spun around. *Damn all soft-footed servants!* "The female?" he snapped. "What do you mean by calling my sister a female? Where is Portia?"

Portia? Timothy felt his courage falter. The earl looked dangerous up on the landing, his eyes glittering in the way they always did when he was on the verge of having drunk too much. Evidently he was laboring under the delusion that it had been his sister sleeping in the post chaise.

"The young woman you brought here, my lord—she is in your bedchamber. You gave no other instruction and as she

197

is not family nor known to us, I assumed . . ." *Assumed you had brought a lightskirt here.* He left the thought unfinished.

"What do you mean, not family?" George inquired icily.

"Just as I say, your lordship. She is not family." Timothy ascended the stairs. "And these," the major domo said with all the dignity of a servant long used to displays of temper from his master, "were found by the undergroom who tidied your lordship's post chaise."

Timothy proffered a pair of gold spectacles that caught the light of a candelabrum on the landing. George uttered a quick oath and took the spectacles. He stared at them for a moment, his expression growing cold, and then he turned to stare at his door at the end of the long corridor. Timothy pulled out the key to the earl's bedchamber—the woman had been most insistent upon leaving—and followed his master as he strode off down the corridor. George tried to open the door and when it would not open, he turned to the major domo, who handed him the key and rapidly retreated down the corridor. The instant the door was unlocked, the earl threw it open with so much force that it crashed back against the wainscoting and wood could be heard splintering.

Jane arose quickly from her place by the fire. "Your lordship!"

George surveyed her in cold silence. She was attired in a demure morning dress, a pale green voile patterned with clusters of violets. "I see that you availed yourself of the opportunity to change after the ball," he said, his hands clenched tightly behind his back.

Jane looked at him in consternation. His face was a blur, as was everything else—the streets outside, the gaslights along the pavement with their halos of light like blobs of creamery butter in the rain. "I . . . I had planned to return to Bath by this morning," she said, her voice shaking with nervousness. "I did not wish my clothes to occasion comment."

He moved closer and she could see that his face was taut with a rage all the more chilling for the polite, controlled way he spoke. "I expect you would like these," he said, holding out her spectacles. She stared at his hand for a moment and then recognition dawned.

"Oh, yes! I said they must have slipped off in the carriage, but your servant did not say they had been found," She put them on and saw the room clearly for the first time. It was large, which she had known, and furnished in a grand and entirely masculine style, all gilt and maroon and heavy wood.

The earl said nothing but stalked around the room, pensively surveying her from every angle. Anger suffused his every movement and animated every feature of his face. Jane found it took all her will not to keep turning so as to keep facing him.

He stopped suddenly. "Explain your presence here."

Drawing a deep breath, Jane said, "I . . . I discovered that my cousin meant to elope with Portia, so I determined to meet him in her stead." She paused. "I meant to let him drive far enough away that he could not return for her before you had returned home."

"Did you?" he said softly. "Did you indeed? And then?"

His handsome face was so distorted by fury that it terrified her. She pulled off her spectacles so that she would not have to see the look on his face. "And . . . and then? Well, Portia is at Lansdowne Crescent, thoroughly chastened, I hope, by the lecture I gave her, and so that is the end of it. Well, except that I did not anticipate that you would take Jonas's place and so we are here now, and . . . and I hope we may simply return to Bath, you and I, and find Portia there, and Jonas, and no one the wiser."

"Do you seriously expect me to believe that they have not gone forward with their plan to elope?" George said, his voice steely. "You created the perfect diversion for their one obstacle, after all, did you not? I have been entirely deceived these last twenty-four hours into believing I had my sister away from that vile man."

Jane blinked. "I assure you, I did not come away to meet the carriage with the intention of deceiving *you.*"

"Then why did you not immediately make yourself known to me?"

"I thought you were Jonas! I did not know that it was *you* until after it could have made no difference," Jane protested, "and then . . ."

"And then?" he inquired roughly.

"I . . . I saw nothing to be gained by it, for I had foiled their plans and that was all that mattered."

A harsh laugh met this statement. "Oh, come, come, Miss Oxenby! Do I strike you as a cretin? Am I some lame, tame country boy to believe you stood in their way? You who have done everything in your power to forward the match since the first time I laid eyes on you?"

"But never by stealth!" Jane cried indignantly. "No, Portia will yet be in Bath, and in the very room where I left her," she declared, "and Jonas will be . . . well, wherever you left *him,* I suppose."

"And you," George said softly, "what of yourself? It is now, what?—fully twenty-four hours that you have been 'alone' with me. Assuming you are unintelligent for a moment, did you not stop to wonder how you would explain your absence? And how you came to spend the night in my company without benefit of a female companion? And why you are here in a bachelor's residence tonight?" His voice was soft but his eyes were like flints. The firelight reflected shards of flame in them as he moved closer.

"But the only ones who know are your servants," Jane said, a quaver in her voice that she could not quite master. "They surely would say nothing. I have found them most adamant in obeying your lordship's orders. Truly, I would have left the instant I awoke this morning if I could have enlisted their aid in retrieving my spectacles and discovering the way out. Other than them, there is only Portia, and she would not gainsay you . . ."

The earl stood directly in front of her now, every line of his stern face clear even without her spectacles. "If indeed the lovers have not eloped in our absence, Portia will undoubtedly have told Jonas what you intended doing, which is tantamount to broadcasting the news throughout Bath. The deaf will have heard of it! Depend upon it—not a single book will have been opened at Meyler's today. Everyone prefers real scandal to imagined ones. No, my naive, country-bred Jane, you are ruined—quite, quite ruined."

"It does not signify," she demurred hastily. "I have no prospects for marriage anyway, and I live beyond society's reach. Truly, all that matters is that we return to Bath posthaste, before the very damage we sought to avert is done for lack of our presence." Jane licked her lips and took a step back as George loomed over her.

The tight skin across his cheekbone flexed ever so slightly as he surveyed her through narrowed eyes. "That will not answer, will it? If they are yet in Bath, the news of your disappearance—along with mine—is common knowledge by now, and if Portia *has* fled with Jonas, it is now too late to redeem that situation. I could almost hope that Portia *has* married your odious cousin, so that the scandal of their elopement might, at least, be capped by a bona fide marriage. But you, Jane—you undoubtedly expected to be ruined, and you also undoubtedly expected me to wed you in consequence. It is what an honorable man would do, is it not? Am I now to marry you? Was that part of the plan?"

Jane curled her toes inside her soft kid slippers. "No," she said, greatly alarmed by his manner and the suggestion he was making, "certainly not. I am well aware of what you must seek in a bride and I am not . . . that is, I do not feel you owe me any duty . . . I mean, after all, it is partly my deception which placed us in this—"

"Precisely," said George, "but however careless you may

201

be of *your* honor, your presence here reflects on *my* honor. It appears that Jonas will have Portia and her fortune, Miss Oxenby, while *you* shall have me. How neatly the trick has been turned, how well the cards have been played. You urged me to delay our departure from Bath until they could complete their plans, and then you told me my sister was ill when all along you *knew* they meant to elope as soon as I left the house! You deflected me from interfering in their true plans, and put yourself in the way to becoming my wife, all in one clean stroke."

"No!" Jane cried, stung by the icy contempt in his voice. "There was no such intent! I meant only to frighten Jonas. I did not mean to place you in a situation for which the only remedy was that you should . . . I mean, I know that you cannot, indeed you *must* not, be joined to anyone with my background!"

George turned away and lifted a decanter from a side table. A tumultuous sense of betrayal filled him. It was as inexorable as a tide, blotting out all else. It had begun the moment he had entered the room and seen Jane standing there, Jane, who had seemed to him as a goddess, a delightful goddess far surpassing every other woman of his acquaintance.

But now she was revealed to be a schemer of the first water. How much more brilliant she was than Lady Judith Percival and others of her ilk, who had attempted to engage his affection with all the subtlety of a mistral breaking directly over one's head. Jane had cast her lures brilliantly, and won his heart without even seeming to try. In that sense, Jane was every inch the nonpareil he had believed her to be.

The rage over what he had thought her to be versus what he now knew her to be threatened to destroy his sanity. That he had loved her unconditionally, absolutely, made the betrayal that much more complete. Worse still, he could not simply order himself to stop loving her. He wanted to shake his fist at the sky, and scream out to be released from the bondage, but he knew such measures would avail nothing, for the fault was within himself that he still wanted her.

He flexed his hand around the stem of his wineglass and heard a faint snap, a distant intrusion on the storm that raged within. His dream was in ashes and he wanted to hurt the source of the flame.

He turned back to face Jane.

"Some wine?" he said. He held out the other glass, and she took it, her eyes never leaving his face. He strolled to the fireplace and drained the last of the wine from his own glass before throwing the ruined thing into the fire.

"It was so logical of Timothy to put you here, so prescient on his part. Of course, Timothy does not know the meaning of the word, but I think one can be prescient without knowing the word, don't you agree? Timothy has ever been a prescient soul. Did I tell you that I bought him as a young boy? He was a jobber's lad on the Great North Road, at a place called the Bear and Barrel. My carriage stopped and in the very spot where I would have set my foot when I alit was a great heap of dung. Timothy threw his smock down over it without hesitation. I decided he would be wasted there. Any lad of ten with such a strong desire to please and the wit to know how to go about doing it—well, the yard of a posting house was hardly an adequate venue for his talents. He cost me twenty guineas."

Jane shivered. "But . . . but you cannot buy people."

"But you most certainly can," George countered in a deadly calm voice. "His parents were glad to accept twenty quid for him. Money is not always the basis for the exchange, however. Jonas has bought Portia with his scheming, and you have bought me with yours. If I did not marry you, the price would be my honor." He walked to her and removed the wineglass from her unresisting fingers. "And do you know with what currency you will pay me for my honor?"

203

Chapter Twelve

Jane shook her head dumbly, transfixed by the anger in his voice.

"You will pay me in pleasure," he said coldly. "Prescient Timothy knew you were here for my pleasure. You are in the lion's den, dear Jane. You will be the lion's prey tonight, and as soon as can be arranged, you will be the lioness."

Jane stared at him. His assuredness made it seem inevitable, but it was the drink talking, drink that amplified a temperament accustomed to having its own way without question or delay. The sweet smell of brandy on his breath was overlaid by the wine he had poured for them. He was not drunk precisely, but neither was he sober. She knew, for she had seen him in both states. Now he appeared to be in the grip of something far different.

He reached out and grasped her shoulder tightly, curling his long fingers around her upper arm. "Since we are to be man and wife, why do we not simply take advantage of this night? Let us be lovers. It is a *fait accompli* after all, is it not?"

Jane shivered and closed her eyes wishing herself anywhere else at that moment. The man who held her arm so tightly was like a stranger, a stranger she had no desire to know better. She told herself that George had every right to be angry. She willed herself to remember how much she loved him. But in the end, the force of his temper, of his indomitable will, reduced her to a trembling semblance of herself, and she was no more capable of thought than a leaf being swept downstream by spring currents.

He pulled away the lace tucker which she had hastily added to the neckline of the morning dress—hours ago? days ago? Time had ceased to have any meaning. She felt his long, blunt fingers moving over her skin, the touch of their lightly calloused tips against her neck, and then they were behind her, unlacing her dress. A sob of misery formed in the pit of her stomach. She had dreamt of this moment in a vague, virginal way. She had thought often of the night in Coventry, and the curious lightness and melting heat which had accompanied his kiss.

Now she felt a coldness which the heat of the fire at her back did nothing to dispel. The room was silent. Even the beautiful fire made no sound, as the hard coal his lordship's servants had arranged with painstaking care burned down quietly and obediently, throwing off heat and light, but no sparks, or smoke to smudge the opulent red damask bed curtains. All around was a conspiracy of silence calculated to make an unreal moment all the more unreal.

She suffered the silence and the hands, aware of the sob deep in the middle of her which had formed but never been vented. Another joined it, and she tipped her chin up to close her throat against them. She clenched her hands and willed the sobs to stay where they were.

She would not cry, for tears would not move the stranger who was touching her. She would not scream, for no one would come to her aid, and she would not whisper, for there was no tender-hearted man present who would heed soft words, and all the words which could be said in the middle range had been said. They had fallen like tears in the black of night, touching no one's heart.

"Open your eyes," George demanded, his voice soft and emotionless.

Jane obeyed, and beheld the terror of seeing a man she did not know inhabiting the face and body of one she loved. Then she nearly did scream, but her lips felt as if they had been sealed together. The deep blue eyes searched her face for a moment and then held her own eyes locked in their gaze. The rich, brown hair, like sable, fell across his high forehead, and the finely wrought lips were parted, as if he might say something more, but he merely stared at her for a long moment. Then he pulled away the flimsy muslin dress she wore, leaving her in the even frailer shift beneath.

Stoke had threaded fresh pin ribbons through the sleeves and neckline only days ago. Now the tiny bow between her small, high breasts trembled, but not from cold. George's breathing sharpened, his nostrils flaring faintly. With an oath, he clasped her shoulders and dropped his face into the curve of her neck.

To be relieved of his scrutiny left Jane weak with relief. She suffered his kisses along her collar bone with better grace for not having to see his face. He was trailing his mouth along her neck now, nipping at it with his teeth, and breathing harshly. His fingers edged their way through her hair, divesting it of pins and the halo of small satin roses still left there from the ball. She had not thought until now of how incongruous they might look with her day dress, but then she had hardly been in a position to waken Stoke and ask her to redress her hair. Another sob joined the ones already clenched within her. How far away such considerations seemed now.

She had some obscure notion that George might expect her to put her arms around him. In Coventry it had seemed so obvious and desirable that she had done it without deliberation. Now her arms felt like lead. She felt what a bird shot out of the sky might feel as it waited on the ground for the hunter to follow his dog's point—terror, resignation, and a fatalistic curiosity about what would happen next.

Her hair came away from her scalp and fell, slowly and

206

heavily, out of the curves and bends into which it had been twisted for so long. George's lips were at her temples now, and he combed his fingers through her hair, forcing it to fall all the way to her waist. Then he uttered a raw sound and his mouth was on hers with ruthless force, plunging her into panic. She worked furiously to retreat from the assault on her mouth, bending backward, but he followed her effortlessly. His mouth was gone suddenly and she clung dizzily to his shoulders, slowly registering the fact that he was kissing the swell of her breasts now.

His cheeks rasped the tender skin, and the invasion of his mouth in that private place was as shocking as the feel of his whiskers. His hand dropped from her shoulder and cupped her breast through the shift. She wanted to cry out and pull away, protest the intimate plundering, but the look on his face kept her from it. It was mere inches from her own, his eyes closed and his jaw taut.

She turned her face away to block out the vision of the man who bent over her on this travesty of a wedding night. She could not—*would not*—hate him. This was not George Tate, the man she loved. This hard-eyed, pitiless stranger bore no relation to the amiable, laughing man she loved. She felt another sob form deep inside and choked it back. This George Tate had lost his reason.

Jane sought refuge deep in her mind, far from the room where the breathtakingly handsome stranger was possessing himself of her flesh. She spun out a fantasy, willing herself to think of what it might be like to receive these same touches born out of love, with warmth and affection. Desperation lent a miraculous potency to her imagination, and she felt her tension easing as she entered into the spirit of her vision. How different it was! Those lips were not thinned out in lust and anger, but murmuring words of love, the hands moving on her not with cold determination but like a gentle breeze.

George dropped to his knees and Jane was jolted from her fantasy as she felt his hands sliding over her ribs and down to her waist, ever closer to a place she rarely even touched herself. She stiffened and then remembered the comfort that withdrawal brought. She departed from cold reality and the hands that slid over her hips became those of her lover, who caressed her with tender words as well as touch. The dream was so real that Jane dropped her hands to rest on the shoulders of the man, and did not flinch when his long fingers traced down her thighs and calves, and caught up the hem of her shift. He pulled off the dainty kid slippers she wore, and stripped away the silk stockings tied loosely above her knees by garters.

Her powers of concentration faltered when she felt her shift rise, and cool air followed in its wake. She looked down in a kind of fogged dismay to see the fabric pooling at his wrists as his hands rose. His dark head mirrored the movement of his hands as he arose from his knees, taking her shift with him. Pure shock drenched Jane as he came to his feet and she was left trembling and naked. It simply could not be happening—but the hostility on the face of the man she had imagined herself to be in love with told her otherwise.

It *was* happening, and it was not over yet. Not even bothering to look at her face, he picked her up and carried her to his bed. Humiliated by her nakedness, Jane pushed her face into his shoulder, and tried again to enter the place in her mind where she could pretend that what was taking place was an act of love. The ruthless stranger dropped her to the bed and stepped back, his legs braced wide and his expression stormy.

She fumbled for the coverlet, hoping he would look away.

George stripped off his neck cloth and flung it to the floor, and then his jacket. Jane saw it as blurs of color and movement. She had no trouble seeing what was most apparent though, which was the wrath in his every action. She hugged the bolster to herself. This man desired vengeance for a sister he thought spoiled and a marriage forced on him by circumstance. She could not blame him for feeling that she was responsible, but she could not bear to be the focus of such anger either, no matter how well justified. Her shivering increased and her teeth began to chatter.

With a strangled curse, the man who was not George but looked like him stopped in the act of pulling off his shirt. He strode to the opposite side of the bed and drew the voluminous bed-hangings down to the end, blotting out the bleary gas lights shining up from the square below. Jane clutched the bolster closer and knew that she must hold herself together, get through whatever was to come. She clung to the knowledge that he was not being brutal, that he had not hurt her yet, despite being in the grip of a fierce and unreasoning rage.

Hunched among the pillows, she watched as he threw aside his shirt and then his shoes and pants. Even deprived of her spectacles, Jane could see that he had a magnificent physique. Broad shoulders and powerful arms gleamed whitely in the glow of the candelabra on the side table. He stood before her, his fists clenched at his sides, regarding her with steely eyes. Reality seemed to be receding again, for the notion of a man standing naked in front of her was so far outside her experience or expectation that she could not believe it was actually happening.

Jane felt a flush of embarrassment. It manifested itself as a heat in her cheeks that spread rapidly outward to cover her whole face. George walked toward the bed and she closed her eyes, hoping that it was not his weight that was making the bed shift, and not his harsh breathing she heard coming closer and closer. She cast about desperately for escape into the imaginary sanctum that had brought her comfort before.

Her mother! The last summer of her mother's life, Jane had just turned fourteen, and they had spoken of love, and Jane had felt emboldened to ask about marriage. Her mother, exquisitely lovely and so gentle, had smiled. It was that smile which came to Jane now, for it had accompanied words she had never forgotten. Her mother had smiled that serene and knowing smile and told her that there was nothing to compare to being with the man one adored, and who adored one in return.

Jane re-experienced the happiness of that day, the feeling that she had in some subtle way been initiated into life's mysteries. She felt George's hands touching her, taking hold of her shoulders and pulling her up to him. She let the sensation be bound up with that golden day so long ago when she had first felt that to be a woman was something special. Jane kept her eyes tightly closed and focused her thoughts. To be a woman was special, and the most special part of being a woman came in the act of being with a man. She loved George. She let that thought save her as he stroked her trembling limbs and kissed her. The touch of roughness she doggedly construed as the impatience of a lover. She could not stop herself from shaking though, and when he drew the last bed-hanging closed, she stubbornly interpreted it as an attempt on his part to keep heat in to warm her.

She felt his hands take possession of her body and lower her to the bed. She lay back and willed it to be an act of love, sinking into the sunshine of that long ago day. It saved her from the cold fear that lingered just outside the sunny circle of memory, and the truth that what was happening was motivated by anger, not love. She felt George's rough cheeks at her breasts again, and a sensation of wetness followed by a tugging that seemed to wind through her chest and lead downward.

George gripped her waist and pulled her down to the center of the bed. The utterly dense, solid reality of his body next to her became mixed with her dreamlike concentration on the sensations aroused by his touch. His breath came hard and fast, and she felt his chest rising and falling, pressing into her upper arm. His hand was roving lower now, and she shuddered as he neared her most private place. His fingers touched the mound of curls that had always struck

210

her as too abundant, repulsive by virtue of their excess. She tried to shrink away but the hand was insistent. It brushed over the curls and stroked the soft skin of her thighs. He slid his hand down, pulling her knees apart. Instinct prompted her to resist.

"Jane," he said hoarsely, a warning note in his voice.

The sound of her name on his lips shocked her. It was not a mere dream that touched her, but a man, a creature of flesh and blood.

"You are going to be mine, Jane."

No words of love—just a proclamation of possession. Jane turned her face into the coverlet as his knee followed his hand to a place between her legs. He moved over her and Jane clenched her lower lip between her teeth as he opened her legs with the sheer strength of his thigh. His weight would have alarmed her even if his intrusive strength had not. She strove desperately to think of his face in kinder times, and managed to blot out the present with a memory of a day when she had made him laugh out loud.

It became that kinder George, the witty and considerate George, who was kissing her. Jane clung to the thought, and even succeeded in magnifying it. His arms tightened around her and she felt it as a protective embrace. Deep in her imagination, she pictured the day when rain had forced them into the shelter of the rock overhang. That George, with the hopeful, ardent look on his face, was fulfilling the promise of that day with these kisses. He began to stroke her with his body, the hair of his chest first tickling and then massaging her breasts. Jane felt a little breathless, and did not evade his kiss.

It felt less awkward now to have him between her legs. He made a sound in his throat and then his mouth was at her ear. He took her earlobe between his teeth, and she remembered them, even and perfect in the openness of a smile. Her breath quickened a little more. She wondered vaguely if it was his weight on her that was making it harder to breathe, until she

211

realized that he supported his weight with his arms and was not resting it on her. He said her name on an exhalation as she felt something pressing up firmly against the tender flesh between her legs. It stroked at her in unison with the rest of his body, giving rise to an oddly compelling sensation that spread outward from the center of her being.

And then, quite suddenly, the small pleasure turned to pain. All the imagination in the world could not rescue her from the sharp hurt as he pushed into her. She gasped and nearly cried out, but bit down hard on her lower lip instead. Tears sprang to her eyes as the hurt turned to a burning. The man above her was oblivious, rocking against her without surcease and breathing harshly. The sobs which had been locked within her were multiplied as he used her body with cold determination, and only pride kept Jane from letting them out. Tears ran down the side of her face, and she endured the thrusting, praying for it to be over, and for the pain to ease.

It did ease, and then she noticed the taste of blood in her mouth. His movements built in intensity, until with a savage grunt and a last deep thrust, he stopped. The sounds of his breathing filled the enclosed darkness created by the bed hangings. He lifted himself up, his powerful arms taut against her shoulders, and then he rolled away from her. Jane sucked in her breath as he withdrew, for it reignited the burning between her legs.

She turned her head further into the sheets as fresh tears ran down her cheek, more from grief than pain. Was that the end of what would happen between them, or only the beginning? Jane did not know, but she prayed for the former. This, whatever else it might be, could not be what her mother had alluded to.

George fell to one side and lay there. A long time passed and his breathing became barely audible. Jane began to wonder if he had fallen asleep, but there was an awake, pensive quality to his stillness. Growing chilled, she wished she dared reach out and pull a cover over herself, but she feared it would rouse George, and that she did not wish to do. At last she felt the bed shift as he sat up. He pulled the bed hanging aside and the sudden light of the fire and the candelabra was enough to make Jane flinch and turn away.

George stood up and pulled on his pants. When he was done, he spoke to the back of her head, his voice flat and cold. "Now I have had what I wanted from you, Jane, and as soon as may be, you shall have what you wanted of me. Wofford shall procure a special license and you shall be Lady Sefton."

Even less than before did Jane desire that. She turned her head and focused on the pale outline of his face.

"No . . . do not, I beg of you," she whispered. Her throat was tight with unvented emotions. "I would rather return to . . . to my home and forget . . . forget that . . ."

Words failed her. George did not reply, nor did he move, but she felt his gaze on her, intent and appraising. It lasted for a long moment, until Jane could bear it no longer and turned her face into the pillow again. It seemed an eternity before she heard his tread on the carpet, and then the door shutting behind him. She rolled over and drew the heavy counterpane with her, wrapping her chilled body in it. She hugged herself as she stared in dry-eyed misery at the fire.

Its light was reflected throughout the room, in the brass pulls on the furniture drawers, in the fine decanter and wineglasses left on the side table, in the silver bowl and picture frames on the mantel, and in the gilt trim on the bed frame. A thought stole into her mind, about the biblical admonition that one could be in want even in the midst of plenty. Now, as never before, she understood the truth of it. She closed her eyes wearily and waited for sleep.

George Aubrey Tate paced from one end of the library to the other. The elaborate pattern of the Savonnerie carpet was burned into his eyes from hours of making the trip back and forth. The thought which had driven him to ceaseless motion could no longer be pushed aside. He drew to an abrupt halt in front of a window and stared out into the night. Belgrave Square lay quiet, the pale glow of gaslights lending an air of calm respectability. It was almost enough to make George put his fist through the glass.

That would bring the watch running. The watch was ubiquitous in the environs of the wealthy, but it was in the slums and the working-class neighborhoods that monsters were said to roam the nighttime streets, inhuman beasts who preyed on their fellow men. Perhaps it would be as well if he *did* put his fist through the glass. Tonight a beast had been loose in Belgravia.

He had raped her.

Dear God, he had raped the woman he loved.

He could put his fist through a pane of glass, and when the watch arrived, he could confess his crime and they would lead him away. Would they believe him? He could easily supply the corroborating details. He would describe for them the haunted look on her face when at last he had drawn back the bed hangings that had shrouded the horrendous deed, the huge blue eyes bright with sorrow and shame.

And the blood. Not virginal blood, although there was undoubtedly some of that, too. No, the small, almost apologetic smudge of it on her lip, and the drop that had swum down to the corner of her mouth and lodged in the crevice there. And of course, he would tell them about the tears that had left their shiny trails on her cheeks. She had bled and she had cried, and he had not even noticed.

George's knees buckled and he sagged into the window seat. Cold air chased over his bare shoulders as he buried his head in his hands. His cursed temper had driven him to madness. Love had made him elevate Jane to a pedestal too lofty for any mere mortal to occupy and her downfall had incited him to exact a draconian revenge. Revenge had been taken, but revenge on whom, and for what? On Jane, for breaking a compact she had not even signed. That was bitter indeed. Had she known that she was perfection in his eyes? Would she even have aspired to hold that title had she been informed?

He had punished her for not being something she had never claimed to be. He had set out to hurt the schemer, but when he looked into her eyes when it was all over, he had seen only Jane, *his* Jane. Cold guilt clutched at him.

At least his father had gone to women's beds at their invitation. Now the son was revealed as a rapist. How much more despicable a sin it was. *Dear God.* No matter what Jane had done, there was no defense for what *he* had done.

He rose and poured himself a whiskey from the decanter on the half-moon table between the two windows facing the square. It choked him on the way down, and did nothing to cool the rage and shame that was churning inside. He hurled the glass at the cold, dark fireplace. It caught the edge of the fender and exploded into countless pieces. The violence of it spoke to some inner need and he hurled another glass, and then another, and finally the decanter. He reached for a vase, and that too joined the growing pile of destruction.

Timothy flitted into his vision, swiftly lighting candles in the room. George stopped and glared at him.

"Beg pardon, your lordship," Timothy said, impaled on his master's malevolent stare. "I assumed you had retired for the night and I gave orders to the footman to close up."

George looked at him, his eyes dark and unreadable, his jaw clenched. Timothy saw that whatever had taken place upstairs had not been satisfactory. The sound of breaking glass had been indication enough that all was not well, but it was not for a well-trained servant to question what his master chose to do with his possessions, nor could that same servant remain abed when the master was awake and might require him. Timothy walked calmly to the fireplace and lit the coals already carefully arranged against tomorrow.

215

"Shall I bring your lordship some articles of clothing?"

"No." The earl's voice was raw and strained. "I do not wish the lady to be disturbed on any account."

"Very good, sir. Is there anything else you require?"

"Brandy," he said shortly. "A great deal of it."

Timothy bowed and exited. By the incipient light of the fire, his master looked like one of heaven's angels stripped of his wings and fallen to earth. For physique and face, there could be few to rival him, but the mouth was touched by surliness, and the eyes spoke of transgressions too grave to be mentioned aloud.

Timothy assembled fresh glasses and decanted the brandy himself. There was no need for other members of the staff to see the earl in this state. The earl had removed him from hell when he was but a boy; whatever he could do for the earl in return, he would do. He retrieved several blankets from a spare room and delivered them to the library along with the brandy.

The earl was in front of the fireplace, his powerful arms stretched out to support his weight as he leaned heavily on the mantlepiece. His head was sunk between his shoulders.

"If your lordship requires anything else . . ."

"Nothing. Leave me, Timothy."

"Very good, your lordship."

He was almost out the door when the earl turned suddenly. "See to the lady's needs in the morning. She is to have anything she asks for—anything."

"Naturally, your lordship."

The earl's expression was bleak, his eyes deeply shadowed. Timothy left, thinking how easily he could dislike the woman upstairs if she was the cause of his lordship's unhappiness.

Chapter Thirteen

George stared out the window. The world was a cold and dismal place. It seemed to have been raining almost from the moment of his birth. It had most certainly been raining since this same time the night before, when he had walked home from his club. Then he had had no more to trouble him than displeasure over Portia's youthful idiocy. Now he was as close to flat despair as he had ever been in his life.

Jane had not descended all day. His major domo had deftly transferred her to the room set aside for Portia's use. Timothy had explained that it was so she could avail herself of Portia's clothes and toiletries, but George suspected it was because Timothy wished for his master to have the use of his own chambers. George had gone up that morning to dress, and he had looked first at the bed. All trace of the hollow-eyed woman he had left there was gone.

He elicited from Timothy the information that a young parlor maid had been found to assist the lady, and that the lady had desired a bath. No, she had not eaten any breakfast, and the lunch tray which had been sent up had been returned untouched. To George's request that she join him for dinner, she had offered no reply, leaving his major domo to shrug when asked if she would be coming down or not.

And so George did not know if he would be granted his

only desire on this rainy day, which was to see Jane. He knew that somewhere in the void that was his heart at the moment, he would have to find some words, too, but how did one find the words to explain rape?

Wofford had arrived from Charlcombe shortly after lunch, and been despatched to disturb the Sunday peace of certain well-connected persons who would see to the issuance of a special license the instant the registry opened in the morning. Another stop had completed preparations for a wedding which would be accomplished in the morning before half the *ton* were even sitting up in their beds sipping chocolate.

His mother's spiritual advisor had agreed to attend them in Belgrave Square. His short, polite reply to George's request conveyed puzzlement between the lines, but on the surface it was all airy congratulations to his lordship. He did not say, nor did George need to be told, how disappointed his mother would be not to be present when her only son married, but George also knew how lucky he was that his mother was not there to witness the disgraceful circumstances of that marriage.

George had waited and waited for Jane to come down to dinner. At last, sometime close to ten o'clock, he had sat down by himself. The food had gone into his mouth by rote and he suspected that he had arisen from the table before the meal was half over. Now he stood again in the library, watching the rain fall, as he had all day. He wanted to see Jane, to find some words to mend what was perhaps unmendable, to take her hand, to swear that he had never meant for it to be like this, and that he loved her.

A soft knock at the door made him swing around eagerly. "Enter."

It was only Wofford.

"I am retiring, your lordship. I believe all is in hand for the morning."

"Thank you, Wofford."

"Please forgive me for asking," Wofford said, "but I

would be remiss if I did not. Shall I send the customary announcement to the newspapers tomorrow?"

George thought for a moment. It was a shabby business from start to finish. His task now was to render it as unexceptionable as possible.

"I believe you should. Not to do so would only encourage more comment, and I dare say we shall have that by the trunkful as it is."

"Just as you say," Wofford replied stiffly. He withdrew, taking his faintly disapproving air with him.

The earl turned again to stare out into the night. Had Wofford ever felt passion for a living creature, for something besides his scholarly interests? Could his secretary understand that love could be deformed by disillusionment into uncontrollable rage?

But what anyone else might think paled in comparison to what really concerned him at the moment. Jane had not eaten all day. Was she ill? Or was she sick in her soul, the way he was, over what had happened? He *had* to see her. Once formed, the intention could not be undone. He went upstairs. What would he say? He would start with the obvious, that tomorrow they would be married in the blue drawing room. There was a light under the door and he knocked.

There was a pause and then a short, heavyset girl opened the door. She had a plain, open face, and looked at George with frank curiosity.

"I wish to see Miss Oxenby," he said, a little disconcerted by the directness of her gaze.

"Yes, your lordship." The girl curtsied briskly and opened the door further. She nodded toward the fireplace.

Jane sat in an upholstered chair. She did not glance up until George stopped a few feet away, and then she looked away again rapidly and removed her spectacles. The exotically lovely face showed no emotion.

"You are well?" he asked.

Another quick glance. "Well enough. And you?"

George shook the question off impatiently. "Yes, yes." He walked around a few paces so that he could see her better. Her face was pinched. The high-bridged nose was as determined-looking as ever, the high cheekbones glowing by the fire's light, but there was a vacant look about her, as if Jane herself was not quite in residence.

The young girl who had opened the door sat down in a cane chair by the window. She lacked the trait of senior servants of being in a room without seeming to listen or watch. George debated sending her away and then reflected that Jane might have ordered her to stay. The thought shamed him and took from his tongue the nascent apology he had composed while staring out at the rain all day.

"I have arranged for a ceremony to take place tomorrow, to make official in the eyes of the church what we have already discussed," he said instead. "It is my intention to leave immediately thereafter for Bath."

"Shall I dress for traveling then?"

"If you feel up to the journey."

"Portia will need me. She will be wondering what has happened to me." She looked up. "Unless you have already thought to send a message to her informing her of my whereabouts?"

George shook his head. Doubt was growing on top of shame. Did she really expect to find Portia at Lansdowne Crescent? Apparently she did. She was looking him full in the face for the first time since he had . . . He broke off the thought. Portia could not have been in Bath all this time, but if Portia and Jonas had returned to Bath from Gretna Green, it would be well to publicly accept their marriage, for Portia's sake.

"*If* she is in Bath, I believe Portia will have need of both of us. Were it not for my sister, I would minimize the scandal of our precipitous marriage by going abroad on an extended honeymoon."

Jane lowered her eyes and turned her face away from him, but George could see her chin quivering. His frozen heart went a degree colder. The little maid was no accident. Just the thought of being alone with him was enough to make Jane cry.

"I assure you, Portia will be in Bath," Jane said softly, "though I know you do not trust or believe me. It is an unfortunate basis on which to begin a marriage."

Not *our* marriage, George noted dully—*a* marriage. It was a mockery before it even began. Would she ever laugh again at something he said?

"If there is nothing more . . ." Jane said, standing up. Her color, never encouraging, faded to the pure white of galanthus pushing through snow.

George lunged forward but the little maid was there before him, her stout frame supporting Jane's weight.

"I'm sorry," Jane whispered. "I can't think what's come over me . . ."

"She didn't eat nothin' all day," the maid said to George, "and I ain't going to leave her, neither, not like this." She looked at him with a challenge in her eyes.

Jane's eyelids fluttered and her head seemed to go loose. "Stand aside," he said curtly to the maid. He got his arms around Jane just as all the resolution went out of her muscles. He carried her to the bed and laid her down. He turned to the maid angrily. "If you care for your mistress, you should have made her eat."

"'Twasn't *me* made her lose her appetite," the girl retorted.

"Nevertheless, it is you who must help her to eat something now," George snapped, a flush of shame suffusing his words with heat.

"Oh, well, then, if it pleases your lordship, I'll try," she said derisively.

George regarded the maid through narrowed eyes, unsure of who he was angrier with at the moment, her or himself. "I'll see that something is sent up immediately." He took a last glance at Jane, who was struggling valiantly to keep her eyes open.

"Don't be upset with Ellen, please," she said faintly. "Truly, it's not her fault."

George knew well enough whose fault it was. He turned away with a stifled curse and strode to the door. The maid followed him, pulling up short when he stopped abruptly with one hand on the doorknob.

"What was your name again?" he demanded.

"Ellen."

"Pack your things, Ellen. Her ladyship has need of someone like you, to protect her from me."

Jane clutched at the small bouquet of flowers that already looked sadly wilted. Her tan day dress and brown velvet spencer were unseasonable, and did not look well with the bright May flowers, but of the dresses Portia had left behind in London, it was the one which best suited Jane's mood.

How joyless it was turning out to be to be married to the man she loved! He sat across from her in the post chaise and slapped his fine leather gloves across a muscular thigh encased in fawn pantaloons. She turned her head and stared out at the passing scenery, feeling her throat tighten. Lying in George's bed after he had left, she had been as lonely as she had ever been in her life. It had had nothing to do with being alone, for she had never minded her own company, but with the lack she felt inside. It was a sort of yawning emptiness that had been echoed by the room around her as the candles burned down and went out, one by one.

She had been intimate with the man she loved, but he had taken her with a subdued violence that had stripped her bare and left her less than she had been before, and not—as she would have expected—more. It was not that it had been *horrible,* for it had not been, but that it had been *nothing.*

It was the perfunctory wordlessness with which he had used her body that had left her empty. The teasing, playful lover she had inadvertently crawled into bed with in an inn in Coventry was the man she had fallen in love with, with his roguish eyes and gentle hands. Perhaps since he had intended to make her his wife it was to be expected that he would treat her somehow otherwise than as a lover. She heard John Marshall's crude words again, from the day at Sydney Gardens when she had eavesdropped without meaning to, about how the earl needed only a good breeder in a wife, someone on whom to get a few brats.

Jane twisted her flowers with clammy hands. Perhaps she was never to meet the lover again. Perhaps it was not good manners, bad *ton* even, to behave like a lover toward one's wife. Tears formed in Jane's eyes. Before she had thought that the earl felt something for her, but now she had no such conviction. He sat opposite her, irritation evident in the way a muscle jumped repeatedly in his cheek. To be held in esteem one day and dislike the next was too awful. She felt as if George had used her with the same ruthless efficiency with which he used his horses—not roughly, not inconsiderately, but as if he had driven her to his intended destination and then dismounted and left her to the ministrations of others while he attended to the next item of business.

That impression was reinforced when they stopped to change horses. George alit from the carriage and ordered a light luncheon without consulting Jane. It was the innkeeper who escorted her inside, the same man she had heard talking to George the night of the elopement. George had evidently informed the innkeeper of her status, for he beamed and addressed her as "my Lady Sefton" over and over. George seemed to prefer seeing to his horses to taking his wife into lunch. He remained in the yard, running his hands over the legs of the grays they had driven from London, and then inspecting the chestnuts as they were led out and put to.

Beyond asking if she had been satisfied with the lunch, George said nothing as they resumed their journey. It had been four hours since they had been married, and not one word of conversation had passed between them. They had nothing to say to one another, where before they had talked of so many things. Now it seemed she was only Lady Sefton,

223

and would serve him in the night, so that he might beget an heir by her. It was a melancholy thought. Judging by his aloofness, George no longer regarded her even as a friend. He would take his real pleasure with this *chère-amie*, and save his affectionate nature, which she knew he possessed, for that other woman. For all she knew, he had even spent last night with her.

They pulled up to the door in Lansdowne Crescent just as it turned two o'clock. Feeling listless, and reluctant to face Portia, Jane lingered in the carriage, but Portia came dashing out the door, her fair hair flying and her pale, pointed face a mixture of disbelief and vexation as she spied George on the pavement and Jane inside the carriage. Ignoring her brother's startled look, she hurried past him and spoke to Jane through the open door of the carriage.

"Jane!" she cried. "Wherever have you been? I have been sick with worry. Why, Jonas declared that you must have been murdered and your body hidden in a shallow grave somewhere! We have not known *what* to think!"

"Lower your voice, please, Portia," the earl said in an undertone. "We will not discuss the details of our personal life on the pavement."

His sister spun around to face him. "But . . . but *you* disappeared too, George! Jonas said it did not at all make sense that you had *both* disappeared!"

George stared at her in his most autocratic manner, the heavy-lidded eyes dark with warning. "Be quiet until we are inside, Portia, or I will clap my hand over your mouth." He held out his arm. "If you please, Jane."

Jane stepped out of the carriage and tried to convey to Portia with a look that she should not provoke the earl. Jane did not think she could give the younger girl any comfort just at the moment if she should be overset by her brother's temper.

Fletcher awaited them at the door. "Welcome back, my lord."

"Thank you, Fletcher. Have the goodness to inform the

staff that Miss Oxenby did me the honor of becoming my wife this weekend."

"Indeed, your lordship, and may I offer you and Lady Sefton my congratulations," Fletcher said warmly. He smiled at them in the manner of someone who had won some money.

Portia stared at them goggle-eyed. "What? Married? You can't mean it!"

"Thank you, Fletcher," George said smoothly. "Please see that coffee and sandwiches are served in the drawing room in half an hour."

"Certainly, my lord," Fletcher said.

George propelled his sister forcefully into the drawing room before she could say some of the indiscreet things it was all too clear she was on the verge of blurting out.

The instant the door closed behind them, she took Jane's hand. "How did this come about, Jane?" She peered closely into her friend's face. "Please, you must tell me all! I have been so worried. Thank God for Jonas or I would surely have gone out of my mind these past few days!"

George stared at her, a hard look around his eyes. "And where is Jonas, Portia?"

"He went to pay a call at Charlcombe, to see if they could tell us anything of your whereabouts," Portia said. "The most shocking thing was that Jonas was set upon on Friday night and left for dead by some despicable ruffians, so we could not help but think that you, too, might have been the victim of foul play! He asked everyone we could either of us think to ask in Bath what they knew of your plans, but no one knew anything more than we did! It was only this morning that he hit upon the notion of calling at Charlcombe."

"So we have Jonas to thank for having communicated to half the world the news of our absence," George said grimly.

"Oh, but everyone was already speculating as to where you both might have gone. There was even conjecture over whether you might have eloped!" Portia had the grace to glance at Jane and color a little as she said it. "But Jonas said it would be the most shocking thing if that was what you *had* done, for you are a peer of the realm and Jane is a nobody!"

George raised his eyebrows, his whole demeanor radiating displeasure. "Pray do not make matters worse by prating to me of Jonas's ill-advised utterings. As Jane and I are both well beyond the age of majority, there can be no question of indecent haste or youthful indiscretion attaching to our marriage. We are quite old enough to be allowed to marry where we see fit." George directed a pointed look at Portia.

Portia swallowed, her eyes going round. "Of course, only . . . only . . . Jonas, well . . . Jonas *did* feel obliged to write to Lady Eugenia Hanover of Jane's absence, and yours too, of course!"

"Of course," George said. "It was the most natural thing in the world that Jonas Biddle should have involved himself in our family's private affairs."

"Well, and so it was!" Portia declared. "Jonas is Jane's cousin, after all. And as for me, well, it was Jonas who supported me in my hour of need. After all, I was locked in my room and left there all night to worry and to wonder, and then, of course, Jane did not come back and let me out in the morning as she had promised! I assure you, I was never so glad to see a friendly face as when Jonas arrived on Saturday!—particularly as Stoke had to fetch Mrs. Briggs to let me out! I do not blame you for what you did, Jane, for I know your intentions were good, but it was mortifying to be found so, and very disagreeable to be forced to contrive a lie to conceal the truth."

George looked at his sister through narrowed eyes. "And would the truth have been so very preferable, Portia?" Portia went a shade paler. "Tell me, do I find you as I left you, an unmarried girl, or do we await the return of your husband?"

Portia drew a strangled breath and dropped Jane's hand. "You! It was you who had Jonas beaten so cruelly!"

George gave a harsh laugh. "Your swain does have a turn for the histrionic. Since when is being got drunk and locked in a cellar tantamount to being beaten?"

"He *was* beaten!" Portia cried passionately. "He was in the most awful state when he came here on Saturday!"

"If he had any marks on him, it was doubtless due to his having fallen down while blundering about in a darkened cellar. What you cannot seem to comprehend, Portia, is that Jonas Biddle is the biggest codswallop imaginable. I assure you, Roger's valet is an accomplished pugilist, but he would not have deigned to exchange blows with the likes of Biddle unless he felt the necessity for it, which I am quite sure he never did."

Portia's mouth worked agitatedly but no words escaped her lips. George strolled across the room and stopped by the pianoforte. He idly leafed through several sheets of music before turning to look at Portia again.

"You do not answer. Did he carry you off and marry you as planned? Or did he perhaps merely spend the night here?"

Portia found her tongue. "You are despicable! We are not married nor has Jonas done anything at all dishonorable! On the contrary, he has sat with me by the hour and held my hand and said everything he could to ease my worries!"

"That would include the interesting suggestion that we had perhaps been murdered and our bodies left in shallow graves?" George asked.

Two bright red spots bloomed on Portia's cheeks. "It was a thought which could not be avoided when we had been two full days with no word from you!"

"Let us cut line," George replied, surveying her coolly. "You *did* intend eloping with Jonas, and would have had Jane not prevented you from leaving the house, and, of course, had I not arranged for Jonas to be waylaid. Have you any idea of the unhappiness caused by your childish impulse?" Portia stared at him mulishly. George walked back across the drawing room and stopped in front of his sister. "Because of your willful stupidity, Jane was forced to marry me, a fate which she finds distasteful in the extreme!"

Jane could not stop herself. "No!"

George turned swiflty. His face went still, his heavy-lidded blue eyes piercing as he regarded her.

Jane faltered under such intense scrutiny. She laced her fingers together and stared at the floor. "When I said I did not wish to marry you, it was because I did not wish you to sacrifice yourself for the sake of my reputation," she explained. "It was not that I had any aversion to becoming your wife."

"Portia, please have the goodness to absent yourself."

"But . . ."

"Now," George said, his gaze never leaving Jane's face.

There was the sound of hoofbeats in the crescent. They stopped outside and Portia rushed to the window. "It is Jonas," she exclaimed. The sound of the front door being opened reached them.

"Tell Jonas that if he has any pretensions to being a man, he will go upstairs and await me in my study. Then you may come back in here and keep Jane company, and you will confine yourself to pleasant topics and not burden her any further with your sophomoric misadventures with Jonas Biddle."

Portia flew out of the room and presumably into the arms of her much misunderstood paramour. George clasped his hands together behind his back and said, "We must talk, Jane. There is a great deal that needs to be said between us, but first, I must humbly ask your forgiveness for not believing you when you told me the truth in London."

Jane slowly lifted her eyes and looked at him. "If all you wish for is forgiveness on that score, then it is yours."

George drew a deep breath. From beyond the drawing room door, they could hear raised voices in the entry hall. "I also wish you to know that I am deeply sorry for . . . for the way our marriage was accomplished."

He stopped, his chest too tight with shame to go on. Jane reached out a hand but he shook his head. "You cannot

228

conceive of how I have cursed myself for letting my damnable temper get the better of me. How much heartbreak might I have saved if I had kept my feelings in check and not . . ." He squeezed his eyes shut and rubbed the bridge of his nose with his thumb and forefinger, as if he had a pain there which would not go away.

There was a knock at the door and Portia put her face into the room. "Jonas has gone upstairs to await you." She tipped her chin up. "He says he has no reason to fear anything you might say."

"Yes, yes," George said impatiently. "I will be done here presently. Please occupy yourself elsewhere for a few minutes."

The door closed. Jane waited anxiously to hear what else George might say. Her spirits had been rising with each passing moment, and she barely prevented herself from going to him when he ran his hands through his hair and a look of profound unhappiness crossed his face.

"I do not wish you to think me a monster, Jane, and yet I behaved monstrously toward you in London."

"I did not think you *were* a monster," she said, gazing at him steadily, "only a man who felt himself provoked beyond bearing."

He stared at her. "Can you possibly mean that? Oh, Jane, I wish it may be true. I have spent considerable time in the past few days pondering how it is that I could have treated you as I did, how I could have so far lost my head as to have—" He broke off as his neck reddened and resumed again only after a long pause during which he composed himself. "I do not deserve your understanding but there is something you do not know, something which in no way excuses what I did, but which may give you some foundation for the generosity you are showing me."

He walked toward a window and spoke to the view outside, his voice firm but emotionless. "I am predisposed to loathe scandal, owing to an incident which occurred when I was quite young. Another man accused my father of

229

seducing his young wife, but my father refused to meet him. The refusal was as shocking as the accusation itself. It became something of a *cause célèbre*, and the affair eventually reached my ears. I believed my father to be an honorable man who was merely refusing to defend himself against a scurrilous lie."

George turned, the lines of his handsome face strained. "I was at university at the time, but I went to London and waited for my father's accuser outside his club. He accepted my challenge, though to give the man his due, he later said he'd been tipsy and had misunderstood my purpose. He'd thought I was there acting as my father's second. He was a man with a great deal of pride. I think that when we met the following morning, he understood that I, too, had a great deal of pride, accentuated, naturally, by my extreme youth. He knew full well that I would be mocked for having defended a father so indisputably in the wrong, and I thank God that he did not add to my disgrace by sending me away with my tail between my legs. We drew blades against one another and he used his experience against my youth so that we both fought in earnest without either of us being seriously hurt. He drew blood and professed himself satisfied, and as a sop to my pride, I think, added that he had no wish to be obliged to flee the country."

George paused, his expression bleak. "Only afterwards did I learn that my father was a notorious philanderer, a fact which my mother had contrived to keep from my sisters and me. My father actually laughed at me for what I had done, and I acquired the sobriquet 'Selfless Sefton' for so stupidly putting myself foward in his place. My mother persuaded me to go away on the Grand Tour. When I returned from the Continent, I had gained in size and wisdom. I silenced my remaining detractors with my fists."

He looked at Jane at last. "I resolved that there would never be another breath of scandal in the family. I tried to lead a blameless life, but then first Horatia and now Portia have nearly brought scandal down on us. I would not have

230

harmed you for the world, Jane, but when I thought that you had colluded to . . . to create yet another scandal, I lost my mind." He paused and added in a barely audible voice, "I would understand if you had no wish to perpetuate what had so abominable a beginning."

Jane removed her spectacles and slowly folded the temples down. "Is that what you want?" she asked. "To be released from this marriage?"

"No! That is, I am not . . . unhappy that we are married." He could not declare his love for her when he had raped her only two days before. It would seem like nothing more than a self-serving falsehood meant to buy back her good opinion. And there was that in his character that would not allow him to abase himself any further than he had already, to admit the shameful truth that revenge and anger and love had become tangled up in the same act.

"I see," she said, staring at her spectacles.

"I have no right to ask it, but is there a chance that you can forgive me for what I did?"

"Understanding and forgiveness are different matters," she said. "One proceeds from the head, the other from the heart."

"And I have forfeited any right to either," he said flatly.

"I did not say so, but when you ask for something that comes from the heart, you must accept that it is not there to be given on the instant. It comes, if at all, only in the fullness of time."

"Will you give me that time, Jane?" He waited, hardly even drawing breath as she looked inward for her answer, the crystalline blue of her eyes dazzling in the afternoon sun streaming through the window. There was a knock at the door and George smelled coffee. "Just a moment!" he snapped.

Jane emerged from her reverie and glanced toward the door. "They will wonder why we do not admit them," she said hesitantly.

"Let them," George said. "This is too important."

231

"Is it?" she asked softly.

"It is to me."

"Then I shall give you the time you ask for."

Jane resisted the urge to bolt and run when she went upstairs and found Stoke organizing her clothes for a transfer to the third floor.

"Oh, your ladyship!" the elderly abigail exclaimed. "May I offer you my felicitations on your marriage?"

Jane glanced behind her to see if Portia had entered the room and then realized with a start that the ladyship Stoke was addressing was herself. She managed to thank the abigail and tried to back out of the door, but Stoke was not quite finished.

"I have been with the family nearly fifty years, your ladyship, and so I make free to say that I am sure you will be very happy. I have known the earl man and boy, and while he has a passionate nature—very like his grandmother, make no mistake!—he is a fine man, with a deep sense of what is owed to duty and honor."

"Yes, I am sure that is true," Jane said uncomfortably. She did not want to dwell on the thought that George was a man with a highly developed sense of duty and honor, for it led directly to the only reason he had married her.

"I shall have all of your things in place in a trice, my lady, with the help of the footman Mr. Fletcher has sent up. You need not worry that you will be at all inconvenienced. What would your ladyship wish me to do with the young person who has arrived from London?"

Jane had to think for a moment. "Oh! Ellen!"

"Yes, my lady, that is what she calls herself, though I think she has a fair way to go before she can call herself a lady's maid."

"No, of course not, or rather, I am sure you are quite right. Stoke, only if you do not have any objections, I shall use her in that capacity. Perhaps I can rely on you to give her some few pointers on how best to go about the job?" Jane asked hopefully.

Stoke appeared to consider it. "Well, she will not do at all for dressing your ladyship's hair," she said firmly. "Your hair is by far too long and thick to be entrusted to a mere amateur. I think it will be best, if your ladyship approves, to engage the hair dresser to come in daily from now on. After all, when one is a countess, it places one under obligation to always appear to best advantage."

"Of course," Jane said unhappily. It had been delightful to dress up and go to balls when she was plain Jane Oxenby, but Stoke pointed out an uncomfortable truth, which was that now she had taken on a much more substantial and visible role. She plucked up her courage and went on to another topic that concerned her. "I am a little apprehensive over how Ellen will manage around Henry."

The light of battle flashed in Stoke's eyes. "There will be no difficulty on that head. Henry is a great deal too accustomed to having things his own way but I will see to it that he does not bully the girl! I shall speak to him, your ladyship, rest assured. There is a very adequate dressing room, and a sitting room abovestairs for your use, and Ellen can see to your needs without ever crossing Henry's path."

Jane thought it important to mention that Ellen was a very forthright girl.

"Good!" said Stoke. "She can very forthrightly tell Henry to keep to his own side of the street then."

Jane lowered her head to hide a smile. "Thank you, Stoke, and thank you for your service to me prior to my marriage."

Stoke's expression softened. "I have served countesses of Sefton nearly all my life, your ladyship, and gladly, but I am grateful to you for not requiring my services upstairs. It is no secret that I am not a young woman. I will be happy to train Ellen for you, and happier still not to have to climb those stairs."

Jane thought of Nanny, of how her joints grieved her, and the way the years had slowed her steps. "Stoke, I hope you will feel free to tell the earl when you wish to retire. That is, I know he is very mindful of the service you have rendered to the family, and I know he means for you to enjoy a comfortable retirement when you feel the time is right."

Stoke nodded with a satisfied look but said nothing, and Jane made good her escape. The thought of her move to the third floor to share George's quarters filled her with foreboding but she mounted the stairs anyway, to see how Ellen was faring. She found the girl in the midst of boxes, trunks and open drawers, struggling unhappily to fold a shawl with tissue between the layers. Seeing her mistress, the short, heavyset girl laid the shawl aside.

"I hope you aren't expecting me to know all about what's to be done just yet," she said, gesturing at the mess surrounding her. "It's a right lot, and that woman, Stoke, has been after me since I walked in the door to do this, that, and the other. I tell you, miss, I can only do as much as I can do."

Jane smiled. "Then we shall be fellow travelers, Ellen, for I am new to my role, too. Just do your best and I will have no complaints—and Stoke means well. I have just spoken with her and I think you will find she sincerely wants you to succeed, and will offer you all the help she can."

An apologetic cough from the doorway alerted Jane to Fletcher's presence. "Beg pardon, your ladyship, but cook wishes to know if you have orders regarding dinner tonight."

"Me?" Jane stared at him, furiously resisting the urge to look around once again in search of the ladyship being addressed. Ellen's plain "miss," though inaccurate, was far more comfortable to her ears. "Well, as it is already so late in the day, I imagine cook is only asking to be polite. What he has on hand is what he will have to prepare, naturally."

"Naturally," Fletcher said agreeably. "And Mrs. Briggs has asked me to say that she will wait on your ladyship at your earliest convenience, to discuss the details of the housekeeping."

"Oh. Could we not simply go on as before? That is, I wish

you will tell Mrs. Briggs and cook and . . . and the rest of the staff, that everything has been most satisfactory up until now, and that they need not consult me unless they wish to."

Fletcher sketched a bow. "Of course, my lady."

Jane turned when he was gone and Ellen went over and closed the door. "Now I know it's not my place," she said stoutly, "but I'm going to tell you, miss, that that's the quickest way to work if you want the staff to take advantage. Don't you be a giving them leave to think they're the masters."

Jane collapsed into a chair. She felt she had gotten off to a fair start with Stoke, mentioning retirement and generally acting as she ought—as a countess ought—but Ellen was obviously not going to let her rest on her laurels. "But I am only used to running a country house," she said weakly. "I have not the least idea what to order for dinners such as the earl sits down to, or what to tell Mrs. Briggs we need to order for such a grand house as this."

"Flowers, miss!" Ellen cried with sudden inspiration. "That's the answer!"

"Flowers?"

"It's what his lordship's mother always orders, great bunches of them, miss! I never saw such flowers until I was hired to work for her—fair took my breath away when I first saw them. Then, when she went away and I was told I'd be working at his lordship's house till she got back, it was the first thing I noticed, miss—no flowers. Order flowers, and tell that butler fellow you expect the staff to do its job proper and not to bother you with nothin' that ain't important."

Jane was so impressed with the simplicity of this concept that she stared at Ellen.

"I ain't said nothing I shouldn't have, have I, miss?" Ellen asked apprehensively.

"Oh, no, no, Ellen, indeed you have not! It is a marvelous suggestion. I shall act on it tomorrow. Thank you!"

Ellen smiled. "And you needn't worry about bein' strict with *me*, miss, for I'll be doin' my best for you no matter what! Though," she added darkly, "that little fellow what serves his lordship hadn't better call me a parlor maid again!"

There was another knock at the door and Portia's face appeared around the corner. "Oh, good—you are here," she said advancing into the room. "I must speak with you, Jane." She glanced over at Ellen, who immediately curtsied and disappeared into the adjoining dressing room, softly shutting the door behind her.

"What is it, Portia?" Jane asked.

"Lavinia Digby is below. She heard you had returned and has come to ask if I can attend the theater with them tonight, since we are back on a normal footing."

Jane gaped at her. She thought of the chaos in the dressing room, with clothes being unpacked and distributed everywhere, of the staff below scrambling to accommodate the unexpected return of the master, and of herself, just married that morning. "Normal, you say. No, I think you must be mistaken," Jane said.

"Well, pooh! I did not mean normal precisely, but only that as you and George are now accounted for, *I,* at least, need not sit about wringing my hands any longer. May I go, Jane?"

"Why are you asking me and not your brother?" Jane replied fretfully.

"Oh, George is still closeted with Jonas," Portia said.

"I do not think it my place to say," Jane protested. "Besides, in view of . . . of . . . what nearly happened, he may not wish you to go out."

"It is not as if I did anything wrong," Portia protested. "I know you will say that it was only because I could *not* do anything wrong, but that is nothing to the point."

Jane could only gaze at her in wonderment. Truly, it was an amazing piece of reasoning. She wondered what George's reaction might be to it and then decided against finding out. "You may go if the Digbys come here and take you up in their carriage—with Mrs. Digby present, mind you—

and bring you back again as soon as the entertainment ends."

"Oh, thank you, Jane! You are my sister-in-law now, are you not? I am very happy you are married to George, you know. I am convinced he loves you," she said cheerfully as she kissed Jane's cheek.

When Portia had scampered off, Jane sagged back in her chair feeling quite sapped by the events of the day and all her new responsibilities. There had hardly even been time to reflect that this was, in fact, her wedding night. The thought gave her butterflies.

George knocked on the half-open door before strolling in. Ellen, who had come back in when Portia left, curtsied to the earl but did not leave.

"Everything is being seen to?" he asked, glancing around. He seemed so tall and austerely elegant amidst the frivolous chiffons and silks draped about the room, and the gloves and laces and slippers.

Jane swallowed nervously. "Yes," she said, "only I must tell you that Portia came to ask if she might go out this evening." George frowned and Jane hastily explained the decision she had reached.

"Yes, I can see no flaw with that," George said. He cleared his throat. "I have told Jonas that I am lifting the prohibition against his seeing Portia, but that if he sets a foot wrong, I will make him rue the day he was born. The next time I have cause to order him thrown into a cellar, he will not wake up the next morning."

"Oh, George! I am so relieved," Jane said. "I mean, not that you anticipate the possibility of having to murder my cousin one day, of course," she added hastily, "but that you will not forbid them to see one another."

"He's still an ass," George muttered irritably.

"Oh, without a doubt," Jane said.

Tissue paper rustling in the corner attracted George's notice. He frowned at Ellen, who gave him a direct stare in return and then bent to her task again. George cleared his throat. "Wouldn't you prefer to have Stoke serve you now?" he asked.

"Oh, no! Stoke is very happy just as she is and Ellen will do admirably for me," Jane exclaimed.

Ellen shot a sidelong look at his lordship that was far less than servile.

"If you should decide otherwise, Wofford could advertise for a trained lady's maid in London," George said.

Jane concealed the trembling of her lower lip by lowering her head. Ellen was the only one to whom she was not some mythical being all of a sudden—"the countess," or "her ladyship." "I . . . I would like to keep her for the time being," she said.

George shifted his weight and looked uncomfortable. "As you please," he said. "I only meant that as her appointment was an interim solution, we might do better now, but no matter." He straightened up and said briskly, "I have received word from Charlcombe in response to a note I sent them. They wish to call on us this evening. I will respond in the affirmative, if it suits you."

Jane nodded, wondering what she had done to put him out of countenance, but he excused himself to attend to other matters and she was left to her speculations. Hugh, John and Roger arrived punctually at nine, just as Jane and George were arising from dinner. John Marshall was his usual bright-eyed self, behaving as if nothing out of the ordinary had happened, and Roger Creighton bent graciously over her hand with a kiss and a nicely phrased wish for happiness. His handsome features were schooled to politeness, but his eyes were alight with appraisal when they rested on her, as if he took some secret delight in trying to determine from Jane's face some snippet of a truth known only to her.

When Hugh had shaken George's hand, he turned to Jane. George watched him closely as he bent over her hand and said something pretty. Jane might have thought he was motivated by jealousy had she not known that George's feelings towards her owed nothing to affection and everything to duty. Hugh's expression was wistful, and there was a hint of sadness in his face, but he said gallant things, and made amusing chat for the balance of the evening.

The Digby entourage arrived near midnight, and Jane and George went outside to meet the carriage at the curb. Jane urged the whole party to alight and join them inside, but Mrs. Digby declined. She leaned forward in her carriage and said to Jane with the warmest of smiles, "Congratulations, my dear! I wish you very happy. I hope you will allow me to call on you in a few days' time, when you are more settled, so that I can hear the complete story of your whirlwind marriage!"

Lavinia sighed gustily. "It is too romantic for words! Oh, to have won for oneself the love of the earl, and then to inspire him to such lengths—Portia has told us that the earl simply could not *wait* to make you his!"

Jane felt her face flame at the unwitting accuracy of Portia's account, but Mrs. Digby saved her from having to answer by saying, "As if anyone could be surprised! La, it was clear to anyone with eyes in their head how it was with the earl. Why, they only had to look at his face whenever he set eyes on you!"

Jane mumbled something unintelligible and backed away from the carriage. The party from Charlcombe announced its intention to depart, too, despite Jane's nervous encouragement that they stay longer. Apprehensive about what would happen when she retired for the night, she nevertheless had no option but to take a candle from the footman and make her way upstairs as George walked their guests out to the street. She parted from Portia on the second-floor landing and continued upward.

Ellen was waiting, perusing a copy of *La Belle Assemblée*. She set the pocket book aside the instant she saw Jane. "Oh, miss," she declared, "you look all done in."

"It has been a long day," Jane said.

Ellen's wise young face hardened. "And neither has the

239

last two days been easy for you," she said. "Come, miss, and let me help you into your night things."

"Yes," Jane said wearily. The effort to be what she was not was taking a toll on her. If all had been right with George, it would have been different, but that was not the case. Despite his apology and her acceptance, there was still a strong undercurrent of tension between them. Rather than think about it, Jane said to Ellen, "Do you frequently refer to *La Belle Assemblée?*"

"Oh, no, miss," Ellen said. "Until tonight, I never knew what it was, but when I went belowstairs for dinner, Miss Stoke, she made me a present of it. She says it's last year's, but that I should study it, and when I know it fair enough, she'll lend me her new one to look at. She says I've got to know fashion better nor you do, if I'm to be of any use dressing you."

"Yes, well, that will not be at all difficult," Jane replied listlessly.

Ellen lifted away the gossamer evening dress of deep blue faille. She hung it over her arm and looked at Jane with great deliberation. "Thank you, miss, for saying as how you want me to stay on. I mean to stand by you as you stood by me, for I know what I'll never tell about what you been through. When I first laid eyes on you, it was like . . . well, like there wasn't no one inside your skin. I thought they'd gone and stuck me with a crazy woman, miss, though I seen soon enough that wasn't the case. I was glad enough when you talked straight, but still, I knew. Men ain't always kind, miss, though I'd as soon you didn't ask me how I know that. If you want, I'll stay all night, like last night, and every night from now until we go where you'll have your own bedroom—back to London, or out to the country, that Henry says."

Jane tried to reassure her with a lackluster smile. "I thank you, Ellen, truly I do, but you mustn't worry for me." She accepted the night rail that the girl held out, slipping it over her head and working her silk drawers off beneath it. "I will manage. I must."

Ellen thrust her chin out but she did not contradict her mistress. Jane washed her face and cleaned her teeth, and let Ellen brush out her hair, all without another word, until the girl led the way through to the bedroom. The room was elegant and gracious, pale sea greens and malachite, and white furniture accented with gilt. It was neither masculine nor feminine, but comfortable for either—or both, thought Jane with an uneasy shiver.

Ellen paused in the act of pulling back the sheet on the low, broad bed. "Are you sure, miss, about me staying?"

"Yes, Ellen, quite sure," Jane said.

She had promised her husband time to see if things could come right between them. What sort of start would it be if she were to pass this night on the divan in her sitting room? Feeling sad and tired and scared in equal measure, Jane lay down and put her spectacles on the bedside table. Ellen went around the room, defiantly snuffing out all but two candles.

"You deserves your sleep," the girl declared. She loosened the bed curtains made of deep green jacquard and lined with plain cream silk. "Since it's mild, I'll just leave them halfway, like so."

"Thank you, Ellen." Jane closed her eyes. The bed was remarkably comfortable, the pillows cool and soft. She lay drowsing, thinking how soothing the light of the remaining candles was, and then realized with mild surprise that sleep was stealing her thoughts away.

Chapter Fourteen

George hurried Henry through the usual routine and Henry was visibly grumpy about it, his expression saying that his lordship should either allow his valet to do his job properly or give orders that he not wait up for him. George paid no attention. His mind was too much on the *rapprochement* he hoped to achieve with Jane. He had apologized to the extent that his pride would allow, all the while knowing how dismally short of the mark it fell, but Jane had been generous enough to accept what paltry repentance he had managed to choke out.

Then he had set in motion every phenomenon he could to reinforce his good intentions—directing Fletcher to seek his orders from Jane as mistress of the house, inviting his friends to call on them and pay homage to her as his bride, gritting his teeth and allowing Jonas Biddle to run tame around Portia again, and sending a note to a certain jeweler in the Strand.

He paused with his hand on the doorknob when Henry was gone. Taking a breath, he turned it and went into the bedroom quietly. The bed curtains were partially drawn and he went to the foot of the bed. Jane was asleep. He felt his body relaxing. She was curled on one side, the long, thick hair streaming out behind her on the pillow.

His heart swelled with the love that circumstance had kept him from expressing. He intended to apologize with his body, and demonstrate his love with his lips and his hands. By bringing her pleasure where he had caused pain before, perhaps he could convince her that he loved her, so that eventually he could say the words without them seeming to be a convenient lie.

But not tonight. He loosened his dressing gown and laid it aside, fighting his disappointment. She looked so peaceful, and he knew she must have been very tired to fall asleep so fast. He gingerly slipped under the covers and settled his weight slowly, so as not to waken her. She seemed so young, and so lovely. He studied her face by the light of the last candle. Just two nights ago, he had turned and seen fear and revulsion on this face. His gut coiled with the memory.

He closed his eyes and drove the thought away. He had been a fiend, but to think about it anymore would paralyze him with guilt. He wanted so much to take her into his arms and begin the love affair he had meant to have with her all along. He reached out and stroked her cheek lightly, wishing that he had not been the cause of the tears that had marked them before.

Jane sighed and smiled, a small smile that made a tiny dimple appear in her cheek. George ventured to move closer, slipping his arm beneath her neck. Her hair smelled so sweet, and her skin was smooth and satiny in the candlelight, the beautiful nose as determined-looking in sleep as ever, and the chin so familiar and dear. He settled next to her gently, trying not to disturb her sleep, and knew that he had begun loving her the first moment he had laid eyes on her. This was what he had been wanting for so long without giving words to it, and now he must go about it with stealth, like a thief in the night, lest she awake and think he meant to hurt her again.

Her soft breath fanned across his neck and he matched his breathing to hers, trying to fall asleep. Sleep refused to come.

His body was too aware of hers, and his heart too alive to her presence. He bent his head and brushed her hair with his lips.

Jane murmured and he went still, and when she settled again, he made himself stay still, too, for as long as he could. Then he raised his hand and ran it over her hair. It was such glorious hair, all riotous reds and golds in the depths of it, flashing and dancing as vivaciously as Jane herself. He combed it through with his fingers, and lightly stroked Jane's back with his fingertips. Oh, how he wished she were awake, so that he could make love to her!

Jane came slowly up from sleep, where she had been dreaming of someone touching her lovingly. Nanny had sometimes patted her back and stroked her like that, when she had been very young and could not fall asleep, but this was different. She wanted the dream to go on, though, and she made a contented sound in the back of her throat.

A thumb traced the outline of her ear and warm breath rushed over it as someone kissed her jaw. It was vivid enough to wake her the rest of way, and quickly. Without even opening her eyes, she knew where she was, and who it was that lay next to her. An icy fear rushed through her. She thought of pushing away and running before it was too late, but then she perceived tenderness in the touch, and it arrested her.

"Jane."

The word was a whisper, a plea—nothing like the cold command of two nights ago. Jane kept her eyes closed and felt his kisses moving across her face. A roving hand captured her hair and bunched it at her neck, all the while he went on kissing her cheek, moving up to her temple. A nervous heat rose in her stomach as he massaged her neck and tasted along her hairline with his lips. It was so astonishingly different from the other night that Jane could not believe it was the same man touching her.

The niggling thought nudged aside pleasure and she whispered very softly, "George?"

He broke away from kissing her and his reply came back on a ragged exhalation. "Yes, my darling?"

Jane had no rejoinder. The sole point of her question had been to be quite sure that it was her husband who was kissing her. Now she knew by his voice that it was, and her astonishment was complete. The gentleness in his voice and the endearment by which he had addressed her were quite remarkable. Hoping against hope that the physical side of their marriage would not be as painful as before, Jane lay utterly quiet, determined to let him have his way without provoking or angering him. Before they had argued, and then she had resisted. Maybe he would go on being gentle if she could just be quiet for him.

Before long, his hands were sliding over her in a way that made Jane shiver with enjoyment. Her body was still heavy and relaxed from sleep, and every part of her seemed ready to respond to his touch. He nuzzled her neck and she felt her pulse quicken. She dared to open her eyes and saw his dark, rich hair falling over the magnificent brow as he moved downward. Tendrils of heat swirled through her as his lips found the indentation at the base of her throat. He shifted and she saw that the three buttons of his linen nightshirt were fastened so that she could see nothing of his chest. It came as a disappointment.

He looked up and saw that her eyes were open. He gathered her into his arms and kissed her. "Oh, Jane, let me love you," he whispered.

The heavy-lidded blue eyes searched hers for an answer. Jane was mesmerized and could not think how to answer. She tilted her head and stared in fascination at his finely chiseled lips. Without any forethought, she closed her eyes and leaned toward him. His mouth descended, and all of his tenderness seemed to communicate itself through the touch of his lips.

He made a throaty sound which jolted her out of her blissful state, until she realized that he was expressing approval. The sound did not tell her that, but his response to the kiss did. He reached for her waist and pulled her firmly up against him. The feel of his arms around her was good, and Jane melted into the kiss further. His mouth was patient tonight, teaching her how much there was to be had from the simple expedient of pressing one set of lips against another.

He cupped the back of her head and tipped it, breaking the contact between their mouths. Jane regretted it deeply, but she soon discovered that it was a necessary prelude to something else she liked. Bit by bit, he unbuttoned her frilled nightdress, and his lips initiated each new area of exposed skin to the shivery pleasure of his kisses. Jane began to feel quite dreamy again, though she was fully awake now, and alive to her husband's caresses. The gradual baring of her skin was so much easier to abide than the way he had callously stripped her before . . . pleasurable even. When he finally slipped the gown off her shoulders, she gladly freed her arms from it.

"So beautiful, my Jane," he said softly as he drew the billowing folds of material down around her waist. There was a depth of conviction in his voice that sent a twisting sensation through Jane's middle.

It might be mere blandishment but she would accept it at face value, and not demur that she was not at all beautiful. She wanted too much to sink into this dream, counterfeit though it might be. If his sense of duty was so strong that it compelled him to do this with some semblance of affection, then she was glad for once for his devotion to duty.

Jane sank deeper into a state of pleasurable anticipation as George's kisses swept her to an ever more sensitive plateau. Her breasts were aching, and she felt an almost irresistible urge to curl her spine so that he would come to them sooner. She wanted to reach out and put her hands to either side of his head, but she did not. Reason asserted itself at a deeper level. The wrong response from her might provoke a repetition of what had happened in London. She

246

knew too little about these matters to take a chance. Not to respond at all was safest.

But as hard as she tried, Jane could not completely suppress the small whimpers of pleasure that formed in her throat when he finally kissed her breasts. Urgent sensations coursed through her when he slid his hand beneath her nightdress and pulled her up to lay alongside him. The smooth palm of his hand massaged her bottom, and it intensified the delirious thrill created by his mouth. He nudged her nightdress downward and she felt it go with no regrets as his fingers played along the length of her leg, and lightly stroked the backs of her knees. He raised himself to toss the gown aside and unbuttoned his nightshirt. He stripped it off and Jane saw it go flying in a blur, leaving him naked. She focused in fascination on the thick, dark chest hair that contrasted with the pale skin of his shoulders and arms. It covered him from collarbone to breastbone and then tapered to a narrower line that decreased until it disappeared where her gaze would not go, below the taut waist.

She began to breathe with difficulty, as if she were running. George took the peak of one of her breasts into his mouth and pulled at it. Jane gasped involuntarily as a wave of satisfaction washed through her. It coursed through her whole body, leaving her feeling hot and weak with wanting. She reached out tentatively to rest her hands on George's shoulders, twisting restlessly. His eyes were closed, his breathing strained, and Jane pushed her hips against him as he cupped her buttocks again. Oh, what the touch of his hand there did to her! It was quite extraordinary, and Jane arched her back to press more of herself along his length. And the feel of him under her fingers—the muscles, so deceptively round-looking, were like iron to the touch, and yet they were covered by skin the texture of velvet!

"Oh, Jane, Jane." The words were mere murmurs, hoarse evocations of the tumult within.

Coiling need filled her. It pulsed out from the center of her body to the tip of each finger and toe. Sounds formed in the back of her throat but she clamped her mouth shut to keep them back. The air which was denied passage through her mouth was forced through her nostrils, and she was embarrassed to hear herself making noises like a horse run too long and too hard.

But George seemed not to notice, or care. He raised himself and kissed her, hard. He greedily took her lips in long gulps, and broke away to nip at her chin. Gasping for air, she matched him, kissing his lips and pulling at them with her teeth when he slid to one side. Something ferocious was building in her, something strong that unaccountably weakened her. George slipped his hand over her belly and she opened her legs to him as he dipped lower, not because she remembered that he had not liked her resistance to it before, for reason was left behind, but because her body demanded it.

His hand played over the abundant curls at the mound between her legs and then his fingers slipped into the heated folds of skin below. Jane nearly cried out, but she bit down on her tongue at the last minute. She threw her head back and felt George's mouth at her throat as he stroked between her legs, evoking swirls of exquisite sensation. He dipped one finger inside her and she gasped.

A raw voice came from far away, breathless and yet concerned. "Does that hurt?"

Jane forced herself to open her eyes and found George looking at her. A frown creased his forehead and she could see his nostrils flaring to the accompaniment of the sharp rush of his breath. Jane shook her head quickly. George drew his fingers along the contours of her inner flesh as he watched her face, the blue eyes heavy with desire as she pushed against his hand. The momentary embarrassment she had felt when his hand encountered the wetness between her legs was gone, too. Even if she had somehow wet herself,

248

as she suspected, it must be normal, for George was using the moistness with great deliberation. She stared into his eyes, restless with longing, and opened her legs wider in unconscious invitation. George drew in a ragged breath.

"Can it be, Jane?" he asked hoarsely.

She wanted him so intensely that she did not care if it meant some pain. She nodded. He kissed her swiftly and smiled, a brief predatory smile that changed him from husband to male animal. Jane spread her fingers across his chest and let them run unchecked through the luxuriously soft hair there as his hand sought out the heat between her legs again. She melted against his exploring touch as he opened her with his fingers, pushing first one and then more within her. She welcomed the increasing fullness, throwing her head back and clutching at his shoulders. Female sounds of wanting squeezed upward through her unguarded throat.

He went still and Jane felt a quick burst of fear. Had she done something wrong? She felt herself plummet from the threshold on which she had been poised. Her heart beat quick and heavy in her chest and she looked at George from under her lashes. He regarded her intently.

"I want you, Jane. Do you want me?" He stroked her softly with his thumb, sending a shudder through her. Shyness reasserted itself as Jane felt the intimacy of what he was doing to her, but desire won.

She nodded slowly. His eyes darkened and he withdrew his hand. He raised himself to his hands and knees, his lithe body suspended over hers for just a moment, and then he was on her, the breadth and the length of him uncompromisingly heavy and masculine. But he kissed her as he settled between her legs, and fear—which had been vying for supremacy over arousal—was replaced by a resurgence of the heated need he had been forging within her.

He reached down between them and opened her flesh for the incursion of his own. His breathing was strained, the gleam of his teeth just visible through his parted lips as he watched her. He sank into her a small way and withdrew, and then again, going deeper each time, until she could feel his body up tight against her mound, and the tightness within of being filled by him. Jane tensed, waiting for pain that never came. He began to move, withdrawing and then pushing into her again so that his body stroked her the way his thumb had earlier.

Jane obeyed the prompting of her body to abet the rhythm. A brief, possessive smile lit George's eyes and then he claimed her mouth. Fire fanned down her throat and across her breasts. Jane kissed him eagerly, and grasped his sides as he thrust into her. The muscles at his waist bunched beneath her fingers, unbearable exciting in their power. Slow, silky echoes of the passion she had felt before when he had used his fingers to explore her were reignited deep inside her.

She raised her hips as he plunged into her. So intent was she on meeting his motion that she did not notice at first that his tempo was determined by the touch of her hands. When she did discover it, she began pulling him to her in a rhythm that answered the burgeoning flame between her legs. Exquisite sensations overtook her, and she was powerless to stop herself from crying out. George made a muffled sound against her lips, and grasped her shoulders as he dropped his face into the hollow between her head and shoulder. Jane strained against him, urgently striving toward a goal she could not name.

When at last she reached it, she cried out at the intensity of it, the sharp pleasure that consumed her, but it was over with unexpected suddenness, a bright burst of ecstasy that pulsed like a flame in a draft and then guttered out. George groaned and pushed into her hard and fast, his rhythm his own now. Jane felt infinitely powerful as she held him, guessing that he, too, was feeling that same bright ecstasy she had experienced, only his went on and on. She embraced him and listened to him gasping for breath as his body went rigid.

His shaft pulsed warmly within her and she felt triumphantly tender. She ventured to stroke his back, and reveled in the dew of perspiration there. In its way, the moment was more intimate than any that had preceded it.

He collapsed next to her at last, pulling her against him and placing small absent kisses along the back of her neck as his breathing gradually slowed and evened out into sleep. Jane settled against him, daring to hope that there had been some hint of true affection in what had happened between them. Afraid to speak or move for fear or ruining the tender moment, she let sleep claim her.

Jane appeared pale and subdued at breakfast the next morning, but she smiled up at him shyly before turning her attention back to Portia's idle chatter, and George was reassured. He had decided it would be asking too much for her to be in the light of day the creature she had been in the night. He had left her this morning asleep in a tangle of sheets, the pale pink mouth softly parted, the high, rounded cheekbones flushed pink, and one slender hand under her chin, the long fingers curled like a child's. Now she was dressed for the day, her hair arranged elaborately on top of her head. She looked extraordinarily fetching in a dove gray dress he remembered having ordered for her at the mantua-maker.

It was in his mind to ask her to join him for a walk but she mentioned the necessity of spending the morning writing letters, to communicate the news of their marriage to her former nanny, and to Lady Eugenia, and to one or two school friends. George arose from the table.

"You remind me that I, too, must attend to correspondence, most notably to my mother in Italy. Shall I see you at lunch?"

Jane blushed a little under his searching, good-natured gaze. "Naturally."

"Oh! Jonas sent round a note asking if he might call here today," Portia exclaimed. "He says he has your permission to call again, which is very handsomely done, brother. May I say 'yes,' and invite him to lunch with us?"

George clung to his good mood with difficulty. "As you wish." He bid Jane goodbye and went reluctantly off to closet himself with a pen and standish. The morning went slowly, and the image of Jane's face kept intruding on his awareness. He knew she had experienced pleasure in his arms last night, though his part in the act had strained him nearly to the breaking point. Holding back the full force of his passion when she had clearly been aroused had been almost more than he could bear, but he would do it again tonight, and tomorrow night, and for as many nights as it took until he felt sure he had driven out the memories of what he had done to her in London. Never again would she shrink from his touch if he could help it.

Trying to communicate to his mother the disgraceful circumstances of his marriage went hard with George. Lady Fanny would never betray any disappointment over the matter, he knew, which only made it harder for him to break the news to her. Most especially did he regret that his mother had been denied the opportunity of being present when her only son wed. Fletcher broke in on his uneasy occupation with an apologetic cough, announcing the arrival of a Mr. Beene. George gladly set aside the task at hand and ordered the jeweler shown upstairs.

Mr. Beene had not had a great deal of traffic with the earl, but he had served Lady Fanny many times, and he ventured to ask after her ladyship when he was ushered into George's presence.

"She is well, I believe," George said, "and as she is not at present in England, I must rely all the more heavily on your guidance in the matter of providing my bride with some jewelry."

Mr. Beene inclined his head, the silver at his temples

lending extra solemnity to a face already carved into a permanent expression of decorum. "I am at your lordship's disposal." He opened a leather chest and withdrew numerous baize-lined boxes which he distributed around the large table nearest the windows. George looked at some of the pieces, idly handling them, and turning them this way and that in the morning light.

"I trust you have at least as good a knowledge as I do of what pieces are within the family purview," George said. "I wish my wife to have jewelry of her own choosing—my personal gift to her, you understand—but I rely on you to tell her what is already at her disposal, especially the formal and court pieces."

"Certainly," Mr. Beene said. "Not having the pleasure of knowing your wife, I have selected a wide assortment, ranging from the very simple to the more ornate. Has your lordship any opinion of what is here?"

George cast a critical gaze over necklaces and brooches, earrings and bracelets. He lifted one piece and eyed it. "No, too gauche, I think. She is very beautiful, and yet she has a manner, a bearing, that is ageless. Let us not make the mistake of adorning her as one would a typical young wife."

Mr. Beene nodded. "Just so, your lordship." It was fully an hour later that he repacked the cases, happily anticipating a return call that afternoon to see her ladyship, with selections that met his lordship's exacting expectations. He left with the strong impression that the earl was very much in love with his new bride, and anxious to please her. Indeed, if rumor was to be believed, it had been the most romantic of marriages, the result of an elopement—almost unheard of among men of the earl's degree! He rode back to his hotel with the serene contentment of a man who was privy to the private life of a very wealthy, highly-placed client, and who was sure of his continued custom. He found himself hoping that the marriage, for all its flamboyant beginning, would suit the earl in the long run.

George descended for lunch and discovered Jonas already in the drawing room. The way the stout young man stood rocking on his heels, coupled with Jane's unhappy expression, gave George a fairly clear idea of what had been under discussion. He set out to counter Jonas's pomposity.

"Jane, my dear, did I mention that Hugh has sent along a small wedding gift already?" he said smoothly. Jane looked up at him hopefully and George turned to Jonas. "Hugh, the heir to the dukedom, you apprehend."

Jonas pursed his lips and a little of the color left his florid cheeks. "I do not doubt that there are many who are anxious to offer their congratulations," he said stiffly. "I was merely saying to my cousin that she must not expect this marriage to be greeted with equal enthusiasm in every quarter."

George clasped his hands behind his back and a wintry smile descended over his countenance. "I daresay we will fare well enough without the approval of those so provincial as to suppose that we require their good opinion to be happy. Which reminds me, my dear," he said, turning to Jane again, "the Prince will almost certainly send a letter of congratulations and a gift, too, when the notice of our marriage appears in the London papers. You need not hesitate to acknowledge it in your own hand, for in my experience, he is only too happy to take up the wives of the men in his particular set, and make them welcome."

Jane shot such a grateful look in George's direction that he felt like Saint George. Jonas appeared thoughtful, but there was still a faintly pinched look about him throughout lunch. Even Portia seemed to find him a little less god-like than usual. It was with relief that they arose from the table at two o'clock and went their separate ways. George thought of waylaying Jane and inviting her to take a stroll in the crescent, but she scampered upstairs and he saw Mrs. Briggs ascend soon thereafter. Covering his disappointment with resignation, he ordered a horse to be saddled and let Henry tog him out for a ride, wondering all the while what it was he had been used to do with his time before he met Jane.

Lady Eugenia Hanover arrived at precisely four o'clock. Jane had spent an hour with Mrs. Briggs endeavoring to answer questions as to preferences which she did not possess, after which she gladly escaped to the drawing room to arrange flowers, gladly, that is, until she realized that to have seen flower arrangements hardly fitted one out to create them. There were quantities of wire, a pair of tin snips, and other oddments laid next to the exquisite heap of flowers left there for her by Fletcher, but she had not the least clue in what way they were pertinent to the task at hand. Lupins, delphiniums, foxgloves—one by one they marched into battle and, with equal precision, went down to defeat. The sad pile of blooms with snapped stems, bruised petals, and crushed leaves grew apace, while the luxuriant mass of unsullied flowers diminished, and only a few survived to stand upright in the vase.

She was just wringing her hands and wondering if she might find among the servants one who had the knack of arranging flowers and who could mitigate the carnage, when Fletcher came in to remind her that it was time to keep the appointment his lordship had arranged for half past three. Blinking back tears of frustration, Jane wiped her hands across her thighs and then remembered with horror that she was wearing a dress of white lawn. She fled upstairs to her sitting room with fragments of wilted fern clinging to her dress and nearly ran into the man waiting there for her.

"Lady Sefton," he said, bowing. "I have the very greatest pleasure to meet you." He betrayed no shock at her breakneck arrival, or the untidiness of her dress.

Jane wished the hasty ascent of three floors had not left her breathless. "My husband . . . said something of . . . your coming, but not the . . . the purpose."

That did raise an eyebrow. "My name is Thomas Beene, my lady, and I am come to present to you jewelry from our firm, Cookson and Beene, of London, for your selection.

Your husband desired me to inform you that certain family pieces will suit for formal purposes, but he wishes you to have your choice of more personal pieces."

Jane stared at him in stupefaction. "Jewels?" She noticed Ellen for the first time, sitting inconspicuously in the corner. The maid was reattaching a piece of beaded trim to a ball gown and smiling in a pleased way over her work.

"As many as find favor with you." The jeweler gestured to a table behind him. "If you are quite ready . . ."

Suddenly the awful day receded—Mrs. Briggs and her interminable questions, Jonas and his patent primness, the veritable massacre of the lovely flowers she had optimistically ordered, the tedious letter-writing. Surely her husband must bear some small affection for her if he had arranged this splendid surprise. Jane advanced toward the table, covered with a baize cloth and surmounted by bracelets and diadems, necklaces and pins. She smiled shyly as she turned to Mr. Beene. "Perhaps you would be so kind as to advise me," she suggested.

It elicited something very close to a spontaneous smile in return. Mr. Beene presented items to her one by one, even venturing to suggest that she try on pieces he thought especially suited to her. Quite dizzy with the thrill of holding one lovely piece after another, Jane could hardly think about what she might actually want at first, so engrossed was she in savoring the memory of George's face as he had offhandedly mentioned over lunch that he wished she might keep an appointment he had arranged for that afternoon. His gaze had rested lightly on her, and she had felt a momentary weakness as his mouth curved up in a private, teasing smile.

With unbridled happiness, Jane now gave over all her attention to the jewelry. A sapphire ring with a matching pendant outlined in diamonds, earrings of pearl and filigree—slowly she set aside pieces which both pleased her eye and suited her. The opulence and beauty of the pieces made her feel very loved indeed, and the afternoon sun

256

bathed the room with a golden glow only slightly less luminous than the glow in her heart. Enchanted and absorbed in the choosing, Jane scarcely noticed when a footman appeared at the door with a salver and a faintly strained look on his face.

"Begging your ladyship's pardon," he said stoically, "but there is someone below who wishes to leave her card and wait for an answer."

"I wish no such thing!" a familiar voice exclaimed. "I demand that you allow me to pass."

A ruby brooch dropped from Jane's fingers. "Aunt Eugenia!"

The imposing figure of Lady Hanover framed in her sitting room door aroused extreme alarm in Jane. Instead of merely breathing heavily from the climb, her ladyship actually seemed to be snorting flames. Her black ringlets trembled and her prodigious bosom heaved as she surveyed the scene in front of her with obvious displeasure.

"I see that I am arrived none too soon," she remarked briskly. She turned to the footman. "Bring tea, and do it quickly." She advanced into the room. "And you," she said to Mr. Beene, "whoever you may be, may leave."

Mr. Beene stared at her frostily. "I am engaged in waiting upon Lady Sefton at Lord Sefton's orders."

"Lady Sefton! Arrant nonsense!" Lady Eugenia declared. "I will have a good deal to say to the earl on *that* head." She turned and examined the jewelry. "I suppose she has ordered up all this without any thought as to what it might cost. Take my word for it—the earl has not the slightest idea that you are here. You are wasting your time."

"I am not sure madam has understood," Mr. Beene said repressively. "I have been sent by the earl to assist Lady Sefton in choosing some jewelry."

"The boy has lost his mind! He cannot be serious!" Lady Eugenia pivoted and fixed a glare on Jane. "Pray, where is the marriage license? Or is this"—here she flicked a scornful

257

glance toward the jewelry—"your payment for services rendered?"

The last wisps of Jane's happiness evaporated. She pulled off her spectacles and let the outlines of her aunt's face dissolve into a soft blur. "We . . . we are *married,* aunt," she managed to whisper.

"Poppycock! George has never gone and married such a nobody as yourself! You are not suited, Jane. You *know* you are not! I do not mean it unkindly, Jane, but you must be the first to admit that you have not been brought up to this high degree. You do not know the least thing about running households of the magnitude and sophistication that George keeps, or how to hold up your head among his peers. And the servants! You should not *ever* be able to properly supervise a staff the size of his, not if you endeavored with all your might! And your parentage, your parentage . . ."

Jane shrank back under this barrage. She knew it all to be true but under the influence of love she had dared to think otherwise. "Yes, aunt," she said faintly, "there is sense in what you say, and yet—"

"And you must not be thinking for an instant of choosing any such jewels as these!" Eugenia went on. "Why, the Sefton jewels are without equal. If George seriously meant to have you to wife, he would order them down from London and allow you to choose from among *them* what was needful for the season here! And Fanny, of course, would present you with something from her own collection as a token of respect for her new daughter. Depend upon it, Jane, she will never do so in your case! Fanny will not consent to this marriage, not in a thousand years. She has had enough and more of scandal in her day. She will not welcome one with your background!"

All Jane's insecurities and fears rose up and began suffocating her. They had been waiting in the wings ever since she had dared to hope that George truly liked her, and would go on liking her when they no longer needed to conduct a masquerade for Portia's sake. She wished she had an apron to throw over her head, a simple remedy open to the lowliest kitchen maid, but not to her. Instead she was forced to see the shock on Mr. Beene's face and the outrage on Ellen's as she stared at Lady Eugenia, her mending dangling forgotten in one hand. The needle swung at the end of the thread, catching the afternoon sunlight that now seemed less a symbol of happiness and more like the glow of flames leaping up around the house to consume them all.

Jane gathered her wits with a stringent effort. "But he *has* married me, aunt," she managed to say. "He . . . he *wanted* to, you see, and . . . and I wanted it, too. I daresay George will know what to say to you about his mother, and . . . and . . ."

Lady Eugenia narrowed her eyes. "I have had letters from Jonas Biddle telling me all I need know about your disappearance, and the appalling goings on that preceded it! I don't doubt that you wished to marry George, but you are wicked and bad if you have let him marry you, regardless of the circumstances. You are just like your mother—stealing a man whom you have no right marrying!"

It was the last straw. Jane sank down on the divan and covered her mouth with her hand. She bit the soft inner flesh of her palm to keep from bursting into tears. A countess could not cry in front of the world. Mr. Beene made a bow in her direction, so rigid that he almost creaked, and withdrew without another word. Ellen still appeared frozen.

"I see nothing to be gained from further discussion," Lady Eugenia declared. "It is apparent that you know all too well that I am right, Jane. I am returning to York House now and I expect you to take steps to right this dreadful situation. It is too, too humiliating to contemplate seeing any of one's particular friends under the circumstances. They will wonder why in the world Fanny ever chose me as George's godmother if I could not discharge my obligation any more creditably than this! I will not linger in Bath. I depart for

Canfield tomorrow morning, Jane—without regard for the hardships so immediate a return journey will work on my nerves—and I expect you to join me, and Portia must return with us, too, or the gossips will make scandalbroth out of her. I will take you up in my carriage, Jane, but"—and here she paused to sweep both Ellen and the jewels with one contemptuous glance—"I expect you will bring nothing which is not rightfully yours."

Tears pooled along Jane's lower lids, turning the sitting room to a blurry watercolor of reds and greens. She tried for some reply but unrelenting misery robbed her of all power to speak. Lady Eugenia turned and sailed out.

As soon as the door closed, Ellen cried, "Oh, miss!"

Jane fished for a handkerchief and found the little maid pressing one into her hand.

"You're shaking like a leaf, miss. It's a sin, that's what it is—her speakin' to you like that, that and the way his high and mightiness did by you! Some people should just be shot, miss, and that's a fact! Why, you'd be better off without 'em all! 'Cept her ladyship—Lady Fanny, that is—she's so sweet and lovely, miss—you'd like her, and I swear she'd like you, so you pay that old dragon no never mind about what his lordship's mother'd think of you. But that still leaves his lordship, miss," she said darkly. "I know I'm far out of place to say it, miss, but he don't care for no one 'cept himself. You can see it in his face, all arrogant and cruel, and not any bit interested in what don't serve *his* interests. He may be handsome, but it's the devil's sort of handsome, miss. I'm terrible afraid for you, I am. I wanted to think these jewels was maybe a good sign, miss, but they ain't his family's, did ya hear? No, these is what he's offered, miss. That lady, your aunt, I think she was right, leastways about *that*. He don't mean no good by 'em, miss. Girls in London knows what to make of fine gents what offers 'em jewelry, and so do I!"

"Thank you, Ellen," Jane managed to say in a voice nearly suffocated by tears. "That will be all."

Please let her go. Jane needed to be alone, to think and to let out the flood tide of tears in privacy. Jane heard the soft click of the doorknob engaging and looked up to find that she was, mercifully, alone. Then a voice called softly from the other side of the door.

"Jane?"

Jane begged God to send George away. *If I see him now, I will make a fool of myself.* There was a moment of puzzled silence at her sitting room door, as if he knew she was within, and then she heard him moving away.

And then, when she was quite sure she was alone, the tears would not come. Jane stared at the wall, trapped within her misery, and with no release from the pain which made her limbs tremble and twisted her breath in her throat. She retrieved her spectacles from her lap and put them on.

Mr. Beene's jewels shimmered and winked at her in the late-afternoon sun. Tight with anguish, she stood and began mechanically repacking the pieces in the cases. She had no idea what should go in which pouch or box, but it hardly seemed to matter. All that mattered was that everything should be returned, however haphazardly.

Lady Eugenia was right. Jane had known all along that she was no more genuine than the actors at the Theatre Royal. Like them she could be dressed for the part and sent on stage, but backstage, when the curtain went down, she was revealed as an imposter. She had even gone to George as an imposter, in the guise of his sister, and only George's sense of duty and honor had compelled him to legitimize the *poseur.*

All too soon it would become apparent to him what a dismal failure she was going to be as a countess. In the name of the love she bore him, she must step down, offer him a divorce—do whatever could be done to sever the connection with honor.

*   *   *

She allowed Ellen to dress her for dinner, but bid her be silent on the grounds of a headache which would be worsened by idle chatter. She went downstairs to meet her husband in the front salon, and tell him that she wanted to give him back his life, his freedom. She was early but it did not matter, because she was so utterly consumed by unhappiness over the forthcoming declaration that she could not have done anything else with herself in the meantime.

Fletcher came in and seemed surprised to find her there so early. He gestured to an underfootman to stir himself and light the candles. Until that moment, Jane had not realized that the sun had set. She thanked Fletcher in a nervous, high-pitched voice, and was surprised when he reappeared with a package on a tray.

"Beg pardon, my lady, but I thought you would like to see this. It is from Lord Hugh."

It was a chrysanthemum plate, a work of art in porcelain. The note reiterated Hugh's best wishes for their married happiness, and added that this gift was only a token one, something suited to those in temporary quarters, and that another one awaited them at Sefton House, for when they arrived home from their travels.

Jane stared down at the blue and white plate in her hands. It had probably cost more than she and Nanny had to make do on in a year. It was beautiful and she loved it. It was truly a gift worthy for the heir to a dukedom to present to an earl and his countess. She was about to set the plate down when she heard her husband bidding her a good evening. She jumped and the plate crashed to the floor.

George smiled, that handsome little twisting up of his lips he seemed to save for her alone, but there was a quizzical look in his eyes. "I beg pardon. I should have had Fletcher announce me," he said lightly.

Jane stared at the fragments of the plate on the floor. "I'm sorry," she whispered. "It was so beautiful."

262

"But replaceable, I assure you." The earl's brows drew together. "Are you feeling quite all right?"

Jane met his gaze and her noble offer to release him vanished. He was everything she had dreamed of in a man— her equal in intellect, amusing yet serious, educated and yet not pompous. Long before she had met him, she had concluded that such a man did not exist, and so it had been easy to give up on the notion of falling in love and marrying. And then love had taken her unaware. She stared into the heavy-lidded blue eyes that could light with amusement or set her on fire with their tenderness, and she knew she could not relinquish him.

"Quite well," she said unsteadily.

Chapter Fifteen

The strain of pretending that nothing was wrong nearly proved to be her undoing. Jane sat upright and dry-eyed through dinner, trying to nod at the appropriate moments, or drop some small *bon mot* into the conversation when it seemed she must speak or appear rude. George shot her any number of questioning glances, but her only response was to look at her plate.

Some chance remark of Jonas's had apparently inflamed Portia or Jane would not have had a moment's respite. Peace would have been too strong a word. She did not look to have peace in her life again until she learned how to fulfill her obligations as George's countess in unerring fashion. The prospect of struggling toward such a goal, and of the endless and embarrassing errors she was bound to make along the way, had such an unsettling effect on her digestion that virtually nothing passed her lips.

"I do not wish to press you, Jane, but are you quite sure you feel all right?" George asked gently.

Jane looked up guiltily. Her husband's dark hair fell carelessly across his brow, and the candlelight burnished it. It put her forcibly in mind of how he had looked as he had taken her into his arms last night. She could not bear to lose him now.

"No . . . well, I have a tiny headache," she said, hedging. She pressed her fingers to her right temple. "Just here. It is nothing, really. I . . . I shall soon get over it," she added uneasily as she pushed aside her fricando of veal.

George's eyes narrowed at the gesture. "Not at all likely, dear, if you do not eat a proper meal. Could you perhaps like something sweet?"

"Yes! Yes, that would be most welcome," Jane said hastily. George made no reply but she saw by the look on his face that he was unconvinced.

The servants removed the dishes and the white linen tablecloth before resetting the table with a display of fruits and jellies, a lengthy process which usually signalled an obligation to converse. Jane fiddled with the hem of her shawl and could not think of a single thing to say. She ignored the plaintive look on Portia's pale, heart-shaped face. Let Portia devise a topic for a change. She was aware of George's gaze on her. Once the footmen had withdrawn, she took a jelly and spooned at it without any serious intention of putting any into her mouth. Her nerves were in such a shattered state that she would almost certainly bring it up again.

"Mr. Beene informed me that you found nothing to please you today," George said when she at last ventured to look up. His brows drew together and he said mildly, "I am at a loss to know how he can have brought his finest pieces all the way from London without choosing a few which could tempt you." He glanced at her bare throat meaningfully.

Jane clutched her spoon and stared at him. Had Mr. Beene said anything of Lady Eugenia's incursion? Perhaps not. "Well, I thought it best to wait and see what is in the family first," she said nervously. "He did say that anything I chose would be additional to the family collection."

If he had seriously meant to have you to wife, he would have ordered the Sefton jewels sent down from London! The ugly words echoed in Jane's head. *Let him say now that he will send for them!*

But he turned his attention back to the orange he was quartering, a trace of annoyance on his handsome face. "I see."

George indicated a desire to remain behind in the dining room after dinner, an unheard-of occurrence, and Jane and Portia left him there. They retired to the drawing room, where Fletcher presently appeared, leading a footman carrying a tray with tea and cakes, but still there was no sign of George. Jane's headache had now become quite authentic from the strain of pretending that nothing was wrong. At last she fled upstairs.

Ellen divested her of her dress, her corset, her slippers, her chemise and her drawers, all with a minimum of conversation. Through the whole process, Jane sensed the girl bristling with things she wanted to say, but Jane was not in the mood to hear any more of the maid's well-intentioned but painful "truths," and she consciously emulated George's most quelling manner, ennui coupled with a strong hint of underlying ill humor. Clothed in her voluminous nightgown at last, Jane bid Ellen good night.

She tied the ribbon at the neck of her dressing gown and tried to set her feet on the path which would lead to the bedroom. She had thought it would be a relief to be alone, but it wasn't. Worry had previously bubbled inside her like the contents of a pot left to sit on a back burner, but now the pot was brought to the forefront.

She was so horribly, horribly unsuited to being George's countess! Earlier, in the drawing room, when the mere sight of him had set her on fire with loving him, she had fervently resolved to devote every waking moment to ensuring that she did not fail. It would be too shocking if she held him to their marriage and then exposed him to ridicule. But she was bound to fail so often that it would arouse comment and make him appear ridiculous, and sooner or later, someone was bound to circulate the fact regarding the circumstances of her parents' marriage. How unfair it was! The best way to serve his interests was to let him go, and yet of all things, it was what she could not do.

The inescapable clash of what she *should* do versus what she *would* do set her eyes to burning and transformed the contents of her stomach into a churning mass of undigested food. She sank down on a chintz-covered chair, bit back a sob and promptly succumbed to copious and bitter tears. Over and over she rejected her own arguments, that she should give George up, that to keep him was ignoble, selfish and self-indulgent. She simply could not bring herself to do it. Tears were still dribbling down her face when the connecting door from the bedroom opened.

"Jane!"

George appeared as a hazy blob in the corner of her eye. Jane struggled to sit up straight. There was concern in his voice, but also a slight edge to it, as if he would not be fobbed off with lies any longer. It made Jane sob even harder, and when he sat down on the footstool beside her, she shook off the comforting hand on her knee, too guilty to accept sympathy from the man she was wronging.

His strong, fine hands swam in her vision. "Why all these tears?" he asked gently.

She hiccupped and took the handkerchief he offered. "It is just . . . just . . . that my head hurts so," she stammered.

"If it hurts so badly as all that, then we had better have a doctor round to look at you," he said. He rose, and while she would have blessed him for not dismissing it as female megrims under any other circumstances, now she dreaded to carry the deception further by allowing him to summon a doctor. She detained him by reaching out and touching his wrist.

He turned and looked at her. "Yes?"

Stifling a last sob and drawing a shaky breath, Jane looked up at him. The heavy-lidded eyes appraised her, the fine chiseled mouth in a straight line as he waited. He was not

267

without compassion; he was merely without explanation, a position he did not at all care to be in. In reading all of that in his expression, Jane found herself committed to still more deception. She managed a watery half-smile.

"It is a type of headache I have had before," she assured him. "I will be quite all right by morning."

George withdrew a step and her hand fell back to her lap. "And yet, I do not believe you have been similarly indisposed since I first became acquainted with you. On the contrary, it has been you who has succored Portia through any number of such indispositions."

Deeper and deeper. "Well, it is more . . . seasonal," she said, thinking quickly. *The flowers!* "I desired Fletcher to order some blooms for me today, and he succeeded wonderfully well, only I believe close contact with them has brought on my usual summer . . . problem."

"Your problem," he said slowly. He carefully clasped his hands behind his back. "And have you any other . . . *problems* I should know about? My godmother's visit, perhaps?"

Jane shrank back, clenching the sopping handkerchief in her hand. "Your . . . your godmother? Oh! Lady Eugenia!" she said with a bright smile, as if she had suddenly remembered a pleasant but inconsequential event. "Well, she did stop, but only for a very short time. She is very devoted to what is proper, you know, and so she did not stay above fifteen or twenty minutes."

"I did not ask how long she stopped," George said in a neutral tone. "I only thought she might have said something she should not have. You need not scruple to tell me if she has. She can be very blunt, I know, and since her only source of information prior to today was Jonas, she might easily hold a distorted view of what has taken place between us."

On no account must she reveal to him that her aunt had offered to take her back to Canfield! He might see an opening to be rid of her respectably, before she could prove herself. "She was not entirely clear on one or two points," Jane managed to say, "but I was able to reassure her that all was as it should be."

"And there is nothing else, nothing at all which troubles you?" he inquired carefully.

"No! Nothing at all." And then she remembered the headache. It was solidly there now, a bright, pulsing pain at each temple. "Except for my headache. I am sure it is the result of attempting to do too much today," she said and flinched. Already she had forgotten her initial lie about the flowers.

George compressed his lips, the skin whitening around them. "As you say." He glanced around. "Surely Ellen could do something helpful, bring cold cloths or some such thing?"

"I sent her away," Jane replied quickly, trying to look less ill than she was starting to be in actual fact. She felt nearly ready to throw up what little she had eaten. "I . . . I will lie down presently, and . . . and with some sleep, it should pass by morning."

A small tremor passed through a muscle in his cheek. "Of course. I will leave you then."

Jane was just able to keep the relief and guilt from her face until he turned away, but he turned back with unexpected suddenness and she felt a jolt of dismay. She quickly schooled her face to a look of mild suffering again, and willed her heart to stop racing. Had he noticed? He looked at her with perhaps a little less charity than before, or so she imagined.

"I will not trouble you with my . . . presence tonight," he said blandly. "There is a gentleman's bed in my dressing room. I will avail myself of it."

George paced the length of the study reflectively. She had lied to him, but about what exactly, and why? In the midst of his hurt, he still felt an insatiable need to go to her. He remembered how she had awoken from sleep and roused to his touch the night before. The mere thought brought heat and hardness. Perhaps he had deluded himself. Perhaps the dark, sweet fire had been all his, and none of hers. He had drawn on all his knowledge of lovemaking, relying heavily on the trait which all his partners had remarked on, which was patience, and the ability to delay his own gratification in anticipation of theirs. He frowned. He had not had much practice in catering to virgins, none at all in fact. On the contrary, it was he who had been catered to from the start. His resolve never to court, never even to come close to, unmarried ladies of virtue had been a miscalculation, leaving him ill-equipped for the situation he now faced.

He absently pulled back a drape and stared down on the moonlit crescent. It had been so short a time since he had taken her in shame and tears, with force and willful degradation. He had set himself the task of remedying that by degrees, but perhaps it was a slate which could not be wiped clean. That possibility was at the root of everything which troubled him. Half-asleep she had responded to him; fully conscious she recoiled from his touch.

Jane had changed fundamentally toward him. She had ceased to behave like herself, and she had ceased to be comfortable in his company. It was manifest in the startled way she had dropped Hugh's wedding gift when he had walked in, in her nervous, quick speech, and the stilted sentiments she had been expressing. The candor, the directness, the easy wit, was all quite gone away. He no longer had any inkling what she was thinking. Before he could have readily divined what she thought from her expression, or simply asked her. No more. It seemed carnal intimacy had taken the place of that other intimacy they had shared, that ready exchange of thought which had bound them to one another more surely than any marriage vows.

When Mr. Beene had reported that a lady had come to call while he was closeted with Lady Sefton, cutting short their time together, and that Lady Sefton had soon thereafter caused all his merchandise to be returned, George had been perplexed. He could not quiz Mr. Beene on whether Jane had liked *any* of what she had seen without suggesting that he was not on speaking terms with his own wife. Jane had said she wished to see the Sefton jewels first, but her words had rung false, as if even she knew that that was no very adequate excuse for not having chosen *something,* if only out of deference to her husband's wishes. And most of all, he had longed to see some lovely adornment on her long white throat, some flash of fire locked in gems that he could remove from her and replace with his own fire at the end of the day. Instead he had found himself tacitly excluded from even sleeping next to her.

George squeezed his eyes shut and the world beyond disappeared, replaced by the smaller universe within his head. Nothing happy found a home there at the moment. It was all treacherous undercurrents, logic and illogic, which wrested hold of him in alternate hours. The one constant was that she had lied to him tonight. His love could have borne almost anything from her except that.

With a muffled oath, he slammed his free hand into the panel that formed the side of the window well. The pain in the heel of his hand suited his temper, and he did it again. Twist the facts any way one liked, the inescapable conclusion was that Jane was desperately unhappy. To see her weeping and lying valiantly tonight had nearly broken his heart. He had given her an open door through which to walk, an entrée to trust, but she had turned her face away. He had apologized, he had shown her all the tenderness and consideration he possessed, and brought her—he would have sworn—some measure of satisfaction in his arms. He had offered her a king's ransom in jewels, and none of it had sufficed.

His wrist throbbed, and a hand grown soft from a lack of sparring practice ached from the blows to the wood. He opened his eyes and stared grimly into the night. Having done the honorable thing, he must now do the even more honorable thing, and give Jane a chance to be rid of him.

It was one of those glorious early June days when each breath invigorated one. Jane tried to feel some of the sparkling vitality that emanated from the little chambermaid who brought her chocolate and the newspaper to the large, lonely bed. Ellen glowed with seasonal well-being, too, and hinted that if she only had three shillings, six pence and the afternoon off, she might have a very enjoyable time walking in Sydney Gardens. Jane allowed the girl to dress her and had just sent her off with a promise to consider the notion when the footman hired to replace Manning announced the arrival of the hair stylist.

Jane patiently submitted to having her hair dressed in a modish style that the dresser felt celebrated "the spirit of the day." She regarded the result dubiously. The spirit of the day appeared to require intricacy of design where Jane thought simplicity would have served it better. A feather and a row of small, elaborate combs thrilled the stylist and left Jane indifferent. Nevertheless, she thanked the man civilly and accepted his congratulations on exemplifying all that was fashionable. As soon as he was gone, she removed the decorations, allowing her mahogany hair to carry the style unadorned.

She ate a quiet breakfast, and saw neither George nor Portia. It calmed her mind and she concentrated hard on what she must do with her time that day. She rather thought a trip to the bookseller was in order, to see if she could obtain a copy of some guide to managing a household. Wishing to seek enlightenment before Mrs. Briggs or cook could ask for orders for the day, Jane hastened out the front door with the new footman in tow. At Meyler's she discovered *The Experienced English Housekeeper*, and was appalled to learn that she should have been ordering a minimum of twelve covers for each of the two main courses at dinner, as well as the dessert.

Feeling quite faint with inadequacy, Jane sat down and memorized the names of sufficient dishes for that evening, including raised giblet pie, curry of rabbits, and beef olives, all previously unknown to her, so that she could be prepared to deal with cook the instant she set foot back in the house. She paid for the book and set out for Lansdowne Crescent. Shoppers were thronging Bond Street and Jane remembered a less pressured day when she and George had strolled there, laughing together, and gently mocking the world for its seriousness.

Well, Jane thought, now that she knew how very much there was to be serious *about,* she doubted she would ever feel that lighthearted again. Lady Montfort emerged from the linen drapers and engaged Jane in a brief exchange of courtesies before gathering the twins to her and moving off. In a lather of impatience, Jane resumed walking, only to encounter Mrs. Digby. There was more genuine warmth in that conversation, and Jane left her feeling a little cheered. Halfway up the hill, anxiety began gnawing at her again, and she wished she dared read her new book as she walked, so as to be more fully prepared to deal with Mrs. Briggs. All those mysterious preferences were discussed in the book, but Jane did not want to antagonize cook by arriving late and ordering all the elaborate dishes that seemed to be required without giving him adequate time to seek out the necessary ingredients in the town.

As she neared Lansdowne Crescent, she recited the dishes over and over: macaroni, sweetbreads, buttered lobster, peas, potatoes, muffin pudding, open tart syllabub. The list went on and on, and for the dessert course, a beautiful pyramid of grapes, nectarines and peaches, among other things. The book even had pictures of how the table was to be arranged, so Jane could speak with some authority on the proper presentation of the meal. Encouraged by the notion that she would be able to order an acceptable meal for her husband that night, Jane entered the house with her shoulders back and her head held high, even feeling a little of the wonderful June lightness that was in the air.

It did not last. In the two hours she had been absent, the sense of an orderly household running peacefully had changed. Footmen and underfootmen congregated at the back of the hall, where trunks and traveling bags were appearing, and housemaids scurried in every direction. Fletcher looked up from the mayhem and greeted her in an unhurried manner greatly at odds with the sense of urgency radiating from the area of the baize doors which led to the servants' domain.

"What on earth is going on, Fletcher?" she asked in bemusement.

"Good morning, your ladyship," he said solemnly. "His lordship's compliments, and he has asked me to tell you that he has been called away on business. My instructions are to remove the household to Sefton Hall. His lordship's apologies for the suddenness, but he asks that you commence your journey immediately following luncheon. Bates assures me that it is a trip of not more than five hours in his lordship's phaeton. His lordship anticipates that he will join you there tonight."

It was impossible to conceal her shock from the staff, but they were better trained than she, for they bustled about their duties without any sign that they had seen their mistress's dismay. Jane turned and wandered into the drawing room. She was to arrive at George's country seat for the first time without him? And what could be so urgent that he could not leave her a private note of explanation in his own hand? The footman who had accompanied her into town wavered after her, undecided as to what he should do with the book he was still carrying.

Jane waved him off weakly. "Upstairs, with my papers."

It all seemed very odd, odder still when Portia hurried in to say that she would not be joining them at Sefton Hall. "George says I may accompany Lady Eugenia back to Canfield, as Jonas is likewise removing to his own home. I must just make a quick trip into town for some sundries which will be unobtainable in Coddington." She paused and looked at Jane with a cocked head. "You seem not quite yourself, Jane. Is your headache still with you?"

Jane blinked. "No, only . . . is it your brother's custom to hop about the country in such an abrupt fashion?"

Portia paused in the act of adjusting her poke bonnet, one with pale pink streamers that brought a suggestion of color to her cheeks. "He is not usually *quite* this harum scarum, but it is like him, yes. He will think nothing of the inconvenience to everyone else, but only of what suits him. That is George all over."

"Ah. Well, I suppose I had better see what is to be done with my belongings," Jane said with an attempt at seeming to take events into stride.

"I would not go upstairs just now, if I were you," Portia said, drawing on her gloves. "Stoke has gone up to your Ellen regarding packing your trunks and I suppose the result will be a great deal of fussing and fuming."

"Yes, too true," Jane said with a shudder, sitting back down.

Great Aunt Serena was carried downstairs in her invalid chair just as Jane was going in to lunch. Fanning herself rapidly with a chicken skin fan painted a lively shade of pink, Serena whispered a quick goodbye and waved cheerily as she disappeared out the front door. Fletcher smiled and bellowed wishes for a comfortable journey as he escorted her to the curb and into the earl's landau. Great Aunt Serena's cadaverous and nameless companion walked through the entry hall and out the door without looking left or right, so Jane was spared the necessity of another awkward farewell.

She sat down to lunch alone, still mystified by the turn of

events. When Fletcher announced the arrival of the phaeton at the door, she went forth with as much aplomb as she could manage. It was with intense regret that she watched the lovely, ordered Palladian vistas of Bath disappearing behind them. Bath might have passed the zenity of its popularity with the *crème du ton* but Jane had found it utterly agreeable, and it was, after all, the place where she had fallen in love with George.

Jane set herself the task of finding enjoyment in the trip ahead instead of dwelling on what was behind. Gently sloping hills, wide open meadows, and timbered fields created a scene of rural beauty outside the carriage. Even the evidence of increasing enclosure—fast-growing hedgerows and the occasional low stone wall—could not diminish the loveliness as they traveled in an easterly direction, and then went north, skirting London.

There was an attractive sense of order to the land, interspersed at intervals by hamlets, villages, and the occasional market town, distinguishable from a distance by church spires. When Bates swung the carriage smartly off the main road and through a pair of iron gates, Jane felt her stomach seize up, though. This must be Sefton Park. They traveled down a long drive, past rustic lodges, and finally, over a stone bridge, after which the drive took a quick turn that ended in a forecourt.

Sefton Hall was at once more imposing and more welcoming than she had imagined. It was a long, three-story house of classical proportions, elegantly simple with its brick facade and slate roof. The staff formed up to greet her, but they seemed as nonplussed as she was by the irregular proceedings, a new mistress arriving without the master. A man who introduced himself as Hicks, a cousin of Fletcher's, made the introductions. Jane went down the long line of staff, a blur of faces and names, and tried hard to act as if nothing was out of the ordinary, as if George's absence from the proceedings was completely to be expected.

Stepping inside, she found the hall gloomy, but Hicks led the way past a massive, unlit fireplace into a more formal hall, with a glazed dome which admitted the still bright light of early evening. Jane soon lost track of where she was as Hicks led her along corridors, explaining all the while that here was the breakfast room, there the library, along down the hall the billiard room, and then a small drawing room used by the family when it was just themselves at home, and a multitude of other rooms. At last he led the way back to the central hall and up a circular stone staircase with a handrail upholstered in dark red suede. It was a sensuous and surprising sensation under her palm as they mounted the steps. On the second floor, Hicks pointed out the nursery, and the old schoolroom where Master George had had his lessons for his first few years, and so on.

Finally, after passing what their guide described as four secondary bedrooms, they arrived at the two principal bedchambers, with corresponding dressing rooms and water closets. All the rooms were papered and attractively decorated, and each had its own marble fireplace. Hicks stood back and invited Jane to enter the last room, apologizing for his lack of more detailed knowledge about the house, and assuring her that when Mrs. Briggs arrived, she would see to it that the new mistress was properly acquainted with the whole house, and not just the east wing.

Astonishment coursed through Jane at the realization that she had only seen half of the house. In a daze, she wandered to the window while Ellen allowed herself to be led off to see her own room. Paved, terraced walks led away from the house, and Jane could just catch a glimpse of a conservatory at the far end of the house. She imagined it would be a treasure trove of botanical specimens, given George's interest in horticulture. The lawns led down to an impressive expanse of water, which took the summer gloaming and turned it into an ethereal water color. Sefton Hall had enough beauty to satisfy a far more demanding expectation than *she* possessed, but it was comfortable, too, for such a large place.

And then the thought of being responsible for its running assailed Jane. She sat down abruptly and nearly gave way to tears. She was tired, she was hungry, and she was baffled by George's absence. She felt a strong streak of self-pity building inside. It was all much too much. She dabbed away a few tears and tried not to dwell on the fact that if no one came to escort her to dinner, she might well starve before she found the dining room.

That sad eventuality was thwarted by the arrival of Hicks. He asked if her ladyship had any orders and, upon hearing that she did not, informed her that her luggage would be delivered presently, and that if it would please her ladyship, dinner could be served the instant she was ready to eat. Concealing her dismay that George was evidently not expected in time to dine with her, Jane allowed Ellen to assist her into a pale saffron evening gown and went down to dinner behind the footman sent to show her the way.

The dining room was immense, and ablaze with as many candles as they might have burned at Longchamp in a month. Floor-to-ceiling mirrors reflected the room back upon itself in dizzying profusion, and the plate and flatware on the table made that which had been carried to Bath for use there look positively plain. All this splendor seemed indecent for one person, and the appearance of an ice swan as part of the dessert course only heightened that impression. Jane sat and poked at dish after dish in a cloud of self-conscious misery, as footmen came and went with each remove.

A clock somewhere not too far distant chimed eight and then nine as the meal progressed. When at last she could arise, Jane breathed a sigh of relief, and turned aside Hicks's suggestion that she have tea in the small salon favored by her ladyship—"his lordship's mother, I mean of course," he clarified. After a moment's reflection, Jane asked that it be

278

served in the library instead.

Hicks covered his surprise well, and Jane let him lead her there. It was with some satisfaction that she saw that it did indeed face the south lawn, as she had remembered, and would provide a view of the forecourt and thus her husband's return. Hicks opened the double doors onto the terrace to admit the evening air and left her. A carpet covered the great expanse of floor, and a red sofa and chairs were drawn up to the now empty fireplace. It was altogether a comfortable room, with endless bookcases surmounted by portraits which looked to have been accumulating, like the books, through many generations.

Studying the faces, Jane detectd likenesses to George, in a finely proportioned nose here, the set of the mouth there, but none of his ancestors seemed to have put all the features together to the same stunning effect that nature had achieved in George. Portia, on the other hand, was also echoed in some of her antecedents, but none of them managed to manifest the less attractive family features in the same unhappy combination as she. A portrait of an exceedingly beautiful blond woman was the most recent addition, to judge by artistic style and freshness of color. Jane moved to stand beneath it, and wondered if perhaps the artist had not taken some liberties. If this was, as she suspected, Lady Fanny, then Portia had every right to rail against fate. A handsome if somewhat dissolute-looking older man stood behind her, seeming impatient to be elsewhere.

Jane allowed herself to be served with a tea tray and then asked Hicks to leave just one footman to see her back to her room. The hour was quite advanced now, but nothing would induce her to retire until George arrived. She leafed through an atlas on a stand and selected books at random to pass the time. The house was profoundly quiet, and Jane was glad to know that another human being lingered just outside the door.

At long last a curricle flashed around the corner of the

drive, the legs of the grays that pulled it a blur in the moonlight. Jane arose, her heart thumping, and saw her husband jump down from the vehicle. A black cape swirled like a piece of night around him and undergrooms appeared as if by magic to lead the horses away. George paused and looked up toward where Jane imagined her bedroom was. His face was illuminated briefly by the glow of light coming from the window there, a tight, frameless portrait of Sefton Hall's master that emphasized his dark male beauty. But Jane also saw something unsettling there, an aloofness, a hardness.

He came rapidly into the house and it was not more than a minute before she heard him striding down the hall toward the library. Jane waited by the cold hearth, determined not to throw herself at him as she wanted to, for fear he would think her vulgar, or that the servants might see and the word would spread that the new mistress was not at all as decorous as a countess should be. She wetted her lips and waited. Through the door came the vibrant sound of his voice but he did not stop to put off his cape or allow the footman to open the door.

Instead, he opened it himself. Jane could not but be glad that she had resisted her impulse to run to him. He regarded her with an impassive eye as the dark cloak furled around him and settled again, hanging straight from his wide shoulders.

"You are still up. Good."

The words sent a shiver through her. He was looking at her without warmth, as if he had found his estate agent there, not his wife.

"I . . . I had hoped to hear some explanation for the . . . move," she said, wishing he did not look so forbidding, so that she could say what she had wanted to say, which was that she had wanted to see *him*.

His expression did not change but he seemed to lose an inch or so of height. He closed the door behind him and threw his cape off, carelessly tossing it toward a chair. It held for a moment and then slithered with a hiss of its silk lining to the floor. He appeared not to care, which made Jane uneasy, for George was usually so precise in the disposition of his clothing.

He went to the fireplace and looked as if he wished there were a fire burning there so that he could jab at it with a poker. Without that distraction, he faced her and said, "I have told Portia that she and Jonas may marry if they still like in six months."

"Oh." It did not explain the dark tension that hung about him. The deep, hooded eyes gave nothing away, added nothing to the bare words.

"That is why I told her she might go with my godmother. She will have an opportunity to see more of Jonas and thus make an informed decision. I would not wish her to marry out of opposition to my opposition."

Not sure that any response was required of her, Jane nevertheless ventured to say, "That was what I feared all along."

"It nearly happened. We sought to avert it, you and I, and landed ourselves in the damnable position we now occupy."

Damnable position. Jane's throat closed up with fear. "I am not sure I entirely understand your meaning."

"The phrase, 'Marry in haste, repent at leisure,' covers my meaning," he replied, "only I do not propose for us to repent at leisure. I believe we have committed ourselves to a marriage which is manifestly untenable, and I see no reason why we should repent of it at leisure."

His words went straight to her bones and left them like jelly. Jane wished she had the strength in her legs to move to the sofa so that she could support herself by bracing her hands on its back. "What is it that you propose?" she asked unsteadily.

He shifted his weight and placed an arm along the mantle, one fine hand resting casually on the edge. "I have spent

281

several hours closeted with a solicitor today, discussing how best to sever our attachment—without undue notoriety, of course."

"Of course," Jane echoed faintly. His expression was commanding, implacable. He was not asking.

"There may be . . . consequences . . . resulting from our brief liaison," he said. Just for a moment, she thought she detected shame on his face, and then it was gone. "I propose to wait elsewhere until it becomes clear whether you have— and please pardon my bluntness—conceived."

Jane felt a flush of mortification sweep across her face and averted her eyes. That was all it had been to him.

"If you have," he continued, "we will perforce remain married for the sake of the child, though I will not impose myself on you again, nor will I in any way impede you from choosing your own friends, or leading your own life. I will live at Sefton House in London, or here, at Sefton Hall, whichever you do not want. All I would ask is that you would endeavor, as I would, to lead a life which would not discredit either our station or our name."

Jane kept her gaze on the carpet, on a square outlined in vines on the pale gold background. Her hands had started trembling halfway through his speech and the palsy was spreading upward now. Discredit his name? Had she failed so miserably as his countess in less than a week that he saw no point in going on? She felt hot and cold by turns, and could not think whether to throw her shawl off or draw it tighter around herself.

"And if I am not . . . with child?" she managed to ask through shaking lips.

"If you have not conceived, and I can only hope for your sake that you have not, I will go abroad for a space of time— the solicitor recommends a year—and then we will quietly petition for divorce. You would be amply provided for if we divorce, and could set up your own household, or remarry if you chose." He flicked a speck off his sleeve.

Why? Why? Jane wanted to abase herself at his feet and beg for an explanation. Was it because of her background? Had she been such a horrible disappointment to him when compared to his *chère-amie?* Why had he asked for time and then given her so little? Had Lady Eugenia convinced him that she was worthless? But no power on earth could impel her to ask such questions in the face of his unbending hauteur. Love, the driving force behind her desperation, was the only power which might have overcome her scruples and her pride, but the love she bore him was so profound that she could not risk hearing that she was unloved in return, or worse, that he despised her.

"Do you wish time to think about this?"

Jane looked up, stiff with pain. She nodded.

He pushed away from the mantle and stood regarding her indifferently. "I'm returning to London in the morning. You can give me your answer at breakfast."

Chapter Sixteen

He was going back to London, back to his *chère-amie*. That was what he had desired all along. Only for pride's sake had he carried her back to Bath, gone through the motions of being wedded for all to see, and now he had consigned her to the country, where she could not embarrass or inconvenience him. She felt ready to die from the misery of it, and scarcely slept all night.

But in the end, there was no answer to be given other than the one he so obviously desired. Jane gave it to him the next morning. She had gone to bed and he had not come to her. She had not even heard him moving around in the room next door, and she suspected the worst, and that he had caused her to be placed in a bedroom as far distant from his own as possible. In distress so abject she could scarcely hold up her head, Jane went down to the breakfast room.

She watched covertly from one side of the doorway as he sipped at a cup of coffee. She would take what she could, even if it meant only the chance to admire the strong, well-shaped hands applying marmalade to toast. She wished she could have stayed there forever, happy just to watch him as he glanced at a newspaper, his expression unguarded in her absence. That hurt most of all, the way his face tightened when she finally walked in.

Once she had spoken, he arose and started toward the door, leaving the rest of the food on his plate as if he had never intended to eat it. As an afterthought, he paused and produced a letter from an inside pocket.

"I nearly forgot—I had Wofford draw up a list of the senior staff, their names, their duties, and so on, so that you will be better prepared to deal with them. He will be staying in London to take care of my business. I hope it will not discommode you to be without the use of a secretary."

"Since I had not the habit of using one before . . ." She could not bring herself to say "our marriage." ". . . before now, I will not miss it."

"You need only ask Fletcher for anything you require," he added. He regarded her with a steady gaze which she returned as if under a spell. "Everything else is satisfactory here? Your room? You are comfortable with Fletcher and Mrs. Briggs? Your maid has not begun to pall on you?"

Jane lowered her eyes so as not to see the mock civility on his face. She was struck by a sudden shaft of longing to beat her breast like some primitive woman, and beg him to be genuine with her again, even if it meant stripping her in honest rage and having her there in the breakfast room—anything but this polite pretense. But she lacked the courage for such a gesture.

"Yes, I am content," she said softly.

"Very well. I must be on my way."

She had run to a front window when he left the house, not caring what the servants might think if they saw the mistress of Sefton Hall with her nose pressed to the glass instead of going out to the front steps to watch her husband drive away. Henry awaited him in the curricle, and as George took the reins, Jane was afforded one last glimpse of her husband. The fearsome male beauty stood up as well in daylight as it had the night before, hard-edged and lean and powerful in the morning sun. The way his jaw was set, his mouth compressed, though, a stranger would have been hard put to believe that here was a man quick to enter into a joke, and ready to smile with little provocation.

And then one deathly quiet day followed another. Jane awoke every morning before the household stirred, and lay watching the white curtains begin to flow as the heat of the rising sun warmed the air and the morning breeze passed through the tall windows overlooking the south lawn. Ellen did not mind leaving the bed curtains open now that it was high summer, but she adamantly closed the windows each night when she left, obdurate in her belief that a miasma might arise from the waters of the lake and cause Jane to sicken.

Sicken Jane surely did, but inside, where none could see. She would arise each night after Ellen left and free the giant windows from their casements, twisting the brass cranks and breathing deeply as the frames swung open. The curtains would move softly in the air, almost as if the house itself breathed through those windows. It evoked a vision of George for her, as he had stood, dark and beautiful, in the library, while the curtains behind him sighed and moved against the blackness of night.

She would stare out over the park, beyond the manicured lawns so sedulously trimmed and rolled by the gardeners, and pray that the ghostly gray horses would appear again and release their spectral master to her. It was easy to forget now that he had entered by a door, easier to imagine that he had emerged through the terrace doors without a sound, a dark sliver of night revealed in human form in the lighted library.

But she waited in vain. From London he had come and to London he had returned. A quick, cold chat with his solicitor to dispense with the awkward marriage entered into only as a matter of honor, a brief trip to discuss conception, and then it was back to London. Undoubtedly he had strained the incomparable Clarisse's patience by keeping her waiting so long as it was, and that even before the notice of

286

his marriage had appeared in the papers, Wofford was kind enough to send along a copy of the announcement from *The Times*. It made Jane weep a little, for it was as if even Wofford saw that the marriage had no substance, and needed paper and ink to give it some semblance of reality.

Conception occupied a central position in Jane's thoughts, though at first the idea produced agitation in her mind and heat in her cheeks. By dint of repetition, though, the thought came to be a commonplace without the power to startle, like a rough-edged tooth grown smooth from countless touches of one's tongue. Jane recalled her mother explaining the patterns of a woman's body, but beyond being relieved to learn that the flux did not signal impending death, Jane at twelve had absorbed little more. A kind letter from Nanny one day, congratulating her on her marriage, made Jane think briefly of confiding in her old nurse, and asking all the questions which she wished to have answered, but then Jane felt the march of time. Nanny had never married, would not know the answers. The child had grown beyond the nurse.

Conception. George had spoken of it nonchalantly, as if it were a matter of indifference to him. Love made her desperate, desperate to see him, to hear him, and to claim him as her own, if only in name. She was reduced to hoping that she had conceived already, so as to keep their marriage alive, but in a guilty corner of her mind, she thought of how she might, if she was not already *increasing,* contrive to get him to come to her again, like he had that night in Bath, for if they did *that* again, it might ensure that she *would* get a child by him.

In the meantime, Jane set herself a pattern. Each day she watched dawn break over Sefton Park and then studied a few pages in the housekeeping book which had followed her from Bath. It served her well in her dealings with Mrs. Briggs and Fletcher but it could not be expected to cover all eventualities, such as whether to order new silk to replace the draperies in the breakfast room. Mrs. Briggs informed her that the ones hanging there at present were not old, not in the least, but that the fabric had not fared well in the strong afternoon sunlight, as anyone might have been expected to foresee. She said it with a faint sniff and a lifting of her brows, so that she did not have to say in so many words that she thought the dowager countess extravagant and impractical to have ordered silk damask for that application in the first place.

Unsure of her position, Jane did not wish to make any decision that she did not absolutely have to. She told the housekeeper she would think about it and then dispatched a hasty note to Wofford, asking him to desire some reputable firm to send samples of suitable fabrics from which she could choose. It was slightly cowardly but also a little clever, as Jane felt sure that a man like Wofford could be trusted to know the drapes in question, and to choose a firm which would send samples, none of which would be a bad choice.

Her other inspiration was to request that Wofford add Nanny Kent's name to the list of the earl's pensioners. She boldly declared that Nanny was owed fifty pounds each quarter, and mentioned in the most offhand way that she rather thought he had better send Nanny some money directly, as she hadn't remembered, in all the confusion, to do so herself in a timely fashion. It settled Jane's mind on one score, at least, and she wrote Nanny a very cozy letter which glossed over the practical difficulties in her marriage, and urged her old nurse to enjoy a comfortable retirement. It was a promise Jane knew she could keep, for had George not said that all Jane's needs would be met whether they remained married or not?

There was precious little else that Jane did which brought an equal measure of satisfaction. She set out every day to be an exemplary mistress of Sefton Hall, but by the time she had given orders and dealt with the seemingly perpetual problems associated with running a large household, she was always wrung out. It almost seemed as if Fletcher manufactured items of business to put before her, to make her feel useful. It did not. On the other hand, she felt something akin to affection for the steward of Sefton Park, Williams, for he paid her a courtesy call and then seemed to manage well enough without any further direction from her.

To escape her endless duties, she would walk the parkland surrounding the house every morning. Beyond the stable, and the mews designed to hold twelve carriages, was a pheasantry, and on the other side of the house were forcing gardens, where the protection of a single thickness of glass sufficed to produce a climate far different from England's own. The head gardener doffed his cap to her when she ventured in through doors largely left open at that time of year, and he ended by explaining in detail the operation of his lordship's succession houses. He listed all the fruits which came to the earl's table as a result of his labors, though he apologized for the paucity of pineapples that year.

"Not more than a hundred, my lady," he explained, shaking his head, "but 'twas the best we could manage, it being so very cold over the winter. The oranges, though—that was very different. Your ladyship has no doubt had the pleasure of tasting the very excellent wine Mrs. Briggs distilled from them."

Jane was forced to admit that she had not, but added that she very much looked forward to trying it soon. "Just to sit in here, out of the weather, must be very pleasant in the cold seasons," she ventured to say.

"Oh, aye, and of course, there's the aviary. That's nice right the whole year round."

Jane meekly allowed herself to be led off for an escorted tour. There seemed to be no end to the splendors of Sefton Park. The steward, upon seeing that she meant to range far and wide, took it on himself to show her the dairy, the fish ponds, and the streams from which the earl's tables were supplied, the kitchen gardens, some four and a half acres of them, the deerpark from which venison could be had, and the orchards.

Rather than adding to her sense of consequence, as Williams seemed to think they would, these further manifestations of George's wealth and position only made Jane more anxious than she had already been. When Bates, seeing her go abroad on foot each day, suggested that she avail herself of a pretty little Arab barb which he led out for her to inspect, Jane nearly burst into tears. The horse was enchanting, with fine, large eyes and lovely paces, but what kind of careless wealth was it that could possess such a horse for no better reason than that his lordship had seen the mare once at a sale barn and liked her? She thanked Bates for his kindness and hurried away without making him an answer.

Jane grew even jumpier after that, shying anxiously whenever a servant appeared unexpectedly. They would curtsy, or tug at a forelock, all with a pleasant smile, and Jane did her best to nod graciously before moving on. They all seemed to take for granted that she belonged there as surely as they did, and she reluctantly dismissed the idea she had had of asking Mrs. Briggs and Williams, very delicately, if the servants could not somehow manage to keep clear of her. She was afraid it would be perceived as awful snobbery when in fact, it was just that she felt she did not deserve their deference.

Without warning, something occurred to completely distract her. Portia arrived, looking very fetching and not a little agitated. She kissed Jane and linked arms with her, drawing her along irresistibly to the small sitting room which Jane indicated she had taken for her own. The door had hardly closed behind them when Portia flung her bonnet onto the deal table behind the tailored sofa.

"Oh, Jane, what a horrid time I have had!" she cried. "You will not credit it, but your cousin has turned out to be the most odious snob imaginable!"

Jane pressed away the smile that rose to her lips. "No!"

"But yes! He is insufferable—not at all what I had thought him to be! Indeed, Jane, I hate to say it, but he has changed, and not at all for the better. He dared to suggest that perhaps we should not wed, not even when six months have passed. 'This havey-cavey marriage of your brother's has cast a shade over the family name!' he said! Imagine! He says he is not sure he should ally himself with a family in which a questionable elopement has occurred so recently!"

"Oh, dear," Jane said faintly, frowning to disguise the fact that she was on the verge of laughing.

"And only picture it—Imogene and Emmaline are forever at one another's throats as to who will have him once he has turned away from me, as they are sure he must."

"How very lowering, to be sure," Jane murmured. "But tell me, have they been so . . . so *thoughtless* as to say so to your face?"

"Well, they are not such cakes as that," Portia admitted, "only one cannot help hearing them whisper and carry on when they think one isn't attending. Honestly, between the two of them they have hardly the intelligence of one sheep!"

"Oh, Portia!" Jane could restrain her mirth no longer. "Please, do not be cross with me," she said. "I think my cousin has been most shockingly bad to say the things he has said to you, only I think he has always been an odious twit. It is just that he has finally revealed himself to you!" She covered her mouth and fell back laughing as a look of consternation knitted up Portia's brow.

"George was right, was he not?" Portia said gamely. "He told me that Jonas would not do. George is worth a hundred Jonases!"

"Well, fifty at least," Jane admitted, sternly resisting the temptation to point out that the brother she esteemed so highly now was the very same person she had been ready to murder any number of times for interfering with her precious Jonas's courtship. How tickled George would be when he heard this!

The thought affected her like a shower of ice water. Just for a moment she had forgotten how it was between them. She had already been composing the story in her head, and looking forward to telling it to him. Her sudden change of mood went unnoticed by Portia, who was engaged in describing how Jonas had also dared to suggest that she adopt less clinging styles, and dress like some aged widow of forty.

Jane was glad of Portia's company, even if it was a Portia in high dudgeon. She had been feeling like a china doll, with the staff intent on soliciting her advice on every particular, and waiting on her as if she would break the instant she picked up anything heavier than an embroidery hoop. Now, with Portia to fuss over too, the staff's attentions diminished by virtue of division, and Portia's choler diminished as Jane's sympathy acted like a poultice on her wounded pride, drawing the heat out of her anger.

Several weeks passed during which Jane heard nothing from London. She was bitterly disappointed when she awoke one morning to discover that her monthly flow had begun. She shed a few tears and wondered if she ought to send a note to George, to notify him that he could set about being free of her. The thought plunged her even deeper into despair. She could picture him with his *chère-amie*, driving in Rotten Row, or taking his coquette to the theatre, and generally enjoying a return to the carefree existence he had led before he met her. He would read her note as Henry laid out his clothes for the day and arranged his shaving things—assuming he went back to Sefton House at all—and casually order his valet to prepare for an extended trip to the Continent.

That would please him, Jane thought as her tears flowed. How could it not? His goal was plainly to put as many miles between them as he could. The sudden and absolute way he had abandoned her in the country was the bitterest proof of all that he was embarrassed by her. Jane abandoned herself to a fit of melancholia, and gave up momentarily on the idea of writing to George, for she was so fiercely unhappy that she could not even contemplate putting pen to paper.

The Earl of Sefton knelt in the tall grass and watched a family of quail peck their way along the edge of a cornfield. It was a perspective of his estate he had never seen before. His shirtsleeves were rolled back over forearms turning a plebian brown from long hours spent in the midsummer sun, and his shirt was loosened at the throat. Squatting down in the hayward, a laborer's pants cuffed above custom-made boots, he was an incongruous sight, with an old cap borrowed from Williams on his head and a Purdey resting over one arm.

The double-barreled gun was broken now, carefully unhinged between stock and barrel, for there was nothing very much he wished to shoot at, though he had killed a polecat earlier, vermin always being in season. The handsome gun gleamed in the sunlight, its wood stock lustrous in the way that only the most skilled of artisans could make it. No one who happened across his lordship would mistake him for a poacher, but that possibility had not even crossed George's mind. If he chose to dress like one of his own gamekeepers and tramp about his property from dawn to dusk, it was his right.

The quail dipped and bobbed past him, a female followed by six chicks. When they had passed, he withdrew into the shade of the trees which bordered the field and pulled a flask of water from the leather pouch he carried. Drinking deeply, he leaned back against a tree and closed his eyes. Life hummed all around him, in the dry rustles of furred animals hurrying through the undergrowth, and the quick darting sounds of birds pecking at the detritus of last year's crop. Everywhere there was life and renewal and hope for the future, everywhere but in his heart.

He had been so arrogant, so high-handed, that what might have been a love match to make the angels envious had instead become a bond of loathing and fear. There was no relief from the barbaric pain of it, nothing left to him but hanging about each day when his wife went walking, and covertly watching her, with a hunger which would not be stilled. The rest of the day he hiked the farthest reaches of his estate, and when twilight came, he shut himself away in the hunting lodge which sat in a copse some miles from the main house.

The papers were drawn up, awaiting events. He had hoped that by offering Jane her freedom and some autonomy, he could lure her back, that the prospect of a civil arrangement would encourage her to continue their marriage, as a loosened rein would calm a green horse. He had had to clench his jaw and keep his fisted hands concealed as he described his requirements to the solicitor. Just to be within the quiet, tasteful precincts of the law offices had been anathema to one who wished the ties made tighter, not eased.

But the gambit had failed. She had gazed at him briefly with those piercingly beautiful blue eyes and then lowered her gaze, addressing her remarks to the empty plate in front of her. The arrangement he had suggested would suit her perfectly, she said, to remain together if there was a child and to divorce if there was not.

That was when he had felt the world go dim around him and had jumped to his feet to keep his blood moving. He called himself every kind of fool all the way back to London, cursing himself for even proposing a plan which had given her a chance to be rid of him entirely. After several wretched days spent maundering around Sefton House, he had remembered Clarisse. No longer interested in any relationship other than the one he had poisoned irretrievably at its outset, George sent a footman to Half Moon Street with a carefully worded letter of farewell, the deed to their *pied-à-terre*, and a bank draft for an amount that had made Wofford pale when his lordship had instructed him to enter the *douceur* into the account books.

Then George had spent the day in sparring at Gentleman Jackson's. Initially he rememberd to use some science, but the bouts descended to mere brawling as his lordship grew exhausted and the self-loathing lurking just beneath the surface got the upper hand. Battered and bruised, he had returned home in midevening. A letter, sent most indiscreetly to number sixteen Belgrave Square, lay on the hall table when he came in. He ignored it and called for some brandy. That was the night he discovered that alcohol was no match for his mood.

Clarisse arrived near midnight, distraught from waiting for him to respond to her summons. Timothy let her in, thinking that his lordship had fallen a way in the world, what with carrying her ladyship off by force and now this, but he did not care to be the arbiter of right and wrong for his master. His lordship was not a happy man. Henry, upon hearing that his lordship's ladybird had come knocking at the front door, went very grim about the mouth. The major domo and the valet had always maintained a jealous distance from one another, but under the circumstances, they kept vigil together belowstairs until they heard the great front door slamming shut in the early morning hours.

Forgetting their dignity, they sprinted up the stairs to the first floor. Standing in the tiled hall, between the twin staircases which mirrored one another as they rose gracefully to the second floor, his lordship held a candle aloft and eyed them with displeasure. As guilty as boys caught nicking apples from a vendor, the two menservants waited for the dressing-down they deserved.

"Expecting a show?" the earl asked in a dangerously quiet voice. Neither man answered. His lordship lowered the candle and the light fell squarely on his ravaged face, its beauty marred by numerous cuts and bruises. "You're too late," he said flatly. "Go to bed."

And when they arose the next morning, he was gone. Henry discovered the earl's dressing room in a state of upheaval, its drawers ransacked, and precious little of any account missing. Brushes, combs, razor, underclothes and a small quantity of linen were gone, but hardly enough to sustain a man of fashion for very long. Firmly allied with one another now, Timothy and Henry made all haste to Wofford, who looked down his nose at them and said that as long as it appeared that the earl had left of his own volition—which it did—then there would be no recourse to the police.

Henry sulked and Timothy glowered, but Wofford remained unmoved, though he was less sanguine when three days had passed and there was still no sign of his lordship. He took comfort from the thought that possibly, just possibly, the earl had reconciled with his mistress and was in residence at Half Moon Street, but that hope was dashed when the woman—Wofford did not for an instant consider her a lady—sent her porter around with yet another tear-stained letter addressed to the earl.

Wofford was more discomfited than he would admit when discreet inquiries to Sefton Hall and Wattier's netted the intelligence that the earl was not at either place. Taking refuge in starchy superiority, Wofford exhorted the staff of the London residence not to be foolish—the earl was not obliged to inform them of his whereabouts, after all—and to carry on as usual, but deep down, he was gravely concerned.

When her ladyship, the dowager countess, arrived unexpectedly at her son's house, the secretary did his manly best to act as if nothing was out of the ordinary. Lady Fanny, whom he had always revered, swept into the grand hall and made it seem small and dowdy in contrast to her own magnificence. Even more influential than her great beauty, however, was her enormous charm. Wofford soon found himself drinking tea with her in the blue salon and telling her a tale which he very much fancied her ladyship needed to hear.

Chapter Seventeen

"For my son to have banished Henry, he must be very badly hipped indeed," Lady Fanny sighed as she pulled off her bonnet and patted the guinea gold curls beneath.

"Henry, Henry," Fabrice murmured. "This Henry, he is a friend of your son's?"

"Oh, no, darling, his valet," she said, grooming the ostrich feather on her hat with long, elegant fingers. She pulled at the soft lavender strands with a pensive expression. "I believe we must quickly contrive some way to lure him out of hiding. Supposition is all well and good, but seeing them in one another's company will be a great deal more to the point."

"Your son and his valet?" Fabrice's bafflement was evident in every contour of his attractive face.

Fanny let out a trill of laughter. "But of course not!" she said. "I wish to see my son with his new bride, of course."

Fabrice responded to her laughter with a brilliant smile. He gently disengaged her fingers from the feather. "Oh, my little dove, how I love to hear you laugh." He encircled her with his arms and pulled her back to rest against his chest. "Most certainly we will arrive at a plan, but for now I am overcome with a wish to lie down with you."

Lady Fanny peered over her shoulder at him with a

mischievous sparkle in her eyes. "You are intent upon scandalizing the staff, no doubt."

"But most certainly I gave no thought to such a thing. It is you who have set me on fire, and you only of whom I am thinking."

Fanny turned within the circle of his arms and drew one finger along the edge of his stiff, high collar. "Dear, dear Fabrice, how sad I should have been not to have met you!"

"And I you," he replied, "but you do not answer my question. I have the greatest passion for you at this moment. Will you lie down with me or do you mean to become one of those so stuffy English ladies now that you are back home?"

"No! I will not allow it," Fanny cried. She tapped his lower lip with one manicured fingernail. "I was never stuffy and it is very unkind in you to suggest it! You know very well that I am meltingly yours, but do you not see that we must immediately set about solving this dilemma?"

"My dearest *signora,* I can deny you nothing, only tell me what I must do to earn your favor," Fabrice murmured, catching up her fingers and kissing them as he spoke.

"Perhaps you could divert Portia," Fanny said a little breathlessly as he nipped at the thin span of skin between her thumb and index finger. "Keep her occupied with questions about the house, or perhaps take a walk with her, so that I can have some private conversation with my son's wife."

"Pah! A walk. It is of all things English the most disagreeable. But," he added before she could reply, "I will do it with exceedingly great pleasure if you ask it."

Fanny's eyes were half-closed, her mouth curved in a rapturous smile as Fabrice lightly tickled the skin of her inner wrist with his mustache. "But then, of course, we have just arrived . . ." She let out a sigh as his arms closed around her and his breath whispered across her palm. "Perhaps we should not disrupt the routine of the house. They will be expecting us to rest, after all . . ."

"Oh, my darling, only to hear you say so sets my blood on fire," Fabrice whispered.

298

And so it was not until after dinner that Lady Fanny began her subtle interrogation of her daughter-in-law. Dinner had gone tolerably well in her estimation. The table was not as unbalanced as it might have been, for Fanny had not only her new husband with her, but his friend, Gandolfo Fiore. Unhappily for the sake of conversation, however, Gandolfo possessed not a shred of English, and so, though their numbers were reasonable, three females to two males, bright, vivacious chat of the sort Lady Fanny so enjoyed was quite lacking.

The dowager countess contrived via the use of raised eyebrows and speaking glances to seclude herself and Jane in a corner of the small drawing room when they withdrew there after the meal. Fabrice took her signals to mean that he should keep Portia fully occupied, and threw himself into the task of charming the girl. Gandolfo looked as if he would have liked to also, but his lack of English reduced him to the role of interested bystander.

"My son said in his letters that you have been all that is kind to my daughter," Lady Fanny said as she settled her skirt around her. "It has been a great comfort to know she has at last found a friend."

"She is very easy to befriend, ma'am," Jane replied, returning Lady Fanny's smile.

Fanny flinched at the "ma'am" and quickly wafted her fan two or three times in front of her shoulders to conceal it. Fabrice treated her like a girl, but as she regarded her daughter-in-law's wan face, she knew that the gap between their ages must seem considerable to Jane.

"George said that you made it seem as if she were the easiest person in the world with whom to talk. I should have liked you enormously for that quality alone, you know." She glanced across the room. Fabrice was gallantly exhorting Portia to play the pianoforte, a request the girl turned down, flushing quite pink and ducking her head. "If only Portia knew how to blush only a little, to be only a little shy, it would work very well for her. This other, this . . . this extreme coyness does her no good."

Jane followed her look and said defensively, "In general, Portia has been much improved. In Bath she was used to dance quite gaily and accept compliments and make conversation very well indeed."

"Then we must hope she will find that facility again," Lady Fanny said.

Fletcher entered, followed by a footman carrying the tea tray. He paused in front of Lady Fanny. "Do you wish to serve from here?" he asked. In the center of the room where the furniture was grouped would have been more logical than the corner, but he honored the tradition of humoring one's mistress.

"Oh, my, Fletcher, it is not for me to say!" Lady Fanny said brightly. "You must ask the countess." She nodded toward Jane.

"Yes, just here will do," Jane murmured. As soon as the butler had withdrawn, Jane looked at Lady Fanny gravely. "Thank you for deferring to me, but I am not . . . that is, I do not believe I am equal to the task . . ." Suddenly she felt very close to tears. "In point of fact, I do not think I shall be the countess very much longer." She clutched her hands together in her lap and stared at them.

"Do you not?" Lady Fanny asked softly, a little shocked. "I wish you will tell me why, for I am delighted to have you for a daughter-in-law and should be very sorry to learn that you were not going to stay." As she said the words, she was surprised to realize that she meant them. She had returned home in a great hurry, prepared to dislike her son's new wife after all that Eugenia Hanover had said in her letter, but since Jane had greeted them in the forecourt that morning, she had been cordial and composed and inherently likable, not at all the pushing, conniving mock-innocent Eugenia had suggested.

"As to the circumstances," Jane said in a choked voice, "I believe it best to leave the explanations to your son."

"Ah, my son," Fanny said. "But where is he to be found,

do you suppose?"

Jane's lower lip trembled. "I am sure I do not know. I believe he has . . . friends in any number of places with whom he might be staying."

Fanny resisted the urge to lay her hand over Jane's clenched ones to stop them from shaking. Instead she picked up the pot and a cup. "Tea? Yes? I think it will help your throat." Jane took the cup to which Fanny had added cream and one sugar. The strains of a Haydn sonata drifted to them from across the room. "Oh, excellent. Fabrice has coaxed Portia out of herself. This way we shall have a little more time to puzzle out the mystery which faces us."

Jane sipped miserably at her tea. "Did he not write to you, ma'am, regarding the . . . the circumstances of our marriage?"

"He did, you know, and in his own hand, which pleased me very much. I have tried to impress upon him any number of times the rudeness of dictating his letters to Wofford, but to no avail. Still, for all that he wrote to me himself on this occasion, he did not relate much beyond the barest facts."

Jane glanced up unhappily. "I would not know what to add to your understanding, ma'am."

"Well, then, allow me to add to *your* understanding," Lady Fanny said in a comfortable way. "My son is not in London—not at Sefton House, not staying at his club, nor with any special friends, either." Having bullied the staff of Sefton House—in her thoroughly charming way—into giving her a complete account of what had taken place there, she had been left with only more questions. She gave Jane a measuring look. "I am the most awful card player, you know. I can never manage to keep my thoughts to myself. I believe it is one of the reasons I am so very comfortable with the Italians. They do not even try to conceal what is within. They live their passions, and speak their feelings. It is so very liberating for one's soul, so very exhilarating!"

Jane was bewildered by the abrupt turn in the conversation. "I . . . I suppose that may be true, ma'am."

Lady Fanny took a sip of her tea, smiling. "Ah! You are thinking that was a *non sequitur*. It was not. You see, I knew your mother, many years ago. Oh, how I admired her! I thought her the most wonderful creature—so vibrant, so marvelously full of life! It was she who gave me my taste for all things Italian."

Jane stared at her. Other than her father and Nanny Kent, she had never known anyone save Lady Eugenia who had known her mother. "Truly, ma'am? You knew my mother?"

"Oh, my, yes. It was shortly before you were born that I met her. I had already married and had George, and I was expecting Horatia."

Jane blinked. "But I am twenty-five, ma'am. You cannot possibly be old enough to have . . ." Jane turned bright red. "Oh! I beg your pardon. I did not mean . . ."

Lady Fanny laughed with every appearance of delight. "My dear child, I think you have just paid me a most wonderful compliment. I assure you, I am quite old enough for things to have happened the way I say they did. When I found myself expecting again, instead of going to London for the season as I had wanted to, I went to Eugenia for a visit. I was most awfully moped by childbearing and child rearing at the time, but your mother was so joyous about your impending arrival that she breathed the life back into me about my own condition. She did not go out except to Canfield, and then only a very few times. I think Eugenia was . . . stuffy, shall we say, about her marriage to your father. She only invited her on my account, since we had our interesting conditions in common. I think Eugenia was more than a little disgusted by me, what with a second child coming so soon after the first." Fanny laughed. "Eugenia was always such a model of efficiency. She had her twins, two children at once with no nonsense, and then I believe she felt she'd done her duty. I don't believe she ever let Henry near her again!"

Jane opened her mouth but only a squeak came out.

"Oh, dear, I've shocked you," Fanny said. "It's only the

truth, though, and I would not have said it to you if you were not a married woman."

"No, of course not," Jane said faintly.

"Dear, dear," Fanny said, setting down her cup. "I set out to know you better and I have succeeded only in talking like a magpie, and saying things I should not. I did so wish you to form a good opinion of me, though, so that you would feel comfortable enough to confide in me."

"I will gladly answer any question you might like to put to me, ma'am," Jane ventured. She found George's mother quite overwhelming, exquisite to look at, assured, and charming. No wonder Portia had retreated to her former shy self—how intimidating to be the offspring of such a nonpareil!

"Then perhaps you would not mind telling me what your feelings are toward my son," Lady Fanny said.

Jane took a hiccup of air and stared at George's mother. "My feelings?" she said slowly. "Well . . . I am honored to be his wife."

"Let me be more direct, my dear. Do you love George?"

"Oh." Jane swallowed hard and stared at Lady Fanny.

"Never mind," Lady Fanny said kindly. "You need not answer. I can see by your expression that you do."

Jane pulled her spectacles off. Lady Fanny's sympathetic air was producing a strong desire in her to cry.

"You look very like your mother," Lady Fanny said, "only I believe you are more truly beautiful than she was. It was her vivacity that attracted one, and gave the illusion of greater beauty than she possessed. She would have been very proud of you if she could see you now. You find yourself in a most difficult situation and yet you are behaving with grace and dignity."

Jane blinked hard, fanning the air with her lashes to make the tears go away, but one slipped down her cheek.

"You are undone by sadness," Fanny said softly. "I am sorry. If you would like to leave now, I will make your excuses for you."

Jane rose and fled. Lady Fanny watched her daughter-in-law hurriedly pulling the door closed behind her and then sat slowly swinging one sandaled foot. Jane was a very dear girl indeed, and Fanny was resolved that she was a worthy successor as countess. Now how to make things right?

What was she to do with the information she had extracted from the steward that afternoon, that George was living alone in the old hunting lodge? Her son was behaving like a virtuous man who had done a very unvirtuous thing, which was precisely what he *had* done, as nearly as she could determine, but how was she to make use of what she knew?

Jane slowly paged through a volume she had lifted at random from a bookcase. Portia was upstairs writing to her old governess, and Lady Fanny was walking in the gardens with Fabrice. Jane had watched them for a while, before they disappeared beyond the hedges where the formal parkland began. They laughed together, walking arm and arm, with many quick, teasing glances between them. Never in her life had she seen a man and woman exhibit such open affection for one another, but it seemed to her that only Lady Fanny could contrive to behave so without appearing vulgar.

The more Jane pondered her unhappy situation, the more she thought about the physical side of her relationship with George. He had expressed no dissatisfaction with her running of the household, had never indicated the least disapproval of her background, had seemed prepared to enter into their marriage fully in Bath, and then . . . And then what?

He had made love to her there, unexpectedly wonderful love. She had been careful to submit to her husband gracefully, striving to keep herself within ladylike bounds even when that soaring, melting heat had coursed through her and set her on fire with pleasure. But she had not kept her reactions within the boundaries of decency. She had tried as hard as she was able and yet she had failed, with the result that she had made those awful panting sounds and moaned when he . . . when he . . . Her mind turned aside the too intimate thought. George had participated without giving rise to the same strange sounds and odd contortions of his body. Jane felt her face flame. And then?

Jane walked unsteadily to a chair and sat down with the forgotten book in her lap. And then the next night he had come to her but he had not stayed. She given him such a disgust of her that he had not wished to lie with her again. She could see that now, could remember the tone of voice in which he had announced that he would sleep elsewhere, and not "bother" her. He had meant *that*. To the extent that she had thought about *that* at all, her only fear had been that she might not be able to keep her responses within the realm of what was respectable as time went on. Now it seemed quite clear that she had crossed that line on only the second occasion of their sharing a bed.

Utterly flummoxed by the realization, Jane did not at first hear the soft baritone voice coming from the direction of the library door.

"Signorina?"

Jane looked up. It was Gandolfo. He spoke again and she nodded, dimly aware that he was begging her pardon for intruding. He advanced into the room, all smiles. She smiled back. Really, he was a most charming sort, with tousled black curls and bright blue eyes alight with the beguiling smile he directed at her as he bowed low over one leg, like some old-fashioned courtier. With a mustache like Fabrice's, he looked distinctly foreign, and yet he reminded her strongly of someone, though she could not think who.

He inclined his head toward the book she was holding. *"Pirotechnica?"*

"Oh . . . yes," she said, absently scanning the title.

Gandolfo gently twisted the book and read from its spine. "Vannochio Biringuccio." He gestured to himself and said something in Italian, smiling broadly.

Jane was surprised at how many of the words sounded

familiar but she was not sure she understood him. Was he saying that he was the author? "No, I am sure you are mistaken," Jane said, turning to the prospectus of the book. "Here—it says it is a detailed account of mining, smelting, and metalworking in the sixteenth century, and that it was published in 1540."

Gandolfo responded with another smile and a rush of Italian. Jane listened carefully. Much of the Italian her mother had spoken to her was coming back. "Oh! You mean to say this . . . this Biringuccio is a countryman of yours!"

"Sì, un paisan!" Gandolfo said, clearly delighted to have been understood. He sat down next to her and expressed great regret when he saw that the book had been translated into English.

"Well, yes," Jane admitted. "Not many people in England speak sufficiently good Italian to read such a book in the original."

Gandolfo treated her to another one of his effervescent smiles, and asked about Portia. Jane searched deep in her memory and summoned forth the words to explain, in a halting fashion, that Portia was busy writing letters. Gandolfo looked abashed momentarily, and then his ebullient charm reasserted itself. He arose and offered her his arm, gesturing toward the terrace outside.

"Oh! Well . . ." Jane stood up.

Gandolfo led her off toward the gardens, going on in Italian at such a rate that Jane quite lost the thread of what he was saying, but nodding and saying "sì" every now and then seemed to satisfy him. Lady Fanny's laughter reached them, a light trill underscored by Fabrice's deeper laughter. Their paths converged near an ornamental pool flanked by stone benches.

"Oh, my dear Jane," Lady Fanny cried. "I see that Gandolfo has found a friend in you!"

"Well, my very limited understanding of Italian has encouraged him to think that I understand far more than I do, I'm afraid," Jane admitted.

"But how delightful," Lady Fanny exclaimed. "I have felt sorry for him ever since we left Italy, but he *would* insist on coming with us, and you can see perfectly well how one can deny him nothing."

Gandolfo took Lady Fanny's hand and addressed her with a spate of Italian, to which Lady Fanny replied in a soothing murmur of that same language. Lady Fanny bent one of her bright beautiful smiles on Jane.

"I see that you are walking in the direction of the cutting garden. Perhaps you would not mind gathering some flowers for me while you are out. I would so enjoy arranging them—that is, if I am not usurping your place. Fletcher tells me you are devoted to flower arranging also."

Jane went pink. "I have tried, ma'am, but I would happily defer to you."

"How lovely! I will send one of the footmen along with snips and a basket. It will give Gandolfo the greatest pleasure to carry them for you, I am sure."

Fabrice tucked Lady Fanny's hand over his arm. "Indeed, my friend wants nothing better than to find a lovely and agreeable Englishwoman to marry, just as I did. How lucky I am to have seen you first!"

"Shameless, shameless flatterer! He is the merest boy!" Lady Fanny declared. She smiled at Jane. "It will do Gandolfo no harm to practice his charms upon my daughter-in-law since my daughter will not give him the least sort of encouragement."

"Daughter, daughter-in-law," Fabrice said with a dismissive wave. "They are both lovely, Fanny. Any man who earns their affection is fortunate indeed."

Fanny tapped him light on the hand with her fan. "If I did not know you were utterly devoted to me, I should be very jealous," she said.

"I am so blinded by your beauty that I cannot even *see* other women," Fabrice said with a heartfelt sigh.

The dowager countess laughed and called back over her shoulder as she allowed herself to be led away, "Jane, my dear, do come and find me when you have done with cutting flowers. We could arrange them together, and there is something I most particularly wish to speak with you about."

Lady Fanny followed up on her intent by sending Fabrice along to collect his countryman not more than a half hour later. A footman took the basket from Gandolfo and Jane allowed the Italian to make her another extravagant bow before he went off, flashing her a last winsome smile as he went.

"Oh, how charming," Lady Fanny exclaimed over the basket of flowers when Jane appeared in the doorway of the small drawing room. She arose from a chaise and met Jane at a table already laid out with the same curious items Fletcher had provided for flower arranging in Bath. "And phlox! I had not thought previously of using it as a cut flower, but it will do very well indeed for background. Thank you, Fellows. You may leave us now."

"I really haven't any idea of how to arrange flowers," Jane confessed.

"Then you may watch and I will explain," Lady Fanny said, expertly segregating the flowers by shape and size.

But it was not flower arranging she talked about. Jane made a sincere effort to note how she snipped a length of wire and deftly inserted it into the frailer stems, and arranged flowers from back to front, cleverly building a pleasing combination of color and texture as she went.

"I so regret that we do not know one another better, my dear, so that I could be sure you would not be upset by what I am about to say."

Jane watched Lady Fanny's long beautiful hands as she manipulated the flowers. "I am not so fragile as I may have seemed last night," she replied. "Please do not hesitate to speak freely."

"Then I will plunge ahead. You see, I have learned that George is at present staying at an old hunting lodge here on the estate. You could walk to it in less than an hour."

Jane stared at Lady Fanny. "He is not in London?"

"No, my dear. He is right here, and has been for some time."

Jane felt her way to the chaise and sat down. Beyond glancing around to see that her daughter-in-law had not fainted, Lady Fanny did not react to her obvious shock. With every appearance of unconcern, she went on snipping and arranging flowers.

"My son does not like ambiguity," the dowager countess said conversationally, "and yet it appears that he has left matters between you in a very ambiguous state indeed. If George has let this uncertainty persist, I conclude that he wishes to remain married to you, but that for some reason he feels you cannot be together."

Lady Fanny glanced around and Jane nodded breathlessly. A stem broke in half and Lady Fanny made a sharp sound with her tongue and set it aside. "The early days of a marriage are fraught with potential for misunderstanding. Too many people who are otherwise quite sensible take the attitude that it is unromantical to simply say what one is thinking or feeling." Lady Fanny smiled as she tucked a lily into the vase. "One hopes that love will conquer all, but it so seldom does." She turned and faced Jane. "Forgive me for prying so into what is, after all, your own affair—and George's, naturally—but might it not be as well if you two were to at least see one another, and talk?"

Jane drew a deep breath, considering how to answer. Just the thought that George was not far away, that he was not with his mistress—had not been all this time—had left her feeling curiously light-headed.

"I . . . I think so," she said breathlessly. "That is, I would like it very much."

"You must do as you see fit, of course, but may I suggest that you seize the initiative?" Lady Fanny said. Her lovely face clouded over and she sighed and set down the snips. "I must confess, a mother likes to think that her children are quite, quite perfect, and so indeed they are for a great many years, but as they grow up, one is forced to see their less than

309

perfect traits. In the case of my son, it is his pride which most vexes me. I have sometimes thought it verged on what the Greeks called *hubris*—that sort of exalted pride which always results in a man's downfall." She picked up a flower and tucked it into the arrangement with an unerring eye. "If you decide you would like to go to the lodge, Bates can provide a groom to show you the way," she said with an easy smile, and then she resumed talking about flower arranging, as smoothly as if she had not just been talking about something far more serious.

Roger Creighton paused on the step of number thirty-two Half Moon Street. He had never been so nervous in his life. The exhaustive assault he had made on Clarisse so far rivaled the effort the British had put forth in the Peninsular campaign, but whether it would be sufficient had yet to be ascertained. A ceaseless stream of candy, small volumes of poetry, flowers and as many other items to tempt and please the woman of his dreams as had occurred to him had been arriving at this very door for weeks.

A footman opened the door to him, and relieved him of his hat, gloves and walking stick. The fact that he greeted Roger by name struck Roger as odd until he raised his quizzing glass and studied the man. "You used to work for the earl," Roger declared.

"I had that privilege," the footman admitted.

The oddness of it faded entirely. Of course George would have provided staff to Clarisse if she desired it. Roger took a last deep breath and walked into the sea green salon draped with chiffon at every window. In the midst of the opulent and seductive room sat Clarisse. She was even more breathtaking than Roger had allowed himself to remember.

"My dear Mr. Creighton," she said, holding out a long slender hand sheathed in pale green kid, "I believe you have not had the pleasure of meeting the Vicomte de Montparnasse."

310

Roger stifled an unpleasant retort. He had not had that pleasure nor did he wish to. The other visitor was of medium height and swarthy complexion. His eyes were wide set, the nose too long, and he had skin which had most decidedly been visited by the pox. The vicomte struck Roger as a man with a knack for eating at the tables of others while never feeling obliged to return the invitations, and his title was the most preposterously fictitious one Roger had ever heard. Nevertheless, he was forced to accept the introduction.

"I am honored, sir," Roger drawled.

"And this, Trevor dear, is Roger Creighton. I know you have heard me speak of him a hundred times. You will likely feel you know him already."

The other man essayed a patently false smile. *"Naturellement,* my love, but of course, any friend of yours may claim my friendship also."

Clarisse smiled a little wistfully at Roger and patted the sofa beside her. "Do sit with me, and tell me all that is new and interesting. London pales so in July, and one has no expectation of improvement in August. Do lift me out of my tedium with some of your witty stories."

"Yes, do," the vicomte added drily.

Roger had envisioned a far different scene but he was too seasoned at dalliance to be put out of countenance by so small an obstacle as the presence of the vicomte. Roger took Clarisse's hand with a lighthearted smile and looked into her eyes.

"We cannot allow you to be moped, can we, vicomte? It is true that this is a dull time of year but there was a most amusing incident the other night at the Daffy Club which you will appreciate . . ."

For nearly a quarter of an hour Roger labored to produce every bit of gossip he knew, every *bon mot,* every *mot juste,* every *on dit,* delivering them all in his drollest style. At the end of it he had coaxed a smile from Clarisse, and her lovely green eyes were shining.

"You see, Trevor, I told you Roger would be a tonic to us

both," she said brightly.

The vicomte, who had been lounging in a chair opposite the sofa, sat up and consulted his pocket watch in a desultory fashion. "Indeed, I am quite revived. I am obliged to you, sir, for raising my spirits."

Roger did not at all care for the vicomte's tone but his annoyance was short-lived since the vicomte followed that remark with an announcement that he must take his leave of them. "I am glad to have made your acquaintance," Roger said in a perfunctory way.

"And I yours," the vicomte replied. "My dear," he said, turning to Clarisse, "I shall give more thought to the matter which concerns you above all else, and if that cannot be resolved to your satisfaction, then perhaps there are other fish that can be made to bite." He flicked a faintly disdainful look at Roger and added, *"Un grand poisson . . . grand et très riche."*

"Oh, but I do so wish for . . . well, you know," Clarisse said, her face falling again. Roger felt ready to murder the vicomte for spoiling the effect of his labors.

When the footman appeared to show the vicomte out, Clarisse lifted a sad face to Roger and asked if he would take some refreshment. Roger, who knew an invitation to extend one's visit when he heard it, accepted gladly.

"Manning, some tea and . . . oh, whatever else. Or do you prefer coffee?"

Roger felt a deep glow of satisfaction that she was inquiring as to his preferences, even though it was over such an inconsequential matter. "Yes, coffee." The footman left and Roger commented on the fact that he had last seen the man in Bath.

"Oh, yes," Clarisse said. "I had a porter before, satisfactory, but not nearly so suitable as Manning. Manning came to me looking for employment after George married. He said it was so very disagreeable to work in a household where *she* was mistress that he gave his notice immediately."

Roger did not generally concern himself with his own servants, never mind those of his friends, but it seemed to him that George had said something derogatory about one of his footmen in connection with Portia's purported elopement. Exactly what he had said, and about which footmen, eluded Roger so he merely said to Clarisse, "He was lucky indeed to have been hired by you."

Clarisse looked a little sad, her full pink lips turning out in a faint pout that became her beautifully. "I had some thought at the time that he might have information regarding *her* that I might see use to advantage. I had thought George would continue to be my *bel ami* after his marriage. Why, I asked myself, has he turned aside from me simply because of *her*? After all, most men do not give up their mistresses just because they take a so insipid little English girl to wife. Besides, George is a potent man, a virile man. Why can he not simply divide his attentions?"

Roger was nonplussed. It was not at all the sort of conversation he had hoped to have with Clarisse, given that Wofford had made it plain that the affair was quite, quite dead as far as his employer was concerned. A rare and scholarly biography on Bacon—run to earth by Roger at no little trouble—had sufficed to woo that information out of Wofford.

"I do not know what you wish me to say," Roger replied. "He is a fool, of course. Any man who has turned away from you must be!"

Clarisse softened her expression. "You are kind to say so, but I fear that it is of little consolation to me. Oh, when the wedding announcement appeared, I was bothered, annoyed, certainly, but I did not think it was of such grave consequence, you see. *Bien sûr*, if he had taken another mistress, I should have been, oh, *très désolée*, but a wife! This, I thought, will be the merest nothing. It need not concern me. How wrong I was!"

Clarisse began wringing her hands with a theatricality that pleased the eye and tugged at the heart. Roger seized her hands between his own without forethought, and saw the surprise in her eyes. "Only let me be your confidant, your friend," he declared with feeling. "I will do my best to help you recover from this loss."

"Oh, you are the kindest, dearest person," Clarisse said. "I wish I could give you some encouragement, but, alas, I am still absorbed by thoughts of *him*. You are his friend. You must know what I have seen with my own eyes, that he is not a happy man! This marriage is no good for him. He came to London when they were married but a week, and he went out and gambled and drank and engaged in fist fights until his poor face was quite in ruins. Are these the actions of a happy bridegroom?" she asked with a catch in her voice.

Roger, to whom all of this was news, had to think for a moment. "No, he said, "on the whole, one must say they are not."

"He is not happy with her," Clarisse repeated emphatically. She pulled her hands away from Roger's and rose. "Oh, I can barely think of it without wanting to wring her neck!"

Roger watched in dismay as Clarisse paced in agitation. The conversation was now as far removed from the one he had wanted to have with her as it was possible for it to be, and yet, he could not see how to turn her thoughts away from George and toward himself. Perhaps if he commiserated with her she would come to the end of lamenting over what had gone before and make a new start with him.

"I am bound for Sefton Hall quite soon," he offered. "I might be able to let you know on my return how I find George, whether he seems content, or well, or . . ."

Clarisse instantly went still, regarding him raptly. "He is there? You will see him with your own eyes?"

"Well, it will be a dashed odd house party if I don't," Roger said with an attempt at lightness. "It was all set months ago, while he was still in Bath, even before he . . . well, before . . ."

Manning entered with a tray and Roger stopped speaking

abruptly, remembering what it was George had said—that Manning lacked a proper sense of discretion. That was George for you, covered in propriety, but still, better to guard one's tongue.

Clarisse sat down opposite Roger when Manning had withdrawn. She poured Roger a cup of coffee, inquired as to how he took it, and smiled at him in a most beguiling way. "This house party, it will be a large one?"

"Can't say, really—didn't ask. George asks, we come. There's always good sport to be had there, and good food."

"I would like very much what you suggested, a report from your own lips as to how George fares. When is it that you will see him?"

"We're expected on Friday next," Roger said. "I will gladly come to you as soon as I return to London, and tell you everything, though if it should prove that he is happy, I will be sorry to be the one to tell you it."

"I want only his happiness," Clarisse said demurely. "If he is happy, then I must be glad for it."

"And if he is not?"

Clarisse shrugged. "Who can say?"

Chapter Eighteen

As Jane got closer to the lodge, she told herself over and over that her reason for coming was to tell George the truth, that she did not carry his child and that he could be free of her. As in Bath, however, the thought of freeing him to leave her behind forever put her into an awful state, one in which her heart's anguish drowned out virtually every other consideration.

She slowed her steps. The map she had desired Williams to make for her had brought her to this point unerringly, where one more turn would take her within view of the hunting lodge. She stopped next to a large oleander and peered through the lengthening shadows of late afternoon. Without conscious thought she left the pathway and walked softly into the lightly wooded area which surrounded it. Mounted and with a groom coming along behind, she would have had to ride up to the lodge without delay, so she had chosen instead to come on foot. A part of her had foreseen this moment, when she would lose her nerve and try to hit upon some compromise.

When she had gone a little way, she was able to see the lodge. She crept to the border of the woods and waited for some sign of George's presence. The half-timbered lodge was dark and quiet, with no sign of habitation. An hour passed and the woods grew dark, although the sun was still shining on the open ground beyond.

At long last George appeared. He walked slowly, as if he had no more desire to be where he was going than where he had just been. How different he looked, though just as elegant and compelling as ever, even in rough clothes. He carried a gun, broken and balanced with unthinking grace in the crook of his arm, the barrel resting over his forearm. He was hatless, too, with just a cloth knotted loosely at his throat. The sight of him, his hair shining darkly in the afternoon sun, his spare, broad-shouldered physique revealed so clearly by the lack of tailored clothing, sent a curious tremor through her, and she found herself remembering the night in Bath when he had taken her in his arms.

He disappeared into the lodge and Jane waited, for what she was not sure. A small plume of smoke rose from a chimney a few minutes later, and George appeared in the open doorway. He stood there with a glass in his hand and his shirtsleeves pushed up on forearms browned by the sun. Jane shivered in anticipation. The other, darker plan, which had never been far from her mind, was taking hold.

If she went to him now and they did *that*, she would have another chance to conceive, another chance to keep their marriage alive. George turned his head and Jane's mouth went dry. Had he seen her? But no. He was only following the sound of something crashing through the underbrush on the far side of the clearing.

Jane felt her breathing quicken as he took a drink and looked up at the stars just beginning to glimmer in the sky. His throat was ruddy from the sun, the underside of his chin still pale. His hair fell back from his face carelessly. He was so different-looking in the open-necked shirt and loose trousers of rough linen, but the whole effect was to make her want to be near him.

She reached out for a tree to steady herself. Would he want to be near *her*? Why was he staying out here when he could be at Sefton Hall? She felt a welling uncertainty. Had she given him such a lively disgust of her after that last time that he had not wished to be obliged to share even the same house with her again?

Jane's eyes grew moist with tears at the thought. If she went to him now, she must contrive to be at her most ladylike. She wanted him to take her in his arms again, with a trembling anticipation that arose from somewhere in the vicinity of her middle as well as from the calculated desire that originated in her mind. If she went to him and he touched her, she must keep the hoarse little cries to herself though, and the heat and the soaring and the pleasure. She must somehow discover a way to behave as a countess should, even while—most especially while—caught up in *that*. A mistress might be able to behave in a vulgar way but a wife must not—Jane felt sure of that. His mistress could provide him with whatever . . . wantonness he desired. She could not, and still lay claim to being respectable and decent, and deserving of being his wife.

George turned and went into the lodge. She concluded from the evidence of the smoke that he was making some sort of evening meal for himself and debated whether she ought to delay until she felt sure he had eaten. Were men not generally known for being in a better mood after a meal? But she could not put it off any longer. There was an edgy impatience in her that was growing stronger by the moment. She took the first step out of the woods and then the next. Now. It must be now, or she would lose what little boldness she possessed.

She walked swiftly across the open meadow to the lodge and then hesitated at the still open door. A lamp inside the main room lit a large shadowy space with a few comfortable pieces of furniture grouped around an unused fireplace. There was certainly no sense of formality here, no entry hall, no grand staircase, no liveried servants. She heard a sound through a door off to the left and then George came through

318

it, carrying a plate with bread and cheese. He saw her and stopped abruptly.

The expression on his face was indecipherable. "Jane."

"I . . . I was just about to knock," she said, swallowing.

"Come in then," he said, "that is, if you are not merely passing by."

"I had not intended to," she said, lowering her eyes. The sight of his face was having the most amazing effect on her insides. The faint shadow of whiskers grown out since morning, which she had never seen on him before, the sharp angle of his jaw, the full, well-defined mouth—she had forgotten how impossibly handsome he was, the rugged good looks that far surpassed Roger Creighton's sort of male perfection in her estimation.

George gestured around him a little sheepishly. "I am come down in the world somewhat, as you can see. I had no taste for London after all."

"I am glad," Jane said, realizing belatedly that she sounded breathless, as if she had run across the meadow instead of walking. "That is, I had supposed you to be far away, and when I discovered you were not far away at all but quite close by . . ." She trailed off as she looked up and caught his gaze on her, searching and intent.

"Quite close by . . . ?" he prompted.

"Oh! Well, then I thought it were better if I . . . I called and . . . and . . ." Her chest felt queerly tight.

George stared at her for what seemed like an age before he broke the silence, a feat which was beyond her. "Well, since you are here, I had better offer you something. Tea? Or perhaps sherry? I think there is some of that about."

"No smuggled brandy?" Jane asked in a small voice.

His mouth twisted up at the corner and there was a hint of warmth in the deep-hooded eyes. It overlaid a curious heat which had been there just an instant before and helped to restore Jane's breath. "Alas, no," he said, "though there has been many an evening when I would have appreciated it keenly." He went to a cabinet and searched among its contents. "Port," he announced, withdrawing a dusty bottle, "though I would not care to vouch for its lineage. Will you try some?"

Jane nodded. She took a step into the room and felt it envelop her in its maleness. George uncorked the port and poured some into a glass. It gave her an odd sensation as he approached and held it out to her. He seemed reluctant to let it go, even when she had gotten a good hold on it. They stared at each other, each holding a part of the glass.

It was he who broke the moment finally, slowly withdrawing his hand and allowing her to hold the glass unaided. "You are well?" he asked, his eyes never leaving hers.

Jane experienced a sinking feeling. Was he asking indirectly whether she was with child? "I am . . . well," she said hesitantly, "though I . . ."

He was watching her intently. *Where had all the air in the room gone?* Jane took a hasty drink and choked on it. Instantly he was at her side, taking the glass and patting her back, but she could not seem to stop coughing.

"Wait here," he snapped.

Tears began to run down Jane's cheeks from the force of her coughing. It was too silly. She could not seem to swallow and set her throat to rights.

"Take a sip of this," George demanded. He put his arm around her shoulder and braced her so that she could be still long enough to sip from the glass of water he held. She put both her hands around it.

When at last she was able to draw a free breath, he slowly released her.

"Thank you," she said shakily. His head looming above hers invoked all the times he had taken her onto the dance floor in Bath. She realized she was still holding the glass of water in both hands, and that his fingers were beneath hers. She let go of it and wiped ineffectually at her face.

320

"Here," he said, his voice rich and soothing so near her ear, "let me." He took her spectacles off and dabbed at her cheeks.

Jane stood stock still, staring up at him. Without her spectacles, she saw small details she had not noticed before—a barely healed cut over his upper lip, a mottled area of green and yellow on his forehead. He was still tenderly drying her face, and without thinking she reached out to touch a fading bruise near his eye. "Your face," she said dumbly.

"It was nothing," he said, pausing in the act of wiping her cheek.

"But someone hurt you," she whispered, still touching the spot.

"Oh, Jane," he said.

Her stomach twisted, wrenching the breath out of her. He was looking at her such that she could meet his gaze for only a moment, and then she closed her eyes. She felt him leaning over her. First his breath touched her, and then his mouth. A flame raced down the center of her being and out to all her limbs. It was so sweet! She felt the beginnings of a moan arise in her throat and she stifled the sound, even though the feeling which had given rise to it grew bolder and hotter by the minute. She fought the urge to melt against him and settled for resting her hands on his chest. She remembered all too clearly the surfeit of dark hair which had been visible at the neck of his shirt. She turned her face to deepen the kiss and resisted using her hands to burrow, to explore.

The handkerchief George held in his hand fell to the floor. He pulled back and took her face in both hands, peering at her with a strength of focus that made her feel very odd.

"Oh, Jane," he said a second time.

Jane felt herself go weak. Oh, let him touch her! Her legs were trembling and she wanted so much to cling to him for support, though paradoxically it was he who robbed her of her strength. His arms went around her and she accepted his

321

kiss not willingly but wantonly, turning this way and that. She felt a tiny flame between her legs that flickered and grew brighter. It was that same flame that had burst and made her cry out in Bath, only now it had started earlier, much earlier.

Think! She must think! Think of smelting ores and . . . and metalworking! She reread a page of *Pirotechnica* in her head as George pulled her up against his chest and massaged her back urgently, pressing her breasts into him. Smelting . . . smelting ores! And . . . and hammering out precious metals to . . . to make them into leaf! Jane wanted to weep with the futility of it. As if ores and smelting and whole rafts of Italian metalworkers could distract her from the heavenly insistence of George's hands at her back!

And yet she must do *something!* Already her hands were finding their way into his shirt, and twining through the short soft curls there, her fingers eager to pull the fabric aside and . . . Flowers! Tin snips! Shortest in the front, taller at the rear! He widened his stance, bracing her between his legs and pulling her within the circle of his arms, his shoulders, his scent . . . And mustn't forget phlox! It was good for arrangements. Lady Fanny had said so!

"Jane, Jane, my own wife," George whispered as he kissed his way past her ear. "I am so happy you are come . . ."

Jane swayed into him, aching cries, mere whimpers really, escaping from her with each rapid exhalation. George pulled away her Kashmir shawl, the fabulously lovely and expensive one he had chosen for her in Bath. It slid to the floor and Jane forgot all about it. She tipped her head back and received a kiss from George that sent a flush of exquisite sensation through her breasts and stomach and on down, lower where . . . Haydn! She squeezed her eyes shut and hummed a melody in her head, one Portia had been playing incessantly of late. George pushed the sleeve off one of her shoulders and lightly kissed the bare skin there and rubbed his cheek across it, murmuring something unintelligible.

322

"Oh, yes," Jane whispered breathlessly. The heat and the hardness of his thighs burned through their respective clothing, and she clutched at the hair on his chest.

"Will you, Jane?" he asked softly, pulling back. "Come and be a wife to me and let me be a husband to you?"

That was what he had been asking. She had hoped so hard that she had heard the question even before it had been properly asked. "Yes, yes," she managed to say. Her lips felt puffy from being kissed, full and bruised and infinitely sensitive. He began to touch her softly with his lips, not kissing precisely, but . . . touching . . . following the line of her collarbone until he found a pulse at the side of her neck that rushed and skipped like a stream scurrying over stones. Oh, it felt so very nice! Her knees went spongy and his breath fanned over her ear . . . Haydn! Base metals! Tin snips. . . .

She had come to him. Miraculously and unimaginably she had found him, God knew how, but all he had felt was fierce satisfaction when he looked up and saw her standing there. Seeing her from within a hedgerow, or from the heights of a tree sturdy enough to support the weight of a man trying to secretly catch a glimpse of his own wife, was no substitute for this.

The lantern's light picked out the golds in her hair, and buffed the prominent cheekbones with light. She looked wonderfully well, if a little thinner. The eyes, so large and intelligent by the light of day, appeared, impossibly, even larger now, in the heavy shadows of his lair. But it was all secondary to the hesitation, the uncertainty in her steps, her tentative crossing of his threshold.

She *had* come, though, and then she had accepted his touches with a certain strained tension, but he could not let it rest there. He had to know, had to ask, if somehow it could be made right with them. Could she allow him to touch her—fully clothed and fully aware? It would be easy for her to

323

walk out the open door again if she did not—could not—accept his touch.

Will you be a wife to me as I will be a husband to you? It had never been asked nor answered between them, except during the painfully subdued wedding ceremony at Sefton House, and now it must be, in private.

How stunning to hear her say *yes*. He went softly with her, tenderly, and felt the stiffness go from her bones, the resistance from her muscles. Dark, furling desire nearly undid him when he heard her sigh, and felt her touching him of her own accord.

He owed her every ounce of control he possessed. Everything else he could offer her would be as nothing if he failed her this time, this time when she came to him of her own free will, and had reached out to touch him first. He gripped her waist as her dress gaped open in the back, drinking in fully the kiss she returned with ardor. The corset was the merest nothing to be done with for hands so feverishly impatient to move past it. He plucked at the ribbon on her chemise with his teeth, and trailed his mouth over the soft swell of her breasts, pushed past the cloth with his nose. She arched and whimpered as he found one nipple, a small, maidenly pink one that furled in his mouth, and made his gut tighten as he swept his tongue across it.

George made a sudden decision and swept Jane into his arms. He was so hot and taut, so ready, that he could not endure to stand there another minute. He would stop, he swore he would stop, if she made the least protest. But she did not. His booted heels rang out sharply on the wide plank flooring as he strode across the room.

The small bedroom was only silver outlines in the very last of twilight, with a silver mass at its center that was linens washed and pressed with care at the main house. But it did not suit him to have the duvet beneath them, soft and bulky. He braced his thigh against the bedstead and twitched the cover away, leaving the plain bed beneath.

Jane had undone his shirt as far as his trousers would allow. George set her down and covered her with his body. It was like a dream to feel her arms come up around him and to hear her breathing, rushed and panicked-sounding like his own as she aimed haphazard kisses at his jaw. He murmured her name and she moved beneath him in invitation. It was past doubting that she wished him to be doing this, that she wished to share in married pleasure with him. The thought hit like lightning, arousing him with a sharp twisting sensation. *Married pleasure.* It *was* pleasure, and they were married. Dear God, how could that prosaic prospect have the power to ignite him as nothing else ever had?

A quiet moan escaped her as he unfastened his trousers and slid them off, and his hand came back to find her clothing. The chemise and dress and corset came off as one, down past her hips, leaving her perfectly silken and naked in the silver light. She stared at him when he paused above her in the act of returning, her eyes wide and full of unanswered questions. Her lips were parted, her brows raised. The lovely breasts moved rapidly in the silver light, in unison with her breath. He lay over her, his elbows braced at either side of her head, and softly pushed his fingers through the dark strands of her hair. He had never been so happy in his life, so undeniably happy to be exactly where he was, doing exactly what he was doing.

"I have been dreaming of this for weeks," he said softly, "to have you in my arms and to touch you." She relaxed beneath him, smiling a little, and he kissed her.

"I . . . I'm glad," she said breathlessly. "I wished for it, too."

He would save the rest of his words for later, for those spent moments when pleasure had left them on the shores of deep cleansing sleep. He gathered her to him and slowly entered her. Her small cries and the answering thrusts of her hips pulled him deeper and deeper, until he could go no further. She was so bright and hot, all wrapped around him, that he felt as if he might burst into a hundred shards of light.

Her hands on his shoulders recalled him to the moment. With gentle force he pushed against her and heard a soft cry of pleasure, a swooning sound belied by the pressure of her fingers on his arms. He gave himself over to it, pushed and withdrew, and felt the tension in her hands increasing with each thrust. Tight sounds of longing grew in her throat and he found that concentrating on them gave him the key he had been looking for, and served as welcome distraction from his own pleasure.

Her cries grew louder and George fought the instinct to follow her pleasure with his own. He could not be sure of her, and he would not release himself until he was. The convulsive movement of her body beneath his was provocation almost beyond endurance. She embraced him from deep within, and the sounds she made touched the innermost part of him, drawing forth a response he was powerless to resist.

He drove into her, hard, and she gasped, clinging to him. She was tossing her head from side to side, as if fighting it. The satisfaction was almost too frighteningly much, even for him, but he would not let her evade her own. She must ride the current with him. He took her lips in a fierce kiss, stilling the thrashing of her head and lifting her body with his own. She moaned against his lips and tried one last futile time to escape this thing they had created but he would not let her.

She began working earnestly to meet his rhythm then, and he exulted in the long, drawn-out sounds of pleasure she made. In the meshing of their bodies there was only accord now, one exultant sensation divided between them. The torrent of pleasure rushed downward without mercy, and he heard Jane calling his name. He had never felt anything like it in his life. Jane panted and cried out beneath him, her fingers winding through the hair on the back of his head. Dear God, if one could die of pleasure, this was surely the moment when it must happen!

Jane's breathless cries filled his ears as she wrapped herself around him. Her body went taut and George felt the swift current carry him into her. It was explosive, flame to powder. He reared back and groaned, a stiff painful sound compared to Jane's sweet sounds of ecstasy, but he was far beyond caring.

Jane came back to herself slowly, out of a deep, swirling place where she had been drawn by George's touches. He had held her tight but then he had pushed himself away from her at the last, with a kind of dazed astonishment on his face and a strangled sound in his throat. Jane lay still breathing heavily, and realized with dismay that she had broken every promise she had made before walking into the lodge, and into George's arms. He lay flat on his back now, his eyes closed, and she clenched her hands at her sides. It was as if he were pretending she did not exist, was not lying next to him. She waited for him to say something, biting down hard on her tongue to keep the tears at bay. She could still hear the echoes of the awful wanton sounds she had made! The flame had been too high, far too bright and hot to resist.

George still said nothing. Hot tears squeezed out from under the eyelids.

"George?" She could not make it louder than a whisper.

The only response from him was a deep rumbling sound. Jane cringed. He had never answered her by grunting before, but perhaps it was what she deserved, to be dismissed with a grunt after the way she had behaved, like an animal.

Her jaw began to quiver. Oh, God, he despised her! He would simply lie there until she left, and then he would get up and go on as if she had never come to his door. He had asked her to be a wife to him, not a harlot! He lay utterly still now, not even breathing heavily anymore. The golden afterglow of pleasure drained out of her, leaving behind nothing but profound misery.

327

Jane felt her face screwing up as a sob tried to burst forth. She froze her face as it was through sheer will, though she could not control the tears which began flowing down her cheeks. The anguished cries that wanted to go with the tears she bottled up in her throat, and they could be heard only as strangled whimpers as she crept from the bed.

She groped on the floor for her stockings and shoes, her dress and chemise and corset. She bumped into a chest at the foot of the bed, and stubbed her toes on the brass bedstand, but there was no indication from George that he knew or cared that she was leaving. Naked in the twilight, barely able to see, Jane did not even glance backward as she slunk out of the bedroom in disgrace. No voice called her back, no soft invitation to return and be a wife.

She did not know what he had done with her spectacles, and the irony was that she could not see well enough without them to search for them. It seemed a mercy not to perceive the world too clearly just now, though. Jane fought down the increasingly strong convulsions in her middle, the ones that wanted to turn into sobs, and struggled into her clothing by the light of the lantern in the main room. The Kashmir shawl was a rich pool of color on the floor and she snatched it up to wrap around her, to hide the inexpertly laced up dress. She was growing short of breath now, from clenching back her tears, and she had to open her mouth a little, just to get some more air.

To her consternation, the strangled sobs became hugely audible. She could not fight them anymore, and as she tied on her stockings, it seemed to her ears that her crying filled the room. She pulled on her shoes, so blinded by tears that she could not even see to lace them properly. At last she arose and stumbled toward the door. Somehow she must find her way through the night, back to the hall.

"Jane!"

She whirled and saw George standing in the doorway to the bedroom. He was naked, all paleness against the

328

backdrop of night in the room behind him. Though she could not see his face very well, her memory and his tone supplied an expression. It was still the shocked, disbelieving one he had worn when she had cried out—moaned!—so loudly toward the last. . . .

"I must go," she said. *And now, before he came any closer and she had to have it confirmed that he was wearing that same look on his face again.* "I'm sorry . . . I shouldn't have . . . it was wrong of me to . . . I cannot be a wife to . . ."

Tears blinded her and she turned and fled, narrowly missing running into the door jamb in her headlong dash to escape the scene of her humiliation.

"Jane! Stop! Come back!"

"No, I mustn't! I'm sorry, I'm sorry," Jane cried. The words were formless, shapeless apologies thrown over her shoulder as she ran, thrown back at the ghostly outline of her husband.

The pale shape followed her into the night with sharp demands. "Stop, Jane—this is madness! You'll get lost! Wait and I will . . ."

But she ran into the first of the trees then, and his voice was obscured by the leaves slapping at her. Oh, if only she hadn't come. Panicked by the branches and leaves that came out of nowhere and grabbed at her and stung her face, Jane raced on clumsily. Her nankeen boots were only imperfectly tied but that fact did not slow her down noticeably, so great was her compulsion to escape. She could not forget the expression on George's face as he had looked down at her when . . . while . . .

She ran and stumbled back nearly the whole way that it taken her almost an hour to walk. Following the silver ribbon of the carriage tracks, past the turnoff to the home farm and beyond that to the village, Jane persisted. Sefton Hall appeared as a huge dark shape in the night, with fat blobs of golden light at intervals in the mass, and slivers of it running down and melting across the terraces and lawn.

329

Ellen bounded up from a chair when Jane flew into the bedroom and slammed the door behind her. "My lady!" she cried. "Wherever have you been? Why, what's happened to you? Your dress, and you . . . It's him, ain't it?" she said darkly. "He's come back and now he's gone and done this to you!"

Shaky and exhausted from running, Jane leaned back against the closed door and shook her head. "Not his fault," she managed to gasp. "Not his, mine."

"Hmph! What you want to defend him for, that's what I'd like to know," the maid declared. "He's like an animal, he is—always at you, a-tearin' at your clothes, upsettin' you. Be better off married to a dustman, you would. Leastways a dustman would treat you like a lady, which his lordship certainly don't!"

Jane closed her eyes. It was she and only she who had disqualified herself from being treated like a lady. "Am I going to be late for dinner?"

She felt rather than saw Ellen pursing her lips. "Well, not if we hurry. Water came up half an hour ago, at least."

"Then we had better hurry," Jane said, tiredly pushing herself away from the door. She had no wish to add further to her disgrace by being late for dinner.

Chapter Nineteen

Lady Fanny sat her horse with perfect ease, blessing her son's impeccable judgment where horseflesh was concerned and thanking the powers that be for Fabrice's complete lack of interest in all things equine, for it had saved her from having to shoo her husband away from accompanying her. She was just vain enough to be glad he was so gallant as to have walked to the stairs with her, though, for she did feel that the blue cheviot riding habit suited her exceptionally well. It was nice to know that one looked one's best when one was tending to such a delicate errand.

Gandolfo waxed eloquent over her appearance and compared her most improbably to several heroines in history. Really, he was so adorable, and so very romantical! Fabrice tolerated his countryman with amused patience, allowing his young friend to kiss his wife's hand several times before suggesting he go off to see whether Portia might enjoy a stroll.

Gandolfo's face brightened momentarily, and then fell with such exaggerated woe that Fanny was forced to raise her gloved hand to cover her smile. "Oh, the Lady Portia is all that one could desire," Gandolfo said. "Indeed, one desires her enormously but how is one to court where words can do no good? Where even words she does not comprehend produce blushes? She is a gentle flower, that one."

Fanny had to resist the temptation to snort. "Fabrice, darling, do see if you cannot contrive to teach this poor boy some few words of English which he could use with Portia, for he cannot go on this way."

"It is true!" Gandolfo declared. "I shall die for lack of love if I do not somehow find a way to say the things which are bursting within my breast."

Fabrice retrieved his wife's hand from Gandolfo's and gave her a confiding smile. "It shall be done, my darling. By this evening you shall be amazed at how he will go on."

When Fanny walked into the hunting lodge, she decided she could very well do for some pleasant surprises that night, for the place where her son had been residing inspired nothing but alarm in her. George evidently cared nothing for what he ate, for there was a plate of bread and cheese gone hard on a side table. An uncorked bottle sat dusty and forgotten next to it, the bed was in disarray, and there was an overall sense of uncaring.

Servants would have to be sent down to make all right, but for this as well as other, more pressing, reasons, she must persuade George to come back to live at the hall. Henry had let it be known through Wofford that he was prepared to come at a moment's notice, even to ride the night mail down if called on to do so, for it pained him greatly to know that his master must be inadequately turned out. However much pain that brought the small man, Lady Fanny had her doubts that he could come down "cheerfully" by the night mail, as Wofford's letter had indicated. The servant no less than the master was accustomed to doing things in comfort and style. It made the current state of affairs all that much more unsettling.

But when George arrived, she set out to upbraid him in the gentlest possible terms, for though the tale of Jane's disheveled and tearful return had reached her through a

332

network of spies Napoleon must envy, now that she came to see the other party with her own eyes, she realized that the groom was suffering quite as much as the bride. She watched him coming across the open meadow and wondered if the gamekeeper's clothes were an affectation he intended to introduce to the *ton,* but there was a certain flatness in his bearing that convinced her the clothes were no affection but rather a complete lack of it. Though the clothes were common, there was nothing common about the man, and Fanny felt her heart swell with love for her firstborn as he came in through the door.

"Mother!"

"Darling boy," Lady Fanny said. She smiled at him tenderly. "Will you not embrace your mother? I am sorry to arrive unexpectedly, but I was finding the Mediterranean heat a trifle oppressive."

"You look wonderfully well," George said, placing a kiss on her soft, powdered cheek. He dropped an empty game bag onto a chair and looked around, seeming to see the place through his mother's eyes. "I wish I had known you were coming. I have—that is, I could make you some tea."

Fanny drew him toward a sofa. "I don't suppose—no, I can't think that any gentleman would stock his hunting lodge with ratafia. Feminine company is so seldom forthcoming in such a place. Perhaps just a glass of cold water?"

She drew off her gloves and smiled at him brightly. It would take too much time for him to light the kitchen fire, and for water to boil. Already she saw his surprise at her appearance wearing off, his defenses dropping into place. If she was to make any headway, she must strike quickly. She heard the rhythmic sound of a pump handle in the kitchen and then he returned.

"Come sit with me, dear," she said, holding out her hand for the water.

"I won't," he said, withdrawing to a chair opposite. "I fear that long days in the sun leave me less than suitable for sitting next to."

He was already proof against any subtlety. There was a hard look around his eyes, and an intractable air about him.

Fanny took a sip of water. *Best to start at the beginning.* "I have met Jane and I want to congratulate you on your choice," she said. "She is a charming girl."

"I know," George said shortly.

Fanny sighed. "I do not wish to pry, truly I don't, but could you not come and stay at the hall? Whatever is the issue between you, my darling, it cannot be resolved if you persist in skulking about out here."

George stood up abruptly and Fanny flinched. She had exceeded the limit of what a mother might say to her grown son.

"The issue between us would appear to be insuperable," George said stiffly. "Proximity can only aggravate it."

"Oh, surely not!" Fanny protested. "You cannot mean to consider yourselves at a stand when you have barely made a beginning."

George's gaze flicked across the room briefly and then returned to her. He gripped his hands behind him and said, "At the risk of being indelicate, Mother, you are well aware that not all things can be mended within a marriage. Such is the case between my wife and me."

Fanny paled. "But surely you have not—you could not even have had the time to . . . to . . ."

"Certainly not," he replied with an edge to his voice, "but that is hardly the only way to prejudice one's marriage. No, in my own misbegotten way, I did worse. Jane has every right to revile me. I revile myself, for that matter. I beg you will not bring her more pain by persisting in trying to repair matters." He turned away, his back rigid. "She came here yesterday. I do not know how she discovered my where-abouts, but that is nothing to the point. She came, and I . . . I misinterpreted her reason for coming here. Never-

334

theless, she made a spirited attempt to . . . to overcome the issue which divides us." He turned back to face his mother. "The encounter was an unmitigated failure, except insofar as it confirmed for me the futility of continuing our marriage."

"Oh, George, I am most dreadfully sorry for you both," Fanny whispered. She stared at the floor for a long moment before rising and drawing on her gloves. "The little mare I am riding—she is a delight, but I must not keep her standing any longer. Could I not persuade you to come to the hall for dinner tonight? I had not time to write and tell you of it before you wrote to me of your own marriage, but George dear, I met a man in Italy who positively made me fall in love with him. It would have been fatuous in the extreme at my age to seek your permission as head of the family to remarry, but I would be so very disappointed if you did not wish me happy, and come to at least meet him."

"You know I wish you happy, Mother," George said, the shadow of a smile lifting the corner of his mouth. "I have always wished that for you."

"Oh, I know you have," Fanny cried, dabbing at the corner of her eye, "as I have wished it for you. Will you come? It seems everyone knows you are here now, and so it would be the greatest insult if you did not acknowledge him. If you do not care for him, I shall understand, but I believe you will see that he is wonderfully good for me."

"Then that is reason enough to acknowledge him."

Fanny smiled a little shyly, glancing up at her son from under her lashes. "He is Italian, very romantic. I can only say that it has been a revelation."

George waited until dusk and then walked to the hall. The whole way he reflected on Jane's having passed this same way the night before. He thought of her slender legs carrying her away from him with such determination that she was nothing but a blur as she crossed the meadow. If he had not touched her in the first place, they might at least have talked, but the heat and the wanting had overpowered him.

His punishment for that weakness was to relive the night in London over and over. Until Jane had arrived at the lodge, he'd almost convinced himself that he had learned his lesson, and that he could control himself where she was concerned. What a travesty. He was a slave to the passion she aroused in him—sweet, beautiful Jane, who no more intended to have that effect on him than he had meant to rape her.

He flushed with shame in the night air, shaking as he strode along. Dear God, she had cried so last night, as if her heart would break, and he had felt her pain so keenly he could almost taste her tears. But that was after he had been stunned into senselessness, turned inside out by pleasure and rendered incapable of staying awake. It was extraordinary to make love to Jane, and whatever else the future might hold, he knew he would never desire another woman the way he desired Jane, nor know that kind of pleasure in another woman's arms.

But where was the compromise? She had tried—oh, how she had tried!—to tolerate his touch. He had felt her respond, even, and the heat that had created in him did not bear thinking about, but when all was said and done, she had regretted it, and had wanted to be away from him afterwards with something like desperation. It would not do. He stopped for a minute and drew in a deep breath, tilting his head back to stare at the night sky. He could never allow himself to be alone with her again, and in the end, he must give her up to someone who had not destroyed her trust, whose touch she could accept without wanting to cry afterwards.

He was full of cold resolve when he arrived at the hall and made his way to his apartments, far from the charming rooms he had ordered the staff to prepare for Jane. A quick bath and he put on the evening attire always left there, along with duplicates of all his other essential clothes. Henry had left it all in such perfect order that even the footman recruited to act as his valet had no difficulty in turning out a respectable product.

George stared at himself in the glass after he had dismissed the footman. Was he respectable? His hair was too long, too many weeks removed from barbering, his hands were remarkably brown against the linen, his neck ruddy next to the stiff white collar. He was not at all what would pass in London as respectable, but it was the darker currents in him, the overpowering passion and ungovernable emotions that disqualified him from the ranks of the truly respectable. He was not his father's son for nothing.

He descended for dinner in a very black mood indeed, prepared to see Jane and yet keep away from her, to prove to her that he could find some restraint in himself. In the breast pocket of his evening jacket was a memento of his dark side, lest he forget it for an instant. He touched the fine wool and felt the shape of her spectacles beneath his fingers. He had been on the verge of directing the footman to deliver them to her when he realized that they were just the token he needed to keep himself in check for this one evening, a reminder of how he had taken them away and swept her up in something for which she had no wish. When he left tonight, he would set them on his dresser with a note to Jane, apologizing for keeping them one more night. She would not understand his motive for doing so—he barely understood it himself—but she would not think worse of him for it. She could forgive, and accommodate, and find the good in one even when one was hard pressed to find it oneself. It was only that, in his case, there was no good to be found.

Such were his thoughts when he spied Jane across the large drawing room, and at her side a handsome, dark-haired man with a mischievous grin and dancing eyes.

"Oh, my!" Gandolfo exclaimed, glancing up. "Who is that exceptionally fierce gentleman?"

Without even one of her lorgnettes—which had been packed hastily in Bath and not found since—Jane had to

337

squint. She saw the footmen in blue and yellow Sefton livery, Portia at the pianoforte, and Lady Fanny with Fabrice, her gold curls shimmering next to her husband's sleek dark head. Lady Fanny turned and held out her hand and it was then that Jane perceived the newcomer. She had to squint a little more to be sure of what the height and breadth of shoulder already suggested. George.

"That is Lady Fanny's son," Jane said in Italian, her voice carefully neutral. "He is George Aubrey Tate, Earl of Sefton."

"How very grand, to be sure," Gandolfo murmured. "He is a splendid figure of a man, is he not?"

"I believe there are many who think so."

Gandolfo peered at her with an impish smile. "You do not like this George Aubrey Tate then?"

Jane could only stare ahead miserably. She could not begin to explain to Gandolfo the nature of the relationship between her husband and herself. "It . . . it seems to me that he is a fine-looking man," she said reluctantly.

"See how he glares in our direction!" Gandolfo said. "I do not believe he cares at all for seeing my poor self in his drawing room. This is *his* drawing room, is it not?"

Jane nodded. George did not move toward them and she felt she would die of shame. It was so painfully obvious that her husband wanted nothing to do with her. "Shall we practice your English words one more time?" she said with an effort.

"Oh, but of course. *Your lips are like roses in spring. Come share the moon and the stars with me! I can barely sleep for thinking of you!*"

Jane giggled. He was so preposterously enchanting, with his earnest declarations of the awful phrases Fabrice had taught him. "That is very good," she said, "but do you have the least clue what you are saying?"

"Not the slightest," he replied, shrugging and grinning most charmingly, "but I shall try them all and see which ones produce the desired effect."

Jane was disinclined to ask what effect he was hoping to produce with such phrases in the girls he courted. Instead she said, "I think I must teach you some additional phrases in English, unless you particularly desire to be slapped in the face for impertinence."

"Shall I be?" Gandolfo asked with good-natured alarm.

"With your looks and manner, yes, I fear you will be if you say those things to properly reared young ladies."

He took her hand before she could evade him. "And you? Would *you* slap me for saying those things?"

"Yes, I would," she said firmly.

"Ah. Then, please, teach me these other phrases, for I would not wish to offend you."

"You are beyond anything," Jane said, laughing.

He smiled, his clear blue eyes crinkled up, the outer lashes tangled where they overlapped. "That is what I wish," he declared, "to see you happy and laughing. You are too often pensive, too quiet, you know, and I would have you be quite gay. Just at this moment you remind of my very most favorite cousin in Italy, with those marvelous eyes. Teach me what to say in English that will amuse you as you are amused right now, so that I can make this look return to your face whenever I desire."

Jane lowered her eyes and looked at his strong, slender hand grasping hers. "First I think you must let go of my hand," she said.

"That is too bad. It is of all things the most enjoyable, but if I must, I must," he said philosophically.

Jane set about teaching him such rudimentary phrases as would allow him to invite a young lady to stroll in the garden, or to play loo with him, as well as the polite conventions of thank you, please, and so on, but it was undeniable that the more improper phrases rolled off his tongue much more convincingly. He did apply himself, however, and when dinner was announced, he had made a fair start as mastering at least some unexceptionable English.

Precedence demanded that George, as the most senior male present, should take his mother in to dinner, while Fabrice offered his arm to Jane. Gandolfo very readily escorted Portia. Without her spectacles and seated at the bottom of the table, Jane could see very little of George. When dinner was at last over, she arose and led the ladies away, leaving the men to their cigars and spirits.

It seemed to be taking a very long time for them to come and join them, for Lady Fanny and Jane drank tea and listened to Portia play an étude, and then another, and a good deal of her Haydn repertoire before Fabrice appeared alone at the door. He spread his hands and said with an apologetic lifting of his eyebrows, "I regret that we will not be joining you." He gestured back over his shoulder with a grimace. "Those two, they are . . . deeply engaged in a . . . a game of chance."

"How very extraordinary!" Lady Fanny exclaimed.

Portia stopped playing and asked, "What is extraordinary?"

Fanny set her cup aside. "It appears that George and Gandolfo have struck up a fast friendship and quite forgotten their duty to us. They are gambling!"

"Oh." Portia glanced wistfully toward the door. "They are not coming in at all?"

"It would seem not," Fanny said. "How dreary of them."

"So sorry," Fabrice said again, bowing his way out the door hurriedly.

"Dear, dear," Fanny said regretfully. "Even the best of men are quite overset by the prospect of a good game of chance."

"How horrid," Portia said pettishly. "Mr. Fiore declared over dinner that he could not sleep for thinking of me and asked if I would walk out to share the moon and stars with him!"

Chapter Twenty

When Jane awoke the next morning, she saw that it was very early, far earlier than she was used to being awakened. Still without her spectacles, she peered uncertainly toward a gray shape by the dressing table.

"Ellen?"

The shape turned and bobbed a curtsey. "No, your ladyship, 'tis me, Daisy."

Belatedly, Jane remembered having given Ellen permission to lie in that day, following a somewhat rebellious reminder that as a parlor maid she had at least been accustomed to having a half day off each week in London. Daisy bustled about, setting things to rights. She had been asked to assist Ellen several times, whenever a second pair of hands was needed, but today she seemed all fluttery, not her usual placid self.

"I'm that sorry if I woke you, milady. I tried to be as quiet as I know how but it's hard, what with what's been a-goin' on."

Jane sat up, resigned to wakefulness. "And what is that?" she asked sleepily.

Daisy gave up all pretense of brushing out a plain blue poplin spencer and drew near the bed to say in a conspiratorial whisper, "Why, his lordship gettin' set to fight

341

a *dool* with that foreign gent! Whole household knows it, milady, and can hardly speak of anythin' but. We watched him ride out not half an hour since!"

Jane's early morning languor deserted her on the instant. "Who?" she demanded. "Which foreign gentleman, and . . . and *why?*"

The maid stared at her, wide-eyed. "As to why, I'm sure I don't know ma'am, but as to who, well, the one as ain't married to her ladyship."

Gandolfo! But why on earth . . . One thought collided with another and sudden understanding dawned on Jane. George had mistaken Gandolfo's attentions for something more than friendship! Jane flung aside the bed clothes with such vigor that she sent the tray holding her morning chocolate flying.

"Oh, ma'am!" Daisy cried, her hands clapped to her cheeks.

"Never mind that!" Jane snapped. "Hand me out a dress—never mind which one—and be quick about it! I must stop them!"

Daisy obeyed after a moment's hesitation, during which her mistress stripped to her bare skin with shocking speed and a complete lack of modesty. With equal speed, she pulled on drawers and a shift, tossed aside the corset Daisy held out to her, and wriggled into a white, embroidered evening gown which had been the nearest dress to Daisy's hand.

Gandolfo thought it fine to have some drama, some heroic challenge cast down, man to man, for in his experience, England had so far been completely devoid of manly men. This George, Earl of Sefton, was proving a welcome surprise. Such intensity! Such bearing! Here was a man with whom one could take no exception. Gandolfo welcomed the opportunity to show his masculinity in a sword fight, for did not a well-made man like himself show to best advantage when dressed in fewer rather than more clothes? To allow for the athleticism of sword play, they had removed their jackets and ties, leaving only the very satisfactory frilled shirts, and trousers supported by braces. It was with just such considerations in mind that Gandolfo had chosen rapiers rather than pistols, since delineating one's physique with white conferred no disadvantage when the fight was with blades, as it did when a single shot decided all.

He glanced around in anticipation of the ladies' arrival, but there was still no sign of them. The morning mist was parting becomingly though, creating a hazy veil of sunshine and shadow in which to enact their drama. The earl was a worthy opponent, a magnificent animal in the dawn's radiance, but as Gandolfo watched him, he began to harbor doubts for the first time, for this English nobleman seemed less interested in presenting himself to advantage than in staring malevolently at his opponent. He wondered if perhaps this earl was a little mad, for he had, after all, thrown down the gauntlet over a lady in whom he had showed no interest whatsoever. It was incomprehensible really, typical of most things English, but still, Gandolfo was not entirely unhappy.

Fabrice made a last, valiant attempt to resolve the dispute, as all seconds must, offering to accept even the scantest of apologies on behalf of his countryman. George turned the offer aside with a crude oath which Gandolfo noted with admiration, meaning to use it himself at some opportune moment in the future. Insults and curses were second in importance only to learning the phrases of love when acquiring a new tongue.

Gandolfo readied himself, noting with keen appreciation the physician standing by a black gig. It lent a certain tragic air, though Gandolfo felt sure that even this most fierce Englishman understood that no one would emerge with any serious hurt. It was simply not to be thought of. This was a

343

match to show manly men in a manly setting, to impress on a lady the difference between their frail sex and the male of the species.

The rapiers were brought forth by a footman, places taken, and at the drop of a handkerchief, it began. Gandolfo made his very best leg to George and noted with satisfaction the form of a female running through the mists toward them. It would be the incomparable, the lovely Jane, and, he hoped, Portia, too. Gandolfo felt his heart swell with satisfaction. It would all have been a waste had they not shown up to witness this drama unfolding in Jane's honor. Why else would he have eschewed his bed at this ungodly hour?

George was struck with horror when he saw Jane come flying out of the low-lying mist. An affair of honor was one thing. To have the lady over whom one fought present was quite another. Even a foreigner like the dapper Italian would understand that under no circumstances must they fight in front of her. George stepped back quickly, dropping his rapier to his side, and was immediately caught in the upper arm for his trouble. Enraged that blood had been drawn in front of Jane's very eyes—though the fact that it was his own counted for nothing—George turned his attention back to Gandolfo with a snarl.

"Gandolfo!" Jane cried.

Hearing this man's name on the lips of the woman he loved inspired George to a frenzied attack that owed little to science and much to passion. He lunged and easily slipped past Gandolfo's guard. The next thrust would have pierced the Italian's heart but for the fact that a brief glimmer of sanity asserted itself in George's mind. He would have to flee England if he killed Gandolfo Fiore, and Jane would hate him for cutting down her pretty boy—these thoughts occurred to George with such speed that he was able to beggar the thrust. The result was a slashing cut in the center of Gandolfo's chest.

Even without spectacles Jane saw the first bright spurt of blood clearly, for both combatants wore white shirts. It was clear, too, that it was George who had sustained the hurt, for he had the advantage of Gandolfo by several inches. Jane sprang forward, her heart in her throat as she perceived that George was injured, but in that instant Gandolfo cried out and fell back. Crimson spread across his shirt front and Jane felt the unfairness of it all. Poor Gandolfo! He had done no more than be kind to her, and George—who did not want her!—stepped in to spoil it all, unwilling to let her have even the most superficially kind words from another man. She raced forward the last few steps and pushed between the two men, heedless of the metallic flashes as their blades caught the morning sun.

"Stop it!" she cried.

George fell back a pace and Gandolfo sagged to his knees. Jane dropped to kneel beside him and held him close so that she could see his face and determine if he still lived. Happily, his eyes met hers with sentience and he seemed filled with gratitude to see her.

"Signorina," he murmured, smiling weakly. He was perhaps shedding a little more blood than he had reckoned for, but the effect was so gratifying, the look on her face so tender and full of concern, that he could not regret it.

"Sir!" Fabrice called out to George as he ran up. "Surely your honor is satisfied!"

Jane looked up at him. "Do not at all rely on it," she said angrily. "The Earl of Sefton's honor is far too precious, too far above that of other men's to be satisfied with merely wounding Gandolfo. No! He will see all his blood drained before he is satisfied!" Jane could not see well enough to discern the expression on George's face but she was satisfied that he was not moving toward them to finish Gandolfo off.

"Will you not allow the surgeon to attend you both?" Fabrice suggested anxiously, not at all confident that George meant to stop the fight.

George turned away without answer. Seeing Jane with Gandolfo in her arms was more than he could bear. To know that all her thought had been for the Italian cut like a knife. The blade, which had gone clear through to the bone of his own arm, as Henry would later tell him, did not cut as deep. He drew himself up and faced her again.

"I would advise you to remember that while you may not have to endure our marriage for very much longer, you are still my wife. You will conduct yourself accordingly, and that includes not flinging yourself into the arms of other men, and most certainly not in my presence."

He calmly handed his rapier to the footman who stood ready to receive it. "I would also advise you that when you *are* in a position to replace me, you not choose someone whose only skill is in the bedroom. I apprehend that this one barely speaks English. Allow me to inform you from long experience in these matters that one must necessarily talk to one's lover, if only occasionally."

So saying, he turned and walked toward his horse, where he ignored the groom's offer of a leg up and mounted unaided. He rode off without a backward glance, leaving those assembled to stare after him with varying degrees of admiration and astonishment.

On Jane's part there was only astonishment. Clearly he was not hurt badly if he could keep to his feet, deliver a cogent and most . . . most *humiliating* public lecture implying all sorts of perfectly horrid and untrue things about herself and Gandolfo, and . . . and . . . Jane felt her face begin to crumple.

"Ah, *signorina*," Gandolfo murmured tenderly, "he has finally deigned to show you some attention and the effect is to make you cry. It is too cruel. What has he said to you? Only tell me, and on another day I will make him regret his words."

Jane shook her head and urged him to think only of garnering his strength. The gig was brought around and

Gandolfo fainted gracefully away as he was lifted into it. Jane reached out to him but Fabrice gently turned her away. "He will be fine. Please, do not worry yourself."

"But it is all my fault that he is hurt," she sobbed.

Fabrice smiled a little ruefully. "Perhaps you will allow that it is also a little my fault," he said. "My friend did not realize that you were married to the earl, you see, and I, who must assuredly *did* know, did not think to tell him he should not . . . admire . . . you quite so much, especially when your husband was in attendance."

"And for that he should be half-killed?" Jane said passionately. "No, it is unpardonable. The earl has the most vile temper! He owes an apology to . . . to . . . *everyone!*"

"But first I think we must worry about stopping the bleeding," Fabrice murmured. "You agree?"

Jane realized that both patient and surgeon were waiting for them to conclude their conversation. "Of course!"

"You will share our conveyance?" Fabrice asked, gesturing to the gig.

"No, no—if I join you, Gandolfo will have to sit upright. I will follow on foot."

Her pent-up fright did not produce a flood of tears in its wake. Instead fright became anger once it was clear there was nothing worth expending tears on. The occasional little shiver passed through Jane, a residue of the fear she had labored under when she had thought George badly hurt and then Gandolfo mortally wounded, but now that it was clear that neither was the case, fury moved to occupy the forefront of her mind.

She was so incensed by the time she reached the house that she stopped by the ornamental fountain, unwilling to go inside while she was in such a temper. She strode back and forth, kicking up small showers of white stones, brooding over just what she should do next. George had treated her very badly indeed. She had never given him cause to hate her, nor—as much as she had feared she might one day

347

soon—had she yet been so dismal a countess to him that she deserved to be reviled. She was quite sure she could never forgive him for suggesting that she and Gandolfo had . . . were . . .

"Ah, dear Jane, you are agitated. Do I disturb you?"

Jane jerked around in surprise. "I wish you *would* disturb me, Lady Fanny," she said, "for with only my thoughts to keep me company, I am afraid I may decide to do murder. You know what happened between Gandolfo and George this morning."

Fanny nodded. "It is very vexing, that is certain."

"How is Gandolfo?" Jane asked.

"Fabrice assures me that as soon as they have replaced all but a few drops of his blood with port, he will be fine."

"I have heard that strong drink will remedy much of what ails gentlemen," Jane said with an attempt at lightness.

"But not what ails gentlewomen, unfortunately."

Fanny watched Jane, and saw the tug of conflicting emotions in her eyes. What was most telling was that she had not asked after her husband. Fanny smoothed over that deficiency by saying, "The surgeon is with George now, but I daresay he will be found to have suffered no great hurt."

"I should not care if he has," Jane said, lifting her chin.

"I see," Fanny said. "Shall we walk along to the succession houses? My complexion suffers terribly from exposure to the morning sun."

Jane fell in beside her mother-in-law. She was within an inch of announcing her intention to leave Sefton Hall—and George—forever, but she was determined to have one last question answered. It appeared that no one was better qualified to do so than Lady Fanny. "I wonder if I might ask you a rather delicate question?" Jane began, feeling her face warm just at the thought.

"But of course, my dear," Lady Fanny replied.

"To do with marriage," Jane clarified, "and husbands and wives, and . . . and . . ."

"You have only to ask," Fanny assured her. "It is most natural that you should turn to me since you have no mother of your own to ask."

Jane drew a deep breath. "Is it acceptable . . . that is, may a lady of quality . . . may she . . . is she permitted to enjoy . . ." Jane broke off in embarrassment, but Lady Fanny simply looked at her expectantly. Jane took heart. "Is a wife permitted to enjoy her husband's . . . attentions?" she asked in a rush.

Lady Fanny paused at the glass doors which let onto the citrus house. "I do not entirely grasp your meaning."

Jane flushed. "It was a question that should not have been asked. Forgive me."

Fanny waved aside the disclaimer. "Please, let us have no false modesty. Is it that you wonder if a married woman may *expect* pleasure with her husband or whether she must resign herself to merely enduring the act? Is that your concern, that you have not yet learned to have pleasure in the act? That must often wait. Some women never know pleasure until they have presented their husbands with at least two heirs and can take a lover."

Jane stared hard at Lady Fanny, wishing she had her spectacles and could see the expression on her mother-in-law's face. "Could you please elaborate?" Jane said carefully.

"I do not understand what it is I am to elaborate on," Fanny averred. "Pleasure? The lack of it? Please, be clear. I am impatient these days with this phlegmatic English way of talking around the subject of lovemaking. It is much too lovely to act as if it does not exist."

Jane cleared her throat anxiously. "Then to feel pleasure is . . . that is, I wished particularly to know whether it is acceptable to feel pleasure with one's husband and . . . and to show it . . ."

"Acceptable!" cried Lady Fanny in amusement. "Why, dear girl, of course it is acceptable. And why on earth should you not show your husband you enjoy his lovemaking?" She saw the look of astonishment on Jane's face. "Can it be that George does not please you?" she asked in consternation.

Jane blushed scarlet and ducked her head. "No," she mumbled, "not that at all."

"Then it is that you have been afraid to admit it?" Lady Fanny's eyes widened in perplexity. "But dear child!" she exclaimed, and then did not seem to know how to continue.

"It is nothing, please," Jane mumbled in an agony of embarrassment. "It is only that he gave me reason to think that . . . that matters were otherwise, or perhaps it was my fault entirely—I do not know. I . . . I hardly know *what* to think at this point."

"Vraiment!" her ladyship declared. "And so, naturally, you ask me. Dear, dear Jane." She put one arm around Jane's shoulders. "One forgets how it is to be young. I assure you, there is no more certain way to please a man than to show him you enjoy his attentions, in this as in all things." She drew Jane along toward the orangery doors. "It is really too bad of the English not to be more frank about such matters," she said with an air of bland detachment, as if she herself were not English.

"Would a man . . . that is, is it possible that one's husband would *know* one enjoyed . . . well, his lovemaking . . . even if one did not precisely say so?" Jane ventured to ask.

"I should think it very unlikely if he did *not* know, especially if one was quite swept away," Lady Fanny said.

They emerged into the open air and Jane perceived a gray shape making its way along the path toward them at a spanking pace. "Good morning, your ladyship," it said breathlessly.

"Oh! Ellen, it is you," Jane exclaimed. Now that the maid was standing directly in front of them, Jane perceived a testy look on the girl's face.

"Footman just brought these to me, miss," Ellen said with a disapproving sniff. She handed Jane her spectacles. "Seems his lordship has had 'em all this time, never botherin' to think as how you might need 'em." She harumphed loudly. "If *he* doesn't know how you depend on 'em, *I* certainly do, and so I wasted no time bringin' 'em to you!"

"Yes, thank you, Ellen," Jane said quickly, hoping the outspoken girl would not malign the earl any further in his mother's hearing.

"I shan't ever get a peaceful half day while he's about, shall I?" Ellen muttered. "First I misses my chance to see Sydney Gardens because *he* says it's time we went to the country, with no more nor an hour's notice, mind you, and *today* he's up and killin' his house guests at the break of day! How a person could have a good lie-in with such going on, I don't know nor never shall."

"Please, Ellen," Jane said sharply, jerking her head toward Lady Fanny.

"Oh, of course," Ellen said. She rounded on Fanny in a business-like way. "Your ladyship, I don't suppose no one thought to tell you, but I'm maid to miss here now, and won't be comin' back to your house like was planned, for which I would be very sorry except that I think she needs me more than your house needs cleaning."

Ellen dropped an inelegant curtsey and hastened off, muttering under her breath about chocolate stains on the linen.

"What an extraordinary girl!" Lady Fanny said.

"Well, yes, she is rather," Jane began, and then decided against trying to explain how she had acquired Ellen, or indeed, anything else about her.

There could be no doubt, Fanny decided, that Jane and George loved one another. It had taken no time at all to elicit that information from Jane, and only a little longer to shape events so that she felt sure George loved Jane in return. Simply watching him while he watched Jane with another man had told her what she had suspected all along. Having her feeling confirmed was gratifying, but the aftermath had been decidedly unwelcome, if not actually deadly. Who could have known that love would drive George to such distraction that he would call poor Gandolfo out? It was really quite out of character for him.

Sailing down the corridor, Fanny arranged her route so that it took her past her son's rooms. She desired to take the measure of things there. Fletcher was emerging but he stopped short when he saw her.

"Your ladyship," he said, looking stricken.

"Is it so bad then?" Fanny asked, feeling a flutter of concern for the first time. When she had seen George returning to the house on horseback, he had looked somewhat pale but otherwise not badly hurt.

"Oh, ma'am, I would not care to answer that," Fletcher said, "but . . ."

Just then a streak of curses reached them, culminating with one Fanny had not previously heard. "Oh, my!" she said.

She heard some crockery smashing, and then her son warning someone against piling any more coal in the grate.

"You see how it is," Fletcher said apologetically. "Doctor said we was to see the room was well-heated, and I'm off to tell Mrs. Briggs that some hartshorn in water is needed, and he's got to have some gruel, for he's never eaten yet this morning, but as to whether he'll let us do our Duty, I'm sure I don't know."

Fanny suppressed a laugh. "Has anyone thought to send to London and tell Henry he must come immediately?"

"That we did, ma'am. Bates has sent young Freddy off— like a race it is, fastest horse and lightest rider. Henry should be here by nightfall, and Mr. Wofford, too."

"What a pity," Fanny murmured. "One would have so enjoyed seeing Henry's expression on the occasion of his being made to make good on his noble offer to come by the night mail."

"Ma'am?"

"Oh, nothing. Do not let me keep you, Fletcher. I am sure you must be anxious to spoon the gruel into your master's mouth with your own hand."

Fletcher looked appalled but only bowed and hurried away. Fanny smiled softly. *She* knew better than to aid in the effort to minister to George. He had a perfectly savage temper at the best of times, and anyone who thwarted his will was bound to come out on the losing end, especially when he was in a temper *and* in pain, which, judging by the bellows coming from behind the closed door, he was. Fanny made a mental note to ask Stoke where on earth her son had come by such a temper, for it certainly had not come from *herself,* or from the late, unlamented earl, for that matter. No matter—Stoke would know. She took herself off to contemplate matters in a more serene setting, and to finish the beauty sleep which had been disturbed by her husband's early arising.

George had only once before been hurt in his adult life, so it came as very hard lines indeed to discover that he was quite incapacitated. It was not precisely as if he were at death's door, though, no matter how the surgeon might carry on, but he was weak enough that when his servants designated themselves the masters, as they did in very short order, there was little George could do to disabuse them of the notion. Each attempt to sit up and throw off the bedclothes, beneath which he felt in danger of suffocating, resulted in profound dizziness and brought forth a veritable Greek chorus of exhortations to lie still.

Chief among his tormentors was Fletcher, who heretofore had been biddable in the extreme but was now intent on inflicting gruel on him in the obviously mistaken belief that it would somehow aid in his recovery. George could only lie flat on his back and wish that the ever so conformable

353

Timothy could be exchanged for the obdurate Fletcher. Still, no amount of wishing could make his head stop swimming, nor quite erase the surgeon's words from his memory.

"Mark my words, your lordship, you arise from this bed prematurely at your peril. This cut lies athwart—as a sailor might say—the wound you took during the Peninsular campaign, and scar tissue is never so amenable to closure as is unsullied flesh."

As the surgeon was just then engaged in the rather painful business of cleaning the new injury, George was forced to clamp his mouth closed and endure the lecture.

"And the amount of blood lost here is not to be scoffed at. I should very much like to cup you but I am of the opinion that an excessive amount of bodily fluid has already been lost. Now bear with me, your lordship, and I will pull these edges together, and make as neat a line as I may."

George thought it wonderfully euphemistic to describe his own part in the proceedings as "bearing with," for no description short of "excruciating" could have fairly characterized what followed. He faintly remembered the surgeon administering a potion afterwards, and then all was hazy until close to nightfall, when he awoke to see Henry sitting at his bedside.

"Hail fellow, well met," he croaked through dry lips.

"Ah! You've come round," Henry said unnecessarily.

George began to sit up but Henry tish-toshed him into staying where he was. It was a suggestion taken with some sense of relief, for George felt leaden all over, and most especially in the area of his left arm, which seemed to be anchoring him to the bed and sending forth ripping great blasts of pain besides. Admitting it could only lower his stock, however, so George chose the only course open to him.

"It is nothing for you to concern yourself with," he insisted loftily. "Bates could tell you that this is the merest trifle. I've known worse."

"Perhaps," said Henry, "but it is the here and now that concerns us, and in the here and now, you have a sword cut which went clean through to the bone. How we shall turn your lordship out to receive visitors decently tomorrow is a matter to which I have been giving some attention. I fancy a sling may answer. Some water?"

George drank from the artfully arranged cup and glass straw arrangement Henry offered and then paused suddenly. "Has that glass tube been nicked from my orchid propagation trays?"

Henry had the grace to look chagrined. "Well, yes, but how you were going to manage to drink without it, I don't know."

"I will replace Fletcher tomorrow," George announced. "Hicks should do very well. I am persuaded the man at least knows better than to tamper with my cymbidiums."

He lay back and cursed the sweltering heat in the room as sweat rolled off his temples. A sudden thought struck him.

"Visitors? Why should I concern myself with dressing to receive visitors? If they wish to come and witness the complete subjugation of a man by his servants, I am powerless to stop them, but I'm damned if I'll dress for the occasion."

"Naturally your lordship would not be obliged to dress for anyone mannerless enough to come calling for such a purpose as his lordship has just described," the small man said punctiliously, "but I am persuaded that you will feel the necessity of at least receiving a few of your guests tomorrow."

"Guests," George muttered irritably. "Tell me who they may be that I shouldn't wish them at Jericho."

"Well, they would include Lord Hugh, Mr. Creighton and Mr. Marshall, Lady Eugenia and Sir Harry, plus offspring, Lady Montfort, plus—"

"Stop! Enough. Why on earth are all these people descending on me?"

"But your lordship, you cannot have forgotten the house party you ordered set in motion before we had even left Bath? Mr. Wofford and I were on the point of coming down for it tomorrow, so your . . . your indisposition . . . has only brought us here one day earlier than we had planned, though not as early as I had *hoped* to be allowed to rejoin your lordship," the valet added in a faintly resentful tone.

George stared at him in horror. "Can you mean to tell me that Wofford went forward with the issuing of invitations despite . . . despite . . . all that has occurred in the interim?"

Henry looked stricken. "Indeed, I am sure he did, your lordship. You never told him otherwise, and it would be more than anyone's life is worth to . . ." Henry broke off with a startled expression.

"To fail to follow my orders?" George inquired with one eyebrow raised.

"Well, er . . . yes," Henry admitted, "though I did not mean to . . ."

"Of course you did not," George said drily, "but now I think on it, perhaps this is a good time for a little truth telling." Henry looked thoroughly alarmed at the notion but George persisted. "For instance, Henry, would you say that I am, in the main, an easy man to work for—reasonable, patient, kind?"

Henry swallowed. "With reference to whom, my lord?" he asked.

George stared back, his brows drawn together. "Why, with regard to yourself, and to the other servants in my employ!"

"Well, that would be difficult to say," Henry mumbled.

"Speak up, man!" George demanded irritably. "Answer the question!"

"Oh! Most reasonable," Henry said quickly, "and . . . and very patient, of course, and . . . and *kind*. Yes! Remarkably kind!"

George eyed his valet with some skepticism but allowed

356

himself to relax a little. "I thought as much," he said. "Henry," he began, in a different tone of voice, "arrange some pillows so that I can at least sit up."

"But your lordship, the surgeon was most clear that you should remain flat abed. There is no way to properly support your arm if you should be upright."

"Curse the surgeon," George said roundly. "Is it him you have to answer to? Of course not! Now be a good fellow and help me up, and tell Fletcher to fetch back all the pillows he has taken away, thinking himself clever to subvert my intention so facilely."

"Certainly your lordship," Henry murmured as George dragged himself up against the headboard. "And if your lordship starts to bleed again?"

"As I see that I already have," George said disgustedly. "Tie it off, stanch the flow, do whatever you must."

But the fact remained that while he had managed to sit upright, his head had not quite come with him, and the effect of the move on his viscera was unpleasant in the extreme. His stomach rolled in a most sickening manner, until he was forced to reach for a small basin left on the bedside table. Sheer perversity kept him from admitting that he was suffering, and he asked for and got the day's paper. The print swam in front of his eyes and he soon abandoned the effort to make sense of it.

The evening progressed slowly, with Henry offering to read to him from the newspaper which lay unregarded on the counterpane. George tolerated such sickroom stuff only because he was bored silly, and was trying hard to marshal his strength so that he could arise shortly and go in search of his wife. He was in no wise clear exactly what he wished to say to her, for he had swung from utter contrition the night before to unthinking fury that morning.

Dinner came and George retched weakly at the very smell of it. He consented to drink some watered-down wine, the surgeon having enjoined all the servants to force liquids down their master's throat. He lay back with a sigh when the tray was taken away. What was it he wanted to say to Jane? Something, surely. Why did the moment never seem right to tell her the truth, that he loved her, and that a heretofore satisfactory and meaningful life had evaporated almost the instant they met, and that now only a life shared with her held any appeal?

His eyes were so heavy. He closed them while he thought. He wanted her laughter, her teasing looks, her witty reproofs. He wanted *her* to read the newspaper to him. He wanted to see those eyes, which could rival the bluest sky nature had ever produced, widen and turn dark as he took her in his arms, the brows arching in scandalized surrender as her mouth opened and she turned her face to receive his kiss.

That was what he wanted to say to her—that nothing else mattered except those things. And he *would* say them, too, just as soon as he arose, which he would do in just a moment, just as soon as his sleepiness passed.

Chapter Twenty-one

Jane was in a perfectly savage temper, except for the moments when she was crying. Ellen sat patiently by, reattaching a section of torn lace to the hem of the white evening gown Jane had worn that morning. The maid's expression seemed to say that she wondered at her mistress's bothering to be so upset, but the one time she had ventured to put such sentiments into words, Ellen had found herself turned on and soundly castigated. Young Daisy arrived with warm water for the evening toilette and sheered off as quickly as she could when she saw Jane pacing like a tigress, her eyes red and her face blotchy.

Jane stopped abruptly and swung around to face Ellen. "I've half a mind to leave here tonight! I see no point in remaining. He has accused me of *unspeakable* crimes, simply unspeakable. I daresay he and his friends may know any number of . . . of . . . *fast* women who would think nothing of breaking their marriage vows, but that he would think it of me!"

Ellen made a noncommittal sound. She set aside the white gown and rose. "Shall I start a-packin' miss?"

Jane was a little startled to find her suggestion taken up so readily. "Yes, I believe you should," she said with sudden resolution.

She found Lady Fanny in the drawing room with Fabrice. Lady Fanny looked ravishing in a pale violet dress that clung to a figure quite untouched by the passage of time. George had not come down yet, which suited Jane very well. She had no desire to see the architect of her unhappiness.

Lady Fanny held out her hand to Jane with a pleased smile when she saw her peering around the drawing room door, but Jane found herself incapable of returning the simple greeting. She received the welcome news that Gandolfo was recovering nicely, and that he was currently sitting up in an easy chair in his room and playing at draughts with Portia.

"I have just come down from seeing him," Fanny said, smiling. "He is quite the most romantic figure. His pallor is just what one likes to see in the fallen hero."

"I cannot accept it all so lightly as you seem to, ma'am," Jane said gravely.

Fanny turned to her husband. "Fabrice, my love, would you mind fetching me a lighter shawl? I am finding this one to be quite stifling."

Fabrice arose and kissed her hand lightly. "I shall just take a moment to look in on Gandolfo, too, if you can bear to wait for your shawl a few more minutes."

"But of course," Fanny replied. "Take all the time you like." She waited until they heard the soft click of the door latch engaging behind him before she said, "Dearest Jane, you are thinking I am terribly frivolous about such a serious matter. Perhaps I *am* too cavalier, but as soon as I knew they would both be fine, I was unable to give myself over to any further worry."

Jane twisted her hands together and stared at them. "I, too, am naturally relieved that no one was seriously injured, but that was only the chiefest of my worries. I must leave, Lady Fanny. I cannot stay even one more night. I . . . I believe I have good reason but I wish you will not ask for particulars. You have been everything that is kind. Indeed, I shall miss you greatly, but I think that in my position, you

360

would do the same."

"Jane dear, do look at me. There, that is better. I shall make no attempt to pry confidences from you which you do not wish to share, but I am vastly unhappy to think of you going this very night. Will you not at least stay until the morning?"

"No! I cannot bear to see George again," Jane said passionately. "He was abominable to me today. He taunted me most cruelly, and made dreadful accusations. I do not believe there is the slightest chance that I could ever forgive him. I have waited and waited for him to come and apologize for the things he said this morning but he has not."

"Perhaps if you gave him a little more time," Fanny suggested gently. "Perhaps he is not feeling quite the thing."

"Gandolfo, who was hurt far worse, is sitting up and playing games," Jane pointed out. "If my husband wanted to, I am persuaded he could have found a way to say that he is sorry."

"Oh, dear," Lady Fanny murmured. "It has all gone so wrong, has it not?"

Jane merely nodded, feeling the sharp beginnings of new tears at the backs of her eyes.

"Well, of course you are at perfect liberty to order a carriage to take you anywhere you like," Fanny said. "You must not feel that I would put the least rub in the way of your doing so, but I admit to some little curiosity. Do you mean to go to Sefton House? There is little amusement to be had in the capital at this time of year, you know."

Jane shook her head miserably. "No, I mean to go back home. I wish nothing more to do with Sefton House or Sefton Hall or the Earl of Sefton, or indeed, anything at all connected with the Sefton name, begging your pardon, ma'am."

"You need not beg my pardon," Fanny assured her, "only have you thought this all the way through? In particular, I wonder if you are quite certain that you are not carrying

George's child? It would be unfortunate to make so definitive a break only to discover that you must reconcile yourself to this marriage for yet a while longer."

Jane opened her mouth to say that she was quite sure she wasn't with child and then realized she *wasn't* quite sure. Only two days ago she had gone to her husband and the results of what had happened between them would not be known for weeks. She stared at Lady Fanny in consternation. "It . . . it may . . . that is, it *could* be that I am . . ." she stammered. Collecting her wits, she cried, "But I must put some distance between us! He was so wretched to me today, so vile, and he has not made the least push to say that he regrets it. I have put up with his . . . his *disregard* . . . more than once already. I cannot do so any longer."

Lady Fanny sighed. "No, I see that you cannot, nor do I blame you. George is far too old for me to apologize on his behalf, but I do anyway, most sincerely. That does not resolve our immediate problem, however. I wonder whether you would consider staying at the hunting lodge for the time being. George's things were removed today and brought up here, so there would be no obstacle to your moving there. You could take your maid—Ellen, is it?—with you. You might find the peace and quiet there a welcome relief."

Jane had grown increasingly nervous that George would walk in and she would be obliged to face him, and hear more of his biting remarks. *That* she did not wish to suffer. She stood up. "It is an excellent solution, ma'am. I will leave within the hour."

"I will be so sorry not to have you here," Fanny said. "May I at least call on you at the lodge?"

"By all means," Jane said, and then with a little more briskness than was strictly polite, she made good her escape from the drawing room.

Fletcher watched her go in some consternation, for he surely needed to talk to either the countess or the dowager countess. He did not know which of them to approach, and yet his soul cried out for the cleansing that only confession could bring. The glowering look upon the new countess's face weighed heavily against ridding himself of his sin at *her* doorstep, so it was to Lady Fanny that he confessed that he had mistakenly given Mrs. Briggs's syrup of poppies to the master instead of the concoction left by the surgeon.

"But I had no idea I was doin' it, my lady!" Fletcher said, almost on the brink of tears. What he would not say, despite all the trouble it had caused him, was that it was Mrs. Briggs who had made the substitution in the wholehearted belief— from what she had heard of the goings on in the master's chambers—that her own draught would be better than the citified stuff left by the medical man, "for if it's needful for his lordship to rest, which everyone says he won't, *my* syrup will do him a great deal more good."

"Is it that rather gummy purple liquid she favors?" Fanny asked with a grimace.

"Yes, my lady," the butler admitted lugubriously.

"Wherever does she purchase it? No, no, you needn't answer that. I fancy the apothecary in the village had the receipt from his father, and from *his* father before him. Well, it will do George no harm to pass a sound night. I recollect that Mrs. Briggs urged some of it on me after Portia was born. I do not believe it did anything other than make me sleep like the dead. Run along, Fletcher, and don't give it another thought."

"No, your ladyship," he said miserably. Her very kind reception of the news of his awful blunder only served to increase his sense of wrongdoing. He slunk away with the intention of pouring out all the rest of the mischief-making fluid, and let Mrs. Briggs see if he cared a fig when she discovered it all gone.

At the hunting lodge, at least, Mrs. Briggs had done her duty handsomely, for it had been transformed since George's removing to the main house from the dusty, neglected hideaway of two days ago into a cottage of gleaming surfaces everywhere one looked. Jane walked through it, absently noting the layout of the rooms.

"Well, Ellen, I suppose it will do well enough, only where are you to sleep?"

The footman, who was bringing in the large trunk filled with what Ellen in her newly acquired sophistication declared were the "bare necessities," pointed out that there was a sleeping loft above, with several small bedrooms for staff.

Ellen, who had formed no very high opinion of the place, declared that she would look at the staff rooms but she very much doubted they would be found to suit. "But then, I am quite happy to sleep on a sofa right here, if need be."

"Thank you, Ellen," Jane said. She wandered after the footman into the bedchamber she had seen only dimly on her first visit to the lodge. It seemed so ordinary a room. Suddenly Jane felt quite moped. She had come to George here at the lodge with such high hopes that somehow things could be made right between them, conducting endless dialogues in her mind of what she would say and what he would say in return, all while she waited at the edge of the clearing. The sound of a pump handle brought her back to the present. All was in ashes, she concluded. Even if she *were* to have conceived a child during those few stunningly blissful moments with her husband, those moments would undoubtedly be the last moments of any happiness they would know together.

Now that he had revealed his low opinion of her character by suggesting she might be carrying on an affair with Gandolfo, Jane had no illusions. What fleeting affection he might have felt for her at one time was snuffed out and irredeemably gone. The most stunning blow of all had been the revelation by Lady Fanny that a gentleman would be *pleased* for his wife to enjoy his lovemaking, and that he would certainly know she enjoyed it—"*if she were quite swept away by it.*" Jane felt very sure that her response had

364

qualified for that description. What then, had she done to displease George if not that?

Something, surely, only he would not tell her—only make his dissatisfaction clear by abruptly leaving Bath, then urging a divorce on her without explanation, and then hurling those hurtful words at her as Gandolfo lay bleeding in her arms.

"Here, miss, have some tea," Ellen said. She urged Jane to sit back on the bed, for there was no chaise or chair in the small room. Jane let the maid pull off her slippers, still damp from walking across the heavily dewed grass from the carriage. "No matter what the morrow brings, we shall see it through together," Ellen said bracingly.

"I fear it will bring only more trouble and misery," Jane said listlessly. "My husband has decided that I have the morals of a . . . a farmyard animal. I have no answer for him. I am utterly unable to refute him except by my unexceptional conduct. If he wants to arrive at such conclusions based on the flimsiest of evidence, then I fear there is no hope at all for me, Ellen. I am utterly in the suds, as the gentlemen say."

Ellen pushed her bottom onto the edge of the bed, wriggling back until she felt in no danger of falling. "You're just blue-deviled, miss, and who's to wonder at it? No, you drink that tea and we'll put you to bed straightaway, and things'll look better in the morning. I've made no secret about how I feel about his lordship, miss, nor ever I will, but that's not to say that he can't be made to come to the rightabout—leastways, if that's what you want. I mean to say, I'll help you to do whatever it is you want to do, even if it's gettin' that devil to be a proper husband to you."

Jane smiled sadly. "I don't believe it's in anyone's power to give me that."

"There now, that's the late hour speakin'," Ellen said briskly. She heaved herself off the bed and soon made good on her promise to rig Jane out for the night. Jane let herself be tucked in with little expectation of sleep, but discovered her error almost immediately.

She had no appetite for the breakfast which Ellen very capably produced for them in the small kitchen the next morning, but she made sure to thank the girl, and remark on what a treasure she was proving to be.

"A treasure!" Ellen snorted. "A treasure would have protected you from that old harpy what set on you in Bath, miss, and that I did not do! I shall be regrettin' that to the end of my days, for the chance to do right sometimes comes but once. It does a soul good to stand firm at the first sign of evil, which I didn't do, nor I doubt I'll get a second chance."

"Oh! Lady Eugenia!" Jane said after staring at Ellen blankly for a moment. "Well, as it turns out, she was not so far wrong about me, you see. At every turn of the way I have set my foot wrong."

"You forget, miss, that I have eyes in my head, and these dangly bits on my head be'n't pieces of my brain which has escaped," Ellen said, plucking at a lock of her hair. "No, I can see who's to blame and who's not."

Jane had a very precise idea of Ellen's feelings on that subject and she quickly announced her intention of going for a walk. She seized her gloves and a hat so swiftly that the maid had no chance to walk out with her. Feeling terribly lethargic, Jane was nevertheless energized by her desire to be alone, at least for a little while. She set off toward the home farm, ignoring—a little guiltily—Ellen's shouts for her to wait and she would keep miss company. The day was overcast and already uncomfortably warm, even for July.

Having no desire to encounter anyone, Jane turned back at the last set of hedges before the home farm buildings. Walking slowly, she presently heard a heavy vehicle coming along behind and moved onto the verge of the lane, hoping to avoid any of the estate's laborers. The wheels slowed behind her and Jane sped up, but a rough cloth seemed to spring out of nowhere and settle over her. Dumbfounded for

366

an instant, Jane tried to puzzle out who would think it the least bit humorous to play such a trick on her, but before she could conclude that no one of her acquaintance would do such a thing, a pair of arms went round her and lifted her off her feet.

"Got her!"

"Come along then—ain't got all day, not with that snoops down by the gate!" came the rather testy reply.

"Well, I like that!" said the one holding her. "I does it neat and clean and all you've got to say is 'op it!"

"Kidnappin' is still a crime, no matter if it's done for silver up front or gold behind," snapped the other. "Now move it, and no more argle-bargle!"

"Put me down!" Jane cried, beginning to struggle at the first mention of the word "kidnapping." The burlap covering her smelled strongly of manure, which greatly disinclined her to draw too deep a breath, but it was unavoidable if she was to raise a cry for help.

"Toss 'er, quick-like!"

"I'll argle-bargle you! Where's the rope? That was all what you had to remember, and where is it?" demanded the man holding Jane.

"Help!" Jane screamed with all her might and then gagged as a fragment of something dry and decidedly unflavorful was sucked into her mouth by the force of her inhalation.

"What'cha doin' to her?" cried the accomplice. "We weren't paid to do no murder—only bring 'er back to Lunnon!"

"Aw, she's just took in a breath the wrong way," scoffed his partner as he wrestled Jane into some kind of conveyance.

Off balance and out of breath, Jane could not put up any resistance when she felt a rope being drawn tightly around her, pinning her arms to her sides. By the time it had been made to go around her three times, she had begun to lose feeling in her hands but through much spitting and thrusting with her tongue, she managed to rid her mouth of the disgusting fragment of what she could only assume was manure.

"Help! I am being kidnapped," she screamed.

A hand clapped over her mouth silenced her. "Gaw, did you ever hear the like?" complained the man holding her. He seemed to be sitting next to her, but despite seeing chinks of light through the roughly woven cloth, Jane could make out nothing of his face nor of their surroundings.

"Din't choo think to bring nothin' to tie over her mouth?" asked the other in disgust.

This query was greeted only by a dignified silence punctuated by a last grunt as the knots were made fast in the rope. From far away, Jane thought she heard something.

"Eh? What's that?" demanded the other kidnapper. The hand was removed from her mouth as he turned away.

"Ellen! Here!" Jane cried. *Thank providence!*

"Grab her, quick!"

Since Jane hadn't moved, she apprehended that the kidnappers were discussing Ellen. Suddenly, the folly of calling Ellen to her was brought home. "Run, Ellen! Run for help!"

But it was too late. The coach shifted violently, there was a thud, and then came the cry. "Throw us a bit of rope!"

"But I only got the one piece!"

Furious and incapable of helping herself, Jane found herself hoping that Ellen, plucky Ellen, would contrive a way to escape. "Kick him, Ellen, as hard as you can!" she shouted.

"Why, I oughter—" sputtered her keeper.

"Never mind her! This one's out cold-like. Give us a bit of rope and we'll be off."

"Hafta cut it from *her,*" said Jane's captor resentfully.

The squabbling was almost as difficult to endure as being mauled about. The knots confining her loosened, there was a rasping sound, and then the rope was tied again, though not as tightly as before. Just in that short time, her arms had gone numb and the return of circulation was so painful that Jane could not speak.

In very short order, the coach was rolling down the road.

"And now, missy, you'll be a'drinkin' summat what will taste good and be good for you," her captor said in a rough voice. He sounded as if he had once been nearly strangled.

"I won't!" Jane declared through the cloth. "And what's more, you'll hang for this! I'm a countess, and the law officers of this shire will know what to do with you when you are caught, as you surely will be!"

"Good Lord awmighty," muttered the kidnapper. "A woman ain't never at a loss for words!"

"I won't be insulted for protesting this outrageous treatment!" Jane cried, lashing out with her feet in an attempt to land a blow on her captor.

"Right then, it's a little taste of me hand you be wantin'!"

"Don't you dare strike me! I . . . I . . . I'm with child!"

"Gor," the kidnapper said on a long exhalation. "She won't be a-likin' *that* news."

"She? She who?" Jane demanded.

"That's enough said," snapped her tormentor. He cut a ragged slit in the bag, the knife point coming perilously close to Jane's face as he did so. A bottle was raised to her lips through the small opening. "Drink, missy, and let's have no more out of yer."

Jane clenched her teeth together but the man applied a bear-like grip to her head, pressing painfully on her jaw joints until she was forced to open her mouth. Much to her surprise, what flowed out of the jar was some still faintly warm chocolate.

"Now, the next thing yer know about anything, yer in Lunnon, and by the settin' o' the sun, me and my mate'll be rich men."

Jane quickly decided that her only chance of escape lay in pretending to be affected right away by whatever they had given her. "Oh . . . oh, I feel faint," she cried in the most pitiful voice she could manage. "Oh!—and ill . . . and . . . dizzy!" she temporized, hoping one of those effects would be what the kidnappers were expecting.

A pheasant exploded from a nearby hedge with a loud cry and a heavy beating of wings. The coach gave a sudden lurch and there was a muffled oath from the driver's box. "Cor, lumme . . . !"

"What's to do?" shouted the kidnapper sitting inside with Jane.

"Get'cher up here," his companion snarled. "Some bird, big as a cow it was, just took off. These is city-bred horses that don't want none o'these wild animals messin' about 'em. I need a hand with 'em."

"No!" Jane said in a theatrical whisper. "You mustn't leave me! I . . . I fear I am becoming . . . becoming . . ."

"Sleepy," her kidnapper supplied helpfully.

"Yes! Yes, that's it! Oh, I am overcome!" Jane said, slumping over in what she hoped was a convincing imitation of drugged sleep.

The coach slid to a stop. "Jake!" roared the driver. "'op it! I don't know which road is ours—nothin' but trees and grass and signs what I can't make out. Not a building nor a stall nor a shop—nothin' to give a cove a clue where he's at."

A creak and a quick slam and Jane was left alone inside the coach. It moved on again quickly, to the accompaniment of a running quarrel between her two kidnappers over whether this road looked the one they'd come by, what pace to set, and whether and how soon it might be needful to change horses. Jane stayed as she was, uncertain whether they could look down and see her through a coachman's trap. The violent motion of the coach coupled with the chocolate on top of an empty stomach was making her queasy, and the stifling damp heat added to the smell of the rough cloth prison they had secured around her was enough to make a person quite ill.

Jane fought the nausea as she worked surreptitiously at the rope binding her arms to her sides. The miles passed and she made progress, but not very quickly. When the rope was finally loosened, she sat tensely, awaiting a slowdown in the hopes of springing free of her restraints and leaping from the coach, but then she was struck by a shocking thought.

What if she truly *was* with child? She might be utterly furious with George, he might not love her nor hold her in any esteem, but the fact remained that she *loved* him, and she could do nothing that might jeopardize their child—if there *was* a child, which she could not be certain there was or wasn't.

A bead of sweat ran down Jane's cheek and she fought back a wave of dizziness. Growing sicker by the moment, she wished she dared throw the bag and rope off and jump. That way at least she could be free to throw up in relative comfort. The heat of the day and her breath were warming the bag and amplifying the smell of manure to an unbearable degree. Jane swallowed several times as her mouth began to water, and then it was too late.

For all that she had not eaten breakfast, the contents of her stomach were considerable. It soaked her dress and the bag, and coated her skin. If she had not already been in the throes of being tumultuously ill, the smell of what had come up—coupled with the smell of manure—would have *made* her ill. But far from becoming drowsy, as Jane felt the nausea passing she became wide awake and furious to an extent that she had never dreamed she could be. Vengeful thoughts ignited in her mind and spawned more. The sound of thunder rolling in the distance seemed merely an extension of her fury.

Angry! Angry beyond all her powers of description to convey! Fury threatened to tear her asunder unless she gave vent to it. First there was George! This was all his fault— *everything* was all his fault—and if she ever laid eyes on him again, she would make him very, very sorry for all his high-

371

handed behavior. And then there was herself. How could she have been made into such a gudgeon by love?

She had spent every waking moment of the last several months trying to please everyone but herself—especially him!—and look how it had all turned out! It was all a hopeless tangle, and no one happy at the end of it, least of all the man she had striven so mightily to please! Well, be damned to him! That's what she had to say to it all, and no more pleasing anyone but herself! Except Nanny, of course, who was quite blameless in all of it.

"I ain't a sittin' out in the wet if it starts rainin'," she heard the rough-voiced kidnapper whine.

"Well, this ain't Lunnun and you ain't drivin' a hack," the other countered angrily. "Try and see if you can spy a cab stand where we could be inside out of it, and a cloth to throw over the 'orses!"

A crack of lightning ripped the sky very nearby, and the coach pitched as the horses fought the traces. Even through the stink inside the bag, Jane could smell the sharp, almost alive scent that followed in the wake of strong lightning.

"Look, see!" the gruff-voiced kidnapper cried. "There's a posting house and no mistake. Pull up, Ned! Hello, the house!"

The coach teetered precariously around a corner and Jane briskly freed her hands of the rope. There was no nonsense left in her. Gravel under the wheels announced their arrival in the yard of an inn. The restive stamping of the horses nearly drowned out the sound of someone running out to attend them.

"What's it for you gents?" A man yelled over a peal of thunder.

Jane threw off the bag with no little gratitude and lowered the window in the coach. "They are not gents!" she said loudly. "They have kidnapped me and I'll thank you to send for the law immediately." She pushed open the door and tumbled out of the coach before the stunned ostler could lower the steps.

"Ma'am!" was all he said.

"Don't stand there gaping," Jane snapped. "Fetch your master, and a gun to train on these two, though I doubt they will try escaping. They have come from London and have not the least idea of what they are about, nor how to get back there."

"Hi now, what's the meaning of all this?" demanded a portly man coming up behind the ostler.

"Are you the innkeeper?" Jane demanded.

"I am," he said, wiping his hands on an apron.

"I am Lady Sefton," Jane announced imperiously. "These two men tried to kidnap me and I want the constable summoned at once. You must hold them against his arrival, but in the meantime, I require your best bedchamber and a large quantity of hot, not warm—hot!—water."

"Your ladyship!" the innkeeper said in some astonishment.

"Well?" Jane asked, lifting one eyebrow. "Am I to be kept standing here while thunder and lightning break around my ears?"

"Oh! No, ma'am, most certainly not! Please, come into the parlor!" the innkeeper said. "My name is Goodwinter, your ladyship, and you have only to ask for anything you want."

"I have already done that in case it had escaped your notice," Jane said testily. "Now send someone for the constable, and for goodness' sake, man, seize the bridles of those horses before these two fiends can scrape together the wits to leave. And where am I, by the by?"

The landlord motioned frantically to the ostler who flew to the horses' heads. Jane gathered her skirts and strode toward the door of the little, lopsided inn. The landlord followed her.

"Why, this is Stetham, ma'am, and this here is the Hare and Hound."

373

Jane paused and looked at a battered sign creaking lethargically on rusted chains. "Yes," she said, her sardonic glance taking in the unpainted facade of the inn. "I can quite see that you must cater to any number of the hunting fraternity."

She briskly declined the use of the parlor, telling the landlord that if he thought she meant to stay in these repellent clothes another instant, he was sadly mistaken. She ordered a tray sent up, repeated her desire for hot water, and marched toward the stairs. The landlord's wife appeared, her eyes wide and staring, and at a few hissed words from her husband, spurted past Jane and led the way up the stairs, murmuring, "This way, your ladyship," and, "I am sure we are very sorry not to have known you were coming so's we could have prepared."

Jane drew herself up outside the bedchamber the host's wife indicated. "My good woman, on the occasion of a kidnapping, one does not receive notice, so one is in no position to give it."

The woman paled. "No, of course not! Begging your lordship's pardon! I had no idea! How very dreadful for your ladyship! I'm sure we never had no one here before who was kidnapped, and that's the truth!"

"I should hope not," Jane declared. "Now, in addition to washing water and some tea, I shall require writing supplies and someone to carry a letter back to Sefton Hall. You *do* know where it is, do you not?"

"Oh, yes, my lady, I'm sure we do, though it's a good long walk from here."

"As I am not proposing for anyone to walk there, it need not signify. I wish it to be carried there by someone on horseback!"

"Oh! Well, yes, that was what I was meaning," the beleaguered landlady replied. "To be sure!"

"Well, then say so," Jane said firmly. "Now, please unfasten this dress and go see that my water is being heated. I do not wish to wait another minute to be rid of this horrid smell!"

When Jane emerged from the small, battered hip bath that the landlady was able to provide for her use, the relief of being quit of the clothes and the smell restored Jane's equilibrium to a certain extent, but she was still in no mood to be trifled with. She desired the woman to produce some garment to replace her own for the time being, and had to be satisfied with the very old-fashioned and well-worn dress that was all the apologetic landlady could produce.

"It's clean, your ladyship, and will cover you decently," Mrs. Goodwinter said timorously. She hated to offer Quality a dress which was, after all, a rag compared to what her ladyship had been wearing, but there was no help for it. Her ladyship looked it over with a critical eye, and as Mrs. Goodwinter said to her husband later, "It was nothin' but good manners what made her ladyship accept it. Oh, such an air she has about her, such . . . such breeding! I would have known she was a countess even if she had come to us in rags and said she was the farmer's daughter!"

Mr. Goodwinter was fully occupied in directing affairs belowstairs, what with assiduously watching over the two sullen kidnappers and anxiously awaiting the arrival of the constable from Littleport. He could only pray that his wife could satisfy their guest's requirements, and recommended her to offer her ladyship some refreshment.

"Port," his wife whispered, glancing around as if the inn were full of other guests from whom such a scandalous preference must be hidden. "She's asked for port as well as tea."

Mr. Goodwinter rubbed the thinning hair on top of his head unhappily and said he hoped his wife knew well enough where to find the best the house had to offer without his assistance. "And best be quick about it," he cautioned her, "for as word of good service can help our business, so could bad word—especially from Quality!—sink us. I expect if her ladyship wants port, it's not for the likes of us to say she should or shouldn't drink it."

By the time Jane had drunk two cups of tea and a glass of port, she was feeling considerably better, though not at all in the mood to eat anything. She adjusted the antiquated dress as best she could, pulling the strings around the neckline so that it gathered along them and settled against her skin. The effect of the ruffle thus created was not altogether unbecoming, and when she had combed her hair through and it had begun to dry, she concluded that the morning's adventure had done her looks no harm. In fact, the landlady was moved to say that her color was much improved since her arrival, and that it was a great comfort to see the healthy shine in her ladyship's eyes.

Jane was on the verge of sitting down and writing to Lady Fanny when the constable arrived. Gathering her dignity and the landlady's best shawl around her, Jane descended. The constable proved to be rather younger than Jane had anticipated, but he was of a no-nonsense disposition and Jane readily decided he would do very well when he surveyed the two villains in the piece and declared that if they hadn't been up to no good, he would be very surprised indeed.

"And so they have," Jane said from the doorway where she stood.

The constable swung round and quickly apprised himself of her identity and what facts she knew in the case. He did not actually tug his forelock when she concluded but his solemn air showed Jane he had a proper appreciation of what was due a countess. He set about questioning her abductors with very little show of sympathy. It was not long at all before they had confessed that they had been hired by a man named Manning to act for a woman they knew only as Clarisse.

"Manning!" Jane exclaimed. "Why of all the—"

"He is known to you, ma'am?" the constable asked.

"He is despicable!" Jane cried. "I threatened to turn him

away without a character after he behaved most reprehensibly in my service, though why and how he has come to be working for *that* woman, I cannot imagine!"

"Then this woman, this Clarisse, she is known to you also?" the constable inquired.

"I only know *of* her," Jane said tartly, "and as far as I am concerned, you may set these two rodents free so that they may return to London and tell her that she is welcome to George Aubrey Tate, lock, stock and barrel."

She pulled herself up to her full height and the constable fell back beneath the onslaught of her brilliant blue gaze. "Beg pardon, ma'am, but I must keep them in custody and act on this information."

"Very well," she said. "Do your duty, officer."

Jane turned and made her way majestically upstairs again. Let Clarisse have George! Nothing was more apparent to her than that the two of them were birds of a feather, and most assuredly deserved one another. She hoped they would vex one another to death with their high-handed ways—going here without warning, going off there without a word, and ordering people kidnapped and drugged! In no mood for sugar-coating her message, Jane sat down and wrote to Lady Fanny, recounting the forced nature of her departure and desiring the dowager countess to be so good as to send along money with which Jane could continue her journey.

> *"I have no desire to return and will find life under the leaky roof I resided beneath when I first met your son preferable to returning to Sefton Hall. I know you will not leave Ellen to suffer under George's regime but please restore her to your own household in London, as I must be quite plain and say that there is no hope of my being able to afford her services in the future. Please desire her to pack a simple dress for me, to replace the one which has been rendered repugnant to me by virtue of the awful adventure I have suffered*

while wearing it. I wish I did not have to trouble you for even this much, but I have no alternative. I beg you will not tell George where I may be found as I do not wish to see him again, nor do I believe he wishes to see me. Please believe that I will ever hold you dear to my heart, and I thank you for all your kindness."

Jane signed the letter with a firm stroke of her pen, sanded it and folded it. Mrs. Goodwinter, when summoned, said that it would go as soon as John the ostler returned from helping the constable transport his prisoners to Littleport, "which cannot take above two hours. It was a shocking tale, your ladyship, and he was wishful to take them where the magistrate may deal with them straight away, and they can be kept secure."

There was nothing for it but to wait. Mrs. Goodwinter urged a hearty luncheon on Jane, and offered to dress her hair, after which the landlady respectfully suggested that her ladyship might want to lie down. Jane was inclined to do so, but when she was alone, she discovered that she was far too agitated to be still. The gathering storm disgorged lightning and thunder aplenty, and she sat by the window and watched the ever-darkening sky. The tension of the approaching storm mirrored her mood though its breaking would, unfortunately, do nothing to relieve the strain she was feeling. Only the pleasure of throttling George Aubrey Tate could do that, and that avenue was not open to her.

Chapter Twenty-two

George awoke to find the morning well advanced and Henry most anxious to shave and dress him. Already carriages had begun arriving and the valet could not bear the thought of his impeccably correct employer lying about in a state of slovenly repose. Fletcher, on the other hand, was of the opinion that the earl should be spoon-fed and sheltered entirely from a host's duties, and went about muttering darkly about the fiend named Wofford who had sent out invitations without first considering whether his lordship still intended to entertain half the *ton* when it must have been clear to anyone with a brain that he and his bride were on stiffish terms.

Fed up with being cossetted and in no mood to receive guests, George crafted a plan which satisfied neither retainer, which was to seek out his wife at the earliest possible opportunity. His arm hurt as if red-hot pokers had been applied to it throughout the night but he was implacable in his resolve to rise. His mother put her head in to inform him that Great Aunt Serena had arrived and was asking after him, but that he was not to trouble himself and that he could rely on her, as the dowager countess, to receive his guests for him.

"And what of my wife?" George demanded, wincing as he

sat up. "Has she declined to be mistress of her own house?"

Lady Fanny bit her lip and regarded him anxiously. "She has left, George, and gone to stay at the lodge."

"The lodge!" George threw back the bedclothes and nearly lost consciousness when he stood up. Henry sprang to his side and prevented him from falling over. "Why on earth has she gone there?" George managed to say as he clung dizzily to a bedpost.

"Well, she meant to leave entirely but I persuaded her to stay there for the time being," Fanny said.

"Then I must go there and persuade her to return," he said as forcefully as his condition would allow.

"I wish you may," his mother replied, "but I hope you will choose your words carefully. You cannot conceive of how unhappy she has been, and I do not quite see what you mean to say to her which can alter her feelings." She paused and her expression softened. "You look most shockingly pale, my darling, and so I hesitate to take you to task, but I must at least say that no one, not even you, can expect to escape the consequences of their own foolishness. Have a care what you say, and think most earnestly of what is best for you both." She wished him a good morning and swept out of the room before he could reply.

George fought back the waves of dizziness that were threatening to turn his fervent intentions into jelly. "Henry, I am up. Clothes, if you please, and Fletcher, take that tray away and do not ever set a plate of gruel down in front of me again or I will draw and quarter you."

"My lord," Fletcher replied with cold dignity, and withdrew.

A young underfootman arrived just as George was slipping his arm gingerly into a sling which Henry had fashioned. The smell of a breakfast more along the lines of the one he usually took was a powerful restorative, and he overlooked the fact that Fletcher had sent the least senior of servants with it. Another day the impertinence might have inspired cool wrath and a rebuke to his butler, but George had room for only one thought in his mind. He mopped his brow and ordered the underfootman to throw a pitcher of water onto the fire blazing in the hearth. "July is quite warm enough without *that*," he said irritably.

Bates only pursed his mouth when George arrived at the stable and ordered a horse to be saddled. If he brought out the least spirited of the mounts from among those at Sefton Park, it was not to be wondered at, and George did not demur when the horse was led to a mounting block. The consumption of a fair-sized breakfast had brought him around to near normal, and moving about seemed to be helping to clear the spongy, absent feeling from between his ears. Any other day he would have spent a great deal of time being angry that he had obviously been rendered unconscious through artificial means, but today he only rejoiced that whatever had impaired him was wearing off. He pointed the horse in the direction of the hunting lodge, and not being a feisty beast, it set a modest pace down the road.

George did not hasten it. He needed time to think. He meant to sit down and talk with Jane in a calm and rational way, but he must organize his thoughts in order for that to occur. The magnitude of his rage following the duel had shocked him, and he supposed it might have shocked Jane, too. He rather thought some directness was required at this juncture, a straightforward declaration of facts not previously brought out, but the words in which to couch them eluded him. He must on no account delay any further in declaring his love for her.

When the lodge was in sight, he reined the horse in with his one good arm and stared. Something was not right. The front door hung open, no smoke escaped from the kitchen chimney, and there was a stillness all around that was intensified by the sultry weather. George's uneasiness communicated itself to his horse, which sidled this way and that as George frowned at the scene before him.

With deep misgiving, George urged the horse forward. He rode right up to the door and leaned over, peering in. Nothing seemed to be amiss but he got no answer in response to his shouted summons. He called again, even louder, but there was still no answer. He reined his horse around swiftly, surveying the surrounding meadow through narrowed eyes. Could it be that Jane was only but taking a walk, and that Ellen had gone with her?

"Blast!" The epithet fell into the silence around him. Every instinct told him that something was wrong, and yet there was not really any evidence to support that conclusion, just something in his gut. If Jane and Ellen were simply strolling in the park, they would be found easily enough. He thought quickly. He would not look foolish if he ordered his steward to mount a discreet search, for he had guests arriving and no one would wonder if his lordship rather thought that her ladyship might have forgotten the time and needed to be fetched back to the main house.

George set out toward the home farm, the likeliest place to find Williams at this time of day. He retraced his route to the point where the home farm diverged from the road back to the hall, and what he noticed this time as he passed made his palms begin to sweat. There were wheel marks in the softer ground by the edge of the road, as if a vehicle had come up from the direction of the home farm and then turned around.

No one in the earl's employ could fail to know that his lordship most expressly disliked to see the turf in any way defiled by careless driving, and yet here were the unmistakable signs of a carriage having turned around without any regard for the adjacent grass. Worst of all was the fact that the wheels were of narrow gauge, most definitely not those of a work cart such as usually travelled the home farm road, and Bates had said nothing about having dispatched any of the earl's own carriages for any purpose.

"Damn!" His horse trembled violently as he jabbed his heels into its sides and set off down the road. If Jane had already left, if she had somehow ordered up a post chaise to convey her away from Sefton Park, then all might be beyond redemption. Time was of the essence. Williams or someone else on the home farm might have recognized a team or a coach which would lead him to one of the nearby posting houses. If Jane had not left too long before, he might still be able to catch her.

Williams was not to be found but George discovered someone else with the information he sought. Old Ned, who had worked at Sefton Park since George's grandfather was earl, was ambling along toward the meadow with a small flock of orphaned spring lambs when George thundered around the corner. The lambs scattered as George reined his horse in abruptly, sending up a shower of dirt clods.

"Ned, isn't it?" George said without ceremony. "My wife! Have you seen her?"

"No, can't say as I have, your lordship," Ned replied, his rheumy eyes screwed up thoughtfully.

"Then anything else?" George demanded. "A carriage perhaps?"

"Now there you've hit on something," Ned remarked in an unhurried manner. "It were nigh on three hours ago, I should say. I sees these two types drive bang through the gates as if they knew right where they was a-goin', but I says to myself, Ned, those two don't no wise belong here. They've taken a wrong turning, sure enough, and we'll soon see the front of 'em again."

"And did you?" George asked with admirable restraint.

"Oh, ay," Ned replied, "though I think it took them a little while to recognize their mistake. I took overlong with the nurslings today. One of 'em was unaccountable slow to take his milk, so I was yet hereabouts when the carriage came back. Then I says to myself, they was up thataway so long, maybe they was tradesmen, with business at his lordship's back door."

"But they were not, that I'll swear," George muttered. He

was in a fever of impatience to go but he held himself in check. "Did you know the horses, Ned, or the carriage?"

"That I did not," Ned said definitively, "but this I can say, there was naught of Cambridgeshire in either of the men. Town sharps, I said to myself, and not country folk at all."

If Ned said the men were from outside the shire, chances were excellent that he was correct. The thought only added to George's uneasiness. "Ned, you must forget the lambs and find Williams for me imediately."

Ned gestured toward the flock. "But they'll come to mischief, your lordship."

George turned in the saddle. Lambs were scattered from one side of the road to the other. Suddenly, far down the road, he saw two of them nosing at something odd in the grass, something pale and wiggling. He reined sharply back the way he had come and found Ellen. She was trussed up like a turkey with a length of rope and her shawl had been tied tightly across her face. She was still groggy from a blow to the head but she recognized the earl right away.

"Oh, it's you, is it?" she said with disdain. "Well, she's gone and out of your clutches now, your lordship, though there's no saying that what the poor thing faces now mayn't be worse than what you've dealt her!"

"Be still and tell me what you know," George snapped.

"Two men, London-bred I vow, took her, and none too politely neither. I thought she maybe expected 'em, for she was a-runnin' away from me and towards them, or so I thought, but then I seed them tie her up and throw her into the carriage, and I knew it wasn't none of hers."

"What did the carriage look like?" George asked, pulling Ellen to her feet with his good arm.

The maid shook herself free of him. "I was just about to be tellin' you that!" she said indignantly.

George remounted with some difficulty after a few minutes, armed with the knowledge that Jane had been carried off in a carriage with a dull red body and drawn by a mismatched team. He pushed his horse to the limits of its speed, tearing straight across the open fields that led back to Sefton Hall. He felt a terror akin to having the earth give way beneath him, and the sensation of falling helplessly through space saturated his senses.

He reined in by the stables and yelled for Bates to bring his curricle around to the forecourt instantly. Freddy leaped to take his horse's reins and George said, "Turn this nag into its box without untacking it if you have to, but be up behind when Bates comes round for me. We need another sharp set of eyes. Her ladyship has been abducted!"

"Yes, your lordship!" Freddy declared, his eyes big as saucers.

George slid off the horse and cursed as his injured arm was jostled. "Tell Bates he's driving," George said, blinking as the pain blossomed anew. He set off at a rapid walk for the house, willing the pain to subside but feeling distinctly muzzy-headed. A few drops of rain landed on his face but did nothing to clear his head or cool his rage. He shouldered his way through the library doors which were just being shut against the approaching storm. The underfootman fell back and begged his lordship's pardon but George was gone from the room before the hapless servant could even compose an apology.

"Fletcher! Henry! My driving cape! Wofford! I require you!"

For all that Sefton Hall was a large house, the staff heard the earl and came running with remarkable speed. Lady Fanny heard doors slamming and the pounding of feet in the corridors overhead and outside the salon door and hastened to the central hall, where George was still issuing orders and surrounded by servants.

"My dearest, whatever has happened?" Fanny cried.

George rounded and there was such a savage look on his handsome face that his mother fell back a pace.

"Jane has been abducted!"

385

"Abducted? No! But how? And why?"

"I do not know why, nor by whom, nor even which way they are bound, but I *will* find her!" George said. He suddenly turned a gimlet-eyed stare on the assembled servants. "Where is Gandolfo?" he demanded. They all looked at him but none seemed able to make him an answer.

Fanny interposed. "I should think he is still abed, George."

"Let us hope that for the sake of his neck he is," George said darkly. "Fletcher! Blast the man! Where is he?"

Fletcher arrived moving much faster than was customary for him, panting and very pink in the cheeks. "I beg your lordship's pardon, but I was engaged in verifying a very alarming message conveyed to me by a member of the staff. My lord, I regret to inform you that the Lady Portia cannot be found."

George's face tightened and a muscle twitched in his cheek. "Do you know, Fletcher, I find I grow weary of hearing you announce that my sister cannot be found," he said in a deadly calm voice. "This is the second time, is it not?"

Fletcher nodded apologetically. "Indeed, my lord, that is the case, but I did not think it right to withhold the information on the ground that it stales with repetition."

"You had better tell me the whole of it," George said brusquely.

Still short of breath, Fletcher panted out his message. "Stoke conveys the intelligence that her mistress almost certainly left the house very early this morning, and that she has taken with her one or two bandboxes."

The sound of carriage wheels in the forecourt drew George's head around, but it was only a chaise bearing the Hanover crest. Lady Eugenia reposed in state inside, next to her husband. Imogene and Emmaline, on the seat opposite, goggled at the facade of Sefton Hall as the chaise drew to a halt.

386

"I have no time for any consideration but my wife's safety," George declared, eyeing the chaise with displeasure. "Ah, Henry, yes, drape it across my shoulders." He stooped a little so that his valet could drop his driving cape onto him. "I am setting off in pursuit of the countess, and God help whoever has done this. Hicks!" he barked. "I need pistols, and quickly—and two for Bates, also!"

The butler's cousin hurried away as a liveried postilion alit and lowered the carriage steps on the Hanover chaise. Lady Fanny was too conscientious a hostess not to feel a pang at not going to greet them but she repressed the sentiment. "George, I do not charge you with any obligation to your guests but I urge you not to go in pursuit of Jane. Only consider your health and allow the authorities to handle this."

George directed a thunderous look at her. "Madam, I will do as I see fit in this instance, and I see fit to track my wife's abductors down and recover her before serious harm befalls her, if it has not already."

"But you are in no condition," his mother protested with a pleading look. "You are entirely without color, and besides, you must stay here to oversee the search for both Jane *and* Portia."

"I will send Freddy to London with a letter desiring every available runner at Bow Street to attend us here at Sefton Park. I will have Williams go for the magistrate and request that he order out every constable in Cambridgeshire. I will even have the militia sent out if need be to find my sister, but I will go in search of my wife now, this instant, and in person."

"Yes, of course dear," Fanny said, fanning herself breathlessly with one slim hand. "I only meant that both Jane and your sister deserve equal attention.

"No. They do not," George snapped. "Jane is going against her will, while Portia, I dare swear, has eloped. She has been endeavoring to escape the tyranny of my custody for the past several months, and if she has succeeded this time, then so be it. She will almost certainly be found with Jonas Biddle, and I wish her joy of him. Her plight, while intensely unpleasant, does not command the same urgency.'

Fabrice appeared and heard the last of this with an uncharacteristic frown on his face. He thought better of delivering the note he carried in his breast pocket and contented himself instead with going to stand next to his wife. Lady Eugenia came sailing in just then, with her husband and offspring bobbing in her wake.

"George, dear, how are you?" Without waiting for a reply, she said, "You will never credit it, but the roads were most appallingly bad the *whole* way here! We hardly dared travel above a walk. And the storm! How we dreaded the prospect of being caught up in it," she announced, drawing off her gloves.

Fanny took one look at George and moved forward quickly. "But how fortunate that you were not," she said, smiling and holding out her hand. "Do let us go and have some tea, or perhaps you would care to stroll the gardens for a few minutes, to restore your circulation." She took Eugenia's arm and could be heard murmuring as she went, "I am afraid we have just received some rather bad news. Come, and I will put you in possession of the whole."

Her soft words were overpowered by the sound of another carriage approaching, this one at a high rate of speed. George strode through the glazed double doors with barely a nod in Harry Hanover's direction, which slight the other gentleman appeared hardly to notice as he wandered off in the direction of the library. Fletcher hurried along behind George, receiving some last orders from his master. The restive movements of the match grays obscured the sound of the three horses that rounded the corner of the forecourt at that moment.

"What ho! Coming out to meet us?" cried a gay voice. "This is certainly a signal honor! I do not recall that he has

388

ever been in such a hurry to see us before, do you Roger?"

George glanced up distractedly and saw his former comrades in arms.

"No, but then perhaps he has heard of your quite remarkable streak of luck at piquet, John," Roger Creighton replied, pulling his horse up with a wry smile. "Perhaps our friend finds himself at a stand and hopes your good fortune will be found to be contagious. I vow, it touched me not a little."

George adjusted his sling in preparation for mounting the high step into the curricle and bid them a brief goodbye.

"But George," John Marshall protested, "never say you are leaving just as we arrive! Why, what's happened to your arm?"

"His face more like," said Lord Hugh soberly. "Dear fellow, whatever is the matter?"

"Jane has been abducted," George said shortly, "and my sister is missing. I go in pursuit."

"Only tell us which direction and we will go with you," Roger Creighton said, his nonchalant manner dropping away instantly. "What else do you know?"

"No more than you, I fear," George said, "except that Jane's abductors have been away from here three hours or more. Damned surgeon gave orders to dose me last night, with God only knows what elixir, else I would have discovered her absence much earlier." George directed a baleful look at Fletcher, who cringed and failed to meet his employer's gaze.

"But why?" demanded John Marshall. "I mean to say, man, what have you done to yourself that you needed a surgeon at all?"

"Duel," George said tersely.

His friends exchanged shocked glances but did not tax him further on the subject. Wofford came flying out the front doors with indecorous haste at just that moment, nearly tumbling down the stairs. "Your lordship!" he cried.

389

"I have just heard the dreadful news!"

The grays harnessed to the earl's curricle shied at Wofford's headlong approach, nearly lifting Freddy off his feet as he stood at their heads.

"Have a care, man!" George commanded. "These are not cart horses."

Wofford skidded to a halt. "No, of course not, my lord," he said, eyeing the grays with trepidation. "I have come for orders. What would you have me do?"

Wofford, with his narrow shoulders and shrinking manner, did not look at all in the heroic mold, and most especially when contrasted with the three former Guardsmen sitting their mounts with steely resolve in every line of their bodies.

"Us as well," Roger said. "Give us our orders of march, George. We are yours to command."

"I should jolly well say so," John Marshall chimed in.

Lord Hugh looked rather drawn but he nodded, saying quietly, "Only form a plan and tell us our part in it. Not for anything could we let Jane come to harm, nor your sister, either, of course."

George looked from one to the other. "Thank you," he said, obviously moved. "I have never had greater need of good friends than at this moment." He considered for a moment and then said, "Roger, I believe it is you who should lead the search for Portia." He summarized his suspicions and recommended that they speak to Harry Hanover as to the likeliest roads one would take to reach Jonas Biddle's residence.

"And Wofford," he said, turning, "discover what else you may from Stoke, and any other of the staff which may have been up at the hour when Portia left. Then I wish you will mount up and lead Mr. Creighton and Mr. Marshall to the magistrate."

"But your lordship," Wofford protested, "I am no horseman."

George began walking toward the curricle. "I have left the tamest horse in Christendom in the stable yard, still tacked up"—here he looked to Freddy for confirmation and received a nod—"and completely blown from a cross-country run. You should have no difficulty at all with him."

"No, your lordship," Wofford said, swallowing.

"And me, George?" Hugh said quietly. "What would you have me do?"

George paused in the act of stepping into the high, two-wheeled curricle. "I believe you had better come with me."

Hugh's face flushed with emotion. "Thank you, George."

George inclined his head and turned away. It was as close as he could come to acknowledging his friend's feelings for his wife. He ordered Bates to spring the horses and the whole party surged out of the forecourt, causing the Digby's coachman no small amount of alarm when he saw them coming. He quickly pulled off the road to let them pass since they showed no sign of checking their progress.

"Oh, dear," Lady Fanny said regretfully, watching them go. "He did not send Freddy to London for the Runners after all." She sighed. "Still, I suppose he knows what is best."

Eugenia knew a prime opening when she saw one and wasted no time in saying, "I wish it were so, friend of my childhood, only it is most certainly not the case. Your son, I regret to say, has shown the most shockingly poor judgment of late!"

Fanny forbore to point out that Eugenia, so far from being the friend of her childhood, was at least ten years older, and adopted a look of benign curiosity aimed at keeping that formidable woman moving toward the garden, where she could vent her spleen without any indiscretions reaching the ears of the staff. She had just ushered that lady out the doors and down onto the terraces under a distinctly threatening sky when she spied a figure striding toward them from the direction of the park.

"Oh, dear," she murmured. Ellen's skirts were snapping with the force of her steps.

Lady Eugenia, having been apprised of what Lady Fanny knew, had not noticed the maid and was saying, "I daresay Jane had not been abducted at all. She is such a scatterbrain she will no doubt have forgotten that the house party begins today and has decided to walk into the village. How very like her it would be, and what better proof that she is not at all the wife for George!"

Fanny made some demurring noise, noting the awful look on Ellen's face as she came closer. She tried to draw Eugenia off to one side of the path around the fountain but Eugenia was implacable in her forward momentum, which carried her on a collision course with Ellen.

"No, it would be difficult to imagine a more ill-conceived match," Eugenia announced, blithely unaware that Ellen had planted herself to one side of the path and was listening to every word. "It will not do, Fanny, which is a fact I am persuaded you know perfectly well for yourself. Even the excessively good breeding of the Seftons cannot be expected to overcome the vulgarity of Jane's background. It is a scandal! The girl has not the least notion of what it means to be a countess. Every endeavor must be made to terminate this union before she can produce children which would taint your line by introducing into it all the qualities in her which render her so completely unfit for all but the humblest of . . . what?"

Lady Eugenia stopped abruptly, her mouth hanging open as Ellen stepped forward. The maid was by far the shorter of the two, but the finger she thrust in Eugenia's face was backed up by a look so hostile that it would have given the devil himself pause.

"You!" Ellen hissed. "You dare say them things about my mistress? I'll tear your hair out, I will, aye, and scratch your eyes out after! You are the meanest, the most cruelest creature what God ever put on this earth, and I ain't

392

a-hearin' any more of that talk from you! I should ha' stopped you in Bath, only the rest of me dint believe what my ears was a-hearin' until it was too late to stop yer! My mistress is a saint, a saint, I tells you, and blameless in all this. What she put up with from his high and mightiness would make a tale you haven't heard, I'll warrant, and you ain't never had no cause to act so mean as you did to her!"

Eugenia had been backing goggle-eyed away from this onslaught all the while Ellen spoke, retreating from the jabbing finger aimed at her breastbone until she was up against the low wall of the pool surrounding the fountain. The sylvan figures graciously spewing water were a decided contrast to the fury in front of them, and her stout captive. Fanny was just wondering whether she should intervene—indeed, whether she *wanted* to intervene—when Ellen planted herself firmly and gave a heave that sent Lady Eugenia Hanover toppling over backwards into the fountain.

A monstrous bolt of lightning cracked across the sky at that instant, freezing the triumphant malice on Ellen's face and the stunned disbelief on Lady Eugenia's. Fanny watched as water dripped from her guest's chin. It was unfortunate but politeness required one to extract one's guests from fountains after they had been set upon by one's servants. Ellen marched off toward the house with a positively beatific smile on her face as Fanny wafted forward.

"She . . . she . . . *pushed* me!" Eugenia spattered. "That girl is out of her mind! Did you hear the things she said to me?"

"Indeed," Fanny murmured, looking at Ellen's retreating back. "What a remarkable girl!"

Chapter Twenty-three

The rain, which had been looming all day, overtook the earl's party not long after they had embarked on the Witchford road. Reasoning that Ellen had probably been correct about the kidnappers' origins, George decided to waste no time in setting out for London, only which road to go by?

"Hi! See here, George, someone's been this way today, and not in a farm cart," Hugh shouted back from down the road where he gone to reconnoiter. They had spent a fruitless and nigh on maddening hour chasing up and down numerous minor lanes and roads in search of just such a sign, but the relief of finding it was short-lived.

"Yes, but where from here?" George retorted, his mouth distorted with anger. "Stretham, Wilburton, Haddenham—they might have diverged from here toward any of those destinations and still be reasonably placed to reach London by nightfall. Damn!"

A cough at his elbow drew his head around. "Begging your lordship's pardon," Bates said, "but did I not hear your lordship say they was driving a mismatched team? And if they knew they was seen by old Ned, as seems reasonable they must might they not be wishful to hire another team so as to be less noticeable?"

"I have no way of knowing," George said irritably. "What is your point?"

"Why, only that if it should be they was wanting a posting house, they must go by the Stretham road, my lord."

Hugh rode up alongside. "It seems we must divide our efforts or throw the whole of our pursuit into one course."

"I find myself unwilling to gamble Jane's safety on an ill-informed hunch," George said darkly, "and yet I must. Why has she been taken, I ask you, and by whom? Whom? If I only knew that, I might better be able to intuit the next logical step in this plot!"

Rain was falling steadily now, not so much as to obscure their surroundings but enough to make the adjacent fields begin to steam with its cooling influence. "It is a damnable position to be in, to be sure," Hugh said quietly, "and yet, if you have no information, perhaps we are better to find that posting house Bates spoke of and see what they can tell us of the day's traffic. If something—or someone—unusual happened nearby today, perhaps it will have made its way to their ears."

Just then they spotted a forlorn figure trudging down the road. Hugh spurred on ahead to question the passerby. Bates drove the horses up even with them and George put a surreptitious hand to his wounded arm. He was glad to note that for all that he was rapidly growing wet on the outside from the rain, the dressing on his arm was still dry underneath his many-caped cloak. He felt surprisingly fit and thought it proved that he had been correct to protest the cossetting of his servants and surgeon.

"Does it pain you, my lord?" Bates asked under his breath.

George turned to his coachman in surprise. "Why do you whisper?"

Bates looked at him stolidly. "I was wishful to know the truth, my lord, but I suspects that if Lord Hugh heard you say you was in pain, he would set you to the rightabout and put you back abed himself. I would keep your secret, but I want to know whether I should be prepared for you to fall of a sudden."

George found something to smile at for the first time that day. His harsh face softened. "It does not hurt more than I can bear," he answered, "and not a candle to the wound I took in the Peninsula."

Bates eyed him in evident disbelief. "I asked, begging your lordship's pardon, because you are of a color to make me wonder, a color very like that same day you just spoke of."

"He's nothing to say to the problem," Hugh reported, abruptly turning his horse back to face them. "I say we make for the posting house."

But George was still loath to abandon the search for some solid lead and turn for the posting house. He ordered Bates to point the horses toward Haddenham, "And if we can make no discovery there, we will turn back and pass along the road to Wilburton, and thence to Stretham."

The rain slowed them to a laggardly trot as it increased in volume. If not for Hugh riding point, they must have been forced to a walk. The downpour soon obliterated any sign of another coach's passing, and in Haddenham, it was the work of ten minutes to knock up someone to answer inquiries as to whether any strangers had passed that way today. The puzzled householder peered through the rain and even bowed to the earl once he realized who it was that sat in the curricle, but the answer was disappointing. No one had come that way today, excepting the ostler from the Hare and Hound in Stretham on his way to deliver an important letter.

They drove on. Even George's driving cape was no proof against the rain after two hours, and by the time they reached Wilburton, the horses were slogging through mud up to their hocks and every member of the party was miserably cold and wet. There, too, the information was that no one had been seen today who could not be accounted for.

George clenched his fists in frustration. It seemed as if all the luck had been with the kidnappers. They had had a clear start, thanks to his having been dosed with that damnable purple stuff. The rain had come along just in time to obscure their escape and prevent a high-speed pursuit. And above all, he had not a clue as to who might have taken Jane, or why. George surveyed his bedraggled party—Freddy's bright red hair gone dark as the rain pasted it to his skull, Hugh sodden and his clothes ruined. Bates's hat discharging water in a torrent from its brim. Before long, the road would become impassable to a wheeled vehicle.

"Bates!" George yelled above the sound of the deluge. "To Stretham! We will unhitch the horses there and I will proceed on horseback."

"But my lord! Your arm!"

"Be damned to my arm! I would as soon be dead as fail in the attempt to find my wife!"

And so it was that the waterlogged quartet arrived at the Hare and Hound, the second party of the nobility to do so that day, which exactly doubled the number of titled persons that Host Goodwinter's establishment had served in its long and lackluster career.

Jane heard the commotion in the yard below and tripped on her overlong, borrowed dress as she hurried to the window. Perhaps Fanny had sent a carriage for her to continue on her way. But although it was Bates who was alighting from the vehicle, he came not with an empty carriage but with a passenger. Her eyes narrowed. *George!* Well, if he had come after her, he was wasting his time! Jane decided to waste none of *her* time in telling him so. She hitched the rough fabric of the dress up and marched out the door and down the stairs in very high dudgeon.

Hugh was just coming in, his dark curls glistening with rain. He stopped abruptly at the sight of her. "Jane!" he exclaimed, moving swiftly forward to take her warm, dry hands in his rain-chilled ones. "You are safe! God be thanked!"

Jane's wrath dissipated upon seeing him. "Indeed, I am,"

she said, "but how is it possible that you are here?"

Hugh still held her hands fervently, and said with much feeling, "We were arriving for the house party when we surprised George embarking on a search to find you. Is it true you were taken against your will? Are your kidnappers here?" He cast a keen glance around the entry.

Jane squeezed his hands. "It is true, but I am perfectly safe now, and the kidnappers are in the hands of the law, but Hugh, I have no great desire to see George. Could you not contrive to make him go away?"

Hugh looked at her in consternation. "Not see George? But he has been half out of his mind with worry! What can you mean, you do not wish to see him?"

Jane sighed. "I do not wish to draw you into a quarrel that is none of your making, dear Hugh, truly I do not. Can you not simply tell George that he may go away again now? Tell him I am safe, and that he has done what duty requires."

But it was too late. George came through the door at that moment, stooping a little since it would not accommodate his full height. Bates and Freddy followed him, and the whole entryway was now filled with sodden men. Water ran off them and pooled on the flags beneath their feet. George stepped forward.

"Jane!"

Jane withdrew her hands from Hugh's. "George," she said frostily.

"You are safe!" he cried. He covered the distance between them in two quick strides and reached for her with his free hand.

Jane shrank back disdainfully. "Yes, I am. Perhaps you will oblige me by going back the way you came now that you have ascertained that fact."

The relief on George's face was replaced by confusion. "But Jane, I have been distraught to know where you were and what had happened to you. I do not think I deserve to be turned away with no more than that."

398

"I find I am no longer concerned with what pleases or displeases you, my lord," Jane said loftily. "In fact, I am resolved that it will play no part in any decisions I make in the future. Ah, Goodwinter," she said, addressing the landlord, who had come in and added his bulk to the already crowded entryway. "This is the Earl of Sefton. I expect he will pay my reckoning since he is here, but that will be the extent of my dealings with him. I will be in my room awaiting a response to the letter I sent."

She gathered her shawl around her and cast one last naughty look at George in preparation for ascending the stairs. Hugh was watching all this closely and seemed on the verge of saying something when George uttered a low moan and slowly sank to his knees. His face, though no more bloodless than before, was screwed up as if he were in extreme pain. "Bates," he muttered weakly, his lashes sinking down. "To me!"

"That's done it," Bates exclaimed darkly, seizing his master by the shoulders. "I make no mistake he's bleedin' again!"

"George!" Jane dropped her shawl and flew to his side. "George, are you all right? Say something!"

The earl brought his lips together. "Jane?" he whispered. "Jane, is that you?"

"Yes!" she cried. "It's me, my darling. Do not give up! You have overtaxed yourself but we will bring you around, never fear!"

"Bed," he murmured, the word barely audible. He sagged a little further in his coachman's embrace.

Jane, who was now whiter than the earl, gestured frenziedly to Bates. "Bring him upstairs! He must be put to bed without delay! Hugh, do you lend your strength. To the top of the stairs and turn right. He must be put in my chamber, for there is a fire burning there already. We must see that he is made warm at all costs!"

George muttered something, but in the rush to pick him

up, no one regarded it. He went limp as arms went about him, and Jane reached out to touch his cheek as they carried him past her.

"Oh! He is like ice," she said, staring down at his immobile countenance in horror. "Goodwinter!"

"Ma'am! Your highness! I mean, your ladyship!" the host stammered, aghast at seeing a member of the gentry being hauled unconscious up the stairs of his inn.

"We must have brandy!" Jane said anxiously. "Oh! And is there a surgeon nearby?"

Goodwinter regarded her dubiously. "We make do with a midwife most times, ma'am, and for the rest, there's a man who has an uncommon good touch with animals."

"A horse doctor?" Jane said, eyeing him incredulously. "I should say not! Freddy!"

The undergroom, who had picked up the earl's hat when it slid from his master's unconscious form, was standing in the background toying with it disconsolately. "Ma'am?" he said, stepping forward, a ray of hope in his eyes.

"You must ride back to Sefton Hall and desire them to send the surgeon who attended your master there to attend him here."

"Yes, ma'am!" Freddy thrust the earl's hat on his head and pelted out into the rain again.

Jane turned to follow the progress of Bates and Hugh as they bore the earl up the stairs. George's head was lolling and he appeared to be in worse case than ever. "Oh, dear! Do be gentle! Yes, that's right, around the corner now, and into that first room." She dogged their steps anxiously, leaning to the left and the right to catch glimpses of George beyond Bates's ample rear as they made their way up to the bedchamber.

A low rumble of thunder outside built in intensity until the very walls of the inn seemed to shake. Jane bit her lip, fearing the place might fall down around their ears, but presently the shaking subsided, only to be followed by a mighty crack of lightning that lit the room. The only thing Jane noticed was George's face. It was a ghastly color.

"Only give us a moment to divest him of his wet clothes," Hugh said to her gently.

Jane left the room and paced back and forth on the small landing. Goodwinter arrived with a tray which Jane took from him. "Make a large fire in the parlor," she said, "and see what dry clothes you can come by for my coachman and Lord Hugh."

"*Lord* Hugh?" the host said. The knowledge that an earl might be only the least of the personages quartered in his modest inn seemed to affect him severely. His left eye began twitching. "Y—yes, I . . . I will," he stuttered, "and I'll send Mrs. Goodwinter to you, shall I?"

Hugh opened the door to the chamber at that moment. "Jane? He's in fit condition for your company now, and seems a little improved."

Jane turned away from the landlord. "Oh, truly, Hugh? I cannot thank you enough for being here, and for helping him, and me, too. I only wish you might have been spared all of this."

Hugh laid his hand over hers and said softly, so that none might overhear, "Indeed, you owe me no apology. You were merely an innocent victim. I only wish that . . . well, when you told me downstairs that you had no wish to see George, I own I thought there might be some chance for me. I was sorely tempted to take you at your word, but the look upon your face when George fainted—but I must say no more! Only know that I am always yours to command."

Jane stood on tiptoe and impulsively placed a kiss on his cheek. "Thank you, thank you," she said, "for everything. It is true that my feelings are . . . well, still engaged."

Hugh smiled ruefully. "George was ever the luckiest man of my acquaintance." He turned away. "Bates, let us go now, and see to these kidnappers. We ride for Littleport as soon as we have fortified ourselves with what food the house can

401

provide at short notice."

"Indeed, indeed," Goodwinter blustered. "I am sure we can make you a meal that will satisfy—not perhaps *exactly* what you are used to but . . ." The sound of their footsteps and the landlord's voice faded away down the stairs.

Jane closed the door behind her and leaned against it. If anything, it was darker than ever inside the bedchamber now, with the storm immediately overhead. She took a long breath and exhaled it with a sigh. George lay in the bed unmoving, but his color seemed reasonably normal by the light of the fire which Bates had built up to roaring proportions. The sheet was drawn up nearly to the broad spare shoulders, and she could see the bandage around the arm which had been supported by a sling before. It seemed to cover an unaccountably large area between his shoulder and elbow for what she remembered as a paltry wound that had bled very little.

"You silly fool," she whispered, "to have ridden after me in your condition."

"Jane? Is that you? Come closer, where I can see you," said a weak voice from the bed.

Jane set the tray down. "Yes, it is me, George. Lie still and conserve your strength while I prepare a cup of tea for you."

There was a slight rustling as she poured and stirred but no rejoinder. She turned to find George sitting up against the pillows, with a gleam in his eyes that might have been either fever or mischief.

"I did not give you leave to sit up," she said crossly. Seeing him looking better caused her anxiety to be laced with a return of the annoyance she felt with him. "You are as weak as a kitten, else I would not have ordered you put to bed."

"Indeed," said her husband, "it was the very outcome I had hoped for."

"What?" Jane peered through the gloom at him suspiciously.

"Nothing. Is that tea ready?" he asked meekly.

She handed it to him. "I am all out of patience with you, George Tate. Do not try my temper any further. I will stay with you until you are well enough to travel back to Sefton Hall and then I mean to go my own way."

"If that is what you wish, then I am in no position to stop you," George sighed, "only might you contrive to help me dry my hair before you leave? It is making me feel chilled."

The sheet had fallen away from the wide shoulders, revealing the whole of his chest, with its abundant covering of dark, silky hair. Jane was quite thunderstruck by the sight, and by the casualness with which he sat and looked at her without any sign of discomposure at being . . . naked. She resisted the faint quickening of her pulse. Despite having seen him unclothed before, somehow this was different. Did husbands and wives—*should* husbands and wives?—be quite so . . . comfortable with one another when in a state of undress in full daylight? Jane bit her lip and glanced toward the window as a gust of rain lashed at the panes. Perhaps since it was not precisely a *bright* day . . .

She turned back to find George's eyes on her, his gaze intent. He lifted an eyebrow and shivered ever so slightly. Jane wrenched her focus away from his unclothed form and took a linen cloth from beside the washing ewer. He closed his eyes when she rubbed it across his damp, disorderly locks. She watched for any sign that he was in pain, or unequal to the task of staying upright in bed, but his handsome face was relaxed, the lips turned slightly upward, as if he was enjoying himself.

"Truly, you are the most exasperating man," she muttered.

He smiled without opening his eyes. "No, that honor, I believe, must go to Jonas Biddle."

Jane smiled reluctantly, softening the intensity with which she toweled at George's curls. "You may be right," she said, "but I can see no profit in agreeing with you."

"Ah, but you already have," he murmured, "and what a

sweet satisfaction it is to me. It seems to me a foundation on which we can build. By the by, he appears to have succeeded in running off with my sister after all."

"Has he?" Jane asked. "I wish it may be so. Your sister used to tell me what a difficult man you were to live with, only I could see no fault in you then, and so did not understand the urgency she felt to be quit of you. Jonas may be pompous but he will not plague her to death with his fits and starts."

"Wicked girl," George said without heat. "Am I to take from that that you accuse me of having an uneven temper?"

"No," Jane said. "An implacable temper. It is your sense which is uneven."

That made him open his eyes. "You began impeaching my character almost from the moment we met," he said with a wounded expression. "I recall it distinctly. Do you mean to go on chastising me for the whole of our married life?"

Jane ceased rubbing at his hair. His words reawakened her sense of having been dealt with unfairly at his hands. She planted her hands on her hips. "There will be no more 'married life' between us, George. I meant to leave you and I will. The kidnappers only hastened me on my way."

He reached out with his free hand and took her wrist before she could evade him. "Do you not love me then, Jane, not even a little?"

"Hah!" Jane said, and then was silent. Denial would be false and admission would be fatal.

His heavy-lidded blue eyes searched hers for a moment before he said softly, "I love *you*, you know."

Jane stared at him. "You do?"

"I have from the very beginning. You enchanted me."

Jane let that sink in and then red-hot indignation boiled up in her. "Well!" she exclaimed. "You have certainly had the most extraordinary way of showing it!" She snatched her wrist out of his grasp and threw the piece of damp cloth to the floor. "You carried me off to London and married me

404

most uncivilly, and . . . and then hurried me back to Bath, and then ordered me to the country without so much as a 'by your leave,' and then you stayed away from me altogether and . . . and . . . you are the most *infuriating,* the most *unreasonable,* the most . . . most . . ."

Jane felt her face begin to crumple, her cheeks puckering alarmingly in preparation for tears. She fought the urge, furiously jamming the full, old-fashioned sleeves of her borrowed dress up to her elbows and thrusting her chin out. "If you have loved me for as long as you say you have, why did you never tell me so before this?"

George regarded her mildly. She looked like some delightful milk maiden in the baggy dress of poorest linen, with shining skin and the huge blue eyes blazing from behind her spectacles. The fierce scowl on her face dissuaded him from taking the situation lightly, though. There was no margin for pride in this room, no earls or countesses, just a man and a woman. He must do his best to bring things back to the way it had been between them in the beginning, when he had first begun to know what it meant to need another person the way one needed air.

"I was afraid that you would think the declaration merely a convenient lie, to keep you by my side when there was that in my behavior which must have driven you away," he said. "Now that you have announced your desire to be quit of me, however, I find I have nothing to lose by telling you."

"But . . ." Jane stared at him, trembling a little with the force of her emotions. The word dangled from her lips as she tried to decide whether he was merely having a jest at her expense. "But you declared *your* intention to be quit of me long before I declared *my* intention!"

"I never wished it so," he said gently. "It was only that we seemed to be at an impasse. From all that I could determine, you did not love me, and—despite my best efforts—*could* not love me."

"Could not?" she echoed. "How can you say that, could

not? Are you some inhuman monster? Did no one ever love you before? Even your mother, who knows your faults full well, loves you. How could you think that I could not . . . or did you think me incapable of loving?" she asked quickly. "Am *I* the monster then?"

"No, certainly not," he said, smiling a little. He patted the bed next to him. "Come, sit. It wearies me to have to make my voice go across the room."

"I don't know whether to believe you or not," she said with a touch of defiance. "I think you have practiced some deception today already."

"Have I?" he asked mildly. "Oh, dear. I wish you will sit down and tell me all about it."

"You are not to be trusted," Jane said stoutly. "You are a practiced deceiver."

"Have we not progressed beyond the part where you malign my character?" George asked, his face a study in disappointment. "Perhaps I shall have to resort to the one foolproof way I know of making you comply with my wishes."

Jane backed away a step. "What way is that?"

"Why, scold you, of course."

"Oh! I . . . I thought you might mean something else," Jane said. She was dismayed to discover that her voice was tinged with longing. "Well! I am not sure I am entirely satisfied with your explanation. For a man who loves me, you have behaved in a very shabby fashion."

"I wish I could deny it," he said. "I have done many things in my life which were not admirable, not up to the standards I set for myself, and some things which I have done proved to be embarrassing in the extreme, but never was I truly ashamed of anything I had done until . . ." He reached out his hand. "Jane, I have long wanted to say how sorry I was about what happened between us in London, only each time it seemed as if I might say the words, something else came about that pushed my intention to the background."

Jane folded her arms and regarded him sternly. "What happened between us in London was the one thing I *did* understand in your behavior," she said. "It is everything since that I have not understood."

"Truly?" he said, looking a little surprised. "Come, sit down beside me," he said tenderly, "and I will endeavor to explain all of it, everything which confuses you, to the limits of my ability." He patted the bed beside him again and regarded her with hopefully raised eyebrows.

"You are a reprobate in the guise of a nobleman, you know," Jane said reproachfully. "And you have the most awful temper."

"Alas, I cannot deny it," George said sadly. "Could I win you over by earnestly vowing to keep it in check for the remainder of my life?"

"That would be tantamount to writing a check on a bank where you have no account. No, I think you had better not promise me that."

"What then?" he said. "Only say the word."

Jane studied him. "Well, I think you had better resign yourself to *my* temper," she said slowly, "as well as . . . as other things about me which you perhaps will not like . . ." Jane felt the heat rising in her cheeks and stopped. "You will just have to accept me as I am, you know," she said defiantly. "I never pretended to be anything other than what I am, and I have grown tired of trying to be otherwise."

George looked genuinely surprised for the first time. "But who has suggested that you *should* be anything else?" His brows drew together and his expression hardened alarmingly. "My godmother! Tell me the truth, Jane, has she made mischief between us? Been unkind to you?"

Jane sniffed and blinked. "Well, yes. She was most awfully rude to me in Bath and I . . . I . . ." Jane dabbed at her eyes with the corner of the landlady's shawl. "You have been beastly, too, sometimes, only when you *have* been nice to me, it seemed as if it was worth any amount of trouble to have arrived at that moment ..." She sniffled again as her nose began to run and fat tears puddled in her eyes. "Oh, George, she made me most unhappy, but I don't love her, you see, and so what she said did not make me nearly so unhappy as the thought that *you* didn't love me, and didn't truly want me to be your wife and ... and ..."

"Jane," George said softly, holding out his good arm, "come and be beside me. I find I cannot bear to be so far from you."

Jane looked at him through watery eyes. "You do not say so out of a sense of duty?" she whispered.

"No duty at all could make me feel as I do right now," he replied, his gaze capturing hers and holding it unrelentingly. "Duty has not the power of love."

"Oh, George," Jane cried weepily and flung herself at him.

His good arm came up around her and he sighed deeply as she nestled against him, sniffling and hiccupping. He had been nearly at the end of what he knew to say to her to make her come to him, and to make her believe that he loved her. He was a master of expressing himself in all respects save the one that was most important—with the woman he loved. Why words should fail him just when he needed them most was a mystery to him, and yet, it was so. All he could do now was *show* her how he felt and then perhaps he could put the nightmare of losing her behind him. Her tears were wetting his shoulder and he smiled, relaxing as he stroked her wonderfully misbehaving hair, all tangled curls of red and gold glitter. How good it felt to be holding her!

He flexed his injured arm experimentally before deciding that any pain caused by using it was well worth it. He tentatively pulled her up to him. "Oh, Jane," he said, "how could you have doubted that I loved you, that I loved everything about you?" He kissed her softly and she looked up at him, her eyes wide and her expression a little wary.

"There were times when I did think you quite liked me," she admitted, "only I could not be sure."

He kissed her again to cover a chest gone tight with emotion. "Tell me which times," he managed to say, "so that I may pattern all my behavior on them."

"Well, *that,*" she said, "the kissing and the . . . touching." She firmed up her lips and said resolutely, "I like it, George. I mean, I like . . . I like . . ."

Her face began to grow quite pink and George nodded encouragingly. "You like . . . ?"

Suddenly she seized his face and kissed him, a little clumsily at first, but with a sincerity of purpose that instantly aroused him. He returned the kiss with ardor, bunching her hair in his hand and welcoming the heat of her lithe body pressing up against him. "There!" she said shakily when at last she pulled away. "*That* is what I mean. I like it, and if you do not care for me liking it, then I wish you will say so, though your mother says it would be most unnatural in you *not* to like it, for she says that, in general, men like it exceedingly well."

"My mother!" George exclaimed in horrified amusement. "You spoke to my mother about my lovemaking?"

"Well, not precisely," Jane said, casting her eyes down, "only in the most vague way, you understand. I would not have at all, you know, had I not been at my wits' end to know how to account for . . . well, for your very odd behavior in sending me away and . . . and . . . then the way you received me at the lodge . . ."

George lifted her chin with one finger. "Do you know, I believe this is something we were better to take action on than to talk about?"

"Oh, happily," Jane murmured as he slid his hand along her shoulder and nibbled at her temple. "Only we must be careful of your arm, and . . . and you *must* not mind if I make those . . . well, those *sounds* again."

"Mmmm, yes, I will not mind in the least," George said, sliding down and picking at the small tie which snugged the dress against her, "and with the storm, I should think no one

409

else will even hear them, so you need not worry about a thing."

Jane laid her hand over his, stilling it. She looked at him anxiously. "But they *might* hear us," she whispered.

"I shall have them murdered and their bodies dumped in a ditch to protect your reputation," George said distractedly, kissing the sweet-smelling valley between her breasts. "Your cousin will tell you that I am quite capable of doing such a thing."

"Oh! Oh, George, that makes me shiver, and yet I am not at all cold," she said breathlessly as he drew a finger over the peak of one breast where it protruded through the linen shift.

"I intend making you do a great deal more than just shiver," George declared, his voice muffled as he spoke against her skin. A great clap of thunder sounded overhead, making the window shudder in its frame and the pitcher rattle in the ewer. Jane let out a startled cry. George reluctantly turned his attention away from the lovely, creamy breast he had just freed from her dress. "Are you frightened of the storm? Shall I draw the shutters?"

"No! Oh, it is . . . *that* . . ."

"This?" George said, resuming his gentle torture of her nipple. He lifted his eyes to watch her response.

She looked at him dazedly, her mouth open and her cheeks stretched taut. "Yes," she whispered. "Most assuredly, it is that."

"Then I shall continue," he said with a wicked glint in his eye.

When Dame Goodwinter mounted the stairs some time later to see what service her ladyship might be needing, she soon came to the conclusion that the countess had no need nor desire for anyone save the earl at that moment. Theirs might be a common enough sort of inn, she told her husband, but she would not be at all surprised if the heir to an earldom was not at that very minute being conceived under their roof.

Epilogue

"Oh, George, I really do feel most dreadfully guilty," Jane said, "lurking about out here while your mother contends with a house full of guests on our behalf." Jane studied the list of arrangements made for the day by Lady Fanny and sent to the hunting lodge for Jane's approval.

George grunted and smiled. The morning sun captured the honey tones in his deep brown hair where he lay against the pillow. Jane knew the sound was meant to fob her off, to make her think she had his full attention when, in fact, he was on the verge of going back to sleep. A half hour ago she had had his undivided attention. The kind of soaring satisfaction he had given her never failed to wake her up and make her eager to face the day, whereas lovemaking had the opposite effect on him.

She spared a tender look for her husband and then drew her wrapper around her while she studied the rest of the note, the part which dealt with matters other than menus and the outings planned for that day. "She says the Montfort boys are running about after Emmaline and Imogene and that Harry Hanover does not stand in their way, nor your godmother. Only think it if they married, George," Jane said in awe. "The Montfort twins married to the Hanover twins!"

"Ghastly thought," George muttered.

411

"Oh, and your mother says John Marshall seems quite taken with Lavinia Digby. That would be most suitable, would it not? He is ever on the lookout for a joke and she is always ready to laugh at one."

"But any man would surely shoot her if forced to endure the sound of her laughter for long," George said, rolling over onto his back. "John is no exception."

"You are by far too harsh," Jane said reprovingly, "and besides, John has not got a great deal of money and Lavinia does. I am convinced they would be tolerably happy together."

George raised one hand and scratched indolently at the center of his chest. "Then I am sure you are right."

"You are sure of nothing of the sort," Jane retorted. "You only hope that if you say the right things, I will not go to Ellen and let Henry descend on *you*. I know very well what your stake is in continuing this conversation."

George made a noncommittal noise which Jane ignored as she opened another letter.

"Oh! Listen to this, George! Roger writes from London to say that a foreign vicomte—something *de Montparnasse?*—has been implicated along with Manning in the plot to kidnap me. Roger saw to it that the authorities knew where he could be found and he has been escorted to Dover and put on a boat bound for Calais. How curious! Roger seems quite indecently glad to have seen the last of him. I wonder why?"

Her husband made a stifled sound and Jane regarded him suspiciously. "You know something which you will not tell me. Very well, I shall simply ask Roger when next I see him."

"You mustn't, you know," George said mildly. "Roger is too much a gentleman to tell you so, but chances are that he is entangled with a woman I once knew and will not like to discuss the matter."

"Oh, you mean, Clarisse," Jane said matter-of-factly. She ignored the choking sound coming from the direction of the bed. "Oh, yes, I know it is very indiscreet of me to admit I know her name, or even that she exists, but truly, George, when one has been kidnapped at the behest of one's husband's mistress, I think one is entitled to dispense with coyness, though I must say that if she had stayed out of my life, I would have been perfectly content to pretend I knew nothing about her."

She took a sip of chocolate as George pulled a pillow over his head and mumbled something.

"What's that, George? I can't understand a word you're saying."

He pulled the pillow away. *"Former* mistress," he said severely.

"Yes, well, of course. It goes without saying that now you are married, you will have no further need of one." Jane said serenely.

George put the pillow back over his head and Jane saw his chest shaking with what she suspected was laughter. She very grandly decided to ignore it, sifting through the other letters brought down from the hall. They had been staying at the lodge for the better part of a month, George having given everyone to understand that his surgeon had advised rest and quiet in measures which could not be had in a country house filled to the rafters with guests. In doing so, he had relied heavily on the fact that the surgeon, when summoned to the Hare and Hound, had discovered his patient to have reopened his wound.

George had had to calm Jane's alarm when she fell back into his arms, panting and flushed with pleasure after their lovemaking, only to see that a trickle of blood had soaked through his bandage.

"Oh, George, your arm," she had cried. "I knew that we should not have . . . oh, but it was so wonderful!"

"Yes, it most decidedly was," he agreed, pulling her closer. "I have shed blood many a time, but never on a happier occasion or for a more worthwhile reason. However, I can see that I shall have to ask my mother to act as hostess for my

413

guests while we stay in seclusion at the lodge. You, of course, will join me there in order to nurse me back to health."

"Sprained ankles, toothaches, and now this!" Jane had scolded. "One might be excused for thinking you were frail, but all these infirmities are only devices for getting your own way."

"You wound me anew," George had said sleepily, which had ended the conversation.

Jane eyed the livid red crease on George's upper arm now. It actually looked worse now than ever, which the surgeon had assured her was normal, saying that it would continue to heal and fade to silver as time passed. She had to admit that she was utterly content except for wishing that they might soon receive further word from Portia. A note had been found after her disappearance saying that she was fine and that when they next heard from her, she would be a married woman. The runners were sent back to London, the constables thanked and sent home again, and the magistrate invited to dine at Sefton Hall as thanks for his role in coordinating the brief search.

Jane eagerly slit open the last letter on the tray when she noticed a familiar handwriting. It bore numerous odd markings, from which she deduced that it had come from somewhere on the Continent.

"This letter is from Portia," she said, reading with care. "It would appear that she is happily married at last."

George stretched lazily. "God knows I hope it may be true. I wonder if she will truly be happy married to that blowhard."

"I apprehend that you mean my cousin, but this note comes from Portia en route to Italy."

George pushed the pillow off his face and opened one eye, mildly interested for the first time. "Jonas had the romantical notion of taking Portia to Italy for their honeymoon? I am sadly outdone, and by a lowly provincial boor."

"No," Jane said slowly, still reading. "It is Gandolfo she has married."

George finally opened both eyes. "I thought you said he had left because he feared that I would come back and finish the job I started."

"That is what we all thought," Jane said absently, "or rather, that is what we thought Fabrice said." She finally looked up from the letter. "How extraordinary. I do believe Portia genuinely loves Gandolfo. In any event, it appears that he is most devoted to *her.*"

"Hmmm. So Gandolfo succeeded in getting himself a rich English wife after all."

Jane stared at Portia's letter, barely taking notice of her husband now sitting up in bed. She read in silence for a long minute, her face alight with amusement.

"What? What is it?" George demanded.

Jane looked up, her eyes dancing with merriment. "I *knew* the name of Fiore struck me as somehow familiar, and Gandolfo said I reminded him of someone *he* knew. How droll!"

George's forehead creased with impatience. "Are you trying to drive me mad? What is the mystery?"

"Oh, George, you will never credit it but it appears that your sister married one of my impoverished relations after all. Gandolfo is my half-brother, only he did not realize it until Portia told him the circumstances of my birth! It seems the Italian side of my family was more forthcoming with him regarding the details of the rest of the family than mine was with me." She looked at the letter again. "Portia closes by saying that we will have to come to them in Italy, and that I will have a chance to meet my other half-brother as well."

"Thank God I have no more unmarried sisters," George declared darkly. "If any of my daughters ever dares to elope . . ." His finely chiseled mouth tightened.

"I suggest you not contemplate quarrels with your

children before they are even born," Jane said mildly, "and may I remind you of the troubles your high-handed manner has led you into in the past?"

"Have I no defense against this continual character assassination?" George asked mournfully.

"None whatsoever," Jane said firmly, "except to remove yourself from my presence."

"Which I have no wish to do," he said. "None whatsoever."